Also by Piper CJ

The Night and Its Moon

The Night and Its Moon
The Sun and Its Shade
The Gloom Between Stars

T0005471

the Dawn and its Light

PIPER CJ

Bloom *books*

Copyright © 2024 by Piper CJ
Cover and internal design © 2024 by Sourcebooks
Cover design and illustration by Kyria and Nigel Smith

Published by Bloom Books, an imprint of Sourcebooks
P.O. Box 4410, Naperville, Illinois 60567-4410
(630) 961-3900
sourcebooks.com

Cataloging-in-Publication data is on file with the Library of Congress.

Printed and bound in the United States of America.
POD

To [an author I'm not allowed to name]
I'm begging you. For the love of the gods, please give us the
final book in your series.
You don't even have to publish it. Just tell us how it ends.
We need closure.

Pronunciation Guide

Characters

Alastair: al-IH-ster
Amaris: ah-MAR-iss
Ceres: SERE-iss
Chloris: KLOR-iss
Dhamir: dah-MEER
Elswyth: ELS-with
Fjolla: fee-YO-la
Gadriel: GA-dree-ell
Kasar: ka-SAR

Malik: MAL-ik
Moirai: moy-RAI
Ryu: REE-you
Samael: sam-eye-ELL
Surya: SER-ya
Tanith: TAN-ith
Yazlyn: YAZ-lyn
Zaccai: za-KAI

Places

Aubade: obeyed
Gyrradin: GEER-a-din
Gwydir: gwih-DEER
Henares: hen-AIR-ess

Raasay: ra-SAY
Raascot: RA-scott
Yelagin: YELL-a-ghin
Uaimh Reev: OOM reev

Monsters

aboriou: ah-BORE-ee-oo
ag'drurath: AG-drath
ag'imni: ag-IM-nee
beseul: beh-ZOOL

nakki: NAH-kee
vageth: VA-geth
vakliche: VAK-leesh

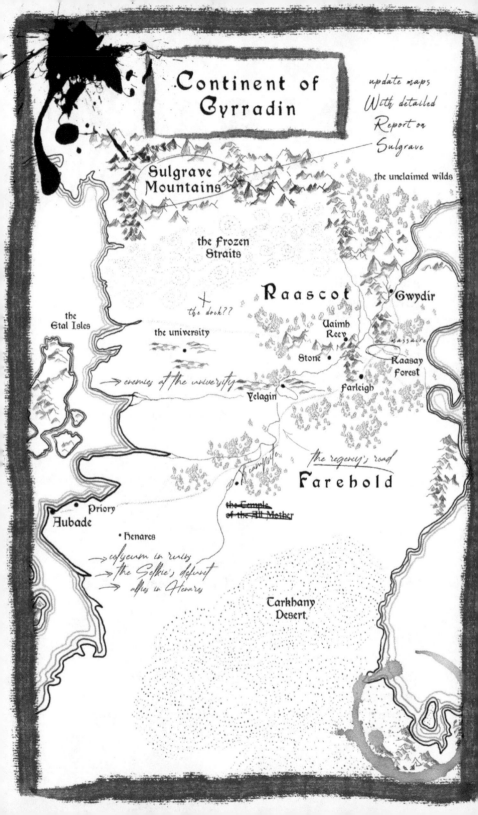

 *the beginning*

east of the sun	*megan dixon hood*
nature girl	*cryoshell*
harpens kraft	*myrkur*
timmarna	*garmarna*
queen of the castle	*victoria carbol*

the middle

be a hero	*euphoria, bolshiee*
fall	*emm*
nothing else matters	*apocalyptica*
freya	*christian reindl, lucie paradis*
wildfire	*ramin djawadi*

 the end

näktergalen	*poeta magica*
utopia	*the sidh*
elixir of life	*leah*
true strength	*john dreamer*
till death	*pi3rce*

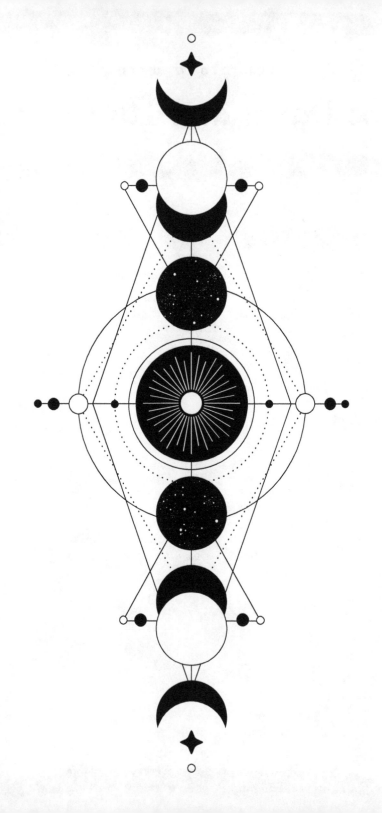

PART I

An Unturned Stone

·One

T HIS IS WHAT YOU DREAM ABOUT?"
       Nox had expected to see battlefields, dragons, glory,
or maidens. She'd even been prepared to step into a nightmare, ready for the horrors of their fight at Castle Aubade
to splash into the general's sleeping mind. Instead, the sweet
smell of dying leaves filled the evening. It was so peaceful,
so picturesque, that she nearly forgot the world had come to
an end.

The corner of Gadriel's mouth quirked in a crooked smile.
He looked up from where he'd been chopping wood. Nox
looked over his shoulder at the gray smoke dancing merrily
from the chimney of the two-story country house, wondering if someone else was home. The ivy that hung on its siding
indicated the oranges and reds of the season. She ran her gaze
over the split-rail fence that enclosed the well-loved yard.

There was no trace of lilac, silver, or moonlight in his
bucolic dream. Her attempts to reach Amaris had been met
with nothingness following the slippery, phantasmal moments
they'd shared on the cliff. Nox had never attempted to visit
anyone else, but when she returned to sleep at long last, she
slipped into her cousin's sleeping mind.

Gadriel wiped the sweat from his brow. Setting down the axe, he said, "This is where I grew up."

A sticky feeling accompanied the statement. Confusion, nostalgia, sweetness, and pain lodged in her throat. He was in simple clothes. She'd never seen him in white before, but his tunic was wet with sweat and clung to his chest. His wings were as prominent as they'd ever been, though they seemed to fold in behind him as if they were even more modest in his memories. Seeing him amidst the oaks and vines with no weapons, no fighting leathers, no trace of military bravado was both jarring and profoundly comforting.

"Is this a memory?" she asked.

"My mother's making apple pie. It's a recurrent dream of mine."

"I…" She deflated. She wanted to ask about Amaris. About Moirai. About the mission, the curse, and what the hell had caused Amaris's dream to wobble like a stone dropped in a pond. She should tell him about Tanith, about the castle, about the Hand and the Hammer. It was too much, too horrible, too difficult to grasp, particularly on an evening this lovely. The longer she stood in the dream, the more her worries began to slip. The smoke, the autumn, the faint scent of apples soaked into her muscles. She relaxed, feeling almost drunk on the pleasantness of the vision. In the end, all she said was "I'm sorry to intrude."

He sat down on the stump where he'd been clearing wood. "I grew up with Ceres's visits. He's the reason I'm a lucid dreamer. Now, when I sleep, I choose memories that bring me peace."

Peace.

Serenity was so rare, so precious, that she struggled to maintain a hold on her sense of urgency. Instead, the calm's intoxicating effect let something gentle slip from her lips. "I've tried visiting Amaris so many times, but I haven't been able to explain the situation to her. It was enough for me to know she was alive… For her, it's just a dream. For me…"

His eyes softened in a half-apologetic smile. A comfortable silence moved between them and she wondered, if only for a moment, what it would have been like to have been raised with her cousin. Part of her felt nostalgia for an emotion she'd never experienced—the pain of a life that wasn't.

He continued talking, saying something about the dreamscapes that he and Ceres would conquer as children. She was only half listening as she sank to the ground, crisscrossing her legs and resting her elbows on her knees. He'd started talking about her—about the reign she had ahead of her, and what a useful gift dream walking was—but Nox had sobered up from the initial effects of the windless autumn. If she was a good queen, she would overcome the temptations of this perfect world. There were nightmares to face. Her eyes fluttered shut so she didn't have to see his face.

"Aubade invaded the north."

Gadriel stopped short. He sucked in a sharp intake of air.

"I wrote to you," she said. "I've been using the quill for hours with no response."

She looked up from her place on the grass, watching his face change from friend to general. He brought his thumb and forefinger to his chin and chewed on the information, his jaw flexing slightly in thought. The gentle pink clouds of a pleasant late hour floated behind his head, casting an angelic haze over the painful realities.

"You're alive," he said. "What's more, it sounds like you already tried to visit Amaris. I'm sorry I haven't gotten the messages. The quill is with her things." His frown deepened as he contemplated the possibilities. "Tell me you aren't dreaming from a prison cell?"

Nox smiled with a combination of pride and victory. The rosy sky matched the glow she felt. "We won, Gad." Her words were so quiet, so happy, they were almost a song. "The Hand and the Hammer met Zaccai and me in the throne room, and we took them down." Her eyes were twinkling as she relived the thrill of battle. "And I was useful. I stood up to

5

my past—stood up for my country. And Tanith… She saved Gwydir. Farehold filled the castle. The men were everywhere. We were overrun. But Ash freed her, and she fought for us. No, that's not quite right. She didn't just fight…she disintegrated the enemy, Gad. Tanith is the reason Raascot stands."

His laugh was a low, breathy sound.

Her brows pinched. "What?"

"I'm just thinking of our early days with Tanith in the dungeon. When you'd said you wanted to turn her, it had seemed like wishful thinking." He shook his head in both disbelief and amazement. His mouth twitched in a thoughtful chuckle, lips parting appreciatively as he absorbed the information. His teeth caught the fading evening light as he smiled. He met her eyes in genuine appreciation. "When I told you that I believed in you as our queen, I didn't realize you'd have to prove yourself so quickly. But goddess, Nox, Raascot doesn't deserve you."

She beamed, head still resting in her hands. She sipped at the dream once more, savoring its buzz. Her smile flickered. He mirrored her expression, waiting for her question.

"What happened in Aubade?" Her tone made it clear that she was asking one very specific question.

Gadriel seemed to understand and gave her what she needed. "Amaris is alive, but barely."

Nox choked on her relief, hand flying to her chest. His words were too serious, too dramatic for the gentle chirping of evening songbirds that flitted through the silhouetted canopies.

Gadriel went on. "Amaris has been unconsciousness for a while now, but she's being cared for. There was a coordinated attack on the south by Sulgrave. Now that I know the north was invaded…" He chewed on the information for a long moment. "Moirai intended for us to come south."

Nox's hands flexed into fists. "What?"

He rubbed at his chin. "She wouldn't have invaded unless she thought our forces would be elsewhere. She wanted the

6

north to be empty. She wanted Raascot's eyes to be on the south."

"It was a trap," Nox said on a low breath.

"One that backfired," he confirmed. "If Moirai had intended for us to intercept her messages about the southern banquet, then the information was easy to find by design. Sulgrave found it as well and showed up in full force."

"Vageth? Ag'imni?"

"Ghouls," Gadriel said, grimacing. "Things unraveled fast. Amaris and Malik went through the front gates with the duke. Yazlyn and I made our way through the dungeons. Once I made it into the castle, the dead had already swarmed. It was mayhem. Moirai's guards stood down while everyone was slaughtered. I've never seen anything like it."

"Malik?" She swallowed the name, fearing the answer.

"Not a scratch on him. I found Malik first. He was helping the unarmed escape. He continued evacuating civilians while I caught my half-feral sergeant dragging Amaris out onto the cliffs. She'd turned Amaris blue to keep her from bleeding out. It was a nightmare, but we made it."

Nox's spine went rigid. "She'd frozen Amaris?"

"Her throat was torn open. It's…rough." He looked away, as if struggling to relay the information. After a beat, he confirmed, "Yaz lowered Amaris's body temperature enough to keep her alive and turned the gash to ice. She is the reason Amaris survived. You might want to get her something nice for her birthday."

Nox's stomach roiled at the thought of Yazlyn freezing Amaris's bloodied, broken body. The world wobbled in response, the very trees trembling as they matched her blooming panic. She looked at her hands and then at the ground, searching for the source of the problem as everything around her rippled.

Gadriel responded to the wavering world by crossing to an apple tree whose branches were heavy with ruby-red fruit. He plucked one, then another, causing the tree to shutter. "Catch," he called, tossing the fruit underhand.

Surprised turned into focus as it arced. The trees stopped wiggling. The world solidified as Nox plucked the object from the air and cradled it in her hand.

The snapping sound of teeth puncturing the flesh of firm fruit pulled her attention upward. Between bites, Gadriel said, "You'll want to watch out for that. Do your best to keep your emotions in check when dream walking—yours, and anyone you're visiting. Strong reactions, particularly fear responses, will wake the sleepers."

She ran her finger over the waxy skin, understanding the distraction. "I guess that makes sense. People sit up in bed screaming from night terrors all the time. I'll do my best to remain calm as you tell me about the army of ghouls and Amaris as a half-dead icicle. Anything else?" Her words were brittle and humorless as she eyed him.

Gadriel nodded, taking another bite. He swallowed and said, "It appears that Sulgrave's efforts were focused solely on the castle. Once Malik and I got the civilians and nobility off the grounds, the citizens were in the clear to escape into the city, with no evidence of the undead beyond castle walls. At least, we assume it was Sulgrave. We weren't able to secure the threat."

Nox lifted the fruit to her lips, then hesitated. "But Amaris…"

"You would have been very proud of her. She did it. She killed the queen."

Nox's mouth twitched, too pained to truly smile. "Please, tell me everything's going to be okay. You can lie to me if you need to."

"She's going to be okay, Nox. I've got her now." He held her gaze solemnly. There was a gravity to his words that she trusted. Gadriel went on: "We've settled at an inn for the night. To our knowledge, the Castle Aubade is still overrun with dead. We're planning to leave it that way until Amaris has healed."

"And everyone is okay…" Nox repeated it back to herself, desperate to believe it. She frowned down at the apple, wondering if food in the unconscious mind tasted every bit as fictional as she imagined. She set the food on the grass beside her as Gadriel continued.

"She and Yazlyn are sharing a room now so that Yaz can keep an eye on her. Everyone else made it out all right, though you'll have to do your best to avoid mentioning crows around Yazlyn for the foreseeable future."

Dizziness caused Nox's vision to speckle before she realized she'd been holding her breath. "What do we do now? Moirai is dead in the south, as are her forces in the north. I know I'm supposed to have some claim to the throne, but what exactly does that mean? How can I sit on two thrones? How would the people even know? And does it even matter while the castle is overrun by ghouls and Sulgrave still lurks in every shadow?"

The musical, pleasant voice of a woman called from the house, and Gadriel turned toward the sound. He offered a hand and helped Nox up from the ground.

"Do you like pie?"

Nox blinked after him. Had he not heard her? She lifted a finger in protest, but he'd already started toward the house. She followed behind him as he crossed the yard and left the fall evening for his doorway. When they entered the house, Nox encountered who she could only assume was Gadriel's mother. Her fae blood made it difficult to put a finger on her age, but the cunning in her eyes belonged to someone who had lived for centuries. The woman was every bit as beautiful as Gadriel was handsome.

"This is my mother, Allua."

The skin around her eyes crinkled with maternal warmth. Nox's hands twitched, unsure how to greet the woman, before she realized Allua had no intention of greeting her at all. Nox deflated slightly, unsure as to why she was disappointed. She reminded herself that Gadriel's dream was a memory, and the memory didn't include her.

Allua hummed to herself, plopping the dessert onto the

table as she continued with her satisfied tune. Heat curled from the sugar-crusted dough in white, smokelike tendrils.

"Do we really just get to sit and eat pie?"

Gadriel grinned as he shoveled in the first bite. "Just wait until you have to hold a meeting with Zaccai in his dreams. I'm told there are wyverns. Battle debriefing in his imagination requires a tolerance of the dramatic. What I'd give to have your power to visit dreams…"

"Come on, Gad, you're the general here. We have to make a plan. Shouldn't you be—"

"Try it." He nodded through a mouthful of pie.

Her eyes narrowed, but she obliged. Sugars and caramels swirled around the bright pop of the fruit as it melted in her mouth. The buttery dough alone had been worth the entire dream. The sleeping mind made each flavor, scent, and sight impossible to discern from reality. If they hadn't established the dream, she may have been able to truly forget herself.

Maybe she'd make a habit of visiting Gadriel.

"It's good, right?" The general grinned with the glowing smile of a son who loved his mother and her cooking very, very much.

"Your childhood home at sunset in the autumn while eating apple pie? Yes. No words do it justice, Gadriel. I'm lucky I got to see this part of you."

He was many things—some that Nox was, and some that she was not. He was Raascot's general. He was a leader, warrior, a winged fae. She'd known him to be tough, stern, and fearless. She also knew that he cared about Amaris. And if he was going to love Amaris, this was the version of him Nox wanted to remember. The wood-chopping, pie-eating man who was easily given over to smiles.

"But the plan—"

He gestured with his fork. "Here's what I would do if I were you. You've won the physical thrones, but there's work ahead of us in getting Farehold to recognize your claim. Call what remains of your circle and discuss the best ways to disseminate

10

information. Use Zaccai. If the curse truly has broken, this will be a game changer for our ability to spread communication between the north and south. Focus on your campaign to inform and inspire the south. Farehold is ours to claim, but first we have to clear it out. I'll take care of it. The ghouls are rather slow, and I'm difficult to kill. I'm not worried."

"And after that? After they're cleared?"

He shrugged, still chewing. "After that, we can have another meeting. You can't be two places at once, so you might need to spend some time thinking about who you want as your spokesman sitting in your stead."

"And then? Will you return north?"

He paused and set down his fork. This was the first time she'd seen Gadriel frown in his dream world. "You're asking questions as if you don't have answers to these. You're in charge."

She was grateful for him. She didn't doubt herself, but she also saw the wisdom in his advice. She stood by her belief that he should be king, and would have gladly stepped to the side if Gadriel had wanted the crown. But the time for those conversations had come and gone. She straightened her posture and swallowed her bite of pie. She was queen, and the only thing he required of her was that she act like it.

"I'll speak to Tanith about the best way to locate the other Sulgrave fae, but to be honest... I think the ones currently on the continent might be the tip of the iceberg. Elil made their arrival in Farehold and Raascot sound like a symptom of the problem, not the problem itself. The demon presence has spiked across the continent like we've never seen. Something has to have spurred their descent. If we don't address the root of the problem, every head we cut off will grow three in its place."

"Are you suggesting what I think you're suggesting?"

"I don't see an alternative. If we do nothing, there will be no kingdoms to rule. One fae decimated Raascot's forces. One fae bound an army of the dead in Aubade. What if they send more? When will it end? After we secure our seats on the continent, we go north to Sulgrave."

TWO

NOX ROLLED ONTO HER SIDE, SAVORING THE WARMTH OF the sheets and the way the pillow had molded perfectly to her head as the last moments of sleep evaporated. She was surprised to open her eyes and see the early purples of morning light through the cracks in her window curtains. Her meeting with Gadriel had taken no more than thirty minutes—an hour at most—yet time passed so differently when she was eating pie in the countryside than it had when she was asleep in her bed.

The temptation to cling to sleep slipped from her fingers, replaced by the need to get up and write down everything Gadriel had said. Her quill—a gray and white feathered quill of non-magical origin—scrawled every detail she might need for their war room meeting. She set down the quill and absently twirled her peppery ring.

She looked between her notes and the clock, marking the time. The hand had yet to strike the six o'clock bell. In spite of all the fear that had gripped the continent and the nerves she knew she was meant to face, a small voice told her that if she rushed to the kitchen, she might be able to beat Zaccai and get an almond pastry before he ate everything.

Everything prepared in the kitchens was wonderful, but the almond pastries contained the added flavor of getting a rise out of the commander.

She put on her slippers and shrugged into a heavy wool sweater before making her way to the kitchen. The attendants' raised brows and curious faces greeted her, and no fewer than three asked if she was feeling unwell or if there was anything they could do for her. She was nocturnal, after all, and seeing her before noon might be cause for alarm.

History tomes, like the castle servants, favored the habits of early risers, which Nox had always considered unfair. She didn't see any reason that someone whose mind and body worked from the lunch hour until the midnight hour should be seen as any less effective than someone whose body only functioned between breakfast and dinner. She scanned the typical platters of breakfast meats, the hardboiled eggs, the fresh arrays of cut fruits, steel cut oats, and kettles of aromatic teas while she contemplated issuing a decree that no one's work day should start before the twelve o'clock bell.

"Ah, ha!" She snatched an almond pastry the moment she saw it.

"Bold selection," said the golden-haired kitchen attendant she'd known as Lee. The young woman breezed behind her with another serving tray, making a clucking sound with her tongue as she warned Nox of the coming storm.

Nox lifted the pastry to her lips without bothering to grab a plate or take a seat. A blur moved just beyond her peripherals before she could sink her teeth into the food.

"Drop it."

Nox spun toward the noise. Her fingers slackened from sheer surprise. Zaccai glared at her from the doorway. A smile bubbled through her. "There are still two more here. You'll get plenty."

"I always eat three."

She narrowed her eyes, though she did so with the

playfulness of someone who was just happy to be alive. "And today you can eat two almond pastries and an apple tart."

Nox bit into it, eyes twinkling as she awaited a reaction. For a fraction of a second, he looked like he might lunge for the food in her mouth and fish it out of her jaw like a dog with a bone. Instead, Zaccai mumbled something unintelligible about monarchs while fetching a plate. His early morning grumbling was interwoven with the same buoyant, drugged feeling she'd felt after surviving their brush with death. Even the kitchen staff seemed to hum with the high of survival from the brink of defeat.

She poured herself a hot cup and slid into a seat. "Do you want to talk about business over breakfast, or do you like to drink your tea first?"

Cai bit into the apple tart and made a face before shoving it to the side. "I don't drink tea. It's Yazlyn you have to worry about before she gets her caffeine fix."

The sergeant's groggy storm cloud of a presence loomed in the room even from the other side of the continent. Nox chuckled to herself. "Don't I know it."

He tapped the tabletop. "Hit me with it."

Nox set down her stolen pastry. "I visited Gadriel last night. He told me what happened in Aubade."

Zaccai stiffened. He dusted the crumbs from off his fingers and leaned in to listen as she relayed the events from the south.

"We need to disseminate information on a continental scale. How has this been achieved in the past?" she asked.

He chewed on the inside of his cheek for a moment after she finished. "It hasn't. The closest we've come is posting proclamations in our kingdom's villages. Raascot hasn't had cause to inform Farehold of anything."

"Great. Add it to the list of things we need to accomplish that have never been done before."

His answering laugh was humorless. "Do you mind if I take these with me? I need to debrief the military and gather information. I'll see what I can have for you by this afternoon."

"Of course not. Go, go." Nox made an agreeable noise while she sipped at her tea, trusting Zaccai to manage his time and priorities. She looked out through the dining room window at the beautiful morning that was coloring its way across the castle grounds. The night before had been one of blind, windswept terror. The blizzard, though destructive throughout the night, had wiped away any trace of invasion by morning. Beautiful, white dunes of blowing and drifting snow danced across the yard. She couldn't help but feel like the snow was perfect symbolism for the clean slate Gwydir had been given. Ceres was off the throne. Aubade had been defeated. The continent was ready for a new era.

The attendants cleared the table after Zaccai left, and she exchanged pleasant looks with a radiant Leona, whose expression was unmistakable. Those who served in the castle were experiencing the same high of gratitude and injection of life that she was currently inhaling by the lungful.

"Is everyone okay?" Nox asked after Lee.

The attendant didn't pause but breezed happily over her shoulder. "We are, thanks to you!"

The corner of Nox's mouth tugged upward in a smile. She had found herself queen in a complex beehive of happy, hardworking individuals, who were hers to protect and oversee. She wanted to do right by all of them.

She rose from the table, belly full, mind buzzing, and wondering where her morning might take her.

Nox wandered around the castle with her tea.

Instead of drifting about in the early morning quiet, she followed the low noise of hushed activity coming from the corridor of bedchambers. The commotion of multiple voices led her to the open door of Ash's room. Nox approached the doorway and paused in confusion at the bodies milling about the room. Tanith's small, supine form was lying in the middle of Ash's mattress. Her wine-red nightdress was the only splash of color against the ivory sheets and the sickly pale of her skin. Ash paced at the foot of the bed. A woman she recognized to be the castle's healer held the Sulgrave fae's hand while the man unrolled a wrap filled with glass tonics and vials.

Nox stepped into the room. "What's going on?"

The healer looked up but didn't answer. Ash crossed quickly to her, speaking with urgency. He seemed to be the only person who wasn't experiencing the joy of survival. His eyes, normally a rich shade of honey, were now muted to a flat, yellow-brown. Worry colored his words.

"Tanith." He looked then back to the sickly young woman in his bed. "She seemed fine last night after the battle. When I woke up, she was unresponsive." His voice dropped with each word of his sentence. Nox pushed past him and approached Tanith's sweat-soaked form.

"Your Majesty," the healer spoke at long last, addressing Nox first. "The reever tells me she used a great deal of magic last night."

"She did," Nox agreed, voice slow with skepticism. She remembered the flu-like symptoms that had drained her after dream walking. It had spurred the act of manufacturing that had led to the ring she still wore. She twiddled it while frowning down at Tanith. "Lightning comes naturally to her. It's her primary ability. She shouldn't be sick if she wasn't attempting an unnatural gift, right?"

The healer and the tall, wingless man exchanged looks at this. Nox wasn't sure if she'd said too much but decided that she needed to be able to trust anyone in her employ.

"Unnatural gift?" the healer asked, looking at the man who still hadn't identified himself. "Do you mean her secondary ability?"

"Not quite." Nox looked between Tanith's clammy pallor and the healer's face, creased with worry. "Tanith is from Sulgrave. She claims they can access the groundwater of magic—that's what she calls it, 'groundwater'—including the abilities that don't manifest organically. She had compared the natural manifestations as freshwater springs, with the access of other powers being more like…" Nox snapped her fingers while she searched for the word.

"A pump?" Ash offered, his tone still strained against his helplessness.

"Yes, accessing other powers was akin to a pump or a well that drew from the groundwater. The Sulgrave compared intuitive manifestations of power to natural springs, where the water broke through the ground of its own volition. Her natural inclination was electricity. That's what she used last night. Why would it have wounded her?"

"Blood magic," the man said.

"No…" Nox's frown deepened.

After exchanging a long look with the healer, the man spoke. "Your Majesty, pardon my poor manners, as we have yet to meet. I'm Belfor. I'm Gwydir's Scholar of Magics. I've been overseeing the magical components of the shields made by the manufacturers for the party that ventured south. The healer summoned me after she arrived. May I speak with you?"

He crossed the room, preempting her affirmative answer. He clasped his hands behind his back while they stepped into the hall, explaining that he had studied magics at the university. He went on to say that there were a number of theories regarding the ability to access unfamiliar powers, but that's all they were—theories.

"It's forbidden," Belfor said, "as it comes at a great cost. Many students died in pursuit of unlocking unnatural powers before the university outlawed it. But given what we know of how secondary abilities often make their user ill, and the nature of the magical deaths, it's believed that accessing an unfamiliar gift requires blood magic."

"But Tanith didn't have the opportunity to…" Nox's words drifted as she racked her memories of the night.

"The user is believed to make a trade with their own lives," he said. "Their own blood is exchanged to access a secondary power. Many fae have found that they can use

17

secondary powers but that it drains them substantially. I have yet to meet someone who can call to any power at will, but I imagine the toll of such a trade would be…substantial. The barter they make for their stolen ability is at the expense of their own life."

Nox looked through the doorway to where the healer spoke with Ash beside the bed. Her gaze remained on Tanith as she asked, "Can you use someone else's blood for blood magic?"

The face he made gave her the uncomfortable sensation that her question had been both inappropriate and worrying. As she'd lacked formal magical education, she had no way of knowing what was typical or decent, but there was no time like the present to learn. Belfor did his best to remain diplomatic, summoning academia rather than emotion as he responded. "Other blood can potentially be used, yes—but if you say she was calling upon her primary ability, I wouldn't know why she'd be using blood magic."

"I don't know what would have caused it," Nox said. "She told us herself that she was predisposed to lightning. She even tried to conjure a rose of such electricity in the war room once before her cuffs were removed. Last night, Tanith summoned lightning multiple times, and because of her ability the castle was saved. Our enemies were fully disintegrated. This shouldn't have required any strength or ability that was new to her."

Belfor's brows met in the center. He rubbed his chin. "You were present when this happened?"

She nodded. "Tanith had first used the ability with Ash in the dungeon. She then helped Zaccai and me clear out the main hall until no enemies remained. All four of us were present by the time Gwydir was secured."

His expression changed. His fingers stilled against his chin before he snapped. "She was summoning a shield. No—if she was protecting all of you, she must have conjured a number of shields." He looked to where her body remained motionless on the bed while reiterating to himself. "She was shielding three separate people while calling on her lightning—repeatedly."

Ash stepped into the hall to join them. Nox hadn't even realized he'd been listening to them before he was standing shoulder-to-shoulder with the man and asked, "What do you mean?"

Belfor continued to watch Tanith as he said, "Her lightning wouldn't have harmed her, as she can speak to it naturally, but if she was calling currents strong enough to evaporate your foes, she was using two abilities at once. Calling an unnatural power is taxing. Calling a borrowed power *and* her given gift simultaneously is a true feat. This young woman…she protected you from her own effects so that you would be spared."

The healer looked up from her place beside the bed. Her hand dropped from where it had remained pressed against Tanith's cheek. The woman shook her head, knowing her abilities had little effect. Healers were nearly unstoppable against mortal wounds, cuts, viruses, and organically occurring injuries. She would be useless in healing the consequences of magical entanglements.

The Scholar of Magics returned to the room and unrolled a leather pouch filled with different-colored glasses, bottles, and syringes. He procured a small vial containing a thick, crimson liquid. The cork made a satisfying popping noise as he freed it from the glass vial and approached the patient. The healer helped to tilt Tanith's head upward so that Belfor could empty its contents into her mouth and allow gravity to carry the liquid into her system. A few ruby drops stood out against her colorless lips, making Tanith look like a vampire fresh from the kill.

"What is that?" Nox's brows pinched in the middle, puckering in rising concern. "It looks like you're feeding her blood. Didn't you just say blood magic…"

Belfor made a low, thoughtful sound. He returned the stained vial to its proper slot in his roll with medical stoicism.

"Yes. It is blood. Technically, this is a rather benign form of blood magic—though try to keep that bit of information to yourself. Blood magic remains forbidden for a reason. The greenstrike, however, is a rather interesting creature with magical healing properties. They're particularly difficult to keep alive. Harvesting their blood is no small task."

Nox blinked back at the information. She wasn't sure what to ask first. "I'm sorry, the scholar's wing? What is a greenstrike? I hate to be ignorant, but I feel like I'm coming up short on my understanding of the kingdom and its functionality."

His smile was neither condescending nor unkind. "Gwydir's library is separated into the above-ground floors meant for the archivists and the general public. The below-ground floors are reserved for the scholars of magic. I'd be happy to give you a tour, Your Majesty. The greenstrike is a rather unimaginatively named leaf-green creature who, for all the world, looks as if it might be a stick. That is, until—"

"It strikes?"

"Precisely."

She took a step toward the bed. "And what does he do when he strikes?"

"If you're lucky, you'll never have to know."

Tanith began to sputter, and all eyes in the room turned to her. Belfor clapped his hands together appreciatively, and the healer dabbed a damp cloth across Tanith's forehead for sweat before mopping up the remnants of blood from her lips.

"You've been more instrumental to the diagnostic procedure than you realized, Your Highness," Belfor said.

"Please," she corrected, "call me Nox."

He smiled in a way that communicated that no, he would not be referring to her by her given name.

Belfor and the healer decided that Tanith would be all right but that she should spend the remainder of the day resting. Before the man and woman departed, Nox requested that a few healing tonics as well as several vials of greenstrike blood be collected and sent to the castle so that they could be on hand in case of emergency. The pair departed from the room, leaving Nox and Ash at Tanith's side.

Tanith groaned, eyes hazy and unfixed, but she appeared to be getting stronger by the second. The rapid recovery was jarring, as her coloring seemed to bloom into her cheeks before their very eyes. Ash caught Tanith's hands in his own, looking down at her with a gentle glow.

The corners of her mouth turned up as she returned the smile.

In a gentle whisper, Ash asked, "You shielded us?"

Slashes of blood colored the spaces between Tanith's teeth as her eyes softened. Voice faint with her musical lilt, she said, "What use is it to destroy the enemy if I'm left without my family?"

✦

It took Tanith the better part of an hour to convince Ash to leave her side. He probably would have remained perched on the bed had she not asked for a cup of tea. She wasn't truly interested in the weak, dirty water the southern kingdoms served with breakfast, but at least it gave her some time alone to think. The sheets tugged around her as she pulled her knees to her chest and sighed as she slid her fingers along the butter-soft fabric. Castle Gwydir's comforts were a far cry from the scratchy sheets and thin cots of the Reds' bunkers. If Raascot could figure out how to brew stronger morning drinks and serve better food, she wouldn't miss anything about Sulgrave.

She twisted the sheet absently and stared into the fire, listening to it crackle as it lulled her into thoughts of far-off retinues, of devotional offerings, and droning sermons. A log popped, shuddering as it crashed into the embers, and the sound redirected her memories to breaking bones, to electric snaps, to terrifying displays of power. She looked down at her hands and stared at the lines that carved across her palm. She frowned as she looked, studying the etchings for a sign of the blood that stained them. She wondered if new cracks were added for the lives she'd taken or if the many splinters had been her predestination as an angel of death. Her eyes glazed over as she waited for her skin to turn as red as her tunic, when movement caught her eye.

Red, yes, but not the color of station or duty. The ginger hair he'd pulled into a knot was the red choice. Ash appeared, tea in one hand, sticky bun in the other, and a crooked smile on his face. "I know you said you weren't hungry," he began, "but it can't hurt to get something in your system."

"Be careful," she replied, accepting the cup. "You're an act away from ruining the reputation I've heard so much about."

"Oh?" He quirked a brow. The scent of dying leaves and apple slices rushed through the room as he settled into the space beside her. "And what will I become in its stead?"

"Doting."

"Ah." He smiled. His amber eyes were honey soft as he said, "Afraid that ship has sailed."

Her laughs were never audible, unlike the others in the castle. She absorbed the feeling like sunlight, letting it warm her lips as she smiled down into the discolored water, inhaling the aromatic steam. The others hadn't learned her laughs, but Ash understood. He winked and gave her knee a squeeze.

"I'm going to need you not to scare us like that again," he said.

She pretended to take a sip, then lowered the cup. "I'm afraid that's a promise I can't make, as I have no idea what frightens your lot."

"Losing you, for start," he said.

Like her laughs, her sighs were also kept inside. She bit the inside of her cheek as she gnawed on his words. She was already on stolen time, after all. She hadn't been meant to survive the southbound trip. She should have fallen to her knees in the Raasay Valley and given up her soul along with the soldiers she'd slain. She shouldn't have been permitted to live when she'd been captured, as the only justice for her crimes would have been death. The reevers shouldn't have intervened when Elil had tried to take her, nor Ash risk his life against his father when the man had made it into the castle. She shouldn't have been pardoned or trusted by Nox, nor freed when Moirai's men had invaded.

Her days had been borrowed from the moment she'd set foot in Raascot, but her wrongdoings had evolved. She wasn't just a thief. Her deception was far viler, and utterly unforgivable, even if it wasn't a crime she'd intended to commit. She'd somehow led Ash and the others to believe that she was a good person. Someone worthy of love. Someone worth saving.

He didn't force her to speak. He plucked the tea from her hands and set it on the bedside table, then tucked his arm around her. She rested her head on his shoulder and inhaled autumn. She decided that no, she would make no such promise. Her life had been forfeited for some time, and she knew it. But she would give everything in her power to protect the others from her fate.

Whatever the cost.

Three

O H, GODDESS, WHY WAS IT SO LOUD? WOULD THEY SHUT
up already? Who was touching her?

Amaris had scarcely been awake for thirty seconds before
she was assaulted with questions and the fussing hands of a
stranger. She found it difficult to raise her head or assess her
surroundings. She wasn't sure where she was or who was in
the room; all she knew was that they were being remarkably
unpleasant. The voices faded until there was one singular,
familiar sound. She did her best to blink away the grogginess
and focus.

Amaris was accompanied by a plump, unfamiliar woman
and the seated shape of a winged sergeant. Yazlyn propped her
feet up on the writing desk and said, "Your queen has been
writing incessant messages, so please do everyone a favor and
let her know you're fine. She can distinguish my handwriting,
and I've been given a royal decree to stop impersonating you
with the quill."

The quill? Her queen? Oh, shit, she was talking about
Nox. Amaris had dreamed about Nox and plums and a face
too lovely for this world on a starlight night. She'd also had
a terrible nightmare. Something about banquets, and bones,

and Moirai, and sharp, painful slashes across her neck. Her hand flew to her throat. A small, slippery bit of skin told her that she'd gained a new scar. She rolled onto her side and asked a single, rasping question. "Do you have a mirror?"

Yazlyn grimaced. "Trust me, you're beautiful."

"I'd like to see the damage for myself," she said, coughing from the effort.

"I'm not so sure you would."

Amaris's heart quickened. The sergeant had clearly had the opportunity to bathe and clean herself after battle. Aside from the pink remnants of a few minor scrapes, Yazlyn seemed to have made it out unharmed.

Amaris was firm. She gathered her strength and pushed herself into a fully seated position. "If I need to start wearing a sack over my head, I deserve to know."

Yazlyn got to her feet. She procured a few coins from her pouch and offered them to the woman beside her. "I'm sure Gadriel will want to speak with you when he returns, but please go get yourself some breakfast."

"And then you'll release me?" the woman asked, voice testy.

"You're not…"

"Held hostage?" the woman finished for her, swiping the coins from Yazlyn's palm. She pushed into the hall, letting the door slam behind her. Amaris stared after the woman's wake, perplexed by the strange interaction. She opened her mouth to ask Yazlyn what it had been about, but the fae had already dipped into the washroom.

While Yazlyn left her bedside, Amaris used the opportunity to take in her surroundings. The walls and floors were made with the familiar cream-colored stones that were common in coastal cities like Aubade. She knew instinctively that they were in no private residence. There was a hum of noise and energy that told her she was resting at an inn. The chamber was large enough for both her and Yazlyn to sleep comfortably and came with an adjoining bathing room.

Amaris pushed the quilt off her lap and realized the night-black sheets had been masking the puddles of discoloration where Amaris had slept. She ran her hands over her body to check for injuries, only to realize someone had changed her into a paper-thin, white slip while she'd been unconscious. She peered over the lip of the bed to find her formerly white clothes stiff with reddish-brown creases of dried blood.

Her eyes lifted from the gory remnants of her once-beautiful gown as Yazlyn approached. She offered Amaris a silver hand mirror and twisted her lips in uneasy anticipation as Amaris accepted the cool disc.

Amaris's eyes bulged at the sight.

"Was I almost beheaded?" Amaris croaked.

"Not successfully, and that's what matters."

Amaris ran her fingers over the thick, white line again and again. It was unnaturally smooth compared to the flesh of her neck on either side, shimmering with the distinctive demarcation of scarred tissue.

"We have matching collars now. It's a pretty exclusive club." Yazlyn attempted a grim smile.

Amaris looked up from the mirror long enough to see Yazlyn tap her fingertips to the metallic band that remained tightly fastened to the middle of her neck. Amaris had thought perhaps the collar would fall off once the curse was broken, but it seemed as though Yazlyn may have acquired a permanent fixture.

Amaris continued to finger the scar, twisting the mirror to see how far the line extended. "Why isn't it pink like my facial scar?"

"Ah, yes." Yazlyn made a long-suffering sound. "That's due to the immediacy of its healing. I helped, but Gadriel has gained himself something of a reputation. I don't know that there wasn't a healer south of the Raascot border he didn't threaten or intimidate into attending you at your bedside. I could be wrong, but it sounded like he physically abducted one from the healer's hall in Aubade and flew her directly to your room."

"Was that why the woman…?"

Yazlyn's lips flattened into a line. "The healers may not like either of you very much. The one you met is on permanent retainer until Gad dismisses her, though I'm not sure she's a willing participant in your well-being."

The door creaked, and both women looked to find the tanned, handsome face of the general. Gadriel's face, smudged with worry and sleep deprivation, lit with intense relief. Without awaiting any sort of invitation, he crawled onto the bed next to her and cradled her face in his hands. His energy was so kind, so familiar, she was tempted to fight him off as an imposter.

"Goddess, you crazy witchling, what were you thinking? How could you take Moirai on alone in the middle of an army of ghouls?" His hand slid from her face to the side of her neck. Gooseflesh chilled her as he ran a thumb over the horizontal scar.

"I'm going to go get the healer," came Yazlyn's hasty words as she scurried from the desk into the hall, door clicking as it closed securely behind her.

Amaris paid the sergeant no mind. She wanted to say something witty, but her words lacked their intended sarcastic lilt. "You forget: I was born for this."

Gadriel's laugh was thick with relief. He hugged her so tightly she thought her ribs were about to break.

She gasped. "Gad!"

He crushed her against him as if she were little more than a doll. "I know you're perfectly capable. I don't doubt your abilities. Just let me worry about you, you beautiful, glorious, talented, stubborn, careless, murderous bastard." He held her at arm's length, then, to eye her, scanning with grinning, appreciative pride. "You really did it. You did what we've fought for, bled for, and died for over the past twenty years. You killed the goddess-damned queen. You fought off a hoard of ghouls. You broke the fucking curse. But damn if you didn't have to scare me within an inch of my life while doing it."

Amaris squirmed as he embraced her once more. "Goddess, who knew you were such a hugger."

"Speak of this to no one." He smiled into her hair.

A glow bloomed within her. "Within an inch of your life, huh? I thought you were hard to kill?" She succeeded in pushing out of his viselike grip.

His low chuckle heated her cheeks. "It turns out I know exactly what it would take to kill me, witchling."

Amaris's mouth twisted into a partial smile. "So, mission accomplished? Do you think the All Mother is ready for me to retire to a life of luxury now that Moirai is dead? I hadn't expected to be washed up and irrelevant on the eve of my nineteenth birthday. I suspect I'm owed a castle in the sky."

The light within him flickered.

She cocked her head. "What?"

After a tired exhale, Gadriel began to explain everything. He spoke of the state in which he'd found her. He told her what had happened with Malik, with the city, and then he began to speak of Gwydir.

"Have you and Nox been speaking?"

"We've spoken, yes," he said with a trepidatious sigh, "but it wasn't through the quill."

Amaris blinked against the amalgamation of foggy memories of dreams about Nox as Gadriel explained dream walking, his meeting, and what was next for their tasks in the south. She lifted her fingertips to her temples and pressed them against the onset of a headache.

"All of my dreams?" she asked.

"Not necessarily," he said, brows meeting apologetically. "You can still have normal, uneventful dreams on typical nights. Dream walking is a very specific gift. You'll have to talk to Nox about it. I'm sorry to be the one to tell you."

Their discussion was cut short by Yazlyn's return. The healer entered the room after her, shooting Gadriel a decidedly dirty glare before assessing Amaris's state. She announced on no uncertain terms that Amaris was fine, then very curtly asked if she was free to go. Amaris wondered what exactly Gadriel had said or done to this woman to have such prompt care, but by whatever means necessary, he had clearly saved her life. She absently wondered what sort of life debt she owed the general.

Despite the ever-growing presence surrounding her bed, the party had not fully reunited.

"Where's Malik now?"

"I'll get him," Yazlyn volunteered, perhaps relieved not to be alone with the two of them.

Malik appeared minutes later, face glowing like the sun when he saw her. He caught her up in another of many embraces since she'd awoken. Emotion laced his words as he said, "I wasn't ready to bury my brother."

"I'm not going anywhere," she promised.

He released her and perched on the edge of the bed near Yazlyn as the group launched into plans. Amaris wished she'd asked for clean clothes. She felt quite childlike as she, the smallest member of the party, remained half under the covers of the large, four-post bed while everyone sat around her. She hadn't asked whose nightdress she was wearing and who had stripped, bathed, and changed her. The outfit she'd arrived in was so stained and shredded, it needed to burn. It was a damn shame such a beautiful gown had met such an ugly end. She grabbed a pillow and hugged it against herself, feeling less naked as Gadriel spoke with a general's tone.

"Moirai is gone, but the task ahead of us is every bit as important. Nox's claim to the throne is tenuous. If we aren't quick to establish a stronghold in the south, our grip will collapse."

Yazlyn inspected her nails, picking dirt from them as she asked, "Is there even a throne? Last time we were in the castle, it was full of the living dead."

Gadriel said, "They're slow and we're skilled. Between you, Malik, me, and a few persuaded guards, we could easily clear the remaining ghouls from the castle. Then we have to figure out not only how to hold the throne but how to let the people know who sits on it."

Malik slumped against the bedpost. "The ghouls will only be half of our problem unless we find out where the Hand and Hammer are hiding."

Gadriel inhaled sharply. "I may have left out an important detail. Amaris is caught up, but keep in mind as I say what I'm about to say: everything ended well and everyone is safe."

Malik went rigid. "Tell me what happened."

Amaris knew Gadriel had years of training in delivering challenging news and was glad for it, given the tense look on Malik's face. Gadriel's voice remained low and in control as he said, "The north was invaded. The reason we saw neither Moirai's captains nor the late queen's forces last night is that we'd fallen for a trap. She'd used her gathering of nobility as a distraction. My assumption is that Moirai wanted us to intercept her invitation for the gathering, hoping that Raascot's forces would leave the castle unprotected. If she was intentionally showing her hand and dispersing word of the southern gathering for anyone to find, it would explain why a Sulgrave fae knew exactly when and where to strike."

Malik remained strangely monotonous as he asked, "You said everyone's okay?"

Gadriel leaned toward the reever. He met his gaze with strength in his eyes. "Nox and Zaccai took out the captains in the throne room. She used her axe."

Shock rocked Malik backward. Confusion and pride battled for attention across his features as he sucked in her name. "Nox..."

"Nox killed the Hand," Gadriel confirmed.

He allowed the moment to soak in before he pressed forward. "I'm told it was Tanith who saved the day. Nox informed me that Ash freed her of her cuffs and she eliminated the Farehold threat completely. From my understanding, it was total annihilation."

Discomfort stirred the room.

"She's free?" Yazlyn asked.

Gadriel shrugged with true, unworried ease. "Ash made a judgment call, and it was the right one. Nox credits Tanith as the reason Gwydir still stands."

Yazlyn wiggled her mouth from side to side as she conjured a memory. She lifted a finger, and the others turned toward her. "If Tanith has the ability to wipe people off of the face of the map, why didn't she use that power in the gully?"

The answer seemed obvious to Amaris. "Because using the monsters allowed for the pure fae to fight, fly, or escape. She wasn't trying to kill everyone. Only the...*unworthy*."

Yazlyn exhaled slowly, sinking into her corner of the bed. "Tanith's so calm all of the time. It's easy to forget she's a homicidal little maniac, isn't it?"

"Nox hoped to turn her," Amaris said. "I didn't think it would end in Tanith fighting to save a demi-fae queen."

"Come on." Malik's mouth quirked in a smile. "You know better than to underestimate Nox."

Their conversation turned as they discussed their plans to clear out Aubade's castle and their options for holding the throne. They exchanged a few ideas for information, but the room shared a confidence that the people of Farehold would be reluctant to hear any sort of news from the northern fae they'd been conditioned to distrust. The events of the previous night could very easily turn into a nightmare for everyone on all corners of the continent.

Gadriel's ideas included a door-to-door campaign. Malik advocated for appointing messengers within each village and township. Yazlyn's ideas seemed a little less sincere, as most of them included some form of threat or violence. While the others conversed, Amaris grew quieter and quieter.

Gadriel raised a hand to quiet the others. He prodded Amaris gently. "What is it?"

She was hardly breathing as her mind scanned her memories. "Tanith. It's Tanith."

Yazlyn folded her arms. "What about Tanith?"

31

Amaris rose from the bed, tussling with the sheets as she escaped their grip. The nightdress was pushed up nearly over her thighs, hugging her tightly as she crossed the room. She tugged the hem of the dress and took four steps to cross to the writing desk. She grabbed her spelled quill and returned to the bed with a piece of parchment, sketching with the magical quill so that everyone could see what she created on the piece of paper. Amaris called on the years of drawing lessons that the matrons had forced upon her as she began to sketch the curved back, the extended tail, the outstretched wings, and then the talons of what appeared to be a large, feathered bird. She sketched in the shading and details in the barest amounts, making it clear that she had created a bird. Their brows furrowed in confusion as the spherical shape gave way to bizarre features. Instead of an owl's eyes and beak, Amaris drew a human's face where the bird's was meant to be. Next to the drawing she wrote only two words: *Use Tanith.*

Malik's lips parted with recognition. "You want Tanith to call the harpies?"

Gadriel nodded appreciatively. "It's perfect. If she can bind creatures to her, this could be the ultimate way to spread information."

Yazlyn's head shake was a firm rejection of the idea. She tapped the paper. "Harpies spread rumors and fears and lies. They're not messenger birds. They don't deliver information. We've all heard their lore—the demons land on trees outside of your window and plant thoughts in your head. This is not—"

"No." Gadriel made a silencing gesture. "That's exactly why this will work. You're right—they aren't messenger birds, but nakki also don't congregate in the thousands to make coordinated abductions. Ghouls aren't intelligent enough to invade a castle. Mud demons…well, you under-stand my point. If the Sulgrave fae can bind the creatures to themselves, Tanith could get the whispering demons to do things we've never seen them do and on a scale we've never thought possible."

Excitement bled into Amaris's voice. "And isn't it better this way? If we were sending out letters or forcing Raascot fae to visit these towns across the south, northern men would be met with suspicion. Instead, people all across Farehold will find themselves knowing that Moirai was an evil, curse-bringing bitch and that Daphne's long-lost heir is now safely on the throne. They may not know where they heard the information, but they'll all be quite certain they heard it somewhere. And with everyone hearing it at the same time…"

Four sets of eyes turned to watch ink blot onto the page beneath Amaris's message. The room stilled as they waited for the handwriting that bled onto the page. Nox's response read:

You're a genius. I'll speak to her today.

P.S. I'm glad you're alive. Come home to me.

Gadriel cleared his throat, politely ignoring the more intimate pieces of Nox's message. "That leaves the question of holding the south."

The statement had barely left the general's lips before Malik laughed at a private joke, shaking his head against whatever had crossed his mind.

Yazlyn spoke for all of them. She flicked her fingers as she made a sweeping gesture. "Do you care to share with the room?"

Malik continued trying and failing to suppress a grin. "Oh, it's nothing. It's just a funny bit. Nox and I had made the joke that the Duke of Henares could sit on the throne as a puppet. He is quite smitten with her."

Amaris and the others stared at him.

Confusion clouded his expression. "What?"

It was as if the oxygen seeped from the room as everyone continued to gape at Malik.

"You…no. You all… *no*. The duke—"

"It has to be him!" Amaris's tone was shrill with the solution.

Gadriel was quick to nod. He rose from where he'd sat to pace with his own carefully contained buzz of emotion. "We'll give him a placeholder title, like the Queen's Steward or something like that. He's a southern nobleman, so I expect he'll be met with little resistance. He isn't actually making a play for the crown, which will make him even less threatening. All we need him to do is temporarily hold the throne while we secure Farehold."

Horror twisted Malik's friendly features into a mask of disgust. "The duke is mindless!"

"That's exactly why this will work," Gadriel insisted. "No one needs to interact with him—"

Malik continued to shut them down, joining the general on his feet as he tried to steer the room out of its descent into madness. "The man has no brain! He would need constant supervision. The duke was a joke for a reason. We couldn't keep him from being immediately ruled out for his incompetence after the first time he sent out letters to the nobility about Nox's breasts."

"They are quite nice," Yazlyn murmured from where she'd remained unbothered on the corner of the bed.

Gadriel crossed one arm, resting his chin in the hand of the other. He tapped his lips and nodded with the solution-oriented mind of a leader. "Then one of us will stay to supervise him. I don't think it could be Yazlyn or me. The Farehold citizens aren't ready to trust a Raascot fae mouthpiece speaking on behalf of their newly seated steward."

Amaris shrugged. "I could stay. I fulfilled my lifelong purpose. I don't really see what good I could serve the cause now that the curse is broken."

Gadriel's brow furrowed. "Your usefulness is far from over, Amaris. None of us know what sort of spells or enchantments Sulgrave could be using to protect themselves or their skill."

Everyone turned to Malik.

His eyes practically popped out of his head. "No! No, I'm not going to stay in Aubade to babysit a madman. It's absurd. There's no way that Nox would want this. It was her joke for a reason. She knows precisely how crazy he is."

Gadriel rolled his shoulders as he squared off against the reever. "Do you want to speak with her yourself?"

Malik frowned at the question. "Speak with Nox?"

The general looked pointedly at Amaris. "Will you ask her?"

Amaris fetched her quill again and wrote a question beneath her drawing of the harpy.

Will you visit Malik tonight? He needs to speak with you.

"Is someone going to explain this to me, or are you just going to keep staring?"

Four

N OX CLOSED HER EYES AGAINST THE FROSTY NIGHT SKY IN Castle Gwydir and opened them to the bright summer sun. Old, wizened trees surrounded the glen like silent sentinels. It wasn't the thick, messy bramble and underbrush she'd grown familiar with at Farleigh but knolls of soft grass ending on the banks of a large, freshwater pool. She took a few steps to where Malik relaxed on the shore.

She bit her lip appreciatively as her eyes grazed his body.

His pants were rolled up to his knees, exposing legs as thick as the saplings around them. The summer sun beat down pleasantly on his bare chest as he lay with his hands folded neatly behind his head. He was firm and chiseled while still having the wholesome useful body of someone who lived a full and happy life. This wasn't the starved body of the vain but the active torso of the useful.

He tilted his head back and caught her staring. He flashed a brilliant white smile. "Good," he said. "The day lacked an angel."

Her heart warmed at his contagious smile. Its heat spread to her cheeks. She kept her voice low and sweet as she asked, "May I join you?"

"I'd be offended if you didn't."

Nox settled onto the grass beside him. She tore her eyes from him long enough to examine their surroundings. "Where are we?"

"The fishing pond. You just missed my father."

"Your dad was here?" She scanned the secluded pond for evidence of another life, but the forest remained still, save for the gentlest rustle of warm wind.

"He took our perch home to clean. I stayed to listen to the birds."

Nox lay down on her back and listened to the papery whisper of the leaves rubbing together in the breeze, the cicada's hum, the warbler's musical melodies, and the sparrow's sharp, short chirps. She was so relaxed, she nearly forgot why she'd come until Malik moved.

"Should we swim?" He was already on his feet, unbuttoning his pants.

Her senses came to her in a bolt. She sat up and gestured for him to return to the grass. "Oh, goddess, um, Malik... we need to talk."

Malik stepped out of his pants and stepped into the water before she could stop him. The glassy pond mirrored the world around it so perfectly, it looked as if he were stepping into the very sky.

Nox heated against the walls-down intimacy of the moment. She tried and failed to look away from Malik's muscled backside as he dove below the glass-smooth surface. She reminded herself that it was indecent to invade the innocence of his dreams unless he understood that she was truly present. She sucked in a breath and readied herself to tell him.

She waited. And waited. And then she began to worry.

"Malik?" she called over the pond's settling ripples.

He burst from beneath the surface a moment later with a dramatic gasp. He ran his fingers through the damp tendrils of hair, slicking it back as he flashed a brilliant smile. He shouted to where she sat on the banks, bewildered.

"Are you coming in?"

She frowned at the water. "Can't you come to the shore? We really need to talk."

He slapped the water's surface and sent droplets to the bank, splashing Nox. "On a day like this? Anything that needs to be said can be said in the water."

She wrinkled her nose. "Aren't there fish and turtles and things in there? I hate water."

"I'll protect you," he said, swimming toward the center.

She remained unconvinced. "Do the fish bite? Is anything in there going to eat my toes?"

"Only me."

"Malik…"

His grin softened as he watched her shrink against the idea of stepping foot into the pond. "I solemnly swear on my life that nothing in this water will hurt you. In fact, I swear with equal gravity that if you get in, you'll have fun."

She looked over her shoulder as if waiting for the All Mother herself to step into the glen and scold her for this invasion of Malik's space. Nox didn't know how to explain to him that she shouldn't be in his private thoughts. He wouldn't have stripped naked in front of her with such aloofness if he realized this was no typical dream. She had meant to meet with him to discuss the situations between the north and south. She had intended this to be a productive dream walk wherein she could disseminate information. Damn, she'd lost control of the dream so quickly. Then again…

"If I swim with you, can we speak about something serious?"

"If you get naked and get in this water, you can do anything you want to me, Your Highness." Malik took a mouthful of water and spit it toward her, arcing it like a fish in a fountain. It came nowhere near hitting her. She lifted her fingers to protect herself from errant droplets, once again caught by the contagious buoyancy of his energy.

"Fine," she said, getting to her feet. His goodness made

her feel inexplicably shy, as if it were her first time being naked before another. Perhaps her fear of water added an element of nerves to the prickle that ran through her. She lifted her shirt over her head and listened to his low, appreciative whistle. Nox wanted to roll her eyes but giggled despite herself. She turned to the side as she stepped out of her pants, giving the reever a profile view of her stripped body.

"Be a gentleman and turn aside so I can get in," she attempted to tease. More than anything, she didn't want him to see the undignified expressions she made as she crept into the water, still not fully certain that sharks and mud demons wouldn't arrive to turn the dream into a nightmare.

He dove obediently beneath the glossy surface, and she hurried to the edge of the pond to join him. She yelped at the temperature, shot a glance over her shoulder at her discarded clothes, and wondered if she could get away with abandoning the dream altogether and just writing Malik a nicely worded letter. He burst from the little lake before the water had fully wrapped around her hips, making her decision for her. Her eyes widened the moment she realized he was headed for her. She tripped in her attempt to stumble backward, pond swallowing her whole as the sky disappeared beneath the rush of cool water.

Mud squished between her fingers and toes as she caught herself on the silty bottom. She sputtered for air, thrashing to the surface with instant regret. Malik emerged like a merman, grabbing her and pulling her deeper toward the pond's middle.

"Relax, water bug." He chuckled against her shriek. "I've got you."

Nox brought her hands down against the surface of the pond in an indignant splash, but her anger dissipated against his playful tug.

She wiped the wet hair from her eyes and did her best to muster a serious face. "Listen! I'm in the water. I need to talk to you."

She'd been prepared to continue volleying with this swimming, cheery version of him. Instead, he turned and wrapped his arms around her, pressing his body into hers. She coughed against the water in surprise. Her mind raced. She needed to focus but felt every inch of him as his body traced along her own from her torso down her legs, with a particularly sensational meeting between her thighs.

Her face and neck cooked, heat consuming her as she lost any semblance of control over the dream. Nox swallowed, digging for the words. Her foot brushed what may have been a submerged tree branch as she attempted to move away. A banshee's shriek tore from her throat, and the world around her began to ripple with her instant jolt of terror.

Malik's face arranged itself with curiosity. He treaded water as he turned to watch the trees and skies waver. "What's going on?"

Oh, shit.

Her fear of water had interrupted the fabric of the dream. She forced herself to calm down. If she could conjure things within a dream, then certainly she could conjure things *out* of them. She meditated on a blissfully empty pond, convincing herself that she and Malik were the only things in the water. She breathed slowly until the trembling world stopped, snapping back into a firm reality. "Malik, this is a dream."

Droplets clung to his hair, dripping onto her as he tilted his head. "Then this is the best dream I've ever had."

Nox placed her hands flat on his chest, pushing against him as she stared into his forest-green eyes. "I need to talk to you, but I do need you to take this more seriously. I know this won't make sense, but please listen to me. I know you see me in the pond with you, but right now you're asleep in Aubade. Do you understand?"

He frowned and slackened his hold on her slightly. He eyed her while he absorbed her words. The wheels behind his eyes began to turn as he traced his mind over each and every bit of information she'd offered. Nox felt the world begin to ripple and worried at her mistake. If her own damn phobia of water didn't ruin their dream, then upsetting him certainly would.

"No, no, shh. You don't need to wake up. Everything is okay. I'm here with you. Please stay calm."

The forest's undulation intensified as the trees, water, and man himself glimmered like the waves in the pond had only moments prior. She forced her voice into a soothing calm, remembering how Gadriel had done the same for her when she'd been alarmed. The existence of a dream was reliant on the state of the sleeper.

She grabbed his bicep beneath the water and stroked his arm with her thumb. "Malik, stay with me. Just relax. You don't need to wake up. Everything is okay. We're fine, see? I'm fine. I'm real. Look at me."

The trees righted. Their private glen stabilized as realization trickled across Malik's face. He leaned into her steadying touch. His eyes sharpened, the playfulness fading from his features. He released her, and the chill of the pond swept in where his arms had been. Her mouth turned down as she reached for his hand.

When he spoke, his voice was rushed with apology. He looked away as he said, "Gadriel said you were a dream walker. I'm sorry, Nox. I didn't realize where we were."

She shook her head, rejecting his guilt. "Stop that. This is a lovely dream. Truly, I am so glad to be here. I wish we were on shore, but…"

"You're afraid of water." He grimaced. He ran a single hand over his face as if covering his regret. "I'm sorry for putting you through this."

"It's okay," she insisted, grabbing his arm beneath the surface. "Since I know it's a dream, I can help to reassure myself that it's perfectly safe. I prefer to think of this as a giant, chilly bathtub. Without soap. And surrounded by grass and bushes and leaves and things. Okay, so, maybe it's not a bathtub."

"Let's get out."

"I'm fine." She tightened her hold. "I promise. I feel safe with you."

His brow remained creased. He moved away from her, keeping his tone serious as the gap between them widened. "You needed to visit me to talk about the duke. That's what I discussed with the others before I fell asleep."

Nox chewed her lip. She followed him until her feet were no longer touching the bottom. She regretted ever telling him that he was in a dream.

Yes, she'd had important matters to discuss. Were they any more valuable than his moments of reprieve? Dreams should remain sacred. She wished desperately that she hadn't ruined the specialness of this place for him. Her heart sank. She was ready to abandon the mission altogether before she caught the hint of a sparkle that had returned to his eye.

"Just to be clear…" A small, mischievous smile tugged his mouth into a crooked grin. "You did willingly get naked and join me in the water while knowing this was my dream?"

Nox cautiously returned his smirk. "I'm a very hands-on queen."

The tension slid from them like condensation escaping a glass in summer. Malik closed the space in two breaststrokes and swept her into an earnest hug.

"You're here," he murmured. He pushed a kiss into her wet hair. "You were supposed to stay in Gwydir so you'd be safe. I never would have left you…"

"I used Chandra," she said proudly as she leaned into his kiss.

"I heard."

She looked up at him under hooded lashes. "Are you proud of me?"

He nearly choked on the staccato breath. The corners of his eyes crinkled earnestly. "Proud of you? Nox, I'm so honored to know you. You're fucking incredible."

She tucked herself against him, savoring the moment.

Finally, he said, "Amaris and Gadriel—they want me to stay in Aubade with the duke while the others deal with Sulgrave."

She nodded and turned to look up at him. His face was so close to hers as the water lapped around them. The chirping birds quieted as if listening for her response. "I think it's the best idea."

Malik deflated, his smile faltering. "I thought you wanted me to hurry home to Gwydir. Even if it's the best for the kingdom, I don't know if I want to be away from you playing babysitter to your puppet. Your general finds the duke's poems more charming than I do. Besides, how am I supposed to hold you at night if I'm half a continent away?"

She planted her hands against his hard chest. She looked up at him seriously. "Aren't you holding me now?"

He made a contemplative face. The birds resumed their songs in the toasty summer afternoon as the tiny waves they created made quiet noises against the bank. It was hard to be anything but happy in this little taste of heaven. Still, Nox began to gnaw on a question. Her silence drew his attention.

"Malik, I know you don't want to stay in Aubade, but let me ask you something very serious. Please don't lie."

He searched her for a tell but came up empty. He waited with patient sincerity.

She bit her lower lip as an impish smile sparkled through her. "Have you ever had a sex dream about me?"

The apples of his cheeks pinked. He failed to fully conceal his expression as he asked, "Excuse me?"

She lowered her face into the water, submerging her mouth and nose as she eyed him and started blowing bubbles in the glassy pond with her own amusement. She popped her face back up and grinned at him. "Answer the question."

Malik continued to redden. "Of course I have. You're the leading lady of every dirty dream."

She pushed away from him and began to swim toward the middle of the pond, leaving him where he stood submerged to his chest. She called another question as she swam. "And why is that?"

"Because you're gorgeous?" he offered.

"Try harder." She rolled her eyes.

"Because I'm madly in love with you," he said.

She clucked her tongue against his romanticism. Her eyes narrowed, mischief growing. "I'm talking about *fucking*, Malik. Why do you dream about having sex with me?"

"Because," he said with some degree of frustration, "dreams are the only place we can safely be intimate."

She eyed him, waiting for her meaning to click. He furrowed his brow as Nox dipped her head under the water, reemerging with her hair slicked once more. He blinked rapidly at her implication.

"Are you saying—"

"Indeed I am."

With unbridled excitement, he plunged after her in the water. She shrieked with surprise as she swam as fast as she could. A scream of joy, of excitement, the first of many.

She wasn't sure if he caught her, or if she let herself be caught. All she knew was that she wanted this. Her eyes fluttered closed as she tilted her forehead to his. He wrapped his arms around her, securing her to him as their lips met. She gripped the back of his neck with one hand, tightening her fingers against his damp locks of hair as she awaited her first time.

It was a whirlwind of firsts, after all. As he guided a hand to grip her ass cheeks, moving her hips against his underwater, she knew with absolute certainty that this would be the only time she'd ever made love—not used, or controlled, or fed on, or drained—but truly *made love* to a man. This was the first time she'd kissed him deeply without worrying that she'd lose control. It was her first time being held, wrapped in strong, tanned arms that had been bulked with exertion and time and felt so safe and so vulnerable all at once.

He paused at her entrance. Her heartbeat pulsed for him,

from her chest to her fingertips to the very center of her being. She wanted him. She tightened her hold and looked into his eyes.

"Are you ready?"

She sucked in a shaky breath. "More than I've ever been."

Her lips parted in a gasp as he entered her.

He paused, looking into her eyes while allowing her to adjust to his fullness. Her brows met, her forehead creased, her eyes squeezed shut as she bucked against the sensation. She felt his eyes on her as he absorbed every micro expression. She melted with pleasure. She grabbed him, wrapping her legs around his hips beneath the water and accepting every inch of him.

"Fuck," he groaned.

She'd meant to say something clever in return, but only a moan escaped her lips.

His movements began gently as she moved against him. He moved with her, using the motion of the water to guide her. Her breathing hitched, increasing in rhythmic intensity until she was clutching at his skin, drawing her fingernails in sharp lines against his back and biting into the muscle against his shoulder to quench her cries. His chivalry evaporated as he clung to her body like she was the last lifeline at sea. He seemed to need her every bit as badly as she needed him.

She was glad it was a dream, if only because no one else was around to hear her scream.

"Goddess, Nox. I—"

"Me too," she gasped. "Me too."

In this moment, Nox knew at least three things about herself. She knew that this felt fucking incredible. She knew that she'd been born to favor women, and that her heart would always belong to Amaris, but she also knew that she loved Malik with an intensity that grew hazier by the minute with each pleasurable, mind-numbing, filling thrust. She begged him not to stop, pleading for the climax to carry her over the edge. And finally, she knew that all of the best things in life existed outside of reason and that she would continue to plant her feet firmly in the gray.

✦

Malik opened his eyes with a smile. He tucked his hands behind his head and looked at the ceiling. Goddess, there were dreams, and then there were *dreams.*

A quick look under the covers confirmed his chuckled suspicion as he headed to the bathing room to clean himself. Under any other circumstance, waking in such a state might have been somewhat embarrassing.

But this was no dream. This was real.

He ran a wet, soapy cloth over his limbs and remembered rippling water. Every splash of fabric into the basin reminded him of gasps, of parted lips, of full breasts, of the most perfect body, of…

Shit. If he didn't get a hold of himself, he'd have to take a few more minutes in the washroom before he was ready to start the day. Then again, coming twice couldn't hurt.

He made no attempt to wipe the grin from his face as he toweled himself dry, or dressed, or as he descended the stairs to join the others for breakfast. He navigated to the corner table with two Raascot fae and the only other reever in Farehold.

Amaris was the first to look up. "You're awake! Did you get to talk to Nox?"

"I did," he confirmed, smiling as he tossed a roll into the air.

"Great," Amaris said seriously. "So, you've come around on babysitting the duke?"

Malik slid into a chair. "Sure, sure," he said, mind elsewhere.

He was glad Amaris didn't press him on the issue. She and Yazlyn seemed preoccupied with their own conversation, which was ideal. He picked at his dinner roll, more or less lost to memory. Gadriel was the only one who seemed to recognize the pleased twinkle in Malik's eyes. The general chuckled appreciatively to himself without bothering to ask any prying questions about Malik's dream as the group made plans to clear the castle.

Pleasures couldn't last forever.

✦

The foursome left the inn and made it to Castle Aubade with a mixture of relief and disgust as they discovered the ghouls were no longer animated. Instead, every hall, room, and corridor was filled with the rotting, stinking corpses of the dead. Whatever Sulgrave fae had bound themselves to the ghouls appeared to have departed, presumably having accomplished whatever they'd set out to achieve. Instead of slaying skeletons, the crew merely relayed information to the castle's attendants and guards and set to work on clearing the castle. The brown and beige clothes neutralized the servants and attendants against the tans of the castle, making it seem as though the stones themselves had come to life as its workers bustled about.

Between sopping bits of rotting flesh and piles of bone, Yazlyn made a few comments about how cleaning out Farehold's castle fell outside of her job description.

"This is on you," Gadriel said, breathing through his mouth to keep from inhaling rotting flesh. Malik watched the exchange while stacking one corpse, then two, then three onto his back. "You hung back to recognize Nox's claim to the throne. You've stuck around to make sure her…how did you put it?"

"Royal ass?" Yazlyn grunted, dragging a body by its wrist bones.

"That's right: her royal ass could fit on two seats."

Malik and Amaris kept to themselves while they worked, though they exchanged a few telling looks. Reever manual labor was clearly different from that of winged, magical fae. You couldn't take up residence at Uaimh Reev while remaining a stranger to grunt work. So the morning ticked into high noon, into the late evening. Bit by bit, bone and muscle and tissue and slush and slime, they worked with guards, attendants, and servants to clear the castle.

Several guards spent the day turning the back stretch of castle soil into a mass grave, and countless bodies later, the pit was filled to capacity. They salted and burned the bones so that if the Sulgrave fae returned to finish the job, they'd only have cremated ashes to call to their aid.

Words were exchanged over how long it would take for the horrid stench to leave the castle, but the servants opened every window, carried in buckets of soapy water, and had flowers brought in from across the city to counteract the atrocious odor permeating the very stones of Aubade.

All things considered, they couldn't decide if their day was better or worse than anticipated. The battle-ready crew would have taken the adrenaline of the fight over the unpleasantness of removing bodies nearly any day. Regardless, by the time the sun had set on Aubade, the castle was clean and their task had been accomplished, with the added benefit of showing a positive face to the castle's wary faithful. Perhaps under other circumstances, the servants would have balked at the sight of winged, northern fae. Instead they spent the day lauding Gadriel and Yazlyn's efforts and voicing their appreciation for their added skill at every turn.

It wasn't Malik's favorite day, but after a night that grand, everything that followed was little more than noise.

Five

NOX MAINTAINED HER COMPOSURE AS SHE SQUARED OFF against Ash. His copper shock of hair stood out like a torch against the castle's navy-blue stones. It was a fire she wanted to put out. She bit back the urge to remind him that she'd been the one who appointed him to watch over Tanith in the first place.

He flattened his palms on the war room table, leaning into his weight as he spoke. "You need her alive and well if she's supposed to help you with the other Sulgrave fae. How is she supposed to help if you've drained her within an inch of her life?"

Nox looked to where Zaccai leaned against the door. He shrugged, folding his wings behind himself as he did so. The iridescent oil-slick flash of Zaccai's feathers blended into the dark rainbow of shadowy colors, only adding to his aura of mystery. The spymaster had offered a few other ideas as to how they might spread the word of Moirai's demise and Nox on the throne, but nothing else held a candle to Amaris's proposal that they use Tanith and the harpies. At Nox's behest, he abandoned his loose leaves of paper in favor of the bird-like figurines that now dotted the war table map. She looked to

Tanith for the go-ahead before concluding the meeting. Ash dissented before Tanith had a chance to respond. His dissent turned what could have been a brief, productive meeting into a battle of wills.

"You're a reever," Nox said, fighting her irritation. "Shouldn't your priority be magical balance?"

"Don't remind me of my oaths." His honey-colored eyes became slits of burning ember. "As a reever, I know exactly how absurd it is to partner with demons."

"Technically," Zaccai lifted a finger, "harpies are red-blooded."

Nox's lips flattened as she fought her smile at the spymaster correcting a reever on beasts. Ash scoffed.

"She just came back from the brink of death," he said, gesturing to Tanith, who plopped her head into her hand as if bored with their argument. "Do you recall how sick she was for weeks in the dungeon following what she did with the mud demons?"

Tanith winced, as if hoping the mud demons wouldn't be brought up again.

"Belfor is sending over greenstrike blood," Nox countered. She turned in her seat and addressed the Sulgrave fae directly. "Tanith, you can say no, and I'll respect your wishes. But I wouldn't ask this of you if I weren't sure your health could be restored. Do you think this is something you could do?"

"Of course I could," she said, voice serene. "You could too, if you accessed your full potential."

Zaccai pushed up his sleeves as if ready to get to work. "All of us?"

Tanith chewed on her thought for a long moment before speaking. She angled her head, razor-straight hair shifting as she did so. "I understand what you're asking. I would have said no before I saw Ash summon the light." She turned away from the spymaster to eye the reever. "Ash, you called upon a power you'd never accessed before just as it was required of you. I thought as a faeling you'd benefit from long life and good health, but nothing more than that." She rotated toward

Nox. "Meanwhile, Nox is in possession of at least two abilities that we know of. It's given me much to reflect on."

Tanith eyed the others with cool, dark eyes. The sound of a clattering pin would have been as loud as a thunder crack in the stillness that followed her admission. Nox knew from the others' expressions that she wasn't the only one remembering who Tanith was when they'd first caught her in the gully and wrapped her in chains.

She wasn't just a faithful servant; she was a zealot, a missionary, and an activist. She had believed so intensely in the importance of maintaining magical integrity that she'd risked her life to cross the Frozen Straits to help restore magical purity to foreign lands. Her beliefs had met the science of lived experience, had been challenged by love, and it had changed her.

Nox attempted to swallow. "Um, that's great, Tanith. Thank you for saying that."

Tanith looked at no one in particular as she said, "I'm merely articulating what I've observed. This has only strengthened my belief in magic and how it knows no restraints. If anything, I was a fool to underestimate the All Mother's abilities to use her conduits. True belief would have been putting my faith in the groundwater rather than judging its springs."

Nox was unspeakably glad for Tanith's progress, but she wasn't so sure others who shared Tanith's beliefs would feel the same. She drummed her fingers on the table and asked, "Do you think the Speaker would be receptive to this development?"

Tanith arched a thin brow. "The Speaker desires unity. Bringing the kingdoms together is a beautiful, honorable goal. Nox, whether you know it or not, you are facilitating the will of the All Mother."

Discomfort wormed through Nox. A cruel upbringing beneath the church's thumb insisted that she keep her conversations about religion academic and hypothetical. She didn't have the patience for Tanith's faith. She shot Zaccai a pleading look to alleviate the awkwardness. He caught her desperate look and nodded in understanding. He pushed away from the doorway and approached the table, abandoning delicate conversational transitions in favor of directness.

"We need you to call the harpies," he said, gesturing to the map.

"But—" Ash started.

Zaccai didn't even look in the reever's direction. He maintained eye contact with Tanith as he said, "The message they carry is vital. We need the beasts to spread the word across the continent that Moirai was an evil queen who cursed the land. Tell the people that Princess Daphne's daughter was discovered once the curse was broken and that she is both the rightful heir and a benevolent queen. Tell the people they are safe and that the new queen is urgently looking for a solution to the beasts overrunning the land. Can you do that, Tanith?"

Tanith continued to eye the middle distance, lost to serenity. "Of course I can."

"And how many can you call?" Zaccai prompted.

It was with cool impassivity that she responded. "All of them."

"Tanith—" Ash begged.

Her eyes sharpened. She smiled as she reached for his hand. She squeezed it as she promised, "We've got this."

Ash deflated, and Nox knew the battle was won. If all went well, Tanith would bind the harpies, and for better or for worse, the continent would know Nox was queen.

✦

Ash was unhappy.

No, that wasn't quite right. He would have been unhappy if Nox had made everyone in the castle wear uniforms, if they were forced to exclusively eat stewed broccoli for the rest of winter, or if some decree had forbidden reevers from using the common tongue and instead immersed them in the unfamiliar sounds and symbols of the Tarkhany alphabet.

This wasn't unhappiness. This was rage, fear, and helplessness. They were putting Tanith at serious risk, and no one
seemed to give a shit. He didn't expect Tanith to be an
advocate for her own survival as the castle's odd man out, but
they owed it to her to exhaust other options before asking
her to fall on her sword for them in the hope that this asinine
harpy plan would work.

Every heartbeat pumped raw anxiety through his veins.
He ransacked Amaris's long-empty room for her bestiary tome
and turned with trembling fingers to the entry on harpies. An
elongated owl with stretched, ostrich-like legs, knife-sharp
talons, and pointed, serrated teeth looked up at him from the
page. It had human hair, a woman's mouth, and a human's
jaw, chin, and cheeks, but there was nothing human about its
dead, dark stare. He didn't care if she was the most powerful
fae on the continent; he didn't want the monsters anywhere
near Tanith.

But no one cared what he thought. He couldn't stop it.
The best he could do was use what was left of the day to
ensure they were stocked with greenstrike blood; then he
watched the clock until the moonless sky descended.

Tanith said with some certainty that the new moon was
a blessing from the goddess. Ash was too angry to make a
mean-spirited remark about how moon cycles worked. He
resented Nox and Zaccai for agreeing with her assertion as
the four of them headed for the roof. They mounted the
spiral staircase in relative quiet, thick furs, coats and blankets
rubbing together with every muted step as they bundled
against the impending chill. The frosted air of a clear, blackened night nipped at them the moment they emerged from
the highest tower onto the flat outlook.

"Is there anything you need before you get started?"
Zaccai asked.

Wind moved the hair around Tanith's face. She flicked
the dyed wool of her crimson hood over her ears and shook
her head. "No. I'm ready."

"You don't have to do this," Ash insisted.

"I know I don't have to," Tanith said. "But it's the right thing to do." With that, she raised her hands before her, meeting her top two forefingers and her thumbs in a triangle as she glimmered with an eerie, familiar shade of blue. A tangible, ethereal magic filled her hands as they remained lofted in a careful parallel to the ground.

Ash hadn't seen anyone wield magic the way Tanith did, so he wasn't sure if holding her hands was an essential step or if it was akin to the peculiar exercises she did that helped her focus. Then again, he'd grown up in Farehold, which had limited his exposure to magic altogether. From the look on Zaccai's face, he gathered that Tanith's technique was every bit as curious to Raascot fae. And because he couldn't change anything by staring at her with his brow creased in worry, he turned toward the dark horizon, and he waited.

For a long time, nothing happened.

The other three looked between Tanith and the eerie glow she wielded as the seconds stretched into minutes. The minutes became ten, became thirty. At half past the hour, he heard something.

The sound was almost as if a wind were picking up, brushing across the drifts of snow and creating a strange rustle with each movement. Ash tilted his ear to the sky as the wind transformed into something akin to thunder's distant rumble.

"Look," came Zaccai's hushed whisper.

Ash stepped toward the spymaster and strained his eyes against the night's inky nothingness. Zaccai's sharp eyes remained trained on something so faint, it might have been a cloud. Ash watched the cloud grow, blotting out the stars closest to the horizon, accompanying thunder swelling with every passing second.

And then the sound clicked.

Wings.

Gloved fingers dug into his forearm as Nox clutched at his arm, eyes wide, lips parted in a noiseless cry. His fingers twitched against the urge to draw his sword. He dared a glance at Zaccai to confirm the spymaster was every bit as rattled as they were. Over his shoulder, Tanith remained in placid focus, her blue glow beckoning the hoard directly to them. They remained glued to the tower in silent horror as the cloud descended.

Wings and legs and talons flapped and flashed. Hideous shapes obscured the walls, the grounds, and the very sky above. If Nox hadn't continued gripping his arm, he would have lost her altogether as she disappeared behind a veil of feathered monsters. He spun on his feet as monstrous birds separated him from Tanith, her glow vanishing behind the tangle of avian creatures.

Enormous, horrible birds with grotesque, human faces cocked and turned atop their owl-esque bodies. The rooftop was alive with beasts, every inch of the castle moving and crawling and squirming with harpies. The cursed animals did not chirp or hoot like any birds of the land, but appeared to be whispering in hurried, horrible tones. Between fear and nausea, he wasn't sure which was stronger.

Ash moved toward Tanith, but Zaccai stopped him with the flare of his wing.

"Don't," came his urgent whisper.

"But she—"

Zaccai's tone was low with warning. "If she drops her control right now, all of Gwydir could meet its end."

Ash looked at the murderous flock of pale skin, womanly faces, and shark-like teeth with renewed revulsion. A thousand pairs of beady eyes that would have been human, if they'd had any whites at all, looked back at him. They were drowning in the fears, lies, and whispers of hell and its demons, and the only thing stopping the harpies from turning on the city was a single, tiny fae. He didn't get the chance to argue. With cool command, Tanith began to speak.

The glow sharpened to a piercing aquamarine as she relayed her message. The harpies stopped their writhing and whispering as they turned to hear their master. Their message was threefold. Moirai was evil. Moirai was dead. And Nox, true blood heir to Farehold and Raascot, was on the throne. With a thrust of her triangulated hands, she dismissed the harpies, sending them back into the sky from whence they'd come. The force of their wings moved the air with gale-force winds, whipping snow and hair and ruffling feathers as they disappeared.

Nox waited until the cloud had nearly disappeared before she whispered, "Now what?"

They had not discussed how long Tanith would be required to maintain her hold on the power. From Ash's best guess, it had already been more than an hour. His muscles remained tense as he eyed her. Nox began to speak, but a curt noise from the Sulgrave fae cut her off.

Tanith grunted, "Once I drop my control, they won't be under my charge. I need to maintain my hold until the message is dispersed."

Ash's stomach twisted. "That could take days."

Tanith shook her head, groaning against the energy it took to speak. "I will have the message distributed across the continent by noon tomorrow," she said, each word coming out in a strained gasp. "You saw how quickly the horde arrived. Their speed is unparalleled. Landing in cities, towns, and villages throughout the continent will take a sore sight longer."

When Tanith closed her mouth, it was with the pursed lips of someone who would not be speaking again. Her remaining stores of power would require clarity.

"Where's the greenstrike blood?" Ash demanded of the others.

Nox's eyes narrowed. "I sent for more when she was sick. I'd planned to get it to Tanith once she was finished and safely in her bed. How was I supposed to know this would take all night?"

"I'm on it." Zaccai didn't wait for an order. He stepped from the ledge, wings carrying him into the night. The commander knew exactly where to find the magical scholars. Ash had no idea how much blood would be required in order to maintain the hold for the next twelve hours, but he said a silent prayer to the goddess Tanith loved so much that it would be enough.

Ash stepped toward Tanith, careful not to interrupt her.

She didn't look tired yet, but she hadn't appeared troubled or sick after taking out Aubade's forces in Castle Gwydir either. It had taken hours for the extent of her magical drain to reveal itself. The illness had acted like a slow virus, planting itself deep in the gut and infecting the body with every pump of the heart as it spread.

Ash played the events of the battle and her following illness with a slow, horrifying realization.

"We stopped her," Ash said quietly.

"What?" came Nox's reply.

"We stopped her in the gully. Who knows how long she planned to maintain her hold on the demons? She was deathly ill following the gully for weeks. Do you remember?"

Nox's lips pinched as she searched her memories.

He looked from Nox to Tanith, noticing the tiny droplets of sweat catching in the light of her unnatural power. She shivered ever so slightly, and he wasn't convinced it was from the winter air.

He understood everything at once. Horrifying images of Tanith's sweat-soaked shape flashed through him as she trembled against the power she wielded. With a gut-sick whisper, he said, "They're dead."

Nox's eyes flared. "Who?"

"Tanith said she came over on a skiff of five, remember? At least two are dead by now. Only two remain unaccounted for."

"Why would you say that?" It was Nox's turn to shiver.

"You've seen it. You've experienced it for yourself. When fae use powers that don't belong to them, the toll it takes on their blood kills them. Tanith would have died if we hadn't cut her massacre short in the valley. Her task was incomplete. And even then, she was so weak she didn't so much as speak for nearly three weeks. Even shielding us from her own lightning during the invasion was so draining I thought she was going to die. If that's true, then whoever bound the nakki forces in Yelagin or the ghouls in Aubade couldn't have survived."

Nox blinked with slow realization.

"They're coming to the continent to die."

They looked at Tanith with renewed horror. She seemed so invincible. Her well of strength wasn't merely in her ability to call on the unseen powers of the world but in her sheer force of will and her quiet resilience. Tanith had believed in her cause with the ferocity of a waterfall as it eroded the world beneath it. She'd been willing to die for her mission.

And here she was, putting her life at risk for them.

Time moved with molasses-like slowness as they waited for Zaccai to return. She was in her second hour of commanding the flock by the time he fluttered onto the roof, landing as quietly as he could so as not to startle Tanith. He'd procured six vials of greenstrike blood and informed them that the scholar believed they could safely harvest only two more vials from the creatures. Any more than that, though, and the captive greenstrikes would perish.

Ash looked down at the life-giving medicine and knew what he needed to do. He picked up a vial and took several cautious steps toward Tanith. With the gentle voice of someone attempting to pet a wild animal, he whispered for her to part her lips. Without opening her eyes, Tanith complied. Ash emptied half of the vial of greenstrike blood into her mouth, knowing their supply had to last them for the next twelve hours. He didn't doubt her capability for greatness. What worried him was the knowledge that Tanith would put dedication toward her cause before her own well-being. Ash had no faith that she would stop if the task turned fatal.

Maybe she didn't value her life, but he did. And he would not let her fall.

Nox waited with them for another hour, shuddering against the bone-chilling cold before Zaccai convinced her that she was of no use to Raascot if she froze to death. The commander stayed on the rooftop, keeping silent watch with Ash.

Zaccai turned to him with the first grays of dawn. "What can I get you?"

"Another blanket for each of us, and a thermos of something hot."

The spymaster departed briefly before the sun came up, returning with three heavy additional blankets. He and Ash both wrapped one around their shoulders, but Tanith remained perfectly still, displaying no signs that she was even aware of the winter weather. Zaccai left two canisters—one of hot tea mixed with whiskey, the other of chicken broth—on the flat stretch of tower beside Ash before turning in for the morning.

Ash shivered beneath his piles of blankets as he kept careful watch of Tanith, dribbling the ruby-red antidote into her mouth every hour, on the hour. The sun's rays didn't offer any heat until the nine o'clock bell. Unfortunately, it wasn't the only thing the sun illuminated.

Tanith was a husk of herself. The ashen bloodlessness of her skin betrayed what she'd spent the night concealing. The harsh morning light made it impossible for her to hide the way her slender limbs trembled. Ash attempted to comprehend holding his hands out straight for six hours on end, let alone the full twelve she'd anticipated. The upper-body strength of the single action was astonishing, and that was before he factored in the demands of calling upon an unnatural power.

His eyes traced from the grayish shade of her face and cheeks to the blue glow her hands emitted. As he stared at her hands, something thin and silver caught the light. The slim band of an aquamarine ring took his breath away. He was moving before he fully realized what had taken a hold of him.

Ash ran to her side and draped a blanket over her shoulders, not caring if it broke her concentration. He knew a blanket would not be enough. He dipped his head in the space between her arms and wrapped her in an embrace, taking the strain off her as she rested her arms on his shoulders. He breathed a sigh of relief when he felt her muscles relax. He held her in an embrace, willing his body heat to seep into her. As his cheek brushed against hers, he felt the icy pallor of death. Closing his eyes, he reached deep within himself to summon sunlight. He'd called upon it before to save Tanith from his father. The light could not fail him now.

Ash clutched her precisely as Tanith had done to him in the dungeon, mirroring the way she'd wrapped her arms around him as she'd saved them from the precipice of destruction. Death called on them now as a familiar face. It was a companion who'd knocked on their door more than once, asking them time and time again to join him in the afterlife.

You can't have her, he said, staring death in the face.

Tanith would never have been in this situation if they hadn't asked it of her. She was willing to die at the whim of their stupid request. He allowed rage to fill him, fury surging from his fingertips as he pressed her into his chest. He gave himself over to his fervor, summoning the power that he wouldn't have known existed if his father hadn't attempted to drown him in his shadow. Tanith was every bit as selfless as his father had been selfish, valuing her own life so little that she would be cast to the side as a pawn for the agendas of nations.

You can't have her! he cried out again as he raged against the reaper.

The sudden soundless eruption encased them in an intense, golden sphere of sweltering, incandescent light. The globe that captured them burned around the pair as the hot, white light heated the earth, causing the very stones on which they stood to glow with summer's baking intensity. His fury and passion and depth of feeling fueled the hot, humming light. Tanith's body relaxed against his as the light alleviated her frozen muscles, healing her with their summery glow.

"I'm not done," she said, voice weak.

"I'm not going anywhere," he promised.

When the high noon bell rang from the city's steeple, she dropped her blue glow with an unceremonious halt. There was no sound. There was no gasp of air or cry of jubilation. Tanith slumped against him as if made of gelatin. Ash dropped his light as he scooped her into his arms. He brought a hand to her throat to check her pulse.

"I'm fine," she muttered unconvincingly. Perhaps the greenstrike blood had spared her from unconsciousness, but exhaustion consumed her, and she surrendered to it wholly.

Ash cradled her with as much gentleness as he could muster as he carried her from the tower. Tanith didn't move a muscle as he navigated the spiral staircase, save for the barely perceptible flutter of her thick, dark lashes.

Tanith had been sleeping in his room ever since Elil had invaded, and there was nowhere else he'd consider taking her now. He pulled back the cover while still clutching her against him with one aching arm. He set her carefully on the bed, perching on the edge while he tugged off her shoes, wanting her to get a full, restful sleep without the discomfort of boots.

Ash turned with the intent of stoking her fireplace when he felt her small, soft hand. Tanith had limply grabbed for his fingers just as he'd attempted to rise. He turned with worried eyes, scared that she was in pain or that she'd grown ill. He scanned her for signs of sweat or strain. Instead, she looked at him with hooded, tired eyes.

"You're not leaving me, are you?"

The silence that followed was not one of hesitation. Ash had been bested in battle on more than one occasion. Amaris, as his favorite sparring partner and brother-in-arms, had enjoyed making a habit out of kicking his ass. She'd knocked him to his back and chased the air from his lungs more times than he could count. Ash had been cut by foes and slashed by enemies. He'd gripped bloody wounds and limped through forests. He'd stared down the eyes of monsters and survived mortality's sharpest edges. In his years on the earth, he'd never experienced the acute blade through the heart that this one small question held.

Her needle-sharp words punctured the protective layer he'd built around his emotions, releasing the dam of feelings he'd refused to voice. She'd won his heart without trying. He hadn't allowed himself to want anything from her in return, no matter how challenging it had been to resist the under-currents of longing when he'd held her. He hadn't permitted himself to look at her with anything but careful protection, despite the traitorous evolution of his heart, the gravitational effect she had on him, or the way his body throbbed beyond his control.

"Would you like me to stay with you?"

Her lip puckered ever so slightly. "Yes."

After a long, quiet moment, he slid in behind her, tucking her small body into the puzzle piece of his arms. He folded around her, wanting her to feel as safe as any human or fae in this world could feel.

"I..." She rolled beneath him, turning to face him. "I want more than...than for you to just sleep beside me."

His breath caught.

Her hair had always smelled faintly of jasmine while he'd cradled her at night. Now that she faced him, he could taste the sweet, sharp spice of ginger root on his tongue. The warm tingle of her breath mixed with his as she exhaled and he breathed her in.

He'd kept his arm around her waist, just as it had been for the nights he'd been the spoon against which she'd rested. Now it hugged the small of her back as she looked up at him with large, doe eyes. His hand slowly flattened against the curve of her spine just above her hips. She parted her lips slightly, and he was flooded with the same jasmine and ginger that had overwhelmed him. He pressed his hand into her lower back, bringing her body closer to him.

"Are you thanking me?" she said quietly, the wet heat of her breath nearly on his lips. Her mouth was so close to his.

"For the harpies?" he asked, moving his hand along her spine. "I don't give a fuck about the harpies. I'm thanking you for staying alive."

Her laugh was little more than a whisper. "I don't think surviving the night is much of a feat."

"Not for most, no," he agreed, "but you are not most. You're brave, and selfless, and reckless, and unlike anyone I've ever met. I'm thanking you for existing." His hand continued to move up her spine, grazing the back of her neck. It began its descent once more as her chin tilted upward, body rocking slightly against the trace of his hand.

She allowed her chest to press into his, bringing her neck closer to his mouth.

He sucked in a ragged breath as he resisted the urge to plant his lips against her throat. Ash dragged his hand up her back once more, resting it on the back of her neck until it cupped her head. He moved her so she looked at him. "Do you know how hard it is not to let myself want you?"

"Hmm," she said with a low, sleepy hum. A hand found his upper arm from beneath the sheets. "And why would you do that?"

"I'm supposed to protect you, Tanith. Nox put you and me together and... I haven't always been a good man. But I'm trying to be."

Her hand worked its way from his arm to his chest. "You're more than a good man," she said.

He knew she'd feel his treacherous pulse if her hand lingered. A familiar, forbidden ache worked its way through him. "I don't feel like one right now," he murmured, eyes fluttering shut.

"You are," she said, leaning into her words. His eyes were

still closed when her fingers pushed his hair back from his face, touching his jaw lightly as her mouth met his.

Months of withheld emotion burst into flame as everything within him ignited against the soft, wet pillows of her parted lips. He kissed her back with the intensity he'd carefully withheld for so long. He sucked in her bottom lip, then released it for her top before crushing her against his. Tanith tightened her hold against him. A single, encouraging moan escaped her throat, and Ash unraveled. He rolled her onto her back, pinning her beneath him. His tongue met hers. Her taciturn serenity did not extend to the way she kissed, each burning point of contact growing with hunger and need. Her hands found the back of his shirt, tugging it up over his head.

Ash rose to his knees, pulling his shirt off the rest of the way. She responded in kind, lifting her arms above her head quietly as she waited. His heart squeezed at the single, most sensual motion he'd ever seen. The unspoken consent of asking for him to remove her shirt crumbled whatever remained of his resolve.

He lowered himself over her, hugging her to himself with a tenderness meant to tell her how deeply precious she was to him.

"I want this" was all she said. No games, no song and dance, nothing but the stripped-bare truth. "I want you."

Their remaining shreds of clothing didn't last long.

Another encouraging moan set his soul ablaze as they pressed into one another, skin against skin. She ran her fingers down his back, holding him close. He froze suspended in the perfect moment, admiring her full lips, the anticipatory pinch of her brows, the way she tilted her chin toward the ceiling as she waited. He wanted to stay in this moment, to savor it, to live in it, to die in it.

The corners of her mouth turned upward as a single hand abandoned his back and slipped beneath the sheets. Perhaps he was content to live in delicious anticipation, but she was not. Her smile widened to a flash of teeth at his groan when she wrapped her fingers around his shaft, guiding him inward. She pulled him close, and Ash felt the wet, warm goddess herself as he slipped inside of her.

She closed her eyes tightly, back arching, neck tilting off the bed as he filled her. The sound she made was sweeter, more beautiful, more moving than any sonnet. He hadn't looked away, soaking in every expression, every movement, every flex of her muscles and flutter of her lashes as she'd accepted every part of him, body and soul.

Her eyes met his again as she slid her hand to the back of his neck, holding on. Her legs wrapped around his hips to bring him close, refusing to let go. He lowered his forehead to hers as he exhaled, shaky and trembling with his own groan of pleasure.

When they connected, it was true union.

She'd become as much a part of him as he had her. Their bodies melded with slow gasps, tenderness and longing. From his cradle of her back to the release of her breath, the clutch of her fingers and motion of her hips, their joining was nothing short of transcendent. It was passion and tenderness, desire and care, want and intimacy wrapped into arms and legs and lips and skin.

This was not a roll in the hay. It was not a drunken night, or release, or distraction.

This was love.

Six

I'M JUST SAYING," YAZLYN GRUMBLED, "I DON'T SEE WHY everyone else gets to experience magical dream walks except me."

"I'm sorry," came Gadriel's wry smile. "I have trouble keeping track of where you two stand. Do you like Nox this week?"

Amaris set down the spelled quill to watch the exchange. They'd only been awake for a few hours but already knew the harpy mission had been a success. The early-morning tavern had buzzed with news of the late queen and her long-lost heir. While pouring tea and distributing bread to her patrons, the barmaid had said something about how she always felt the queen was wicked, as she had a sense for such things. Southern citizens on the street were muttering their fear of the influx of monsters and their relief that the new monarch was focusing her efforts on the problem. Everyone seemed to be exchanging a shared message: Moirai was dead; Princess Daphne had a benevolent, hidden daughter; and Nox now held the seat of power in Farehold.

It was almost too perfect.

Amaris had remained in the dining room only long

enough to hear the patrons before scooping up a muffin and returning to the room to inform the north. Nox had been quick to respond with a detailed letter explaining the events that had taken place in the tower, from the horde of nightmares to the need for greenstrike blood.

"Are greenstrikes a southern thing?" Yazlyn had asked, peering over Amaris's shoulder.

Malik responded for her. "They're tropical, and blessedly rare. I didn't know their blood had magical uses, did you?"

Amaris thought of the greenstrike's entry in her bestiary tome. The horrid little creatures were rumored to shoot into unsuspecting humans and animals with arrow-like speed, burrowing beneath the skin in their hunt for blood. It was ironic that the creatures' own blood should turn out to be so valuable.

"No," Amaris confirmed. "To be honest, I know almost nothing about blood magic. What do the fae know of it?"

Gadriel leaned against the desk's ledge. "That it's forbidden."

"In that case, our current assignment is to break the law. Nox said the most urgent task right now is to acquire more greenstrike blood. Any ideas?"

"Don't look at me." Yazlyn lifted her flattened palms. "I'm not from here."

"None of us are from here," Amaris said with a sigh. She pressed her palms against her forehead to fend off a budding headache. "Malik and I will see what we can do. I think it's best if you and Gad avoid going out as much as possible. The south no longer sees you as ag'imni, but you'll still draw a lot of attention when we're trying to be clandestine."

The next several days passed with aching slowness. Malik and Amaris continued their fruitless search for exotic animals, apothecaries, or eccentric scholars. Gadriel and Yazlyn split their time between the inn and ongoing restoration efforts in Castle Aubade with the staff who'd already accepted their presence as allies. They bided their time until the arrival of a raven—one of seven intended for each of Farehold's noble families—appointing the Duke of Henares as Nox's steward and recognizing Malik as the steward's hand.

The letter marked the end of their time in Aubade.

Malik prepared to move into the castle to commence his full-time job as a glorified nanny.

"Where will you go from here?" Malik asked while packing what remained of his meager belongings. The others had already cleared out their earthly possessions as everyone was poised to leave.

Amaris watched her brother move across the room, doing her best to keep the pity from her eyes. From the slump of his shoulders and dull expression on his normally sunny features, his feelings about his new role were no secret. She'd had the answer to their next steps for days and had waited with bated breath, hoping Malik wouldn't ask. Now that their departure had arrived, she dreaded the conversation.

"Ultimately?" she asked, keeping her tone light. "We have to get to Sulgrave. We're not just dealing with a few errant tyrants. The issue lies with whoever is dispatching them across the Frozen Straits. But I assume you guessed as much."

Malik sighed. "I don't see how it's fair that you're going to make the trip to unseen lands and I'm supposed to stay behind. Does Ash also get to go?"

Amaris made a sympathetic face. "He has to go. We can't get to Sulgrave without Tanith—both the journey, and once we arrive in the mountains. And we both know Ash won't leave Tanith's side."

He finished his task and sank onto the corner of the bed. "I'm going to do my best not to hold this against you, though I do feel that Samael would want all of the reevers to stick together."

Amaris chuckled. "Oh really? Are you sure he wouldn't say that a reever presence in the fragile southern lands was essential?"

"No, he'd definitely say 'Malik should get to see Sulgrave,

because there might be cool monsters and new magics and he is the biggest and strongest reever.'"

"Wow, your impression of him is uncanny."

Malik looked to the corner, where Gadriel had been ignoring the reevers while he sketched maps from memory and tried to ascertain the best route from Aubade to Sulgrave. After a stretch of silence, Gadriel looked up from his work.

"Are you waiting for Yazlyn to return so you can say goodbye? I'm sure she'll appreciate that."

Malik nodded, but Amaris wasn't sure if she believed him. She couldn't recall a single conversation between her brother and the sergeant. She'd convinced the others that it was her turn to try to hunt down greenstrike blood, since the reevers had been unable to locate any. Now her absence was Malik's final reason to drag his feet.

"Has Tanith sent any information about where her skiff was docked?" Malik asked.

Gadriel frowned down at his maps. "She has not. I've been waiting on the information. I think there's a good chance that she wouldn't know how to find it on a map. My hope is that Tanith will show Nox the exact location in one of her dreams. But it remains to be seen."

Malik grabbed his satchel of belongings and rifled around until he found what he was looking for. He procured a pocket watch no bigger than his palm and held it out for them.

"Yazlyn won't return any faster by watching the clock."

He pushed out a breath. "No, this belongs to Nox. It's a manufactured item, I believe. It's spelled to act like a compass of sorts."

Amaris accepted the object and turned it over in her hands. It had the twelve numbers, a single pair of hands, and the consistent, monotonous ticking of a perfectly ordinary watch. Her lips puckered in a frown. "Shouldn't a compass point north?"

"Tell it to show you where Gadriel is," Malik said.

She listened to the rhythmic click, click, click for several moments. Voice heavy with skepticism, she looked down at the watch and said, "Show me Gadriel?"

The response was instantaneous. The hands spun wildly, slowing as the minute and second hand triangulated Gadriel's position. They landed with arrow-straight precision, pointing directly at the winged fae. Amaris's eyes widened. She looked from the magical item to Gadriel, who shook his head expectantly.

"Well?" he asked. "What does it do?"

Amaris's attention returned to the watch as the hands fell from their point as if a latch had snapped. They swung and bobbed until the hands returned to the proper time like a perfectly ordinary pocket watch.

Malik got up from the bed to swipe a few fruits for his satchel. He pocketed a pear and said, "It's a magical item that's meant to tell you where you want to go. Ask it to show you where the ship is docked, and it will take you there."

Amaris blinked at it. "Why do you have this?"

He shrugged. "It belongs to Nox. She gave it to me before I made my trip to Uaimh Reev so that I could find my way back to her. I probably should've returned it."

"I'll give it to her," Amaris said absently, turning the piece over in her hands.

Gadriel stiffened. Amaris's heart plunged into her stomach as she realized what she'd done. She winced as Malik spoke.

His voice was tightly controlled as he asked, "Why do you say that?"

Amaris looked at Gadriel long enough to see his warning glance, but it was too late. The moment she'd been dreading had come. She swallowed, struggling to find the right words. "Well... It isn't just Tanith and Ash who are heading to the docks. See, Zaccai is staying behind in Raascot with the military. He feels confident that he'll be able to serve as temporary steward in the north, just as the duke will in the south."

Amaris's dismay spread through her like poison. She

offered Malik an apologetic grimace, only to see that he hadn't breathed. He lowered the apple he'd been about to stash in his bag.

His voice was acidic. "Are you telling me Nox is going to cross the Frozen Straits?"

Gadriel set down the quill entirely and angled his body for the coming storm.

Amaris gestured for Gadriel to stand down. She lifted her hands as if Malik were a bull ready to charge. "Listen: it would be the first successful diplomatic mission in a thousand years with the lone ruler of the continent—"

Malik's temper erupted. He chucked the apple onto the bed. "No! Absolutely not."

"Malik…"

"I will get on a horse in the next ten minutes and can be in Raascot to hog-tie her to the throne. She cannot leave the continent for the goddess-damned arctic graveyard."

She squeezed her eyes shut. "About that…"

"No," came his loud, firm reply. She'd never heard anger in his voice. She may not have been at fault, but she'd kept it from him for exactly this reason. And right now, she was the only place he could lay his blame. His volume increased as he said definitively, "Amaris, no. I don't want to hear your arguments. She can't go."

With a sharp breath, Amaris dropped the other shoe. "They've already left."

She cracked an eye open to see the slack-jawed shock on Malik's face. An instant later, his expression shifted. His face reddened. She gritted her teeth and waited for him to throw things, to smash whatever remained of the fruit, to get it off his chest. Gadriel was on his feet, wings flaring slightly as if to protect Amaris from incoming shrapnel.

Malik's horror only swelled. "What sense does that make? What power does she have that would keep her alive on the ice? Why would she leave Gwydir? Do you *know* why people don't cross the straits, Amaris? Do you know why no one goes to Sulgrave? Because they die! Everyone who attempts to cross dies!"

It was Gadriel's turn to try. "Malik," he began.

The reever spun toward him. "You go! You and Tanith are the only two who need to go!" Returning his attention to Amaris, he gestured toward the general and said, "He has the power of heat, and she's from the cursed mountains in the first place. What the hell are you, Yazlyn, Ash, and Nox supposed to do apart from freeze to death? Do you want me to leave flowers on your icicle corpses? What kind of general would allow this! What kind of plan is this?"

"Listen," Gadriel ordered with cool command.

Amaris decided in that moment that she'd take a beseul over the anger of a gentle man any day. Practically frothing, Malik spat, "There's no logic to it. Zaccai and I stay on the continent while everyone else goes on a suicide mission? Why would you put the *continent's* queen in such a vulnerable position? What good can she do for you on the ice? What possible rationale would compel you to bring Nox!"

Gadriel's nostrils flared as he attempted to contain the reever's temper. "Malik, calm down."

Amaris groaned. Not once in recorded history had anyone's temper abetted by being told to calm down. She saw it the moment Gadriel did.

Malik was a reever, but Gadriel had the lightning reflexes of the fae. Malik wound up his fist to punch the wall, but Gadriel caught it the instant before he turned the bedroom into kindling.

Malik turned his aggression on the general, growling, "You're sending your queen to die, Gadriel. How am I supposed to feel?"

Gadriel relaxed his hold on Malik's clenched fist. He kept his voice level as he took a halfstep to reposition himself between Malik and Amaris. "It was Nox's idea. It's the right call. We have a chance not just to unify Farehold and Raascot but to make peace for the world. Imagine the political weight she'll carry when she's arguing the continent's cause. She's the monarch, Malik, not me. I can't tell her that she isn't allowed to go on a diplomatic mission. Especially when it's the most important mission of the millennium."

Malik headed for the door. Over his shoulder, he said, "That's fine. You don't have to tell her. I will."

Gadriel raised a hand to stop him. "Amaris told you: they've already left. Since none of them are winged, it'll take them longer to get to the crossing point. They need the extra travel time."

"Then I'll search the forest."

Helplessness strangled Amaris as she watched her brother struggle.

"I can intercept them if I leave now."

Gadriel remained firm. "You're nearly two weeks away on horseback. Amaris, Yaz, and I will be flying. The three of us will be at the dock in a few days. You need to stick to the plan and stay here with the duke."

Malik grabbed handfuls of his own hair. He looked at Amaris. "Give me the quill."

She shook her head. "It's done, Malik. They haven't been in Gwydir for days."

His eyes bulged with his anger. It was such an entirely unfamiliar emotion on his kind, warm face. "Days! Why didn't anyone tell me!"

Amaris's temper flared to match. Malik was a fool if he thought he was the only one angry, the only one worried, the only one with feelings. She moved from behind the wall of Gadriel's wings to gesture at the mayhem. "This is why! Look how you're reacting!"

Yazlyn knocked on the doorframe and poked her head in. "Am I interrupting?"

The room snapped in a chorus of conflicting answers.

"No—"

"Yes—"

She grimaced at the energy in the room as she sidled in.

Everyone turned to watch Yazlyn, emotions ranging from Malik's rage to Gadriel's stoicism. Amaris held in her next battle-ready words.

Yazlyn may as well have been waving a white flag. She grimaced apologetically. "Okay, well, do you want to hear what I learned from the apothecary, or should I let you get back to your fight?"

When no one responded, Yazlyn jutted her chin toward Malik. "What's wrong with him?"

Malik's eyes darkened. "I've just learned that you're all sending Nox to her icy grave while I'm supposed to sit here at the castle with her love-drunk duke."

Yazlyn yawned. "Oh, that. There's a reason she didn't tell you. She knew you wouldn't be happy. But she's a big girl." The sergeant changed the topic with unceremonious boredom, leaving Malik to simmer on his own. "Okay, so, on to the more pressing information. According to the nearly four shops I've found, unless we want to go into the wild and attempt to find the creatures themselves, our best chance to find captive greenstrikes will be the bestiary stables at the university."

Amaris practically choked. It was a morning of problem after problem. "Oh, great. They love us there."

Malik made a purely disgusted noise that he was being dismissed.

Maybe it was the humor in Yazlyn's quirked brow, or exhaustion over bumping up against walls before their journey had even begun, but Amaris's irritation leaked from her. She crossed to Malik and chafed his arms twice before pulling him in for a hug. "I know you're only angry because you're worried. But I love her too, you know. I promise you that we'll be fine. You're needed here. Nox trusts you. There's no one better to watch the entire southern kingdom. You're doing something no reever has done before."

He grumbled about how no reever had visited Sulgrave either, but as he succumbed to the hug, she knew he'd resigned to his fate—reluctant though he was. He was smart enough to know that no amount of yelling or throwing fists toward the heavens would change the course of their rapidly unfolding destiny.

They returned their keys to the innkeeper and abandoned their home away from home as they readied themselves for the road. First, they opted to accompany Malik to the castle and peruse the weapons and wares that supposedly belonged to Nox as Farehold's new ruler. Malik's mood changed ever so slightly as he realized he might be able to find the sword that had been taken from him nearly eight months prior.

While Malik searched the armory, Amaris took a trip to the stables to search for Cobb, Nine, and Fourteen. She spotted the reevers' common mares on the far side of the corral amidst several far nobler horses of regal breeding, but there was no gray to be seen amidst the black, white, and chestnut steeds. Amaris let herself into the stables and found the dappled gelding in a corner stall lined with clean straw and stroked his neck fondly. Her eyes watered as she thought of the first time she'd spotted him in Farleigh's courtyard. Odrin had swung her onto the horse's back, and they'd taken off to begin the rest of her life.

"Are they being kind to you here?" she asked. "Do you get enough exercise? Are you happy?"

Cobb whinnied. He pushed his velvety nose into her hand.

Amaris turned away only long enough to fetch a tin bucket of oats mounted on the wall. She hung the pail on a hook on the inside of the horse's stall and sighed. "I wish I could take you with me," she said softly. "Where I'm going isn't safe for horses. But when I get back to the continent, I'll give you the kingly life you deserve. I'll try to say goodbye before we leave."

She wiped a tear from her cheek and left the stables, doing her best not to think of Cobb drinking water from the basin in Stone, of him tethered to a tree the night she found two winged fae, of the animal who'd been there for her rebirth time and time again. Now the best she could do for him was ensure that he stayed comfortable, and castle life was a good life for a horse.

Amaris was still battling the sniffles when she entered the castle. She'd chosen the wooden door closest to the stables and was unsurprised that it led to the wing meant for the help. She rounded two corners before she spotted a flash of black feathers. Yazlyn was hard at work pillaging the kitchen. Amaris was hit by a wave of heat from the stone oven as she entered. Bits of flour hung suspended in the air, dancing amidst the iron pans, ropes of sausage, and bushels of herbs hanging from the ceiling. Shelf after shelf was dedicated to spices, to jars, cans, bags, and grains as if she were in a library of perishable goods. She'd never seen this much food in her life.

"Make yourself useful," the sergeant commanded by way of greeting. She tossed Amaris a potato sack before resuming her raid of cured link sausages, of smoked venison jerky, of rock-hard lumps of cheese, a jar or two of pickled vegetables, apples, dried apricots, and little loaves of white bread.

An attendant who introduced herself as Agatha appeared with an armful of loaves. Amaris was ready to explain herself, but the woman was utterly unbothered. "We've been baking bread all week to help combat the smell of the dead," she said, plopping the rolls onto the counter. She returned to her task without waiting for Amaris's reaction. Over her shoulder, she said, "Take as much as you can carry."

Gadriel appeared a moment later with a leather satchel whose contents gently clinked and tinkled within its belly. He set to work shredding burlap sacks and wrapping the healing tonics so they wouldn't shatter in transit.

"Where's Malik?" Amaris asked.

Gadriel jerked a thumb to point down the corridor. "He's off charming the attendants in the throne room. They're thrilled that they don't have to interact directly with the duke. You should have seen their faces."

"I want to say goodbye to him before we leave. Give me a moment and I'll meet you there."

Amaris took a piece of parchment and placed it on the wooden butcher's block. She wrote a quick note with the magic quill before jogging after the others.

We're helping Malik settle into the castle, raiding its supplies, and then we'll go to the university for greenstrike blood before we meet you at the crossing. Malik knows you're crossing and is mad at you—or mad for you. It's hard to tell. You might want to talk to him. Also, I don't know if I've told you this, but Gadriel and I may have made a few enemies at the university, so I apologize in advance if the mission doesn't go well. I'll check in soon.

She pinched her nose as she navigated the halls. The castle did smell markedly better, but the unmistakable rot of decay lingered, no matter how many fragrant bouquets lined the halls. The servants offered a curt, uncertain bow as Amaris joined the others in the throne room.

"If it isn't my wife," came the duke's singsong voice as Amaris entered.

Horror struck her as she realized people might recognize her from the role she'd played as duchess on the night of the castle's infiltration, but not a single servant looked in the duke's direction. It took her all of five seconds to understand that the entire castle staff was already exhausted by the duke's endless string of obnoxious bullshittery. Malik had been within the castle walls for less than an hour, but everyone had already turned to the steward's hand—the duke's blond, bright, sensible "cousin," who, bless him, had been touched by the sun as a child for staring at it too long.

Amaris eyed the servants curiously as they interacted with Malik. Relief poured from them as tangibly as sweat as they spoke to the kind, reasonable, handsome man who was to act as the duke's mouthpiece. She wondered if the bait and switch of introducing the duke first and then ushering Malik in on his heels had been intentional or pleasantly coincidental.

"Did you find our swords?" Amaris asked.

Malik excused himself from a conversation with an attendant and looked at her apologetically. "I'm pretty sure they were melted down before we'd even been handcuffed. I did grab you a jeweled dagger, just for the hell of it." He plucked the ornately decorated knife from his belt and handed it to her. "What about you? Any luck in the stables?"

"Happy and healthy," she replied, still looking at her new treasure.

"All three of them?"

Amaris nodded. "Want to walk us out and see for yourself?"

"I do. But Agatha was saying that if you're about to be on the road in the winter, the three of you should help yourselves to the castle's furs." Malik gestured to a woman in beige linens who, given the shocking shade of red splotching her upper chest and cheeks, had perhaps never been referred to by name in court. She turned away, if only to conceal her blush, and gestured for the crew to follow.

"Oh my goddess," came Yazlyn's murmur a few minutes later.

Amaris whistled appreciatively as the attendant led them deeper into a collection of extravagant robes, cloaks, and furs. She ran her fingers along fox, mink, and some cloud-soft wool she couldn't quite name. Amaris plucked a fluffy white pair of mittens from a shelf when she heard Yazlyn over her shoulder.

"It's lynx!" came her gasp. Amaris turned to see Yazlyn spin in a spotted fluffy coat. It bulged ridiculously over her wings, but she pranced to the mirror to inspect her find.

"Actually," the attendant corrected quietly, "it's snow leopard."

"As unethical as it is beautiful." Gadriel chuckled from the far side of the room. He'd snatched a few more practical finds from a cedar chest and held them out to Amaris and Yazlyn.

"Pants?" Yazlyn pouted.

"Fur-lined."

She shrugged out of the white-and-gray coat. "I'm from the north, you know."

"Yes, and Raascot is infamous for people dying in its arctic temperatures," came his dry retort. She took the pants with a sigh. He collected as many scarves, gloves, and cloaks as could be practically rolled and stashed into a sack.

"Are you sure we can't take the snow leopard?" Yazlyn continued to pout. "Just because we're cold doesn't mean we can't be pretty."

"We already have to carry food, medicine, blankets, and Amaris."

"Sorry." Amaris made a pained expression. She didn't love being dead weight, but there wasn't much she could do about it now.

"I'll have you carry whatever we find for warmth. Can you fit anything else in your sack?"

Amaris set to work emptying her bag to stuff it full of her new collection of wools and furs. She stuffed half the winter things into the bottom and began carefully replacing the supplies she'd gathered in the middle, intent on tucking one final blanket overtop to secure everything. She'd finished with the food and had just reached the quill and folded piece of parchment when she noticed a response in Nox's careful, looping handwriting.

Why doesn't it surprise me that you've found a way to make enemies at the continent's only university? I hope you haven't departed from the castle, because if you've left, I'm going to need you to turn around. I know of something that was stolen from the university long ago, and I'm quite sure they'd be willing to overlook your indiscretions and barter for their greenstrike blood. Go to the stables and look for a carriage that was owned by the Hand. It's manufactured for fast travel. If you figure out how to tap into its power, you could be at the university by tonight.

"What is it?" Gadriel asked.

"An excuse to go back to the stables. Shall we?"

They emerged from the castle into the cool, coastal afternoon. Malik spotted Fourteen the moment they approached the horses. True to her promise, Amaris said a final goodbye to Cobb before turning to the attendant. Though a kitchen attendant by trade, she'd appointed herself as their escort as they navigated the castle grounds.

"We're looking for a carriage—one that would have belonged to the Hand. It was black, and—"

"I know the one," Agatha said.

She led them behind the stables to a sheltered stretch of royal carriages. While the others shimmered in the crimsons and golds of Aubade, one glossy, black coach stood out like an ominous warning. The memory that hit Amaris was practically a nightmare.

She stopped short of the carriage. "I've seen this before."

The others approached the boxy death trap on wheels and ran their fingers along its exterior. The attendant had excused herself when they'd arrived at the stables, but he approached with the help of a young stable hand with two chestnut horses in tow.

Amaris's voice dropped a register. Even the horses were familiar. She continued looking into her memories as she said, "Not once, but twice. This was the only carriage other than the bishop's white-and-gold carrier that ever visited the orphanage. This belonged to the Madame."

Yazlyn's fingertips dropped from their resting place near the latch. "Didn't Nox's note say it was stolen? Or that it belonged to the Hand?"

Amaris was insistent. "I'm sure of it. This belonged to the woman who had intended to buy me. This was the carriage I was meant to get into. This was one of the last things I saw before I ran away and became a reever."

She glanced between the others, then dropped her gaze. Gadriel's face had remained unreadable. Amaris had volunteered very little about her life prior to her training at Uaimh Reev, save for the brief, pained statements she'd made outside of Farleigh. They knew that she and Nox had grown up in an orphanage together and that one had gone north to train with assassins, the other south to a life in a pleasure house. Uncomfortable puzzle pieces were clicking together as they eyed her. Amaris's eyes swam with memory.

Amaris scurried from the discomfort she felt by changing the topic. She looked at the stable boy. "We won't be able to return these horses."

Malik asked, "Do you want to bring Cobb?"

Her face fell. "No. Any creatures we bring will have to stay on university soil. I'd rather know Cobb is here. We'll be trading the stolen carriage and two sturdy horses with the university's masters for our weight in greenstrike blood."

Yazlyn made a face. "Do either of you plan on telling me what you two did at the university to make so many enemies?"

They exchanged looks. "We may have gotten into an altercation with the Master of Beasts and the Master of Magics."

"You *may* have?"

Gadriel waved his hand. "Words were exchanged. Magic was thrown. Promises were broken. Escapes under the cover of darkness were made."

Yazlyn leaned against the carriage as she expressed her amusement. "Ah. So, we'll be among friends. You two make traveling the continent truly wonderful. Now, shall we get to it?"

Malik approached Gadriel first. The two clasped hands but said nothing else. He took a step toward Yazlyn, but her casual, two-fingered salute cut the interaction short. Finally, he turned toward Amaris. Stoicism be damned; she wasn't going to be robbed of her goodbye. She wrapped her arms around him, soaking in the warmth of his hug one last time.

"Take care of her for me?" Malik asked.

Amaris pushed out of the hug. She held Malik at arm's

length and attempted to scowl, but any stab at irritation evaporated into a chuckle. "Hey, I'm your brother in arms. Aren't you supposed to be worried about me?"

"We both know you can take care of yourself." Malik crushed her in a final embrace.

"Make sure there's a continent for us to come back to," Amaris said quietly.

And though she wished he'd turn and go into the castle so he didn't have to see the glossy threat of tears in her eyes, Malik waited outside as they climbed into the carriage. He waited as the horses began to pull them down the road. He waited until he was little more than a dot against the custard stones of Castle Aubade. Then, he offered a final wave.

As the carriage jostled and bounced down the road, Amaris took the moments she needed to pull herself together. Gadriel busied himself with the rather curious reins that ran from the bit, to the tug buckle, to a slim hole within the carriage, allowing the driver to sit comfortably inside and steer the horses down the road while watching them through a narrow windowpane. Neither fae interrupted Amaris's reverie. When she faced them, it was to two questioning expressions.

"Do you have any idea how this works?" Yazlyn asked.

"If it's manufactured," Gadriel began, "then it's already imbued with the magic it needs. The only thing missing is…"

"Intention," Amaris finished for him.

They guided their horses from Aubade, and once they were well on the way, they did the only thing they knew how: they set their intentions and hoped for the best.

Between the spelled quill, the protective wards, the pocket watch, and every other manufactured object she'd come upon, no magical item had taken any specific tricks to manipulate. An element of their power seemed to be the simplicity of their operation. They collectively held their breath that the same would be true of the carriage.

It would prove challenging for Amaris to explain what

happened between Aubade and the road to the university. In one moment, the carriage window was filled with cream and caramel rocks, plants common to the coast, and blue glimpses of the ocean between buildings. In the next moment, sleep descended upon the coach like a fog. Amaris yawned, intending to close her eyes for only a moment. When she opened them, she battled fatigue to look out the frosted window toward gray stones, deep green splotches of moss, and snow-crusted hills.

Seven

W E DID IT," AMARIS MURMURED.
       The view beyond the windows was the rolling
hills and jagged rock she'd seen from the back of the ag'drurath. Amaris was hit with the familiar scent of pine and the
mist that clung to the land as frost sparkled on the needles of
the trees and frosted the edges of boulders.

She watched as the others bobbed their heads, stretching and yawning as they stirred from a deep, enchanted
slumber.

Aubade's climate had felt more like a lovely spring day
compared to the northern realities of winter. Though the
elevation near the university wasn't as dramatic as that of
Gwydir, the region's low-lying clouds kept the air heavy
with chilly dampness. Freezing fog clung to every rock, leaf,
and tree branch on the windless day, white, crusted hoarfrost
spiking from each conifer needle around them. Amaris wasn't
alone in her thankfulness that they'd taken so many winter
supplies from the castle.

"I'm not sure I'm ready to be back at the university," she said.

"Perhaps Yazlyn should do the negotiating," Gadriel
agreed.

Amaris dug through her bag until she found her warm, white hat. She tugged the fur over her ears and wrapped her arms around herself. "We're on the same page. Honestly, Yaz, it might be best not to mention that you know us."

Yazlyn's dark chuckle was equal parts amused and impressed. "What *exactly* did you two do here?"

"Don't worry about it," Amaris said unconvincingly. "Fortunately, Gadriel was perceived as ag'imni when we were here. I have no idea what they do or don't know about the status of the curse, but I assume you'll be the first Raascot fae they've seen in true form in twenty years. So, be charming."

"I'm always charming," she quipped.

They took their belongings from the carriage and stashed everything, themselves included, behind an outcrop of lichen-covered boulders surrounded by conifers. The pair gave Yazlyn a list of names and who they suspected would be good resources for bartering.

"Master Neele will be your best bet for locating the greenstrikes. She's the Master of Beasts."

"And she's probably still mad that they didn't get to keep me behind bars as a pet," Gadriel grumbled. "My escape was a blow to academia."

"Got it," Yazlyn said. "And if the carriage isn't enough, I'll just send them your way to take you away in cuffs, since they want you so badly." She said she'd brainstorm ways for them to make it up to her later, then disappeared down the road without them. They watched as the glossy black carriage, two strong horses, and its winged fae driver vanished.

"And then there were two," Gadriel said. He folded a wool blanket so that half rested on the damp earth and the other half snagged against the support of the boulder behind them. He took a seat and lifted an arm for Amaris to warm herself beside him. She obliged, but the gesture would always tug her heart to her memories of Nox. It was impossible for her to so much as accept the affection of a lifted limb before her mind was flooded with images of

Farleigh and the way things used to be before they became so very, very complicated.

Amaris rested her head on his chest as he tucked his arm in closer, folding a wing for added heat. She'd felt a lot of emotions regarding the general. She'd been afraid of him. She'd hated him. She'd loathed his very existence. She'd longed for him. Now she was just grateful to be held by him. Their story had not been a conventional one.

"Have I told you lately that I appreciate you not dying?"

She turned her head to look up at him. "I did my best."

He smirked, but the irreverent expression did not extend to his eyes. They softened as he said, "Your best was more than enough. You killed the queen, witchling. Now, if you can continue to stay alive, I'd consider it something of a personal favor."

It was challenging to distinguish the time of day behind the thick gloom of the clouds, but the falling temperature told them that night was quickly approaching. Gadriel warmed himself easily with his gift, and Amaris sighed appreciatively as her muscles relaxed. She eventually heated enough that she was comfortable taking off the hat and mittens and leaning into him while they talked of everything from war and family to their favorite breakfast food, how he'd become friends with Yazlyn, and why someone as charming and handsome as Zaccai hadn't found a partner.

Conversation idled, and with a slow exhale, Gadriel asked, "Will you tell me what you were talking about earlier? When you identified the carriage?"

Ah, that's right. Millicent. The brothel. The beginning of the end.

It had been so long ago that she had been nearly able to remove herself from it emotionally. She would have been able to tell him without a second thought, except that she understood what her choices had cost.

She rolled the memory around on the back of her tongue for a moment, wondering how much she would tell him.

But they had nothing but time, and she supposed these were things she wanted him to know. She kept the emotion from her voice as she said, "Our orphanage was a child mill, but I've told you as much. The matrons made their wages from buying and selling children. Most of the children came from poor families or mothers who couldn't support a newborn. The kids would often mock one another that their mother had gotten pregnant just to sell them, but I doubt that was ever the case."

"Children are cruel."

Amaris's lips twitched up in a humorless smile. "They are, they are. But they were products of the matrons. Nox was already there when I was purchased." Gadriel made a controlled expression but refrained from interjecting. She noticed the way his jaw knotted, but she carried on. "Nox says my arrival is her earliest memory. She was three...maybe just shy of four years old when the thief came with me. I'm to believe it was sometime after my first birthday, but I have no way of knowing the timelines. None of us have birthdays, which is just a byproduct of being raised without families."

She took a slow sip of air while she collected herself. He'd remained tense as he waited.

"Anyway, I don't know if you've noticed, but I look... unusual."

He smiled at that. "You don't say."

She rolled her eyes. "This is how the story goes: the woman you met? Matron Agnes? She knew I'd fetch a high price because my features are...commodifiable."

He sucked in a sharp breath, and she almost thought he was going to interrupt. Once more, he said nothing.

"They set me aside for the bidders with the deepest pockets. This meant that I wasn't trotted out on market day like the other children. The matrons put me through a variety of lessons in case I was to be sold to nobility or needed to have the advantages of the upper class. They also didn't want any members of the church spotting me in case I was recruited to serve in a temple. If I was swept off with the bishop on one of his visits, Agnes wouldn't be reimbursed for her investment. In the end, it was the madame of a brothel who put a deposit on me."

His eyes darkened. "How old were you?"

"I didn't go, Gad—"

There was a murderous calm in his voice as he repeated the question. "How old?"

"I was too young to go with her to Priory at the time, but I knew that after I bled, I'd be sent to the pleasure house. I looked exotic enough that she was pretty sure she could sell my maidenhood for a small fortune. The day she came for me, I did this."

Amaris gestured to her scar.

He shifted his weight away to observe her fully. His tone was one of genuine shock as he eyeballed her most prominent scar. He'd commented on her scars before, but she'd given vague, dismissive responses. She couldn't quite read his expression as he asked, "These scars? You did them to yourself?"

Pride bloomed within her as she looked back on the memory. "The matrons had been so careful to make sure I never got a scratch. I was unmarred. Soft, valuable, their perfect little prize—a flawless payday. Nox and I planned to run away. We had packed, we were ready, we were going to take to the woods that very morning. When the madame came, I did the only thing I could think of to destroy my value. Then I ran off and became a reever. Looking the part of a tough, war-hardened hero probably didn't hurt my credibility. But yes, these were self-inflicted."

He adjusted his hold on her, tucking her in more tightly. His thumb moved in slow, comforting movements that she wasn't entirely sure he was aware he was making.

She hadn't expected any emotion to find her. She'd been detached from the story for so long that she let her guard down over one final detail. Water lined Amaris's eyes as the lid on the box within her cracked open. Her throat knotted as she choked out the words that had haunted her for so long. "I told her to wait."

She felt Gadriel's frown against her hair. "Told who to wait?"

A single hot tear carved a path down her cheek. It cooled as it touched the outside air, tracing a chilled line to her chin. "The morning we were supposed to run away, I told Nox to wait for me. I didn't know about my persuasion. I didn't know about my commands. I didn't know I left her stranded, stuck to the back door for Millicent to find. I thought that when I took too long to join her, she'd take off for the trees. I was so sure she'd escaped. But I told her to wait."

Silent tears fell freely, pooling at her chin before they dripped onto her shirt. Gadriel tightened his embrace, holding her close, but he made a single, uncertain sound as he did so. She sniffed and looked up at him.

"You think Nox went to Priory in your stead because you commanded her to wait?"

Amaris wiped at her tears with futility as they continued to pour.

Gadriel took his time answering. His voice was gentle but firm as he spoke. "Amaris, Nox has strong fae blood. Your command wouldn't have worked on her."

Amaris shook her head. "But…"

"She didn't wait because of your power. There was no compulsion in her decision to stay. She didn't wait because you made her. You didn't hurt her, or curse her, or ruin her."

"But she stayed."

"Because she didn't want to run without you. She waited because she loves you."

Amaris wiped at her tears.

"Have you spent all this time thinking that she went with the Madame because of you?"

She choked back her sob. "She never would have gone with that woman if I hadn't run off and left her behind. The Madame had already put down her deposit, and she wasn't going to leave without getting what she came for. It should have been me."

He hugged her more tightly. "Nox doesn't blame you, Amaris. You got out. You were resourceful. You became a reever. You broke the damn curse. And now look at her. Does it look like her life is in shambles? She's the queen of the whole damned continent."

Amaris sniffed again as she reined in her emotion. A small, sad laugh escaped her lips. "I guess things have turned out all right for her."

He laughed at that, relaxing around her. The honest, thorough vibrations of his chuckles comforted her as his chest moved with the sound. "That they have."

Gadriel cupped her face gently. He used his thumb to wipe away what remained of her tears. She closed her eyes and leaned into his hand.

"You were both robbed of your childhoods, but you were not the one who took hers from her. The matrons did. The Madame did. A kingdom that allowed for the buying and selling of children did. You did not do this."

Amaris took a ragged breath. "You know, I kind of like you when you're not being an asshole."

He smiled. "I'm not so bad. Now, please let me know if I can murder Matron Agnes on our way back to Gwydir. I'd very much like to see her head on a spike."

Her mind wandered to a vision of decorative skulls, each the bleached remains of those who had wronged her. "There is a kind matron at Farleigh. Her name is Mable. She'd do a wonderful job turning the place into a proper orphanage. Maybe we can see about a regime change and make Agnes spend the rest of her days scrubbing the floors."

He looked profoundly disappointed. "Manual labor? I was hoping for something more violent."

"I don't want to traumatize the orphans. In fact, I'm hoping some of those children follow in my footsteps. Imagine Uaimh Reev filled with orphans. The only pain I want to put those kids through is the agony of running up and down that mountain."

And while she joked, she felt a weight escape her she hadn't realized she'd been carrying. The tightly guarded box had burst open, and once the beast within had been addressed, it lost its power. The lightness it left in its wake was better than a belly full of wine. Perhaps they were sitting against a rock in the fog poised to cross the straits, but as far as she was concerned, life was pretty damn good.

She exhaled the last of the baggage and breathed in comfort, hope, and certainty. She relaxed against Gadriel, losing herself to the soothing strokes as he ran his fingers through her hair. A warmth akin to being wine drunk spread through her as she let herself desire one more thing. Maybe she was in the mood to celebrate, maybe it was the high of being alive, but right now she felt safe, and wanted, and loved. Gadriel moved his hand from her hair to her arm, continuing to trace his fingertips along her in slow, intoxicating patterns. A tingle spread through her, forcing her toes to curl.

"While we're asking favors…" She let her voice trail off, feeling a nerve tick behind her ear. He cocked his head in interest.

"Ask your question, witchling."

"Well," she said, exhaling slowly, "in addition to healing age-old traumas, I've beaten a dragon, killed a queen, and I've mastered my shock wave. As my trainer, you should be very proud. There is something on my to-do list that I've been trying to tick off for some time."

His crooked smile sent a thrill through her. Emboldened, she pressed on. "And you should also allow yourself to touch me without worrying that I'm going to damage the castle. In fact, we are in the forest…"

His chest shook with a laugh, though the sound was noiseless. "Oh, Amaris. When I do finally fuck you—and believe me, I will—I'm not going to bend you over a rock in the woods while we wait for my sergeant to run up on us. And it won't be because you're feeling sad and in need of comfort. I'm neither quick nor gentle. When I finally have you to myself, it will take me all damn night."

The air escaped her lungs. Her cheeks burned.

His hand began a slow ascent from her knee up her thigh as he continued speaking in a low, husky voice. "You'll feel safe. You'll feel cared for. And you'll feel loved. Because you are, Amaris. Deeply."

She squirmed, and his hand wrapped around her thigh, holding her still. "Then when you feel unsafe, it won't be because of the past, and it won't be memories of someone else. It will be the hand on your throat as I see whether or not you're going to be good, or if you're going to make things very, very hard."

Amaris let out a sound she could only describe as a whimper. Her hips moved on instinct, begging him to touch her. She wanted him more than she could say. Her eyes remained closed as she leaned toward him. She felt the heat of his breath as his lips moved against her ear.

"I'm very much looking forward to taking my time with you."

She stopped breathing altogether, leaning into his touch with her every inch and curve and muscle. His hand continued to climb, tracing idle circles as he felt nearer and nearer to where she wanted so desperately for him to touch her. Her back arched against the rock. She'd been so focused on the hand working its way up her thigh that she released a small gasp when his other hand slipped against the tender skin where her neck and shoulder met.

"Do you know why I gave you a safe word?"

She attempted to swallow as she shook her head slightly. Her heart did its best impression of a hummingbird's wings, the fog of lust, fear, and adrenaline eliminating all capacity for thought.

"Because I like it when you struggle."

"Sadist," she said on a ragged breath.

"Something like that." He kissed her hair.

She had no interest in waiting. She twisted and swung

her thigh over his legs, straddling him in an instant. She plunged her fingers into his hair and slammed her mouth into his, pleading, demanding. He crushed her into the hard wall of his chest, clutching her tightly as his tongue made a perfect circle against her own. He broke the kiss, dragging the heat of his mouth down the outside of her throat. Her hands fumbled for the clasp at his belt, but he snatched her hands easily and held her wrists together behind her back.

"Give a witch an inch, and they take a mile."

She gasped against the sudden halt. She did her best to flirt between her staccato inhalations. "I'm a goddess, not a witch, remember?"

She was met with a dark chuckle. His words came out in the low rumble of a growl. "No, no, witchling. In the bedroom, I'm god."

Oh, goddess damn this man.

She hated how much she wanted him. He was infuriating and terrifying and beautiful, and she loved every second of it. She wanted to punch him in the face just to be bested in battle by him and feel his crushing weight on top of her. To meet the All Mother with his hand on her throat would be a heavenly way to die.

Instead, she was met with a far less pleasurable kind of death. It was the soul-sucking slap back to reality that came from Yazlyn's voice carrying from down the trail.

"Why did you two have to hide so blasted far!"

The smile stayed on his lips as he muttered, "See? What did I tell you?"

Amaris offered a small laugh. "It's not my fault she has the worst timing. She's your soldier."

"I don't claim her."

"Hello? Am I about to come up on two dead bodies?" Yazlyn continued calling from down the path. The boulder they'd rested against had sheltered them from prying eyes.

Amaris dismounted with a defeated sigh as Gadriel stood

to get Yazlyn's attention. The rush of cold air in his absence sent a chill down her spine, and not the pleasurable kind. She couldn't get into her mittens fast enough. Tucked into her furs, she squinted through the final steely grays of dusk as she waited for Yazlyn to emerge from the fog.

"So?" he asked, dipping his hands into his pockets and leaning against the boulder with the unruffled ease of an alley cat. "How'd it go?"

Yazlyn lofted a small leather satchel over her head. "I don't know how many was a good trade. I asked for two vials in exchange for the horses and magical carriage. Did I get swindled?"

"Yes, you're very funny," he said, voice tired and wry all at once. "Everyone finds you exceedingly charming and clever. Now, report."

She sighed at the lack of an appreciative audience.

"Well, as you can imagine, they were surprised to see a carriage that was stolen from the university nearly thirty years ago ride up into their lawn. Did you know the carriage's creator was murdered by its thief?"

Amaris's thoughts drifted to Millicent. "That doesn't shock me."

"Of course, I had to insist that I'd come by the carriage honestly and that I deserved to be fairly compensated, since I have nothing to do with whatever shadowy dealings happened decades prior. I invested my hard-earned savings in this carriage, after all. They were…reluctant. It seems as though they felt some property right over the stolen goods."

Gadriel's jaw flexed with controlled irritation as he did his best to humor her. "Are you going to tell me how many you received, or are we going to continue playing this very fun game?"

She opened the satchel to display a dragon's hoard of glass vials filled with red liquid. Whatever Yazlyn had said or done had clearly gone exceedingly well. Additionally, she'd done what Amaris and Gadriel could not and managed to leave the university without making powerful enemies.

"Amaris, can you see if Nox has written anything about the docking location? We still need to know how to find this skiff."

Amaris pulled her quill and parchment out and set them on the blanket but was disappointed to find the parchment blank. She wrote a note.

Your advice was sound. We were able to trade the carriage for greenstrike blood. We're at the university now waiting for further instructions on where to meet. Please advise as soon as you've learned more from Tanith.

"Can't we use the compass?" Yazlyn asked.

"What's the use if Tanith isn't there? We won't get to Sulgrave without her," Amaris said.

Yazlyn made a face while she observed their surroundings. "Are we supposed to just camp here in the snow when there are perfectly warm dormitories and buildings just over the hill? We're about to spend weeks in the freezing cold. Doesn't one last night in shelter sound nice?"

"Ah yes, and those weeks will fly by if you spend the whole time complaining." Gadriel was already hanging a second blanket over a low-hanging branch. The makeshift tent would help to capture this supernatural body heat. Between the insulated feathers of the fae, the night might not be too terribly unpleasant.

"Are you going to make me cuddle?" Yazlyn asked.

"I'm not making you do anything. Lie over there and be cold."

Amaris rested her head on Gadriel's chest as he tucked her against him. Yazlyn's protests were short-lived and all for show, as she was quick to take advantage of his furnace-like ability. The sergeant's blackberry scent mingled with Gadriel's natural dark cherry and leather cologne, creating a delightful cloud of heat, security, and wonderful fruits. It was as safe and comfortable as she'd ever felt. He draped his other arm around his friend, and the three of them slept as soundly as they might have on the softest feather bed in the castle.

Eight

A MARIS REACHED FOR GADRIEL AS SHE OPENED HER EYES but found she was no longer on the forest floor. There were no fae, or wings, or trees to be found. She slowly let her eyes adjust to her surroundings until she recognized her room in Castle Gwydir. She turned a sleepy face to the logs popping merrily in the fireplace and savored the soft, warm sheets.

A soft sound came from the far side of the bed. Before she had the chance to turn toward the noise, she inhaled a luxurious, unmistakable plum-laden perfume. For the first time in her life, she understood she was asleep without being told. Amaris rolled onto her side and looked into the most beautiful face in the world.

"We're dreaming, aren't we?"

Nox was in a black nightdress that barely grazed the top of her thighs, propping her head up with her arm on one pillow. She settled soft, slender fingers on Amaris's waist and looked into her eyes. Amaris expected her to smile, but she didn't. Instead, she moved closer.

"That we are, Snowflake. Do you know where you are?"

"In real life? I'm quite certain I'm on a forest floor outside of the university."

"Real…" Nox repeated the word. "What makes one experience more real than the other, I wonder?"

Amaris didn't know how to answer. Truth be told, she wanted this to be real. She and Nox had spoken regularly through the quill, but the last time she'd dreamed of her face had been the night she'd almost died. Even then, it had been a good dream. She tilted her head. "To what do I owe one of your famous dream walks, Your Majesty?"

"We had a deal, remember?"

Amaris did.

She remembered their fight. She remembered their words, their anger, and her promise. Nox had said that she couldn't know if what they felt was real, or if they'd been tools of destiny born to undo a curse. Amaris remembered her solemn vow to kill Moirai and break the curse if that's what it took for them to find out.

"The curse is broken," Amaris responded quietly.

"It is." Nox nodded. She lowered her head, touching her forehead to Amaris's.

"Why haven't you visited me like this before?" Amaris asked.

"I have," Nox replied. She looked up at her through her lashes. "It's not my fault you have no control over your sleeping mind… I think if I'm honest with myself, I've been visiting you for a long, long time without understanding that I was dream walking. It's my secondary power, I suppose. It's meant to make me sick. And it did once. The first time I truly understood what I was doing, it nearly killed me."

Amaris's brows knit, but she knew Nox wasn't finished speaking.

"For years, I was at the Selkie, so there was no shortage of ways for me to replenish my strength. I suspect that's why I had no idea I was tapping into a secondary power. If I'd stayed there, I may never have noticed I was using a new ability. But when I think about the times I've dreamt of you…there were so many times we were together like this. Almost together, anyway."

Amaris's eyes scanned for recognition. "So many times where we nearly kissed?"

Nox sucked in a breath. She so rarely looked caught off guard, yet this small piece of information seemed to rattle her. "So, you do remember them."

Amaris laced her fingers through Nox's. "Do you remember all of the times we used to sit on the other's bed at Farleigh? How we'd hide from the others and whisper and spend all of our time in our own little bubble?"

Nox exhaled a single, soft laugh.

Amaris didn't know if there was a right or wrong way to ask the question on her mind. She slipped her hand over Nox's, fingers grazing the soft skin of her wrist. "Did you always feel this way about me? Did you always know that you loved me…in this way?"

Nox's face grew more serious as she released a long breath. "Amaris, I loved you from the first moment I saw you, but love can take so many shapes. It was you and me against the world—set apart without truly understanding why. All we had was each other. I didn't think about boys the way some of the other girls did. But…back then? I don't know. Maybe on some level, I knew."

The very fire quieted, as if the flames leaned in to hear what Nox would say. She was sharing something that would change Amaris's life, one way or another. Whether she left feeling full or with a broken heart, the time had come to speak their truths.

"Why didn't you say anything?"

Nox's pause was considerate. She looked down at the pale fingers that rested on her wrist and picked up Amaris's hand, turning it over in her own before she interlaced their fingers. "Because it felt like a betrayal, in a way. I wanted you to be able to love me and trust me without agenda. I didn't want you to think that the reason I cared for you was that I wanted anything from you…because I didn't. I still don't. I wouldn't ask anything of you if I knew that you were happy. If all you'd ever wanted from me was friendship and family, then I would have been that for you until my dying breath, and I wouldn't regret a moment of it. That's still true."

Amaris chewed on her lip. "I don't think it's fair."

Nox flinched. She averted her gaze.

"No," Amaris amended, squeezing Nox's hand. "I don't think it's fair that you kept this to yourself. You didn't give me the opportunity to fully see you. You didn't trust me to still love you regardless of whether I returned your affection. I won't even get into how infuriating it is that you didn't trust that what we felt was real until the curse was broken. The bed is too soft and the night is too nice to pick at old wounds. But this is something else."

Amaris may have claimed she was irritated, but her face told a different story. Their story was one that had taken years, a curse, two kingdoms, and a continent to unfold, but they had been inevitable. There was no anger, or regret, or sorrow. What she felt was deep, and singular, and beautiful. Nox's stare had remained fixed on their hands, but she tilted her head slowly, grazing up the arm, the shoulder, the neck, until she finally met Amaris's patient eyes.

"Bygones?"

"Bygones."

It wasn't poetry, but it was all they needed.

Nox untangled their hands and dragged her fingertips along Amaris's jaw.

Amaris said, "It's not fair that we had all of those years together when we could have been sharing moments like this."

She brought her hand to where Nox was still touching her hair and squeezed it, closing her eyes with emotion as she did so.

"Come to think of it, how did we spend our entire lives together and never discuss anything romantic? What friends avoid the topics of crushes and sex and love as if it were the plague? I mean, I understood why we were better off avoiding talking about Yazlyn—who is asleep an arm's length away from me at the moment, by the way." Amaris bit back her smile. A thought tickled her mind, and she shifted topics. "Can I ask you a question?"

Nox perked.

"You and Malik…?"

"Oh my goddess, *that's* what you want to ask?" Nox threw herself onto her back with a grin, covering her eyes but not her smile. The giggle that emanated from her was infectious.

"We're overdue!" Amaris insisted with a shove. Her eyes widened as she watched Nox squirm. "How? You don't like men!" She shook her head in conspiratorial disbelief, matching Nox's grinning energy.

"I don't know what to tell you. It truly just happened the other night. In a dream."

"You can do that?" Amaris asked, surprise colored ever so slightly with a jealousy she hadn't expected.

Nox peeked through her fingers. "That's what you and I are doing now, isn't it? Dreaming?"

Amaris thought of the countless dreams where they'd lain in bed, just like this. There had been so many times their lips had almost touched. So many kisses that never were.

Nox said, "I've never been able to be with a man without him dying underneath me or turning into a husk. Well, you've met the duke, so you know exactly what happens. Honestly, it was a great arrangement given my profession. That, and considering I generally find men vile creatures. Their death was fortuitous. Honestly, life was simpler when I hated all men. I'm irritated with you and your reevers for robbing me of that."

"We'll talk about murder later," Amaris said, rolling her eyes. "And? Nox the Killer Queen falls for a man! How was it?"

"Ah, damn. I knew I was missing a title when I sent out those decrees: Killer Queen. Not quite as catchy as your title, Queen Killer." She hedged. "Are you sure you want to be talking about this?"

Amaris made a serious face. "Since when have we kept things from each other? You know, other than you keeping your feelings from me a secret. And that you were a succubus. Actually, come to think of it, do you tell me anything?"

Nox gave her a look.

"Tell me," Amaris said again, and she was surprised to find that she meant it. Friends were meant to share their lives with one another. And they were so much more than friends.

Nox covered her face again, still smiling. Amaris gaped at the sight. She'd never seen Nox at a loss for words—never seen her flustered, or giddy, or anything of the sort. "It was incredible. It's completely different from being with a woman—not better, just different. I won't be fancying men anytime soon. But it was certainly an experience. How is it with the general?"

Amaris twisted her mouth. "We haven't technically…"

Nox's eyes narrowed. She relaxed the weight of her head against her hand as she propped herself up once more. "I don't believe you."

Amaris sat up so that she could cross her arms across her chest. "It's not for lack of trying. Honestly, I think I'm attracted to him for some of the same reasons that I'm attracted to you. You're both quite formidable."

Nox winked. "It doesn't surprise me that you like domination. You've always been a brat."

"Now you even sound like him. Except, he says truly the filthiest things."

"Oh, dirty talk turns you on? I'll make a note."

Amaris blushed and averted her eyes. "You're taking notes?"

Nox's smile widened. She was taking entirely too much pleasure in having flirted Amaris into shyness. With a saint's solemnity, she said, "I have a moral obligation to ensure that our first time is spectacular. Especially if it's your first time with a woman."

Amaris scrunched her face. "First time with anyone, technically. Fully, anyway."

"Liar!"

"Hand to the All Mother."

"I didn't realize I was sharing a bed with someone so pious! A goddess, sure, but a maiden as well? After all of those years living with your burly, handsome assassins? My, oh my."

"I did attempt to crawl into Ash's bed once...but that's a story for another time."

Nox laughed. "I guess, technically speaking, I also tried to take Ash to bed—for entirely different reasons."

Amaris's eyes bulged.

"You know," Nox sighed, "we were robbed of this. As friends, as partners, as anything. We never got the chance to laugh and exchange secrets. Not like this. It's..."

"Nice."

"All that fancy education and the best you can come up with is 'nice'?" Nox clucked her tongue. "So? Why haven't you?"

Amaris made a sputtering sound as she considered the many reasons she was the most pious person on the continent. "You know how it usually takes a great pain or trauma or near-death experience to get someone to access their powers?"

Nox frowned. "Go on."

Amaris groaned from embarrassment. "Mine is tied to near-death arousal. Literal choking, biting..." She flinched preemptively before her final words came out. "Some rather rough...play? That's what brought on the shockwave that destroyed my room. It's made him...wary of instigating much more with me."

Nox picked up her pillow and slammed it back down. "You were destroying *my* castle! And you didn't tell me!"

"We were fighting." Amaris laughed. "Plus, you hated me. And I wasn't sure if this was the kind of thing we'd ever talk about. This is...atypical."

Nox sighed. "I don't want to keep things from you anymore."

Amaris rolled her body onto Nox's stomach, propping her hands up beneath her chin just beneath the girl's chest. "It's just…here we are, working through what we feel for one another. Is it weird to spend that time talking about other people?"

Nox looked truly unbothered. She rolled her shoulders. "You're my best friend and have been since long before I knew how I felt about you. Besides, us discussing sex and our partners is no weirder than an orphaned escort taking the continent while a demigoddess breaks the curse and falls in love with their queen. I don't think a conventional life was ever in the cards for us."

Their smiles faded. The camaraderie softened as something else took its place. Amaris had expected to be afraid. She'd thought cowardice would take her when the moment for honesty came, but instead, she had never felt more sure of anything. She leveled her stare as she said, "Nox, I almost died to break the curse to prove that this is real. We're real. And…I'm ready now. If you aren't, I want you to know that's okay. We've been through a lot. But you should know, I have no intention of letting this go. I'm going to keep chasing you if it takes the rest of my life."

Nox's mouth twitched in a smile. A second turned into two, then five, then ten.

She didn't answer with words. Instead, she flattened a hand on Amaris's back and gently rolled her to her side. She lowered her mouth ever so slowly, a hair's breadth from Amaris's lips, hovering in the space above them as she had in so many dreams. The air passed between them as the thin fabric of their nightdresses remained the only barrier. She didn't complete the descent, letting Amaris feel the energy charge of anticipation.

Amaris recognized this moment. This was where their dreams had always ended. She'd awoken time after time without knowing if Nox's lips tasted of cinnamon, or her tongue of plums. She was owed this moment. When their lips met, it would not be a teary kiss between iron bars, or a confused, emotional kiss of reunion in the town house when their lives were on the precipice of disaster. She wanted a slow, intentional, perfect moment. She wanted this.

Amaris's fingers balled into fists of the papery fabric that clutched Nox's hip and took the plunge.

In that moment, she tasted twenty years of apprehension, hope, longing, love, and passion. Between gasps for air, wrestling for closeness, and the desperation to be nearer, she was consumed with a need so deep that it could only be described as wanting to crawl into the other's skin and live within them. She wanted to melt into Nox, fusing to her so that nothing could tear them apart again.

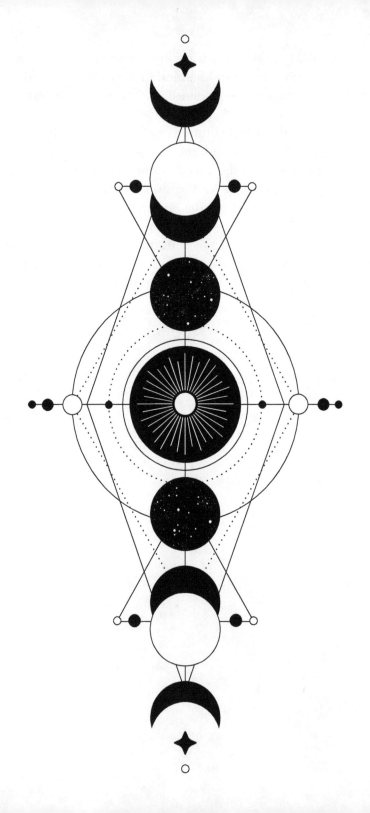

PART II

Into the Impossible

Nine

WET CLUSTERS OF FALLING SNOW STIRRED AMARIS FROM her sleep.

Her hand flew to her mouth, dragging her fingertips along the lips that had been ablaze only moments ago. She winced against the chilly kiss of a snowflake as it melted on her cheek. It took her eyes a moment to adjust to the soup-thick bank of gray morning fog.

She turned her head to the general who still slept beside her, his arm tucked over her for warmth. His pocket of heat created a protective dome as the damp, cold morning pressed in around them. Her eyes fluttered from the Raascot fae sleeping soundly to the provisions resting on the edge of the makeshift tent. Next to the burlap sacks and satchels, a single, loose-leaf sheet sat quietly absorbing snowflakes, each droplet liquifying on impact.

"Oh, fuck," she cursed, sitting up quickly enough to rouse the other two. She grabbed the piece of parchment and continued a string of panicked vulgarities as sections of the paper were rendered useless with wet splotches of runny ink.

A darker blotch appeared on the page, slipping from the parchment and dripping onto the wool blanket. Nox had to be writing to her to ask what had woken her, but portions of her message were illegible. Beside it, lines began to form, becoming shapeless as they bled into the water.

"Shit, shit, shit."

"Give it here!" Yazlyn snatched the paper and began to blow hot puffs of desperate air over their only means of written communication. They crowded around what appeared to be the scarcely discernible edges of a map. Amaris recognized the outline of the continent, along with an *x* marking their current position at the university. The dotted border that separated Farehold from the north smeared before they could see the plot point that truly mattered.

The best they could tell, the wobbly blob appeared to be a direct shot northeast to an empty space on the edge of the Frozen Straits. While the carriage had saved them more than a week of travel, it was challenging to gauge how much time in the air it would take them to get to the lip of the straits. Even the best scholars' maps contained little more than conjecture when it came to cataloging the straits and the Sulgrave Mountains beyond. A smeared approximation hastily drawn by a queen and ruined in the snow was far from reliable.

"Why did you leave it out?" came Yazlyn's accusatory hiss.

"It's too late now," Gadriel snapped back. Then to Amaris, he asked, "What about the compass? If it works as well as Malik claims, it should still get us where we need to go."

Amaris dug through the bag until her hands closed around the cool, round object. "It'll point us in the right direction, but that's about it. We have no way of knowing if we have a week of travel ahead of us or if we'll get there by nightfall."

Yazlyn looked between them. "So, do we ask it to take us to Tanith or directly to the dock? Was Nox showing us where to go, or telling us where they are at present?"

Amaris bit back the urge to remind Yazlyn that they were looking at the same piece of parchment, and that they had the same amount of information, but she resisted. Instead, she attempted to write her question, but the quill punctured through the weakened page.

"We're still at the university," Yazlyn said. "I'll go ask for paper."

Gadriel's jaw ticked as he considered her proposal. "It will open you up to interrogation about why you've hung around the property for a night and day. I think we're better off looking for tree bark or a different writing surface. Keep your eyes peeled for birches and willows, okay?"

Amaris frowned. She was no botanist but was quite certain their topography no longer supported the sort of thin, papery bark they needed. But pessimism wouldn't serve her, so instead, she said, "Let's point ourselves in the right direction and hope for the best."

Emotions remained strained as they packed up their makeshift tent and divided the supplies. Yazlyn was to carry the extra blankets and food while Gadriel carried Amaris, who would do her best not to drop the very important satchel of greenstrike blood. Thanks to the carriage and its fast travel, they had barely touched their assorted traveling foods. This was both good news for their supplies and bad news for Yazlyn's upper body strength. The sergeant made no fewer than eight grumbling comments about the awkward bundles she held, but before long, they were ready to take flight.

Amaris was quite sure she'd never get sick of flying.

She admired the world below her as it unfolded. The land around the university remained mossy shades of red and green as the snow melted the moment it hit the ground. The fogbanks cleared as they flew, revealing shadowed pockets of snow and icicles clinging to stones. The days were short this time of year, and by the time the afternoon sun turned from bright, clean light to yolky orange, they'd made it far enough north for the ground to transform into rolling blankets of white, broken by shrubs and trees at the crevices between hills.

"Yazlyn's losing altitude," Gadriel said through the wind. He nodded toward the black dot in the distance where his sergeant had begun to dip.

Amaris couldn't tell if his tone was one of irritation or concern. His expression changed the moment they landed. Yazlyn's face was a violent shade of pink. Her chattering teeth made it difficult for her to spit out her words. Amaris recognized the early signs of frostbite when she saw them.

Gadriel ran to her, quick to summon his warmth. Over his shoulder, he asked, "Amaris, can you build a fire?"

Yazlyn remained stiff, limbs frozen as he did his best to chafe blood and warmth back into her arms. Amaris left them to it while she ran for the brush. This was no thickly abundant forest. The trees had thinned the more northward they'd flown. The existing branches and brambles were so damp, she knew they'd smoke for hours before offering a true fire. She tucked a few wet logs under her arm, then focused her efforts on straw-like weeds that poked through the snow and pinecones scattered beneath what remained of the sparse evergreens. If she could get the fire hot enough with smaller twigs, she could make the logs work. By the time she returned to get the campfire started, she'd expected Yazlyn to have made more progress. Instead, she came up on a worried general while the sergeant continued to shiver.

"How long for you to get the fire started?" Gadriel asked, scarcely looking up.

She frowned at her supplies. Her heart ached at the memory of the only father she'd ever known as she recalled Odrin's lessons. He had forced her to practice starting fires with flint and sticks, but they'd usually had a supply of dry firewood at the ready. "Ten minutes to get the kindling going," she said. "Another ten or so before the fire will accept the logs."

He nodded but continued using his ability to help Yazlyn keep her fingers. "We'll make shorter flight paths from here on out. We'll cap our airtime at four hours before we stop to warm ourselves—less, if Yaz needs us to land."

"I'm sorry," Yazlyn said through her shivers. She wasn't making eye contact with either of them, which made Amaris feel horrible. Of all the shitty things Yazlyn had done, the very reasonable act of getting cold did not rank. Amaris felt responsible for hogging the general's ability to produce heat for so long. She hadn't even felt the slightest chill as they traveled while tucked in his arms.

"You have nothing to be sorry for," Gadriel replied.

Amaris knew enough of their relationship to understand that Yazlyn wasn't just his troop—she was family. If anyone understood surrogate family, it was Amaris. She'd only spent a few years in the keep and would die for any of her brothers in a heartbeat. When it came to the fae before her, the two of them had been friends for longer than Amaris had been alive. She wasn't about to let herself be the reason Gadriel lost a sister.

The sun had taken on a richer shade of reddish orange by the time the three were comfortably thawing around the fire.

"Do you think you can go for a few more hours tonight?" Gadriel asked.

"I'm fine now," Yazlyn insisted.

He pointed to the pale crescent moon that decorated the sky well before sundown. "We'll land when it hits its peak, okay?"

They were in the air again before the sun dipped below the horizon, leaving them alone with a pale silver splinter and a white-dotted sky. Amaris peeked at the pocket watch every once in a while to ensure they were on the right track to find Tanith. By the time the moon hit the highest point in its arc, they were ready to touch down for the night.

They stopped in a shallow valley. Trees were few and far between, but Yazlyn was able to use her ability to manipulate ice to help them create a cave-like shelter. Amaris offered to pluck the yellow-brown traces of long-dead grass that poked through the banks of snow, but without wood, the fire would do very little. Instead, they lined the bottom of the shelter with one wool blanket and draped another over the shallow cave's entrance to capture what they could of Gadriel's heat. The snow insulated their shelter and gave them a reprieve for the night, but it was with eerie certainty that Amaris realized they wouldn't have made it through their first day without Gadriel.

Spirits dampened as they settled in for the night. In the moments before sleep, Yazlyn said, "I'm already a liability and we haven't even reached the ice."

He chastised her quietly. "You aren't a liability. It's objectively cold. We need to operate within the conditions we're given."

Every word seemed too loud in the small cave of their own making. "And what conditions will we be given on the straits? Malik was right. No one goes to Sulgrave for a reason. It's a death sentence."

His tone shifted from that of a friend to that of a general. "We have me and my heat. We have healing tonics, food, warm clothes, and a near-bottomless supply of blood for Tanith and everything the little vampire can access. We have more resources than you realize."

No one spoke for an hour or so as they tried and failed to sleep. Amaris couldn't turn her mind off as every thought hinged on Malik's angry words. He'd said it himself. Nox was both the most valuable and the most vulnerable party member. How was she supposed to make it across the ice in one piece if Amaris with her reever training and Yazlyn as a powerful fae were already struggling to remain functional?

She could tell from the uneven breathing that the others weren't sleeping either. They listened to the night, disquieted by its silence. There were no hooting snowbirds, no rustling mice, no howling coyotes. They were still on the Farehold side of the border, and the land was already too inhospitable to support even the heartiest life.

After an eternity of silence, Gadriel spoke. "If we get on the straits and it truly seems like a suicide mission, we'll turn back."

Neither Amaris nor Yazlyn said anything in response. She knew she should try to sleep, but she couldn't quiet her mind. A loud voice clanged between her ears, insisting that they couldn't make it this far just to freeze to death. They couldn't slay demons, unseat a monarch, slash through ghouls, and claim two kingdoms only to walk out onto the arctic waste and die in an unceremonious, icy grave.

Beneath her gloves, Amaris counted the hours on her fingers. In warmer weather, it may have been sixteen hours of nonstop travel—twenty at the most. But they'd vowed to fly for no more than four hours at a time before stopping to warm. Their short trip segmented into such frequent stops would take an eternity.

She probably slept that night, though she couldn't swear to it. Her rest was so shallow and unsatisfying that she may as well have stayed up all night. It set the tone for three of the slowest, most miserable, sleepless days of Amaris's young life.

Each night, the only shelter was whatever Yazlyn was able to manipulate from the snow around them. The crescent moon waxed overhead, welcoming a crystal-sharp sea of stars, every speckle piercing the darkness as too-bright metallic shards cut through the clean, clear air, with each of them gaining minutes to the hour in snatches of fitful rest. It had been days since she'd seen her last tree as the world below them tipped like a can of flat, white paint.

For a while, Amaris was convinced their compass had broken. No matter how far they flew or how long they traveled, their manufactured pocket watch remained firmly stuck just past the two o'clock hour, insisting that they not budge from their northeasterly flight plan. A honey-colored sun melted over the horizon, sending dull, buttery beams in an infinite line in either direction. The sun set, leaving them with the dull reflection of moonlight over an endless expanse, flat and empty of snow. There were no signs of life.

No sun rose on the fourth day. The light changed from the steely pewter of twilight into a dull, flat gray. They gnawed on their frozen provisions, packed their blankets, and set northward without a word.

By high noon, the world had all but disappeared. The ashen, flat sky melded with the endless, wintery earth in an absence of color. If it hadn't been for Yazlyn's wings and chocolate-cherry curls, there would have been no break between the monochromatic nothingness. Amaris's eyes unfocused until the sergeant was little more than a charcoal smudge on a white canvas.

Yazlyn didn't wait for Gadriel's feet to touch the ground before she started yelling. "What if we're already on the straits?" she barked, voice hoarse from the frosty air. "What if we passed the dock?"

Amaris shook her head, tucking her hands under her arms. She looked at the sergeant's cherry-red nose, her wind-chafed cheeks, her flaring temper and winced. Amaris was miserable, and that was with the consistent benefit of Gadriel's gift. She pleaded with Yazlyn. "Malik said this compass—"

Yazlyn bit back like a wolf tearing meat from a carcass. "What does he know? Malik isn't here! Maybe your goddess-damned compass doesn't work in the cold! Maybe it—"

Gadriel rubbed at his temples. He spoke over her. "If the compass says—"

"What have you been asking it?" Yazlyn demanded, temper rising with every word. She marched toward them, snow crunching beneath her boots. "Are you sure it isn't taking us straight to Sulgrave? What if we missed the others entirely? If you're asking it about Tanith, it could very well be taking us to her home or her people or her family!"

Amaris opened her mouth to interject.

Yazlyn lunged for the object, and Amaris jerked her hand away. Amaris reacted on instinct, grunting as she absorbed Yazlyn's disarming strike with her forearm. She returned the punch before she knew what she was doing, her furry mittens acting like boxing gloves as they softened the hit, Yazlyn's winded nostrils flaring. Her angered cry was not one of military training or controlled attack but of desperation and misery. She shoved Amaris, sending her backward onto the snow. Amaris yelped as the sleek metal object slipped from her grasp. Both women turned in horror to watch the pocket watch skid over the snow like a rock skipping over a pond's surface.

Gadriel snarled at her. "Sergeant!" He bit the title in a halting command. Any semblance evaporated as he pulled rank.

Yazlyn froze. She straightened her spine as she squared off against her general.

Gadriel bent to help Amaris from the ground. The look he gave Yazlyn was colder than the winter winds. His lip twitched against a snarl as he began, "If it's broken—"

Yazlyn's temper had not abated. She growled, "If it's broken, then what? What are you going to do? *Not* take me farther onto the ice in a land with no shelter where everyone is guaranteed a certain death? Do it. Go without me."

Gadriel leveled his stare. "You won't make it back to Raascot alive."

Yazlyn refused to relax. With a snarl, she demanded, "Then how long? How much longer will we look?"

Amaris peeked up from the shelter of her gloves just as the wind picked up to bite her exposed bits of skin more. Gadriel took two steps toward Amaris and tugged at her hand, looking at the precious piece of enchanted metal within. He pointed north. "Two more days."

The sergeant stamped her foot, but the tantrum was wasted on the soft crunch of snow. "One."

"Yazlyn—"

"This isn't a fit over discomfort, Gadriel! If we don't find it by the end of tomorrow, we have to turn back. None of us have slept more than a few minutes on the hour. We're freezing. Even if *you're* staying warm, you can't travel for days without resting. Fae and humans alike die without sleep. We'll have enough supplies to get back to Gwydir if we leave before the sun sets tomorrow. I'll already be lucky if I make it another day with all of my toes intact. Maybe you've stopped caring about me, but consider whether or not you want Amaris's blood on your conscience. The cold won't spare her either."

The day was miserable, though that was nothing new.

The travel was multiplied by three in every aspect. They were three times as cold. The wind was three times as strong. Every second, minute, and hour took three times longer to pass. Fatigue became dangerous as they pressed on. Gadriel's head nodded as he struggled to stay awake, dipping dangerously toward the earth before he'd jerk his head upright and course-correct.

No one spoke when they landed for the night.

Despite their bone-aching exhaustion, the howling wind and bitter cold prevented true sleep from finding them. Another in their line of endlessly long nights passed in disgruntled, nearly sleepless silence, with nothing to pass the time aside from listening to the wind and its howling threats.

She was both relieved that night came to an end and despondent as a new day of suffering began.

Amaris recognized the expressions looking back at her when they packed up their blankets as they were greeted by another overcast day. Gadriel muttered something or other about how it might be good to get their blood moving before they took to the sky, so for thirty minutes, they walked. As they shuffled, Amaris knew these faces, these movements, this lifeless animation on the corpses limping through Castle Aubade. She was traveling with the living dead.

"We'll find them today," Amaris promised dully, though she had no reason to believe what she said.

"I'm cold." Yazlyn dropped her sack to the frozen earth. She looked up at Amaris with expressionless eyes. "There's no wood for fire. I'm the only one of the three who can't benefit from Gadriel's heat. We're at each other's throats. But that isn't the worst part."

Amaris opened her mouth to ask what she meant, but she didn't have the energy to form the words.

"The worst part is that at least you two will get to die on the ice together. At least you have each other."

Gadriel finished packing up the blankets and looked up from where he knelt on the snow.

"Even if we reach the others, you'll find your childhood friend, or whatever the hell she is to you. Gad will find his cousin. Who will I find? A woman who hate-fucked me for a few months until she grew tired of calling on me."

Amaris's expression was half pity, half sleep deprivation. "That isn't..."

"If we make it and then we succumb to the cold, Ash and Tanith will get to die in each other's arms. How fucking romantic. And the only woman I've ever loved is probably stretched on the Etal Isles, sketching mermaids and sipping water from a coconut. What do I get to do? Continue north until my wings freeze and I die on the straits, alone."

She shouldered her bag. "Four hours," she said and set into the air before either Amaris or Gadriel could respond.

Gadriel's sigh was one of bone-deep sorrow as he extended his hand for Amaris. "I'm sorry. To both of you."

"We'll be fine," Amaris said, stepping into his arms for another day of travel. "Yazlyn will be too." But even as the words left her lips, she wasn't sure that they were true.

She knew topography was morally neutral, but this terrain felt cruel. The wind was wretched. The barren tundra felt decidedly evil. Maybe they wouldn't find the docks. Maybe they'd quit before their journey began. Maybe leaving the hateful Straits behind wouldn't be so bad.

They'd barely been in the sky for thirty minutes before Amaris checked the watch.

For the first time in days, she felt something. She jolted with such shock that she nearly dropped it. Gadriel jerked, dipping dangerously until he got control of his wings. She could barely find her voice as adrenaline seized her.

"Stop!" she shrieked, horrified at what she saw. "Land! Land!"

Gadriel looked from Amaris to the metallic circle in her hand. His face set with purpose. His wings beat with a thundering force, tripling his pace as he darted in front of Yazlyn, cutting her off so that she understood the signal. They were on the ground a moment later, all three staring at the pocket watch with wide eyes.

"South," Amaris said, shaking her head. "It's behind us."

It took less than a second of looking to spy exactly what they thought they would see: absolutely nothing.

Amaris tilted the watch from one side to another. She spun around, keeping her eyes on the dial. "Did we pass over it?"

"We haven't seen so much as a rock in days." Yazlyn glared.

Amaris remained resolute. "We have to go back."

Yazlyn's nostrils flared. "Give it to me."

Too tired to argue, Amaris extended her hand. "Here. Take it."

Yazlyn muttered to the frozen, spelled accessory, taking off her glove and tapping its glass twice with her fingernail to confirm that it was indeed pointing backward. Gritting her teeth, she took off into the air without them. The others ran to catch up as she flapped her wings, looking down at the watch in her hand every few moments. They'd been airborne for less than fifteen minutes before she stopped mid-air, beating her wings backward twice to hover. Her chestnut curls whipped around as she eyed the snow. Yazlyn shot for the ground.

They crashed to the frozen earth and took off running after her. Amaris grunted against the impact but was quick to her feet. Yazlyn was fast, but her muscles were stiff. The sergeant was losing her mind, and Amaris knew it. She pushed through her reserves of energy and closed the distance between them. She grabbed Yazlyn's arm and gave it a yank. "You have to keep it together."

"It's broken!" she cried in response. Her tone was a

cocktail of betrayal, fatigue, hysteria, and rage as she spun on them where they'd landed. The space beneath her eyes was purpling with the darkening bruises of sleeplessness. If Amaris had thought they looked like ghouls before, she'd been too hasty. Yazlyn's mind was slipping.

"Look at me," Amaris demanded.

"Look at you?" Yazlyn retorted with wide, wild eyes. "Look at the clock! Your stupid fucking compass has been leading us in a fucking circle!"

"No," Amaris insisted. "Check to see if it's working. Ask it to point to Gad—"

"I don't want to find Gad!" Yazlyn screamed, chucking the watch directly into the snow at her feet.

"For fuck's sake!" Amaris shrieked in surprise. She dropped to her knees and began to dig for their most precious possession. She didn't bother to look up as Gadriel tried to shake sanity into his sergeant. She couldn't worry about their fights, their hurled obscenities, their enraged shouts.

"Come on, come on," Amaris begged. The early signs of a sob knotted her throat. Tears lined her eyes as handful after handful of snow came up empty. "Come *on!*"

Yazlyn's fury punctured the monotonous sound of dry snow and ice scraping over dunes as the wind blew through the bitter, white void. The cold had clearly done more than freeze her fingers and toes. It had encased her mind and encrusted her heart. The only warmth she found was the burn of bottomless, unrelenting rage.

Tears found Amaris at long last as her fingers hit cold, hard metal. Unable to grip it through the mittens, she yanked them from her hands and plunged her fingers into the ice to dig out the watch. Within moments, the skin of her ivory hands grew to a violent, painful shade of red, contrasting against the snow as they throbbed. She struggled through frozen joints to get one hand back into her mitten, then the other. All the while, the battle continued overhead as the fae remained locked in an angry death match.

"This piece of shit has taken us nowhere, Gadriel! Our blood is on your hands! We're in the middle of nowhere, and there's no damn ship! Where's the skiff, Gad?! We're going to freeze to death out here, and—"

Deserts are said to contain mirages. Dark caves have hallucinations. And the Frozen Straits, it seemed, came with the soft, familiar call of the continent's only living monarch.

"Yazlyn?"

Ten

A SINGLE WORD—A NAME—SNAKED OVER THE COLD, vacant emptiness as a lone, bewildered question. Amaris looked up from where she knelt on the snow. Gadriel and Yazlyn went still, all craning their necks with jaws on their hinges in shock to see...something.

It was impossible.

Nox was there, but she wasn't. Amaris squinted against the blinding horizon, struggling to understand the sight. It was Nox's face. Nox's dark hair whipped in the wind, moving about her shoulder, her neck, obscuring her mouth as it blew. But where her body was meant to be, there was nothing. No hands. No legs. Only a face.

The three gaped at her, uncomprehending.

Perhaps Amaris had been too judgmental when she'd assumed Yazlyn had lost touch with reality. Clearly, hers was also cast to the straits, dead on the ice. A collective illusion, a phantom, a wishful thought, a strange, disembodied fantasy was all that remained of their cracked, broken minds.

Then an arm appeared. Nox extended a hand and beckoned them toward her.

Amaris got slowly to her feet. She took a single step, but Gadriel snagged her elbow. "Wait."

She shook him off, and he didn't fight her. As she moved, Nox's features came into sharper focus. Her eyes and nose were pink, but not with the cold as Yazlyn's had been. Her bloodshot eyes made it look like she'd been crying.

Nox's hand flew to her mouth as a single, choked sob cracked through the wind.

Apparition or no, if this was death, she wanted them to spend it together. Amaris broke free from her shock. She took off across the snow, sending particles of ice and the cold, dry crystals into the air as she nearly slipped on the surface and crashed into Nox's arms. Nox enveloped her in a hug, clutching her tightly in return.

"You're real," Amaris sobbed.

Nox untangled one arm, lifting it and gesturing to the others. "Come in! Get in here!"

Amaris made no attempt to hold back her tears as she stepped free from the hug. Her eyes struggled to adjust against the peculiar, dark rectangle that contained Nox. She squinted as she looked over her shoulders at the fae. Gadriel stepped up behind her, eyes wide. A shape caught her attention as she turned back to Nox, noticing another fae—a second Gadriel—slowly approach. The men extended gloved hands at the same time, touching gloved fingertips.

"It's mirrored," Gadriel breathed, resting his hand against the glassy surface. Amaris's lips parted, eyes wide as Yazlyn stepped up to the reflective surface. She turned away from Nox long enough to see the furry white hat she'd taken from Castle Aubade, and hair just as white to match. Her cheeks, her forehead, her chin were strawberry-pink as the cold stung her skin.

It truly was a mirror.

"Get in, get in," Nox insisted through sniffles. Amaris looked back at Nox to see tears freezing the moment they fell. "I need to close the door."

Nox ushered Yazlyn and Gadriel through the tall, dark rectangle but continued to clutch Amaris, breathing her smothered sobs into Amaris's shoulders while the others watched helplessly. Nox closed the door behind herself to prevent any more of the wintry cold from leeching in. The relief was immediate. Given the days they'd had, the warm, windless shelter was as every bit as comforting as a hot cup of chocolate and a warm blanket by the fire.

"I can't see a thing," Yazlyn said from somewhere within the blackened gloom.

"Give it a second for your eyes to adjust," came a male voice.

"Ash?" Amaris asked. She lifted her hand to her eyes as if shielding them from the sunlight, but it was a useless gesture.

With everyone safely inside, Nox broke down completely. "I've been writing to you for days. When you didn't write back, I knew you'd never find me. How could you see us? This ship is built with the intention to never be found. I wrote, and I wrote, and I wrote... I tried to visit one of you—all of you—*any* of you every night. I didn't know how you could possibly find the cursed ship—this goddess-damned thing... I knew you were on the ice, and..."

Amaris lifted the watch. Nox gasped, snatching the spelled object from her hand.

"We haven't been sleeping long enough to dream," Amaris said with quiet apology. "We've tried every night, but if sleeplessness didn't kill us, I'm pretty sure Yazlyn was about to."

"And you would have deserved it," Yazlyn grumbled from somewhere in the shadows.

"I thought you had already died," Nox said, looking up from the watch. Amaris understood why she'd been crying. "All of you," she emphasized.

"I'm so sorry," was all Amaris could say, and she meant it. Her heart ached as she thought what it would do to her if she'd spent three days believing Nox to be dead.

In the time it took for Nox to appreciate her enchanted treasure, Amaris's eyes adapted from the harsh, white light to the cabin. She shrugged out of her coat, letting it drop to the floor. The hull of the ship was dark, save for two small, double-paned glass slits on either side to provide limited visibility. Ash offered a wave the moment her gaze settled on him, then slid to where Tanith stood on the far end of the ship's interior.

Amaris kept her eyes on Tanith as she asked, "Your ships are invisible?"

At her side, Gadriel had taken off his gloves and let his heavier layers fall to the floor as he inspected the hull. She noticed where his eyes had landed. The ship appeared to have been welded together at conventional joints, creating an arrow-like shape, but the walls themselves contained no bolts, screws, or visible rivets. She took her mittens off as well and placed her hand against the chilly, metallic sheet. She withdrew her fingertips and surveyed the window. It was scarcely more than a peephole, no more than one finger tall and three fingers long, letting in slivers of light on either side of the vessel.

While Amaris canvassed the ship, Tanith said, "Our skiffs are made of a reflective silver—yes. I suppose it's like your hand mirrors on the continent. It's effective camouflage."

Gadriel's dark eyes flashed with genuine ire as he glowered at the Sulgrave fae. "You don't think that would have been useful information to share before we set out on this journey?"

Tanith shrugged, utterly dismissive of his anger. "It didn't seem relevant."

Gadriel's temper flared. "How can it—"

"Let it go," Nox said with a sigh. "I've spent the last three days yelling at her. Whatever you have to say, she's already heard it."

"Shouldn't it be cold?" Amaris asked. She directed her question at Tanith. "Aren't we standing in a tin cup? Metal freezes when it's on the ice."

"In the southern kingdoms, you use the word 'manufactured,'" Tanith said.

Amaris looked at the wall again, wondering what combination of powers could turn silver into a ship. It wasn't exactly toasty, but at most, it was only as uncomfortable as a poorly insulated room.

"How far into the straits are we?" Yazlyn asked.

Tanith frowned. "We aren't."

Yazlyn shook her head. "What do you mean? We've been flying over snow and ice for days."

Tanith cocked her head to the side. The expression was not condescending, merely curious. She often eyed the continent's fae as if they were sentient creatures who'd learned the gift of speech, as if she couldn't fault them for their lack of understanding. "We're on the wintry dunes of the dock. The Frozen Straits are the remnants of what was once a great, dark sea. The ice is as clear as cracked glass. The dunes are an anchor. That's why she hasn't moved an inch since we left her here. Nox hasn't permitted us to leave the dock."

Gadriel took a seat on the floor and leaned his head against the wall of the ship. He addressed Tanith. "How did you and your companions make it across the snow alive? You didn't have vials of blood or tonics to replenish your power, and there's no way you all possessed the ability to heat or heal."

"We didn't."

Nox's lips parted. "You said you came over with a team of five."

"I did," Tanith answered.

Yazlyn threw up her hands and spun on the seated reever. Her voice had a blade-sharp edge as she growled, "Ash, I've been ready to murder someone all day, and it might as well be Tanith. Deal with her before I kill her."

Ash took a calming breath and motioned for the others to leave it to him. "Tanith, can you use as much detail as possible to describe how you crossed the straits, who you crossed with, and how you got from the skiff to the mainland? Paint me a picture so it feels like I'm there."

He shot a quick glare toward the others as if to belittle them for how easy it was to talk to her like a person. He was met with the crossed arms and narrowed eyes of four unsympathetic faces.

Tanith made a small nod before she told her story. Her airy, musical voice was calm, recounting the memory as if it held no emotion. "It was summer when we left. Four other Reds and I departed from the church on our mission to the continent. We knew none of us would return to Sulgrave. The goddess values our sacrifice, and we honored the All Mother with our obedience."

Amaris sank slowly to the floor, back against the cool wall. Nox joined her as they listened.

"It took my companions and me four days to descend from the mountains and reach the docks. Sulgrave has a number of ships for a variety of purposes. Silver skiffs have been around for three thousand years. The church is the only institution that still uses them."

"Only the religious cross?" Gadriel clarified.

"That's not what she said," Nox responded carefully. "Sulgrave has other ships for the straits, Tanith? Is that what you're saying?"

She looked at Nox. "Which is it? Would you like to hear my tale, or discuss my country's engineering?"

"Both, ideally," Nox said, "but please, finish your story."

She sucked in a breath. "Velin was the strongest in faith but the weakest with groundwater. He did not make the crossing from the docks onto the continent. The cold took him in the night before we could build a fire. His partner would not leave his side after he fell, which was disappointing to us all. Their love for one another was great, but it should not have been greater than their love for the All Mother."

Yazlyn raised a finger to object, but Gadriel snatched her hand and lowered it. Given that Yazlyn was a smartass even when she was in a good mood, it was probably for the best that she not interrupt when she had homicide on the brain.

"Once we reached the thawed lands, the three of us who remained divided the continent among our missions. We trusted that the All Mother would provide opportunities so that we could critically assess the scenarios allowing the fae and wielders of magic to remain unharmed until the goddess embolden more to Her divine purpose."

Ash kept a comforting hand on Tanith as he turned to Nox. "If I'm right, and their powers took them, then no more Sulgrave fae remain on the continent."

"You say that so often," Tanith said lightly. "You say 'the continent,' but you mean Raascot and Farehold, correct? Do you think of the desert kingdom? Of the islands? Of the mountains beyond the ice when you refer to the world?"

Amaris didn't have time for a lesson on linguistic inclusivity. Her brows met as she turned to eye Ash. "You knew there might be no more Sulgrave fae on the continent?" Then to Nox, she said, "Ash told you this, and you still wanted us to go north?"

Nox straightened her spine and addressed the ship. "We've all seen Tanith's abilities. Some of us more than others."

The energy within the hull grew taut. Amaris took a step closer to Gadriel as she awaited an explanation.

Nox looked at the general. "Gadriel and I spoke about this weeks ago. Sulgrave is a threat not because of five zealots. Demons have been increasing across the continent for years, and we've seen exactly what Tanith and her people can do with these monsters. Their deaths may be cutting off the head of the snake, but three more are sure to grow in its place. Is the entire population of Yelagin, half of Raascot's military, and an assault on Castle Aubade nothing? That was achieved by only three Sulgrave fae. What if three more venture south? What if all five make it next time? Or ten? Or twenty? I can't be the queen who let two kingdoms fall."

Yazlyn shook her head. "But if they're coming on suicide missions..."

129

Nox had started quietly, but her voice rose with authority and certainty. "We've seen how accessing unfamiliar powers drains them. I, myself, was at death's door when I first realized I was dream walking. But I got better. I adapted. We can't wait for infiltrators to call their groundwater and die. We can't risk them acclimating to new powers like I did."

Amaris flinched. Perhaps it was the cold, the sleeplessness, or the exhaustion against any ability to maintain a semblance of lies, but she couldn't help herself. "Gadriel, do you have any plans of telling Nox why her dream walking no longer drains her?"

Without saying a word, Gadriel gave her a look that said *Don't you dare.*

She leveled her stare and mouthed, *Try me.*

His jaw ticked. Out loud, he said, "I don't see how that's helpful information."

Amaris shrugged, emboldened. "It seems pretty helpful to me."

"Now is not the time," he said, eyes darkening. A thrill ran through her, equal parts obstinance and pettiness. She did not back down.

Nox clenched her fists. She looked between them. "I suggest one of you make it the time."

Gadriel's lip twitched. He sighed. "Nox, I want to make it clear that I respect you—"

"That's how all great conversations start," Yazlyn grumbled humorlessly.

His hand opened and closed reflexively at his side, betraying his tested patience. "Your ring acts as a funnel. It connects you to the siphons worn by Amaris, Yazlyn, and Malik. Apart from Zaccai, myself, and the manufacturers, I'm pretty sure Amaris is the only one who knows."

"We know," Tanith said with a dismissive flick of her fingers. She looked up at Ash, then back at the queen.

While Nox battled her confusion, Yazlyn became incensed. Her lips pulled back in a snarl. In one moment, she tore her mittens from her hands. In the next, she began attempting to yank the ring from her frozen finger. She growled against the stiff, painful joint that stopped the ring from budging.

Nox looked down at her peppery jewel, eyes wide as teacups.

Fury burned through Yazlyn as she snapped at the general. "You!" she grunted, "gave!" still twisting, "me!" an exasperated cry, "a siphon!"

Regret prodded Amaris in the side. She was exhausted. Her emotions were raw. She'd given in to the urge to stir the pot and knew she'd pay for it later. She avoided looking at Gadriel, knowing what she'd find on his face if their eyes met. Instead, she tried to calm the irate sergeant. She swallowed. "Yazlyn, it doesn't siphon your power. The ring doesn't hurt you at all. I've kept mine on well after learning, even when I hated her. It's a succubus thing. It's meant to help Nox access our affections. You know—so she doesn't die."

"How could you do this to me?" Yazlyn's question hung heavy with betrayal.

Amaris snatched Yazlyn's hands in her own. "I should have told you when I learned what they were. Believe me, I was just as angry. Look, I'm sorry, I—"

Yazlyn's chin quivered as she looked at Gadriel. Amaris followed her gaze to the general's face and regretted it instantly. The look Gadriel gave Amaris let her know that she was in for an unholy punishment.

Yazlyn smoldered for another furious minute before the cold, the exhaustion, the fruitlessness of her rage overtook her. She let out a pitiful, choked sound before sinking to the floor. Her wings draped around her with unnatural deflation. She gave up on the ring, brought her knees to her chest, and buried her face in her hands.

This was Amaris's fault. It had made sense in the moment. Nox couldn't rule, couldn't make informed decisions about Sulgrave and unnatural gifts, if she wasn't given every piece of information. Still, she hadn't considered what the knowledge might do to anyone else in the boat.

With a heavy sigh, Amaris fished a wool blanket from her sack. She draped it around Yazlyn's shoulders, but the sergeant did not look up from her quiet slump.

"I shouldn't have told you like this. It should have been weeks ago, when we were safely at the castle and could go to the pub for drinks. We could have laughed about it and gotten drunk and you could have kicked my ass in rummy. I'm really sorry."

Beneath the curtain of auburn curls came a short, tear-damp laugh. "You really are garbage at rummy."

Amaris's face scrunched with empathy. For as long as she'd known Yazlyn, the woman never seemed to be able to catch a break, nor did anyone extend her grace when she needed it. She didn't deserve the way her heart was constantly wrung and crushed between their hands and beneath their feet, but here she was. She followed, she fought, and she served. She was their friend, and she deserved more than they gave her.

Cool metal chilled her knee. Amaris looked up from her place on the floor. "What do you say, Tanith? Can you turn water into wine and give us all a round?"

Tanith quirked a brow. She took an uncertain step closer.

"She's kidding," Ash said abruptly, halting her advance.

"Fine," Tanith responded, half curious, half idle with boredom. "If I'm not making drinks, then does anyone plan on asking me how to get the skiff off of the docks anytime soon, or will we be staying on shore?"

Yazlyn's fingers knotted in her hair. Nox threw up her hands. Gadriel sucked in a tightly controlled breath. No one seemed to have the patience for Tanith, save for Ash. He spoke with her in hushed, hurried tones. Their back-and-forth remained under their breath before Ash turned to address the room.

"I don't suppose any of you can speak to wind?" he asked unhelpfully.

Amaris was ready to curl up on the floor and let unconsciousness take her. She knew Gadriel must be every bit as exhausted as she was, but he kept a cool head. He responded, "Does this ship have a sail?"

Ash nodded and gestured to a device on the ceiling. It was one of the few disruptions in the flat, reflective hull. It appeared to be a metallic crank adhered to the roof. Ash said it would raise the mast and release the sail.

Gadriel looked at the shape, then back at the reever. "We can't manipulate wind, but Tanith can, right?"

Ash made a face. "Technically, she can do anything. Be very careful of what you request of her. No matter how much greenstrike blood you brought, it will eventually run out. Don't waste it on making wine."

Gadriel motioned toward the crank. "Unleash it. We need to make sure it's fully functional."

Ash set to work while Gadriel redressed and headed for the door. Amaris got to her feet and joined Ash, each grunting against the effort as they turned the crank clockwise. The crank's rhythmic clicking changed intonation as it locked into place. They exchanged a look, then nodded at the general. Gadriel dipped his chin in return, then pushed against the seam that had allowed them to first enter the ship. A blinking white light pierced through the cabin. Bitter wind rushed into the space as Gadriel stepped outside. The door closed behind him, leaving the others to wait.

He was gone for several moments before knocking.

Nox hurried to the door and let in a bewildered Gadriel.

"How do I open this from the outside? It has no handle!"

Nox looked at the Sulgrave fae. "Tanith did it before. I've only opened it from the inside."

"Tanith," he said tersely, "everyone is going to need you to be a little more forthcoming. Make yourself useful." Releasing an agitated breath, he regarded the others. "I can do it."

Nox frowned. "Do what?"

He rubbed his hand down his face as if trying to wipe away the fatigue. "I can stay outside and generate the wind we need for the sails by flying. I can stay warm and keep my wings going through the day."

Tanith interjected quietly from the corner of the ship. "We won't be moving at night?"

"We're barely functioning as it is," he said. "Now that we have a safe shelter, everyone needs to be sleeping. Besides, we can't exactly have Yazlyn take over during the night, as she'll freeze."

Tanith looked away without responding.

Gadriel continued, "We'll move slowly unless the wind is at our back. We can collapse the sail and I can stay heated while pushing us forward."

Yazlyn lifted her head. "They don't know what you're implying, Gad. Tell them what you're saying before you damn yourself to die outside."

His mouth formed a tight line. "It's no different from someone kicking a float in the ocean for their raft to get to shore. Only this time instead of legs as paddles, we have wings and a sail."

She glared up from the floor. "It's no different? You'll be pushing the weight of a skiff, five bodies, yourself, and the supplies. Do they realize what you're going to put yourself through?"

The skin around his eyes tightened. "If the wind is against us, we'll anchor. If the ice of the straits is as clear as Tanith says, then momentum will carry us forward. The hardest part will be pushing away from the dock and getting out of the snow drifts. We could skate on the ice for long stretches of time with only a few beats of my wings. If we're smart about our rations, we'll be fine." Then to the others, he asked, "Before we get started, did you three bring food?"

Ash nodded on behalf of their party, gesturing to where his weapons and Chandra rested against two burlap sacks. They broke open their provisions, picking at the assorted proteins, fruits, and grains until they'd eaten enough to keep them going.

He clapped his hands together. "All right, Sulgrave. You're up. Care to show me how to push off from the docks?"

Tanith scooped her outer layers from the floor. She grabbed Ash's as well and handed him a coat. "It will require everyone to get us out of the banks and onto the ice."

Gadriel said, "The sooner we start, the sooner we'll finish."

"Fine," Yazlyn grumbled, rising from the floor. "But I want ten unbroken hours of sleep tonight. I'll slit anyone's throat if they snore."

The light blinded Amaris as they opened the door and she and the others stepped onto the frozen tundra. A thick, mirrored rod rose from the ship's center. The canvas sail blended in with the world around it. She sighed as she looked at their only hope for survival, then got to work. It took three quarters of an hour of cursing, countless vulgarities, a few fingers burned against the frozen metal, and several strained muscles before the ship shuddered, groaned, and began moving. After another hour of watery eyes, numb limbs, and burning lungs, the ship made a new noise.

Amaris jumped away from the skiff as it skated forward of its own volition. Panic lanced through her. She gasped as the ground opened up to swallow her whole—but her feet remained firmly planted. She tapped her foot uncertainly, slipping as she lost traction on the dark expanse. Over her shoulder, pearly dunes moved and shifted. Nothing but clear, glassy ice stretched before them.

The ship continued onward as if steered by a phantom crew. She craned her neck to find a row of metallic blades welded to the ship.

"It's on skates," she said, watching the skiff as it sailed on without them.

At her side, Nox laughed. "Have you ever seen anything like it?"

The others watched their handiwork as it moved too slowly to escape them but just fast enough to assure them that their plan would work. Amaris looked for signs of relief on everyone's face, then back at the ice.

"Welcome to the Frozen Straits," Tanith said.

Amaris had expected the cold. She'd known there would be wind, snow, and ice. What she hadn't anticipated was the infinite expanse of black and blue, laced with threatening cracks that had shattered and refrozen over time. Though the surface was as smooth as glass, each shard pierced the ice like a broken mirror, plummeting into the depths until they were too far beneath the surface for the naked eye. She couldn't fathom how deep the water below must be, just as the ice was incomprehensibly thick. Unlike the dunes behind her, the straits were too slick for snow to find purchase. The ice crystals that drifted across the glass were nothing more than dry, brittle snakes slithering across the surface. She watched the serpents dance until movement pulled her attention.

"Shall we?" Tanith asked, a rare playfulness in her voice. She jogged after the skiff, lunging for the ship's starboard side. With two sharp, successive bangs with the side of her fist, the door popped open from the seamless, mirrored boat. She extended her hand to help the others in as one after the other, they caught up to the skiff and hopped inside its protective shelter.

Amaris was the last one on, save for Gadriel. While the others were safe and warm, the general remained outside, gripping the mast as he continued to push.

"What do we do?" Nox asked, holding the side of the ship for balance.

Amaris leaned into the space beside her. Nox wrapped her arm around Amaris's waist as she rested her head on Nox's shoulder. Amaris said, "Now we stay sane long enough to get to Sulgrave."

Yazlyn returned to her place on the floor. Ash and Tanith curled up in the corner. Nox and Amaris were left to sink against the wall, watching the twin slits on either side of the hull as they grew dimmer as the afternoon waned.

"How long do you think he'll stay out there?" Nox whispered. It was the first time she'd spoken in…Amaris wasn't sure how much time had passed. The sky was no longer slate gray, though she hadn't watched it closely enough to see if the clouds were truly dissipating. It wasn't until the soft lavenders and pinks of sunset washed the cabin in rosy tones that she knew they were free from the oppressive overcast skies at long last.

Everyone in the skiff had been too drained to so much as speak; meanwhile, Gadriel had continued working tirelessly. Amaris thought of the centuries of training combined with his ability to generate warmth, but she knew no matter how powerful or disciplined he may be, he'd pushed far beyond what could reasonably be expected of him.

"Should one of us go get him?" Nox pressed.

Yazlyn spoke for the first time in hours. Her voice was low and emotionless as she reported, "The wind was blowing from the southeast. It's not exactly at his back, but I assume he'll stay out there as long as he has the advantage."

A few tenacious stars poked through the indigo sky in the minutes before the sun disappeared altogether. By the time the light vanished, diamond shards decorated the space beyond the window. Amaris nodded in and out of full consciousness before a sound rattled the ship. Gadriel banged against the side of the ship in quick succession, presumably as Tanith had done. When the door did not open for him, Tanith left Ash on the floor and opened the door. Eventually, Amaris would have to ask Tanith to give everyone a proper lesson on the latch. For tonight, however, what they truly needed was sleep.

Gadriel sank into the space beside her while Tanith returned to nestle into Ash's arms.

"Are you okay?" Amaris asked, quiet enough not to disturb the others.

He summoned what he could of a smile, but if the weariness hadn't been plain on his face, she would have heard it in his words. "I'll be better after a good night's sleep."

She gave his arm a squeeze before returning her cheek to its comfortable perch on Nox's shoulder. Her eyelids grew heavy as she stared at the bright cluster of stars through their small window. From where she sat, she could just barely make out a milky, paintbrush-like stroke through the sky's body, connecting the various points of light in a cloud of stardust.

Nox shifted her weight and pulled Amaris into her lap. Perhaps she would have gone on admiring the stars, but her weariness lapped at her like water, pulling her beneath its waves. Gadriel's steady breathing told her that he'd already succumbed to sleep. And though they were on the Frozen Straits skating toward unknown lands, though the climate was arctic and perilous, and though they'd been at each other's throats and on the brink of ruin at the day's onset, for now, at least, they were safe. She nuzzled into the warm pillow of Nox's thigh and drifted into a deep and perfect sleep.

Eleven

AMARIS YANKED HER HAND AWAY FROM THE SAND AS IF she'd touched fire. Tiny particles trickled through her fingers, falling noiselessly onto the beach below. She squinted at the nearby sand dunes and watched as the seagrass rustled against the hot breeze. A sandpiper darted from its shelter as it sprinted for the calm, sparkling sea. She turned to watch the bird, only to find she was not alone.

"Now I know I'm dreaming," Amaris said.

Nox beamed. She flashed brilliant white teeth in response. She was in little more than her underthings—black, strappy bits of fabric that left little to the imagination. Amaris took in her similar state of near-nakedness. She shrank away from the sun, fearing it would scorch her pale skin, but found no evidence of pink or sunburn beneath its happy rays.

Amaris soaked in her summery surroundings. The reddish, custard stones in the distance told her they were somewhere near Castle Aubade, though they were too far from the city to worry about passersby. Clay roofs dotted the hillside homes, each house little more than a barnacle clinging to the cliff. She looked back at Nox. She shook her head, mouth open in bewilderment. The salt air was heavy on her tongue as her jaw remained on its hinges. "We…we're in a ship. It's winter. You're asleep next to me in the real world, aren't you? This seems ridiculous."

"It *is* ridiculous!" Nox agreed with a laugh. She pushed up from her seated place on the sand, kicking up a cloud in her wake as she ran for the waterline.

Amaris lifted her arm to protect her eyes from the sand spray, then pulled her arm away from her face and stared at it. She shouldn't have been able to feel the tiny bites of discomfort as sand hit her skin. She shouldn't have had to squint against the harsh sunlight. She inhaled through her nose, wondering at the absence of dying fish and the foulness of rotting weeds. Instead, the breeze was clean with warm wind and something fragrant—hyacinths? Gardenias? She looked around for their source, but her back was to a cliff, with no bushes or flowering trees to be seen.

While she remained in quiet awe of her surroundings, Nox escaped the blistering sun by splashing through the water.

Amaris shouted to her from the shores. "This isn't real!"

Nox turned to regard her from where the waves lapped at her thighs, the only speck of color breaking up the infinite blue stretched behind her from above and beyond. "Isn't it?"

Magic.

The word clanged through Amaris as everything clicked into understanding. This was more than a dream. This was Nox's magic. Amaris had seen Nox's serenity and semiconsciousness. She'd witnessed her frustration. She'd seen her predatory, battle-ready, tired, and sad. Never carefree. Not like this.

While Nox carried on playing with the crystalline waves as if she were a kitten with a ball of yarn, Amaris got to her feet. She performed a less-than-graceful tiptoe across the scalding sand. The balls of her feet cooled instantly when they reached the water.

"Get over here," Nox teased, wading farther into the water.

Amaris eyed the waves. She'd never gone in the pond behind Farleigh. Uaimh Reev had been as far from the water as the moon had been from the earth. She had seen water, of course, but she'd had as much reason to dive into lakes as a human had to take to the sky. The air was meant for birds and winged fae; the water was meant for sharks and ships.

She said, "I can't swim."

Nox waved her hand with a swish. "Sure, you can. This is a dream. *My* dream. I'd never let any fish or weeds or sharp rocks exist in these waters. Would you prefer somewhere else? We could drink at a pub? Back to bed? Or, what if, for now, we just enjoy being warm for what's left of the night?"

Amaris looked at her toes beneath the shallow, aqua waters near the shore. "Here goes nothing," she whispered to herself as she walked out to sea. She approached Nox and asked, "Why here?"

Nox winked. "I thought you'd died and that we were all about to freeze before our crossing. We've earned a reprieve."

Amaris returned the smile. She closed her eyes and tilted her face toward the sun. "Goddess, yes. I am so tired of being so cold." She raised her arms and soaked in the sun's baking rays. "Why does it feel so real?"

Nox shrugged. "Because it is. We're here, aren't we? Can you feel this?"

Nox pinched her.

Amaris flinched at the small hurt. "Hey!"

"Or this," Nox asked, grabbing Amaris's hand. Amaris's heart spiked at Nox tugging her close. The ocean waves licked around her, adding to the tingle that spread around her body.

"Or this?" Nox's voice lowered into scarcely more than a whisper. Her hands ran down Amaris's sides and landed on her hips, pressing her body into Amaris's. Her breath caught in her throat as the space between them vanished. Her lips were so close, Amaris could almost taste the words.

"Or—" Nox didn't get the chance to finish her thought. Amaris flattened one hand against the sun-warmed small of

Nox's back, slipping the other onto the back of her neck. She stood on her toes, clutching Nox as she pressed her into a kiss. Her lips moved in tandem with the waves. The salt and sweat mingled with the ripe, dark flavors of cinnamon and nutmeg and plums. Nox's mouth was the Yule holiday. It was forbidden orchards. It was every sweet fruit and dark spice she'd ever craved, and the seawater only deepened her thirst.

It was real. All of it, from the sun's blistering heat on her shoulders and the waves lapping against her legs to the slick, pleasurable need that ached between her thighs. She molded her body against Nox's soft curves. Her lips were alchemy, her kiss turned to gold on her tongue.

Amaris had kissed three people in her life. She'd jumped into Ash's bed out of a desperation to feel accepted, fueled by a fear of rejection and a longing for closeness. She had kissed Gadriel with lust, primal hunger, and a craving that demanded satiation. But with Nox, her mouth moved with the sort of intimacy that shaped space and time around them. Together, they were the summer in the depth of winter. They were the innocence in corruption, the midnight sun, the glacier that carved the continent.

A chill shot down her spine as Nox's salt-slicked hand slid up her back. She picked up her knee, stepping between Nox's legs and applying glorious pressure to the apex of her thighs. Amaris arched her back encouragingly as the opposite hand slipped beneath the strappy bit of fabric clinging to her hip, creating slow brushes of anticipation as she grew nearer and nearer to her sensitive places.

Their mouths parted as Amaris tilted her face toward the sun once more, gasping at the sky as Nox dragged fire down her neck with passionate kisses. With a flick and a tug, the piece of clothing covering her top snapped loose. Naked from neck to navel, she was bare before the sun, the sea, and the one she loved. She released a slow, sensual moan as her soft lips moved south, closer and closer to her breasts.

Between the heat, the sun, the joy, the pleasure, it was difficult to differentiate one sensation from the other.

Until it wasn't.

The cold hit her like a bucket of water. Amaris jolted awake, gasping for air as if she'd just broken through the water's surface.

"Fuck!" Her eyes flew open. Heart pounding, she used her free hand to swat at the gloomy, shadowed air. "What!"

Her shoulders trembled with anger as her eyes battled to adjust to the ship's dark hull. The sound of waves was replaced with the rocking creek of a skiff. Her nipples peaked beneath her shirt from cold and arousal alike. In the absence of seawater, she was left with the damp, telltale sign of the pleasure she'd savored only moments prior. She flipped like the pages of a book between confusion, fury, and fear while she struggled to discern the silhouette of the small fae girl who had woken her.

Tanith was staring at her, dark eyes wide in the gloom of the ship.

"What?" Amaris demanded once more.

"There's something outside," came Tanith's hushed voice.

Amaris scanned the ship to confirm the others still slept soundly. Her eyes shook the sleep from them as she focused on Tanith.

"Why did you wake me and not Ash?" she whispered. She could barely make the redheaded reever's shape but noted how his arms remained splayed open as if the Sulgrave girl had crawled away from his spooning hold. Even Gadriel or Yazlyn would have been a logical ally against a threat beyond the ship.

"The others won't be able to see," Tanith said.

An uneasiness wrapped itself around her spine at Tanith's chilling words. Amaris gently removed Nox's draping arm, careful not to wake her. With any luck, she'd get to remain in a dream of the tropical ocean and its waves.

Amaris rolled onto her knees. "There's something on the straits?"

143

Panic was an emotion she'd never heard from Tanith, regardless of the situation. Fear leached into the fae's plea as she gestured for the window. "Please, look."

She rocked onto the balls of her feet and took careful, silent steps toward the window. She shivered as she reached the slot, wishing she were under the wool blanket, praying that there would be nothing to see. She squinted against the bright, silver moon. Her fingers ached against the frozen metal as she leaned into the slotted window. She stared for a long time, seeing nothing apart from the twinkling stars and their reflection. Seconds ticked into minutes before she was able to differentiate the dark ice from the hard line of the horizon. She shook her head, ready to dismiss Tanith altogether when she noticed...something.

She jerked her face away from the glass but did not look away. "What is it?"

Tanith moved closer to peer out the window. "I heard it thirty minutes ago."

"You haven't slept?"

Tanith shook razor-straight hair. Her voice was ominously low as she responded, "The cold isn't the only reason we don't cross the straits."

A shape—a blur of blackened shadow—shot past the ship. Amaris sucked in a gasp. "What is it?"

"I don't know," Tanith replied. "It can't be seen."

"Why wouldn't you tell us this!"

Tanith merely stared at her. "The Raascot fae were cursed for twenty years, were they not? Was discussing their inability to be seen helpful to their cause? Would Farehold have been receptive to that which they could not perceive?"

She chewed on her inner cheek as she considered Tanith's words.

Amaris was sucked into a memory. Samael had looked at her at Uaimh Reev many years ago and said, "...*with those eyes, I'd love to see what gifts of sight you possess.*" That's why Tanith had woken her above all others.

"Listen." Tanith brought her hand to her ear, allowing the sounds of the wind and quiet of the night to press in on them. The steady breathing of four sleeping bodies accompanied the wintry sounds of the straits. "I know what it sounds like."

Together, they pressed their cupped ears to the windowpane. Whatever was beyond the ship, Tanith was afraid.

"Are there tales? Myths? Does Sulgrave say anything about what's on the ice?"

As if in response, the ship groaned. A low, rhythmic popping followed by a metallic ripple wasn't enough to wake the others, but it was more than enough to enrage Amaris.

"What do you want me to do about it?" Amaris hissed.

Tanith had no response. There was no answer that would satisfy either of them. "I'm sorry," came Tanith's muted reply. "But someone else needed to know."

With that, she crept back toward the empty space within Ash's arms.

Amaris's fingernails bit into her palms as she battled her frustration. She wanted to sleep. She wanted to be awake, to be battle-ready, to fight. She wanted to relax. She wanted to go into the snow and face her foe. She wanted to be knee-deep in a deliciously warm, sensual dream. More than anything, she resented Tanith for bringing problems without any hope of solution. Perhaps that was the irritating blow that forced her to clench and unflex her fists. As annoyed as she was and as helpless as she felt, she understood. Maybe she couldn't fight the creature or save the day, but she could join Tanith, reassuring her that she had not lost her mind.

After all, she knew no greater pain than being alone with one's nightmare.

Twelve

TANITH STAYED IN HER PUDDLE OF SHADOW AND WATCHED as Amaris fell into a fitful sleep for the rest of the night. Perhaps she should try to sleep as well, but she couldn't.

Her eyes were still open and stinging from sleeplessness when the hull turned from pitch black to slate gray. She listened as the others stirred, curious to see if Amaris would mention the night, but the reever did not. Tanith hadn't told anyone for the same reason Amaris kept her mouth shut. If they didn't know what was beyond their ships, nor the threat it posed, then it was both useless and unkind to worry the others. Not when they already had cold food and colder spirits.

And the crossing was miserable enough without the added stress.

She gnawed on a breakfast of hard-boiled eggs, half a loaf of rye bread, and a tin cup filled with snow that would soon melt into drinking water. At least the southbound trip had better food, even if the company had been quieter. She and the Reds had spent much of their time in prayer, and when they weren't reflecting on the All Mother, they were going over their strategy. They had detailed maps of the southern kingdoms and had little trouble planning their mission.

It was more than could be said about their current journey north.

She knew she was their only resource for Sulgrave, its people, its practices, and its geography, but she knew if she told them the truth, they wouldn't do what needed to be done. The others attempted to ply her for information so they might be prepared for their arrival, but in lieu of useful information, she told them that Sulgrave's mountains made Raascot's look like anthills, that everyone would speak the continent's common tongue, though it was not their preferred language, and lastly, there was a strong, dark drink, bitter and more powerful than tea, that Yazlyn would absolutely love. While the others found her anecdotes interesting, she knew these tidbits were utterly useless. Her vagaries resulted in a swift end to the conversation more often than not. They pressed her for information about the church, the government, and the beasts of the land, but Tanith remained committed to evasive nonanswers. She didn't mind taking the brunt of their frustration. She'd tell them what they needed to know when the time came. She was doing them a kindness, even if she couldn't explain why.

But they still had time. She had a few more days where she could simply be with them before everything fell to pieces.

The days and nights fell into rhythmic consistency. Every day, Gadriel would steer the ship for six hours, pausing for nourishment and for anyone who needed to escape the ship for any brief reprieve, whether to answer nature's call or to sprint toward the horizon, screaming in anguish at the gods as if chased by the hounds of hell that were edged on by the madness of being alone on the ice. Usually, it was the former. Occasionally, it was the latter.

The general's emotional control was as unsurprising to Tanith as the sergeant's lack thereof.

She understood that Yazlyn had been precariously perched somewhere between sanity and snapping for days before arriving on the ship, and the fragility of her mental state increased with each passing day. Still, she rallied her spirits, leading the others in stories, lore, and songs. The sergeant expressed disappointment that no one had thought to bring cards, as it would have been ideal to teach Amaris how to play rummy, but Yazlyn knew a few hand games meant for drinking and forced Tanith and the others to play along until everyone was entertained and enjoyed the competition.

Tanith found Nox's cheery demeanor surprising, given the circumstances, but perhaps the queen's levity came in the wake of three days of crying over whether or not Amaris, Gadriel, and Yazlyn had died before making it to the docks. Their survival buoyed her despite the cramped conditions, flavorless food, and barren landscape. Tanith had never considered pleasantness and likability to be important qualities for a leader, as long as they did what needed to be done, but Nox's warmth had her reconsidering her position. Her winsome personality certainly hadn't hurt in gaining Tanith's loyalty, after all.

Tanith enjoyed the third day of travel as she listened to the others venture into gossip and conjecture, inventing a few blasphemous rumors regarding the continent's bishops that they promised to spread when they returned. The fourth day, few found the energy to chatter.

The nights were kinder than the days, as Gadriel would set his intention for warmth and allow it to fill the hull as they drifted off to sleep.

It wasn't until the fifth day that the journey reminded her of her southbound crossing. They spent the hours in silence as a beautiful blue, cloudless sky and a snowless surface provided nothing to see and nothing to look at beyond the slits of their windows. While she didn't mind the quiet, she knew the others were tired of each other. They were tired of bread and cheese and dried fruit. They were tired of the monotonous scenery. They were tired of the chill. They were particularly tired of knowing that they were less than halfway into their voyage, as a week or more of sameness stretched before them.

And while she had been prepared for the emotional toll, she knew the others believed themselves doomed to a hell of same after same after same. And perhaps they would have been, had it not been for the fifth night. When the moon rose over the razor-straight horizon, everything changed.

✦

The sky that night wasn't just clear. It was singing.

Amaris had pinched herself into wakefulness for at least a few hours later than the others each night. She'd been able to tell from Tanith's rigid posture that the Sulgrave fae was getting equally little sleep as she spent each night straining her sharp fae ears against the creaking sounds of the metallic hull, listening for a presence. This meant she was awake the moment the sky came to life, flooding the hull of the skiff with a strange emerald glow.

She leaned forward, eyebrows bunched, squinting as she worked to discern the eerie, whirring hum seeping through the ship's walls. Amaris got to her feet and crept to the window to inspect the source of the peculiar high-frequency sound that scraped and echoed across the ice. Her eyes widened against the peacock array of greens, blues, and iridescent purples. In a flash, she was on her knees, shaking the others awake.

"What?" Nox blinked groggily.

Gadriel was alert and on his feet without fully understanding why he'd been called to action.

"Is everything okay?" Ash asked, rubbing the sleep from his eyes.

"You have to see this!" Amaris ran to jostle Yazlyn, unable to keep the excitement from her voice. "Get up! You have to see this!"

"Someone had better be dying," Yazlyn groaned.

Amaris ran to the door.

Gwydir, she'd learned from her months in the kingdom, was said to be built on the stones that had captured the northern lights. On clear nights, the distant horizon would occasionally reflect the beautiful glow of fae lights emanating from the sky rather than earth, often shifting between a midnight blue and a glimmering forest green on the distant horizon.

And now she'd caught the rainbow she hadn't realized they'd been chasing.

They burst from the ship and stood directly beneath the twisting, dancing snakes of the aurora borealis. It was dragon made not of flesh but of light, of beams and diamonds and magic. It took a moment for everyone to stir from their sleep, but once the entire party was awake and pressing against the window, it required only one loose suggestion that they go outside before everyone was on the slippery black ice dancing below the swirl of the magnificent rainbow that twisted and twirled through the sky.

They'd reached the end of their rope and collectively cracked as they'd tumbled into collective insanity. They were lunatics freed from their asylum as they sprinted, slid, and twirled across the ice on a drunken buzz as potent as fine wine.

They laughed like children who first experienced music, or the man who'd discovered fire, each lit by the verdant glow from above that banished the shadows of the night. It was hard to tell whether they'd been so starved of entertainment that this was genuinely as brilliant as they perceived it to be or if they were actually in the arctic chill of the music of the gods and their lights. The twinkling, grating melodies mixed with the altos and sopranos of the stars clashed in unfamiliar rhythms, scraping in their own tinny alien music. Amaris hugged Nox until the half-wild general had grabbed the both of them and spun them in a circle against the ice, pressing his body heat into them. Yazlyn had shot into the air, and it took him only a moment to join her, both of the Raascot fae soaring into the frigid air after the angelic greens and purples and pinks of the strange lights.

Each laugh came with the sharp, cold mint taste of ice as the inhalations burned their lungs, but they didn't care. The cold was not their enemy tonight. It was their angel. It was the music and poetry and lights of the old gods, the All Mother, of everything good and beautiful on the continent. This was the hidden, sacred gem of the Frozen Straits.

Ash and Tanith shared a grin under the cover of their blanket-wrapped embrace. Over the black ice, Amaris heard his murmur as he pointed. "Look. It's aquamarine."

Tanith responded with a lovely, airy laugh—a sound no one had heard from the solemn Sulgrave fae.

Amaris yelped a second later as Gadriel dove and snatched her from Nox's arms. The queen shouted after him with a toothy grin and half-hearted objection, but Yazlyn—drunk on the joy of the color and change and wildness of the music—swooped in, spinning Nox in a tight ballerina's twirl until she was beaming once more. Amaris watched their joy until Nox fell into Yazlyn's arms in a healing, much-needed hug to bridge whatever unspoken hurt had lingered between them.

"You're green." Amaris laughed, looking into the emerald glow reflecting off of Gadriel's skin as if it'd been carved from the gem itself.

"You should see yourself," he said in turn. "Fuchsia and sapphire are really your colors."

"How high can we go?" she asked. "Can we touch it?"

"Should we find out?" Gadriel replied, eyes sparkling. With several powerful beats, they continued their upward flight until their heads swam from the dizzying heights.

She stretched her mittened fingers toward the sparkles. His wings held their place in the air as if he were treading water in the sea as his gaze met hers. Her childlike joy faded when she absorbed the look on his face. He wasn't staring with any sort of intensity she recognized. It was something new, something unfamiliar. Something that if she didn't know better, she may have thought was uncertainty.

She placed a white-fur glove on either side of his face. "Kiss me?"

And before the question had time to escape her lips, his mouth was on her own. It was no lover's gentle press. This was passion and possession. The press of his mouth was as much a declaration of ownership as it was of affection. Her body tensed reflexively as she had the sensation of falling, but the butterflies she felt had nothing to do with gravity. She relaxed from surprise into submission as she melted into his kiss. Between the whir of the singing lights and the thunder of his wings, there was only him. In that moment, the world below was so far away, they might not have existed at all.

When he broke the kiss, he kept his face close to hers. She tasted blackberries on his low groan.

She swallowed. "Gadriel—"

He brushed his lips across her cheek. "For now, witchling, just have fun."

With that, he began their slow descent to the ground. They returned to and rejoined the festivities. She'd expected laughter and shrieks, but the energy that pulsed between them was something else entirely. Something subdued, sacred, and beautiful. Yazlyn had either lost her mind or had finally found whatever remained of her joy, as she'd taken to singing an unfamiliar song in a minor key. Amaris stepped out of Gadriel's arms and slipped her arm through Nox's.

Amaris was so surprised to hear a male voice that she nearly jumped. Not one but two, as both Ash and Gadriel joined in on the eerie lullaby. The general carried the bass, and Ash knew the melody on the chorus. Yazlyn's voice abandoned the main tune and found the complementary harmony.

Nox's and Amaris's eyes widened as they looked at each other. Nox asked, "Did you know they could sing?"

Amaris whispered back, equal parts surprised and hypnotized, "I didn't even know they were *capable* of song."

Amaris hadn't heard the song of the winter fae and her

babe, and from the curious tilts of Nox's and Tanith's head, it seemed she was not alone. It was the ominous tale of a mother on the drifting snow as she sang to her child about the world of ice and stars with a haunting lullaby.

"How do you know that?" Amaris asked of the group, grabbing Nox's hand as they stood to listen. She rested her head on the young queen's shoulder.

"Didn't your—" Yazlyn began to ask. Ash touched her arm, but they all knew what the sergeant had intended to ask.

No, her parents had not sung her lullabies. There had been no songs, whether joyful and merry or soulful and minor in the orphanage. She realized her mistake the moment it left her lips.

Gadriel returned to the women, once again enveloping them in his wings and warmth. "I'll teach it to you."

To Amaris's surprise, he kissed her head. He kept the other arm draped amicably around Nox as he did so.

She wasn't sure why the air abandoned her lungs or why her chest tightened. Amaris blinked several times to see if Nox had witnessed the exchange.

With a chuckle that was part nerves, part epiphany, she realized none of it mattered. The entire castle had known that Amaris and Gadriel had been sharing a bed long after they'd traveled together and trained together. Amaris and Nox had intimately discussed their dalliances in a rather sensual dream that she bitterly regretted the inability to complete. Still, having Gadriel show affection in such an enclosed space felt wildly forbidden. Perhaps she'd read too many of Tanith's romance novels. Or maybe she'd created rules where none existed.

He winked at her, as if understanding precisely what fear this would instill.

Sadist.

With a low chuckle, Gadriel left them to twirl Yazlyn once more.

She looked up at the musical, frozen rainbow, watching

spring-green, amethyst, and magenta lights perform as if putting on a show for them alone.

"It's perfect," Nox said.

"What is?"

She touched her head to Amaris's, holding her close. "Everything."

And for a few moments, it was. When Amaris thought back on that night, she wished she hadn't wasted a second of their beautiful minutes on worry. After all, they were the last precious moments before everything fell to pieces.

Thirteen

DELIGHT PLAYED ON THEIR FACES AS THE PARTY RETURNED to the ship, happy and exhausted. Nox hadn't realized how desperately she'd needed a night like tonight, but it felt like her cup had been refilled. The only sound belonged to the flickering aurora borealis, as if the display had tired them and their show had ended for the night. Their glow was dimming perceptibly, hiding the reflective corners of the skiff as it began its fading journey back to the stars from which it had come.

She nuzzled into Amaris, still sipping on joy when Amaris came to an abrupt halt. Nox's smile faltered. She looked between Amaris and the way the light bent and shifted over the reflective ship. They were less than thirty steps from the warmth of the skiff.

"What is it?" Nox asked, giving Amaris's arm a squeeze. When Amaris remained still, seriousness clouded her tone. She squinted her eyes, looking into the distance in an attempt to discern what had caught Amaris's attention. She repeated, "What?"

Out of the corner of Nox's eye, Tanith caught her attention. She'd similarly frozen in her steps, palm outstretched for the ship. In a quiet, anxious voice, Tanith asked, "Amaris?"

At her side, Amaris dipped her chin in confirmation of whatever secret the two shared.

Tanith's swallow was almost audible across the still, windless night.

Nox wasn't alone in her demand for answers. Ash and Yazlyn murmured their questions as all eyes remained on Tanith and Amaris. She might have pressed further had Gadriel not raised his hand to command silence.

It worked.

He was below Nox in rank. He had no power over the reevers. Tanith would never yield to his or anyone's authority. Even still, his centuries of training carried gravitas. Nox didn't know what was happening, but whatever it was, Amaris's mouth remained open on an unspoken word, her eyes wide in silent shock. She hadn't so much as blinked.

Nox was about to squeeze her again when she took one careful step forward, then another, shifting her weight so she made no sound as she moved. She moved free of Nox's hold and extended her hand wordlessly to Tanith.

If Nox hadn't been afraid before, this single act raised her hackles. She was certain that Tanith and Amaris working together would ring alarm bells in the others as well.

Tanith matched her cat-like movements as she took slow, careful steps toward Amaris. Nox searched Gadriel's face for answers, but he shook his head. He had none. Ash and Yazlyn remained motionless on the ice as they waited for... something. Anything. Answers. Explanations. Perhaps a loud laugh over a confusing practical joke. Anything was better than this nauseating, petrifying brand of anticipation.

Nox strained to listen as the reever and the Sulgrave fae met in the middle. Voice scarcely more than a whisper, she heard Amaris ask, "Do you know anything that could be helpful?"

Tanith joined Amaris in staring at the dark, empty horizon direction. Her pointed ears seemed to twitch once, as if she heard a sound, a clue, perhaps a crunch against either snow or ice that no one else could hear.

Darkness seeped in like water. Contrasted against the northern lights and their brilliance, the first-quarter moon was insufficient. For all she knew, by the time their eyes had adjusted to the change in light, it might be too late.

What Tanith said next chilled Nox to the bone.

"It survives on the ice," came the fae's urgent whispers. If it weren't for the windless night, Nox wouldn't have heard it at all. Tanith's hushed words tumbled one after the other. "It thrives at night. It is neither man nor fae. It withstands all manners of cold, snow, frost, and wind. I do not know what it is, what it eats, or how it hunts. Only that it has not been merely wind and ice that has tattered ships and destroyed passages. No one has recorded its appearance. I'm not sure that it can be seen."

Cold flooded Nox's lungs with her sharp inhalation.

She watched as Amaris turned to the other reever, but Ash only shook his head, uncomprehending.

They may have remained frozen in perpetual, anxious confusion had it not been for the crack, snarl, and explosion of sound and snow that sent everyone into a panic. Tanith turned for the ship, pushing Ash forward. Amaris slipped on the ice, catching herself with a grunt as she reached for Nox.

"Get to the ship!" she shouted.

Nox fought for traction as she ran. She yanked Amaris to her feet as they sprinted for the ship. A loud, bone-chilling growl, a snap, the thunder of ice, of teeth, of *something* sent everyone into the side of the skiff. They thrashed at the wall as Tanith battled to the front, pounding at the entrance and sending the door swinging on its hinges.

"Go, go!" Gadriel shouted. They dove into the cabin. The general pushed the others into the darkened entrance, remaining behind until the last person dove inside. He slammed the door behind them, then leaned his back against the door as his chest heaved.

"What is it?" Ash demanded.

Amaris answered, but the squeak of her panicked words was a jumble of syllables and vowels.

"What?" Ash pushed.

Amaris sucked in a loud lungful of air. A loud, cracking noise broke across the ice. A thunder accompanied by a thump and shudder shook the skiff. Knees buckled, the floor twisted and dipped, and half of them fell to the floor as the ship rocked.

Amaris's voice came out in a strangled gasp. "Aboriou!"

Ash was the only one who reacted while everyone else gripped the floor, the wall, each other for stability. They remained tensed in horror as the other reever reacted.

"They're not real!"

The ship rocked again as something outside of it struck.

"Whatever it is," Nox said through gritted teeth, "it feels pretty fucking real to me."

"Everyone, be quiet," Amaris pleaded. She lowered her voice to a stab of quiet panic. "If it strikes the ship again, don't scream. We need it to lose interest."

"But why—" Yazlyn began before slapping her hand over her mouth. The ship rocked again as something brushed against it.

"I don't know," Amaris said, her answer scarcely more than a whisper. The aurora borealis had winked out altogether, leaving aching silence in their absence. She didn't have to raise her volume beyond that of a secret as she said, "If I had to guess? Our noise drew it. Aboriou are not supposed to exist. Their entry in the bestiary tome is only a sentence or two, as if the authors thought their lore wasn't worth mentioning."

"And?" Yazlyn lowered her voice to match Amaris's intensity. She looked between the reevers. "Were they two *helpful* sentences?"

Amaris closed her eyes as if reading from the tome etched on the back of her eyelids. She said, "The aboriou is claimed to have found a home on the desolate wastelands of otherwise uninhabitable ice and snow. No description of the creature exists. Something, something, something….and then I remember the second part because the author made a joke. She said: either this monster is indescribable because it is too deadly to permit survivors or for the more likely fact that it, like the boogeyman, is a fiction crafted by those who demand explanation for the tragic—but natural—deaths of their companions."

Nox dropped her voice for a chance to rib. "Seems like Amaris was a better student than you."

Yazlyn looked to Amaris. "Who was this author?"

"Is that important?" Ash answered for her, rife with irritation.

Hands flew out to support their bodies in unspoken synchronicity as a loud crack broke their conversation. The boat rocked with impact more as the creature rammed into its side. Yazlyn stumbled, as others struggled to maintain their footing. Everyone looked at Amaris with glaring intensity, as if she were personally to blame. Tanith lowered herself to the ground, hands gripping what existed of the lower portion of the mast. Amaris, then Nox, copied the motion, clutching the bottommost portion of the mast as they crouched. The others followed suit, bracing themselves against the walls or floor of the ship so that their bodies would not betray their presence with any sudden movement.

A new sound broke the silence.

A brushing noise seemed to indicate that the creature was rubbing against the reflective exterior of the skiff. This was not the reptilian noise of the demons of the continent but the coarse, bristle sound of hundreds of thousands of straw-like strands of hair as they scraped. The creature might have been alerted to its own noise, as it repeated its motion once, then twice, crawling along the edge of the ship, listening to the way its hair dragged on the metallic structure.

No one dared move or breathe, hoping the creature had given up.

Nox peered through the oppressive darkness, scarcely able to discern the others' silhouettes. The next noise was a calming gust of wind, conjuring the familiar sound of isolation. She had nearly relaxed when another thunderous hit came against the skiff, rocking it up before it slammed down.

Gadriel tried to keep his voice low as he fought for answers. "What can be done?"

Tanith answered, "If we want to survive the night, the best we can do is go undetected."

"It already knows we're here," Yazlyn retorted.

"Be quiet," Tanith snapped.

Silence. Tension. Stress.

With no way to know or believe that it had truly gone, everyone in the cabin remained stiff for nearly an hour, but the beast did not hit their ship again. Nox's last thought was the certainty that her eyes would remain fixed on the starry slot to the outside world all night. The next thing she knew, morning light cut through the hull in hard beams.

Her first conscious thought was gratitude that they'd survived the night. The second was that it was goddess-damned freezing. She shivered, clutching her arms as she looked at the others. Puffs of breath escaped their lips. Gadriel, as it turned out, had been unwilling to risk drawing the creature to a heat source. Nox hadn't realized how hard he'd worked day in and day out to keep them warm until waking stiff and trembling in the absence of his heat.

The morning was a mixture of grumbling attempts to warm one another and accusations hurled at Tanith and Amaris.

"You two knew?" Yazlyn asked, rejecting her bread after the first dissatisfying bites. She tossed its half-eaten remains back into the sack and leaned against the wall, arms crossed.

Tanith kept her eyes on her breakfast. "We believe as many fae have been killed on the crossing by the animal as they have by the cold."

"But you traveled here with Nox and Ash and didn't mention a beast to either of them. You said nothing to any of us," Yazlyn pushed.

Tanith's face fell. "I did tell someone. Our first night on

the ice, I woke Amaris. She saw a shadow, and from what she saw, I made a guess at the reason we have never possessed a description."

Gadriel furrowed his brow. "It's hidden? How can a creature have an enchantment?"

Tanith pinched a piece of loaf between her fingers, picking at the bread one bit at a time. She shook her head, still unwilling to meet their gaze.

Ash chewed on the information. "Creatures cannot conjure enchantments."

Yazlyn's irritability resurged. "We know."

"No," he pressed, "a creature couldn't do this. But clearly, it's been done. If this were simply an elusive beast, Amaris wouldn't have seen it when the rest of us couldn't. It has to be magic. A spell, a curse...I don't know. Who would benefit from enchanting the beasts on the straits?"

Nox frowned. "Are you implying...?"

He nodded seriously. "Perhaps someone felt that the ice was not enough of a deterrent between Sulgrave and the continent below."

Nox considered the implication. An unseen beast lurking on the icy wastelands would be a nearly invincible foe to any hopeful adventurer. Even if they braved the cold, managed the supplies, had the ship and had prepared the heat necessary for survival, no one could shield against something unknown and unseen. The aboriou, whether one beast or a litter of many, had been the final ingredient necessary to successfully cut off Sulgrave from the rest of the world.

"Why would that stop anyone from Sulgrave?" Nox asked. "You can bind beasts to your will."

Tanith's shoulders rolled forward, slumping into her helplessness. It was an expression Nox had never seen on the fae. Defeated, Tanith said, "We can't bind what we don't know."

"So now that you have its name...?"

"It doesn't work like that. I need to visualize the creature, along with the image of what I want it to do. I was able to see the harpies come to me, and then I created the image of them covering the continent with their message and made my will into a reality."

Somehow, Nox found this information doubly unnerving. Tanith wasn't just controlling beasts; she was manipulating the world around her by creating reality from imagination.

"So, what?" Yazlyn asked. "We just live in fear now?"

Gadriel got to his feet. He headed for the door as he said, "We do what we'd always intended. We survive the crossing."

He let himself into the gray morning, leaving silence in his wake.

Nox had heard that bad things came in threes. The aboriou, of course, was a very bad thing. The wind shifted, forcing them to collapse the mast and sail, which was the second bad thing. Gadriel continued pushing, with Yazlyn joining him for hour-long intervals before she came in to thaw. Once she'd worked blood and life back into her limbs, she'd go outside to help once more. This method was more or less effective for two days of laboring on the ice. They took turns sleeping in shifts at night, the waking party straining to hear for any signs of danger.

Nox wondered at the third bad thing. Maybe it had already happened, she thought. The others had overshot the skiff initially, leaving her to think they'd perished. That had been bad. The parchment had gotten damp, and they were forced to rely solely on the pocket watch, preventing them from sleeping. That had been unfortunate to be sure. She'd spent days unable to reach them in their sleep, which had been bad…

She counted their misfortunes on her fingers and frowned at her outstretched palm. Bad things came in threes, yes. But did they come in multiples of threes? Nox didn't know. So they did the only thing they could and pressed on.

While several insisted it was their eighth day on the skiff, others were sure it was now their ninth morning. Supplies were dwindling, and the ice had been too barren to catch snow for their tin cups. Mouths were dry and spirits were low as the wind continued to whistle across the desolate wasteland. Despite the chill, the depression, and the looming threat of a beast on the ice, the dwindling food, and the overall misery of life on the crossing, Nox thought they were managing as best as they could.

Until the tenth morning.

Fourteen

Nox SHOT TO ALERTNESS, AND SHE WAS NOT ALONE. Everyone scrambled for readiness, certain they'd been discovered by the beast. They ran to the window slots to perceive their coming demise and were met with a solid wall of white. They'd awoken to a blizzard so total, so punishing, that the straits had disappeared. A howling gust caused their ship and everyone in it to quake.

No sky. No ice. No horizon.

The ship lurched and swayed as it was slammed by the wind's violent gusts.

"Fuck!"

"Goddess damn it!"

Several concurrent cusses filled the ship just as the skiff tipped up on its blade, then slammed back onto its base. Nox's heart ached as she understood the third bad thing.

"What if it knocks us over?" she asked, eyes wide.

"If the wind capsizes the ship?" Gadriel asked.

"We're not in water," Yazlyn bit. "It can't capsize."

But Yazlyn's argument reassured no one. Perhaps they wouldn't sink beneath waves, but they were one disaster away from their shelter cracking, their transportation shredding, and their lives scattered like snowflakes in the storm.

The western wind picked up speed as it barreled across the flat, open straits, meeting no obstacle to stand in opposition to its force or speed until it hit the small, metallic skiff. The wind screamed as if banshees had congregated beyond the walls of their ship, wailing with terrible anger. The dry, brittle snow particles that typically skated across the glassy surface of the frozen sea hit the silvery structure with such intensity that the impact of each snowflake reverberated through the ship as if arrows were embedding themselves into the very walls.

"We need to anchor it," Gadriel said, raising his voice so he might be heard over the storm's relentless banshee wail.

Yazlyn grabbed his arm. Her eyes flashed red as she hollered, "If you try to set foot outside this skiff, I will knock you unconscious myself."

He didn't have time to retort before the second shudder of hurricane-force gusts.

"We can't do nothing," Nox said. Her eyes shot to the blinding white patch of window. Every moment that passed seemed to anger the storm. The wind rocked the skiff onto one blade, but this time it did not slam to the ground. The ship began to tilt.

"Hold on!" Ash yelled.

"It's going to tip the ship!" Yazlyn cried out at the same time.

"No!" Gadriel grunted. "Get to the port side!"

The response was instantaneous. Each threw their weight to the far side to counteract gravity, but their efforts came a moment too late. High yelps, low groans, shocked attempts to catch limbs and wings and tumbling sacks created a blur of chaos as the skiff rolled, tossing its crew backward into the hard, unforgiving metal of the starboard side. Nox cried out as she hit the wall with bruising intensity. The crunching smack of flesh on arctic metal rang through the hull as the others fell victim to the storm. The pearly flash of hair drew her attention as Amaris went limp against metal sheet.

"Amaris?" She inched toward the reever. Nox attempted to wipe the hair from her eyes, but the sharp sting of tears hit her before she felt a nauseous wave, followed by a thumping, swollen ache in her arm. Jaw clenched, she forced herself to ignore what very well might have been a broken arm. "Is everyone okay?"

At least, that was what she'd intended to ask.

Her question was stolen by a renewed violent gust as it pushed the flat edge of the ship sidelong across the ice. She cried out against the painful sound of scraping metal as the blizzard took its arctic hands and pushed the skiff far from its path. The crack and pop of silver and ice made hearing nearly impossible. She grunted again as she tried once more to drag herself closer to Amaris. One window was planted against the dark ice. The other slit directly overhead provided a dull light as the port side was now lofted toward the white, furious sky.

Nox split a healing tonic with an unconscious Amaris, knitting her arm together before dribbling what was left between Amaris's lips.

Then they sat, and they waited.

What followed was cold, agonizing, mind-numbing impatience, anxiety, frustration, and misery as they waited for the worst snowstorm imaginable to ebb and see whether or not they'd been buried under a mountain of snow and ice.

Day lasted into the night, then stretched well into the eleventh day. The blizzard raged with no indication of ebbing until they'd been stranded in the cabin for two full nights and the early parts of the twelfth day. They had food, but there had been almost no water remaining in their canteens from the melted snow previously gathered. Tanith used her abilities to conjure water from air once, filling all of the skins, but the taxing act required that they dip into their precious greenstrike vials.

"How do we get it back on its skates?" Yazlyn had asked.

"It doesn't matter while the storm continues," Gadriel said, voice bitter against his own helplessness. This wasn't a foe he could battle. They were left to wait, and to hope.

Their chapped lips and dry hands confirmed what they already knew: they were in a frozen desert. The very ice below them was salted. As they weren't sure what it would take to get them out of their predicament, they urged Tanith to save her powers.

By the night of the twelfth day on the Frozen Straits, the storm showed the first sign of ebbing. Nox was the first to draw attention to the dying winds. She looked into the exhausted faces of the others. "If the storm dies," she said, "we're sitting on the door. How the hell are we supposed to get out and fix the ship?"

The others looked at their new floor.

"Listen," Yazlyn commanded. She cupped her ear for emphasis, and Nox understood the gesture. It was quiet. The wind was no longer flinging chunks of snow and ice against the skiff. They'd survived the blizzard. "I can do it." Yazlyn blinked against exhaustion—a tiredness that was every bit as existential as it was physical.

Nox winced against the hopeless look on the sergeant's face. "But what if you—"

"I said: I can do it."

She didn't leave room for dialogue. Yazlyn pressed her hand into the cold, downward-facing wall and called the ice beyond the ship as if summoning a hand from the frozen sea itself. The others tumbled downward as the ice scraped and pushed the ship into an upright position. A terrifying, unfamiliar cracking noise shook the party as the skiff thundered onto its true bottom.

"You did it—" Gadriel began his praise.

"Not yet," she said, teeth bared. Her first act of magic had righted the ship but trapped them anew. Yazlyn manipulated the ice once more, struggling to control something she could not see. She worked through the wall on the vertical barrier that blocked them in, forcing it to crumble.

Gadriel clapped his hand on her shoulder. "Take the compliment, Yaz. You did it."

"But what did I do?" she mumbled, voice low and miserable. She may have righted the ship, but Nox understood her question. With slow, stiff muscles, everyone braced themselves for whatever awaited them. They opened the door for the first time in days and stepped in the fading evening light to assess the damage.

Nox tipped her head back, tilting her face toward the sky. They'd survived. The clouds were already parting, revealing pockets of pink and orange as the weather relinquished its terrible hold on the straits.

"I found the source of the noise," Ash called behind her.

She wanted to savor their survival for a moment later, but she was a queen. It was time to let responsibility make her miserable every moment of every day for the rest of her life—or whatever it meant to be a royal.

The cracking noise, Ash explained, had belonged to the blades beneath the skiff. As Yazlyn had set the ship back on its base, the brittle metal that had allowed them to skate for the first ten days had splintered and collapsed beneath the sudden thud. The right side of the ship was no longer the nearly invisible reflective surface it had once been, as the scraping against the ice had created indentations and gouges through the mirror, revealing the darker silver of the metal beneath.

Gadriel rubbed at his temples. "Tanith? Can you fix it?"

Ash opened his mouth to interject, but everyone, Tanith included, shut him down.

"Yes, I believe so," Tanith said. She rested her fingertips on Ash's forearm. "It's just hard to know what to tackle first. If I'm using my ability to lift the ship, then calling on a second ability to repair the metal will be…challenging. I've used two powers simultaneously, but only when one of the two was my naturally occurring gift."

"No," Yazlyn said with some confidence, "you only have to speak to metal. I can lift the ship—make icy stands, or something of the like, to make the underside available for you to repair. Then you only have to call on one new power, right?"

"Right," Tanith agreed.

Nox felt worthless in their situation, but that wasn't a new emotion. Her powers were useless in combat, in storms, in cold, and in ship repair. She struggled to keep her mind from wandering down an unhelpful path over her own helplessness.

"Who has the compass?" she asked. A moment later, she set forth to make herself useful. A quick consultation of their pocket watch had told them they hadn't gone too far-off course, though they'd need to angle the ship northwest in order to compensate for how far the wind had taken them.

Determined to continue to help, she wandered away from the ship to fill their canteens with the low-moisture snow. Nox knew it would take several trips of melting and refilling before they had enough to drink, but she'd be damned if they'd weathered the elements only to die of dehydration. She was feeling quite a bit calmer underneath the sunset's final stages of pink, glad for the moon that had appeared with its pale gibbous between the dissipating clouds. She closed her eyes and breathed in through her nose, appreciating the clean air, the biting cold, the sharp scent of survival. Bright evening stars dotted overhead, urging her to be grateful that they were still alive.

She took another step into the liberating feeling before something crunched underfoot. Nox's lips and brows pinched as she cocked her head, examining the curious bit of snow near her foot.

"Hey, someone?" she called.

The others had better things to do, of course. Yazlyn and Tanith ignored her as they focused their efforts on repairs, eyes scrutinizing the blades of the ship from where it remained elevated. Nox appeared to be standing over a small, windswept drift of snow.

"Amaris?" Nox beckoned the reever toward her.

"One second," Amaris shouted from her place below the ship.

"Could you come look at this?" Nox called. She could

scarcely make out Amaris's pale features against the snow, though she sensed the flash of inconvenience. Urgency worked its way through her words as she stared at the snow and pressed, "I think it might be important."

Fifteen

G O," GADRIEL SAID.

Amaris frowned as she looked between the general and the ship. "I just feel I could be more useful—"

"*Go,*" he repeated. "I have plenty to do. Yaz is going to need help."

He didn't wait for her to respond before he jogged over to meet his sergeant. Amaris abandoned the ship and made her way toward Nox, slipping every time her feet hit slick ice instead of snow. She saw the question on Nox's face long before she reached her side.

"Are you okay?" Amaris asked, slowing with cautious curiosity as she approached. They had a few minutes of dusk left before they were left in darkness, but there was just enough light for her to absorb Nox's expression.

Nox's face remained twisted in frown. "What does that look like to you?"

Amaris *hmphed* as she closed the distance between them. She tilted her head, spying something curious. While normally they were met with the vacant blackness of the frozen seawater beneath them, save for the grayish slashes carving downward as the ice had cracked and refrozen, there appeared to be a shape beneath the ice. She didn't understand why Nox found it important, but curiosity got the better of her. Amaris kicked at the drift in an attempt to clear snow from the interesting shape.

"No," Nox stopped her foot. "Don't kick at it."

Amaris redirected her frown. She'd been doing her best to reveal the interesting shape in the ice. "I can't kick at it." Amaris gestured at the odd shape.

"The print. You're disturbing it."

"What print?"

But the moment she asked, she saw it. There was an impression in the snow. If she didn't know better, she would say it almost looked like a paw print. It was the width of at least three human hands, with the jagged punctures of what could only be claws pressing themselves into dots against the surface. Nox knelt to examine the print. It was a curious impression to be sure, but it wasn't half as interesting as whatever remained below them.

"What do you think is in the ice?" Amaris asked.

Nox glanced away from the paw print long enough to shake her head, disinterested. "There's nothing there." She resumed her study of the print, trying to get the reever to focus on the enormity of the impression in the snow.

"The thing you called me over to see," Amaris reiterated.

"It looks like a footprint, doesn't it? Like an animal?"

It was as if Amaris had been punched in the gut by Nox's innocent words. She grabbed Nox's hand and pointed with urgency. "There. Right there below us. What is that?"

Nox made an irritated face. "Stop it, Amaris. There's nothing there. You're the animal expert here. I know you've pored over those bestiary tomes. Does this print look like anything to you?"

Realization lanced through her like molten iron.

Amaris gave Nox a hard shove, pushing her with all her might just as the sun fully set over the horizon. She tried to shout for them to go but was fighting Nox's baffled resistance every bit as hard as her own scrambling flails. She slipped in her attempt to force Nox forward, knees cracking against the ice. Stars flashed in her eyes and a nauseous roil in her stomach revolted against the quick pain.

"Nox, go!"

Nox dipped to help her instead. With an exasperated pant, Amaris got to her feet and grabbed Nox's arm, jerking it with joint-popping intensity. Nox balked. "Amaris!"

But she didn't have it in her to respond. She'd lost the capacity for language as she tugged at the queen, shouting the only two words she knew at the others. Her two words echoed across the empty plains of the Frozen Straits as Amaris pumped her arms and legs, dragging Nox forward.

"It's here!" Amaris screamed.

A confusing, echoing sound similar to the metallic snapping of cords interfered with the night's otherwise peaceful silence. The sound had the frequency of something that faded in and out quickly, like a swelling bubble of singing whales, or a smothered, elongated hooting of owls. It was the sound of ice slowly popping as the enormous sheets of frozen seawater began to snap, shuddering the water below it. Amaris was running from the source of the sound as fast as she could.

"It's here!" she cried again. The arctic night was minty and painful as ice filled her lungs in a gasp of sheer panic. Adrenaline took over, pumping from her head to her toes as her entire body was numb and alive all at once. She knew only one responsibility in that moment, and it was to get Nox away from the monster.

"Come on!" Amaris snarled, fury and urgency doing their job. Nox still blinked with abject confusion, but allowed herself to be dragged forward.

Gadriel looked up at them from where he'd joined the others at the skiff's stern. Why wasn't he running? Why wasn't anyone moving? Amaris looked in horror at the skiff. It remained lofted above eye level so that Tanith had access to the boat's underside. Ash remained on the far side of the ship, kneeling in the snow while the strange symphony of noises continued. His eyebrows knit together at Amaris's sudden outburst, but no one spurred to action.

She yelled again, but it was too late.

The cracking, scraping sound of the explosion through the ice's surface layer hit their ears before they understood Amaris's warning. She was almost fully to the ship, Nox in tow, when the aboriou broke free. The others gasped and cried out as the volcanic eruption of ice and snow alerted them to something powerful and enormous.

White fur. Teeth. Eyes. Big. So, so big. Holy *shit*.

She had to fight it. How the fuck was she supposed to fight it without weapons?

Everyone's swords and bows were still resting within the walls of the lifted cabin. Neither she nor anyone else would be able to get inside in time to arm themselves.

"Get them somewhere safe!" Amaris cried. She trusted Gadriel to understand her meaning. To her surprise, it was Tanith who broke free from her manipulation of the metal and emerged, fists clenched at her side, to posture against what she couldn't see. They had only a few seconds before the beast was upon them. Tanith looked exhausted. Gadriel hadn't moved. No one had jumped into action. Why weren't they acting?

A thunder and roar tore from the creature's throat as it finished breaking through the ice.

They had thirty seconds at most before it reached the first of them.

A second wave of understanding stripped the horror from her. She couldn't panic. She couldn't be afraid. The others were going in blind. Amaris knew with cold certainty that it was up to her to direct the battle.

Her voice came out as a rasp as she shouted to the winged fae. "Go! Fly them!"

That was all it took for their military training to click into place.

Yazlyn grabbed Tanith ungracefully by an arm and a leg and darted skyward, away from the reflective ship. Gadriel dove first for Nox, protecting his queen before he attempted to swoop down for the remaining reever, grunting as he hoisted Ash by the collar of his shirt.

Amaris was alone, sans weapons, armed with only the true sight of her lilac eyes and hand-to-hand combat training.

Three more explosive sounds crashed against the ice as the beast tore for Amaris. The others could not defend against what they could not see, but she could.

Amaris was alone, and she knew it.

"Come and get me, motherfucker," she said, readying herself for impact.

Fifteen seconds if she was lucky. Thirteen. Ten.

She saw every pump of the beast's arms and legs as if it were moving in slow motion. The horned, white beast was an amalgamation of every horrific beast. It snarled with the enormous maw of a wolf. It ran with the lithe, feline movements of a predatory cat. Each jolt of its muscle forced the white shag fur of snow bear to ripple and move as it ran.

She'd studied the tomes inside and out. She'd memorized every beast on its pages. Yet nothing would have prepared her for the deep-set eyes behind the gigantic, toothy snout of this predator. She tensed in a half-crouch. She was out of options, but the motherfucker was huge, and she knew its strength had to be its weakness. The monster flicked its eyes up with brief disinterest. With the others skyward, it focused its attention on its only available meal: Amaris.

She forced herself to stand still as the monster frothed, closing the space between them as if it had been born to sink its teeth into her flesh. In four steps it would be atop her.

She remained motionless as it sprinted for her.

"Three," she said, choking out the count.

The star-studded sky and gibbous moon reflecting on its eyes, its teeth, its claws.

"Two." She wiggled her fingers, bracing herself for the final impact.

Another snarl tore from its mouth as it locked her in its sights.

"One!" Amaris screamed as she dove to the side, dodging the aboriou's path as it brushed past her close enough for its hide to rub against her airborne boots. Unable to stop in time, the beast careened toward the skiff, ramming its body into the icy stilts Yazlyn had made for the boat.

Now was her chance.

Amaris slid as well, the side of her body thumping painfully against the ice as her hip, arm, and shoulder took the brunt of her fall. But her tactic had worked. She'd knocked the beast off of its footing. Even its padded paws and giant claws could not dig themselves into the ice in time for a swift stop. The beast groaned as it slid into the ice and metal, taking a moment to adjust itself and shake off the hurt of the impact. It shuddered, bits of snow and ice flying from its fur coat.

"Come on!" Amaris shouted at it again, drawing its eyes to her. The moon refracted against its dark eyes as if two more moons were joining the night sky before her.

Her attention was diverted for the barest of moments.

Above her, Gadriel's grip on Ash was slipping. Flying with Nox alone would have been easy enough, but she knew maintaining air while holding two would be damn near impossible. Gadriel's wings beat fast and hard as her brother twisted overhead to grab on to the general's clothes. The men exchanged words before Gadriel began to lower Ash to the roof of the ship. She was certain it would be only long enough for him to adjust his grip, but horror dripped through her. The beast had been staring her in the eye, fangs glinting as it snarled, when the clanging sound of Ash's feet on the metallic skiff caused it to whip its head toward the noise.

The others couldn't see how the monster had turned its attention, but she could only hope her answering cries would do as much for them as they did for the creature.

"No! No, look here!" She waved her hands from where she stood on the ice and snow. She took speedy, backward steps to position herself on a snowdrift, seeking more traction than the black sea ice offered. She couldn't let it get the best of them. There was no other choice.

Desperation rose within her as she watched the beast lose interest. It turned away from her, and her voice, her calls for it to look at her, her jumps, the frantic waving of her arms told the tale. It had fixed its sights on the others. Ash had taken too long. His feet were still on the roof while they repositioned themselves.

"The ship!" she screamed, looking at Gadriel. "It's climbing—"

A metallic crack and pop as it sank its weight into the skiff cut her short.

Amaris screamed for the general to go, and Gadriel quickly grabbed Ash, but he couldn't find the air he needed. Their momentum shot them to the opposite side of the ship, falling almost instantaneously downward as they careened toward the ice.

Amaris saw great wings disappear behind the ship, then the thud and impact as they reappeared in the window created by the space beneath the ship. Nox cried out as she struck the ground, rolling several arm's lengths away as Gadriel skidded onto the surface of the sea. Ash was first on his feet, running to lift a wide-eyed Nox from the snow. The wildcat-like beast dug its claws into the hull of the ship with the loud, splintering sounds of cracking glass and scraping metal as the skiff crunched beneath its enormous weight.

The aboriou locked its sights on the three.

Amaris made no attempt to keep the powerless, angered cry inside. Her tactic wasn't working. The creature was going to eat her friends, and they'd have no way to see what was coming for them until they were between its teeth.

"Please," she begged, both of the beast and of her friends. *Please get up. Please run. Please escape.*

Please don't eat them. Please turn around. Please choose me instead.

Amaris continued to uselessly call for the creature's attention, but as it mounted the skiff and the ship buckled beneath it, the only thing it cared about was the motion on the ground. Gadriel had found his feet and was set at a dead sprint for the others. Nox was still getting to her feet. If the creature didn't look at her, she had ten seconds before she watched Nox die.

Amaris would have gone on raging against the wind, had Yazlyn not made a quick choice.

A flash of black blotted against the moon and stars. Amaris held her breath, horrified as the sergeant dove like a bird of prey. She was heading directly toward the roof of the skiff—the last noise, the last indentation, the last evidence of the monster. Amaris knew the fae didn't know the monster's head from its invisible body, yet she and Tanith plunged toward the creature, legs outstretched for impact. The moment they landed, it whipped its head around and thrashed for them with enormous, sharpened claws, but they were already off.

As its paw lifted for the swipe, Amaris caught the glimmer of something metallic on its front leg reflected in the gibbous moon. The creature was neither cursed nor enchanted: it was wearing a manacle. It roared in a harsh, ear-splitting sound as it swatted.

The reever's eyes widened as she chased after the shape of the sergeant's enormous wingspan and the stars that blotted out behind her. Amaris screamed at Yazlyn, "Do it again! Aim lower! Starboard, starboard!"

The sergeant made another sweeping dive to hit the creature on the right side of the ship just as Gadriel was taking off into the sky again. Yazlyn's feet found the creature, and she clung to Tanith as she attempted to push it off, but this time when it swung for her, it struck.

Yazlyn went down, careening toward the ice with an incredible force.

"No!" The horrified cry that ripped from Amaris's throat

was one of guilt, shock, and panic. She had given the very command that may have caused their death. The fae was a bird swatted from the sky by an angry, prowling cat. The sergeant remained immobilized where she landed. Tanith sprinted to Yazlyn's side and grabbed for the winged fae's head, trying to shake her awake as the beast descended.

There's no time.

"Tanith, shield!" Amaris shouted.

She'd scarcely said the word, and Tanith obeyed without hesitation. She thrust a hand overhead, casting a sphere so that when the beast lunged for them, it bounced back against the obstruction. Tanith looked toward the place of impact, whether feeling its ripple against her magic or hearing it clang against her protective bubble. It tried to swipe for them once, but if the goddess was good, she would allow Amaris to try one final tool.

Amaris raised a fist and begged for her magic not to fail her.

She slammed her shockwave into the ground.

The explosive ripple moved the snow, the ice, the very world, with Amaris at its epicenter. The creature stopped mid-thrash as it absorbed the power of her wave. The straits sounded a sharp, loud splintering noise as the black ice popped and snapped below them, sending a vertical shard of white into the depth of the slippery surface. The echoes and waves drew the aboriou's irritated gaze and the beast shifted for her, unleashing another roar. When it came for Amaris, she called her magic again, hitting it horizontally with her shockwave. Just as Yazlyn had been rendered unconscious from the collision of her impact, the beast flew backward with an incredible force and smacked its great head against the ice.

It struggled, bobbing its head as if dazed as it tried to get to its feet.

But Amaris had one last plan.

The reever ran for the monster while it planted its front paws on the ground in an attempt to stand. She sent another wave after the beast the moment it lifted its maw. Her shock-wave thrust the beast's mighty skull into the ice with a crack. Collateral damage whined and shuddered as the ice that had been supporting the skiff collapsed, sending the dented ship diving for the ground beneath.

She had a split second to make a decision.

Amaris wasn't sure if she should run for her sword now that the door to the ship was in reach or if her best bet was to go for the beast. Chilly wind and the dim glow of the clear night's stars pushed down as she made her choice.

She groaned and tore after the creature, screaming for the general. "Gad, I need you!"

She trusted him, and he did not fail her.

He dropped Nox and Ash near Tanith, allowing her shield to cover them, and was at Amaris's side in a flash.

"Tell me what you need," he said.

The beast was groaning through its daze. No blood shone on the ice, but it was fighting for consciousness. Amaris closed the space between herself and the creature, skidding as she halted against its furry hide.

"Here!"

She grabbed his wrist, forcing his hand onto the silver shackle fastened around the beast's leg.

"The lock!" She coughed as frigid temperatures scraped angry fingers on the soft tissues of her throat.

Without a moment's hesitation, Gadriel summoned his power for locked doors. The manacle crumbled to the ground. Amaris knew her tactic was successful a second later as Gadriel, Ash, Nox, and Tanith reacted to the horrid snow beast.

She'd gambled, and she'd been right.

As the piece fell to the snow, Amaris realized she'd achieved more than ridding the creature of its invisibility. The shackle was no simple silver cuff. It had been lined with spikes on its innermost layer that had bitten into the monster's flesh, as if to prevent the shackle from slipping. The spikes were coated with a layer of fresh blood, presumably agitated by the motion of its recent attack. A red bracelet of blood and scabbing tissue smothered the white fur near its paw. The aboriou groaned again as it attempted to raise its head, but the danger had not passed.

Amaris had one last command. "Tanith! Can you bind it?"

Two things happened at once. Tanith nodded weakly, moon illumining her battle to stay conscious, but she would do what was asked of her. In the same moment, Ash slid across the ice and ran for the ruined ship, sprinting toward their supply of greenstrike blood.

Perhaps it was cruel to ask this of her given that in the past hour alone, Tanith had manipulated metal, summoned a shield, and was now attempting to tether a creature, but the way Amaris saw it, either Tanith could be brought to death's door or every one of them could die between gnashing teeth.

A blue glow emanated from Tanith's fingertips as she lifted her hand. Ash reached her with the leather satchel just as the beast came to its senses. It rose onto its four, gigantic feet, but something was different. Amaris couldn't be sure, but it seemed to lack the bloodthirsty urgency it had possessed mere moments prior.

"I've got it," Tanith panted, slumping into Ash's arms.

The monster shuddered again, shaking what remained of the ice and snow in its fur. With the binding that calmed it, what had been a brush with death a mere thirty seconds ago was suddenly a humongous, tame beast. She didn't want to leave it alone without certainty that it wouldn't harm them, so Amaris reached a cautious hand toward the beast to touch it. Her hand disappeared beneath its hairs as she continued to plunge deeper and deeper, discovering fur so thick that it took an entire arm up to the elbow to attempt to reach the aboriou's hide, yet it did not react. Amaris backed away from the snow beast, confident that, thanks to Tanith's power, she would have been perfectly safe even if she'd opted to crawl onto its back.

She looked at Gadriel. "We did it."

"You did it," he replied.

Sixteen

Nox cautiously approached Amaris, the general, and the creature. "What are you doing?"

"The runes…" She shook her head. "When we settle down to live a long, boring life, I really want to study manufacturing. I wish I understood what these meant."

She ran a finger on torturous spikes that had lined the inside of the cuff. Nox listened as she said the beast was no demon—no trace of sulfur, of black ooze, of the demons of the continent. The aboriou's blood ran red like that of a fae, human, or natural-born animal. Her face twisted as she examined the fresh drop on her finger.

"Do you need to warm up?" Gadriel asked.

Nox shook her head. "Go help them fix the ship. I want to stay with Amaris."

It took a while for the others—primarily Tanith and Gadriel—to repair and warm the half-crumpled cabin to the best of their abilities. Nox and Amaris joined them just as they were forcing a healing tonic down Yazlyn's throat. The sergeant coughed and made a face against the astringent flavor of the medicine, but they knew she would be fine.

They'd survived the attack, but they were not yet in the clear.

They salvaged what they could from the ruined ship and took the rope meant for the sail to harness the animal. The blades on the skiff's underbelly had been repaired, but the hull and sides of the boat remained crumpled and scratched. Thankfully, they didn't need a perfect ship as long as it could be towed. The beast happily carried them across the ice as Tanith retained her tethering control, urging the creature toward the docks in Sulgrave.

"She's fine," Nox said, watching how Ash monitored Tanith with the concerned patience of a physician.

"I'm confident everyone would say that—including her—right up until she dropped dead." He didn't distract her as she guided their newly tethered mount and its claws tore across the ice. The aboriou changed everything. The beast padded along like a happy dog guiding a snow sled at four times the speed they could have hoped to achieve from wings or sail. The aboriou did not tire, maintaining its speed for the remainder of the night before Tanith said through clenched teeth that the creature should rest. She would call to it again after night had fallen once more.

After their brush with a grizzly end, everything almost seemed too good to be true.

"All right." Amaris clapped her hands as night fell. "Now that you know what it looks like, can you call the aboriou to help us again, no matter where it is?"

"I can do anything," Tanith responded. She emerged from the ship with the others at her side. Binding the beast with magic was one thing, but it would require the physical labor of the others to harness it and secure it to the skiff. A few minutes later, the snowy beast was at their side, licking at its paw.

"Wait," Nox said, stopping Gadriel before he could move forward with the rope. "Can I try something?"

She felt the weight of everyone's anxious gaze. Gadriel and Amaris shared a cautious breath—one she recognized from the matrons and the madame alike.

She narrowed her eyes. "Let me rephrase that. I'm your queen, and I'm going to try something."

"Oh, come on." Yazlyn rolled her eyes.

"You can cast a shield around me if you like," Nox said to Tanith, "but I am just wondering if the creature could be won to our side."

"Nox, don't be absurd," came Gadriel's scold.

Nox shrugged. "I seem to recall being met with similar resistance when I wanted to win Tanith to our side. How are you doing, Tanith?"

"I'm cold and would like to get back in the ship," Tanith replied.

"See?" Nox lifted her brows. "Best of friends."

Amaris repositioned herself between Nox and the aboriou. "I know you couldn't see the creature for half of the battle, so clearly you don't fear it as you should. But—"

Nox waved her away. "We did free it from its shackle, didn't we? I was thinking I might offer it some meat without Tanith's control. Just as an attempt."

Gadriel tried the tone of a general, the concern of a father, the bartering of a friend, the command of an authority figure, but Nox ignored him completely. His variety of attempts covered the time it took for her to fetch a sausage link from the skiff and return from the ice. He could fret all he liked. He'd had his chance to take the throne, and he'd turned it down. She could do whatever she wanted.

"It was in pain," she argued. "It's been in pain for a long, long time. You said it yourself: it's not a demon. It's an animal—one who was wounded. Think of it as a snow horse. Or a big snow puppy."

"A snow horse with talons and fangs and a thirst for blood!" Gadriel's eyes widened, temper flaring. "This is not a puppy, Nox. We did not make it across the straits for you to freely lose your head to a monster. Be reasonable."

"I can hold the aboriou, or cast a shield around Nox," Tanith said, "but I cannot do both."

"Drop your tether," Nox said. "I'll take the shield. But let the creature make up its own mind." They watched on collective, bated breath as Tanith unbound the creature, but it did not run. Instead, it limped idly around the skiff.

Nox grinned at the calm creature, then at the others. The sky overhead was bright, fresh, and clear, as the moon was only a few days away from its fullest, which seemed to her like a very good omen. The stars burned with their white fire behind the head of the beast, casting quite a lovely light on the aboriou.

It was a large cat, she thought. A cat with curious horns—horns that no longer looked threatening but instead as merely a necessary sheltering tool for its embedding in the ice. Even its claws reminded her of the continent's moles and their need to burrow through the earth more so than that of a true, angry predator. In its calmed state, everything that had been perceived as a tool to shred, kill, and destroy looked like the easily explained defenses of life on the Frozen Straits.

Nox twisted her mouth for bravery as she took several pieces of dried meat from their food supplies.

"Please don't," Amaris urged.

Its head snapped up immediately as it bared its teeth, a low growl rumbling from its throat.

"It's okay," Nox shushed the creature. She tossed a dried sausage onto the ice in front of it and watched as its ears flicked. It kept its teeth bared defensively as its dark gaze went from Nox to the piece of meat. The beast took a hesitant step forward and sniffed the meat, ears still down as its sharpened canines remained exposed in a threatening pose.

Nox's confidence grew. Certainty took root within her as she continued to make calming sounds. She knew no one around her had relaxed. They'd made no secrecy of their tensed postures and anxious gazes. She was pretty sure that Gadriel's hand was on the hilt of his weapon, but she was confident he wouldn't need it.

The furry creature licked at the sausage and took it into

its mouth, swallowing it whole. Nox grinned at her small success. She made another encouraging noise as she tossed a second sausage onto the ice.

"That's our food," Yazlyn said.

"Shh," came a second voice—or third, or fourth. Nox couldn't be certain who was stacked for her or against her, as her interests lay elsewhere.

"Hey," she said with the soothing voice of a mother speaking to a child. "I'm Nox."

The beast relaxed its lips, no longer baring its teeth as it limped closer. It snatched the meat off the frozen surface. Its great shoulders relaxed, housecat, family dog, farm horse, she couldn't quite land on a comparison. Its mannerisms did seem dog-like as it eyed her with cautious curiosity. Nox took a few daring steps closer and watched the creature flinch against her approaching presence, but she stretched a sausage out on her hand. If she had been listening, she would have heard Gadriel's demands, or threats, or whatever it was he was saying. He could keep it to himself for all she cared.

The beast eyed her speculatively as she took a few more forward steps. She was within arm's reach. Keeping her voice quiet and gentle, she called back to the ship.

"It's hurt."

"Nox, come back to the ship." It was not a request, and she did not care. In fact, she was quite enjoying the looks on everyone's faces—Gadriel's included—as they collectively discovered the one area where the general did not respect his new queen's judgment or decision-making. Nox bit back a smirk, wondering how familiar he was with being ignored. She had more important things to do than explain to him that this was life with her as queen and cousin.

"I think it's only angry because it's hurt," Nox said. "I can't imagine how long this manacle has been torturing the poor creature. The pain it must have endured… It's so cruel. Who would do something like this?"

Seeing as how Gadriel had been met with little success,

Amaris called out across the ice more calmly, "Nox, you've had your fun with the monster—please come back to the ship."

Nox directed her attention to the only reasonable member of the party. "Tanith, can you heal its paw?"

Tanith attempted to match the gentleness of Nox's tone with her own low, musical words. "Not while maintaining your shield."

Nox smiled. "Please try. It won't hurt me."

Gadriel looked like he was about to disregard everyone's wishes to abduct Raascot's new queen, but Tanith obliged. She dropped the shield she'd been casting in order to send healing energy toward the creature.

The result was immediate.

The creature exhaled with a loud, happy huff. It took a step, testing its weight against its leg. The aboriou made a few careful motions, experiencing pain-free steps for the first time in what may have been centuries, for all Nox knew. Her face went from hopeful, to surprised, to worried, to overjoyed as the creature took off for the horizon, spinning in tight circles as if it were chasing its tails. It leapt into the air toward the moon and grabbed for it like a cat chasing an insect. The aboriou returned to Nox then, and from Gadriel's sprint to action, he must have been certain it was diving for the kill. Instead, it halted in its sprint and nuzzled its great head into her.

She laughed and produced another sausage. "Look at it! It loves me!"

"Nox—"

"And I love it."

Gadriel sounded like he might cry. "You can't be serious. Please, for the love of the goddess—"

She returned to the ship grinning, covered from head to toe in stray white hairs.

"I want to keep it."

He closed his eyes, head hitting the ship's inner wall with

a quiet thump as he succumbed to his exhaustion. "Of course you do."

✦

Four more days.

That was their estimate as the Sulgrave Mountains began as little more than shark's teeth on the horizon. They grew with the aboriou's help at night, and Gadriel's work during the day, until they were a distinct, jagged shade of purples and blues in the distance.

"We're going to reach Sulgrave soon," Nox said. "There has to be something you can tell me before I meet with officials. Something about government, about culture, about—"

"I have nothing to do with the comtes," Tanith had said dismissively. "I am with the church alone."

Nox struggled not to feel annoyed.

She knew Tanith was far from useless. She was powerful beyond measure. Her answers, however, frustrated everyone apart from Ash. Fortunately, there were other things to occupy their time. The sight of something on the horizon lifted everyone's spirits. And, thanks to the aboriou, the journey was going much faster and requiring far less mental and physical exertion as they completed their trek.

Fjolla. That's the name Nox decided on for her new beloved pet. It was a name that, in the mountain dialect, meant snowflake. Nox loved the name nearly as much as she loved her new best friend.

She was the only one.

Amaris made no attempt to conceal how the appropriation of her nickname made her feel. It also wasn't lost on Nox that Gadriel seemed every day like he was growing closer and closer to claiming for all the world that she had died on the ice and he'd taken the throne for himself. She wished Malik was there, knowing he would not only delight in the aboriou's presence but support her adoption of the creature.

Amaris expressed specific annoyance that Nox should get a marvelous snow beast when it had been the reevers, her in particular, who'd spent years studying and obsessing over bestiary texts.

"It's not fair," Amaris had grumbled.

"Stay mad." Nox had shrugged.

Despite their protests, Fjolla grew gentler and more excited to see Nox with every day that passed. The aboriou would wiggle excitedly until she offered their remaining sausages, quickly sacrificing the supplies intended for the cabin crew for her new pet. As a lover of beasts, Amaris found the aboriou interesting, but it wasn't worthy of four days of nonstop amazement.

At the very least, Fjolla's presence was a break from monotony. The creature's addition gave life to the final stage of their journey, until at long last, their time on the desolate wasteland came to an end. It was equal parts exciting and terrifying. They had yet to reach the fabled mountains, but they'd survived the straits. They'd done the impossible, and they'd done it unscathed.

When they docked their ruined skiff, it was in no uncertain terms that Nox announced she would not leave her new best friend behind. Once they were free from the ship's protection and no longer on the ice, the aboriou had nowhere to burrow. It would curl up behind Nox when it was ready to rest, offering its immense warmth to her as she napped against the creature. In practice, the others hadn't decided if they were amazed or annoyed. Regardless of their personal feelings of inconvenience, they were already whispering when Nox wasn't listening about the legendary tales that would be told of the orphan girl who claimed two thrones, tamed snow beasts, and crossed the Frozen Straits.

Gadriel had amended the conjecture of legend with a quiet mutter. "Claimed the thrones, tamed the snow beast, crossed the straits, and wooed a goddess."

"Demi-goddess," Amaris corrected. "Or…something."

Ash and Tanith seemed the least irritated by her new pet. They joined Nox in cuddling against Fjolla when they needed warmth and rest, even if it took excessive reassurance from Nox to get them there. Fjolla eventually calmed enough to accept their company and shared its body heat and depth of fur against the remainder of their frozen crossing. Gadriel, Yazlyn, and Amaris were left to the wool blankets and body heat generated by the general while the others cuddled into their monstrous snowflake.

Something curious took root as they journeyed, and Nox knew she wasn't the only one who felt it. The more excited the others became, the quieter Tanith grew. It was not the lofty serenity they'd come to expect, but a strange, withdrawn energy. Talking to her about it seemed to make it worse, which was no surprise to Nox as she regarded the frustrating, elusive fae.

"How long is the walk from the docks?" Ash had asked.

Maybe it was because he'd been the one to ask it, but Tanith had answered, "Five days."

Gadriel and Yazlyn expressed frustration over their inability to fly, but it would be fruitless for them to take two forward and return for the remaining members. It would only expend their energy and, to Nox's dismay, make Fjolla feel abandoned. Instead, they walked.

They walked and walked and walked.

Their legs ached as they left the flat, slick surface of the sea and found themselves trudging through the snowdrifts and piles nearer and nearer to the mountains. It was through some muttered surprise that the snow grew damper as they neared Sulgrave, as Gadriel had been quite sure that if the climate had been arid on the straits, it would be only worse the farther north they ventured.

The excitement they'd felt upon abandoning the ship dwindled as the walk went on and their provisions depleted. Their stomachs ached with the gnawing hunger of knowing they wouldn't be filled. Their stock would have been running low even if Nox hadn't sacrificed so much of their meat for her new beast. She'd tried to offer Fjolla some of the cheese before Yazlyn wrestled it from Nox, loudly announcing that she'd sooner defect from Raascot and renounce Nox's claim on the throne than give up their cheese to a monster.

"Keep your rations," Nox said, procuring a wedge of crumbly white cheese. "She can have mine."

"Fine," Yazlyn snapped. "But if we run out of food, know this: I will be the first to kill your aboriou for its meat."

This achieved two things. Nox refused to speak to the sergeant for the remainder of the day, and she no longer attempted to steal food from their dwindling supplies to give her snow beast treats.

So, on they pressed.

As they walked, the air changed into a curious, unseasonable spring. It became warm enough that they had to shrug out of their cloaks. By the evening of their third day on foot, hardy trees began to sprout from the snowy cracks in rocks around them. Cheery, tenacious yellow flowers poked up from their hiding place beneath the remnants of snow. It was the first time they'd seen a living thing in weeks. At least, a living thing that wasn't trying to eat them.

"Is there a mountain pass, or will we have to climb?" Gadriel asked, looking at Tanith.

He exchanged looks with Nox when Tanith said nothing. Nox lifted a single shoulder. She'd been unable to get the Sulgrave fae to say anything useful since the journey began.

His jaw ticked. "You've been getting quieter for days, Tanith, but your cooperation is vital. Will you please—"

To everyone's surprise, it was Amaris who defended her. "This won't achieve anything. If she doesn't want to talk, she's not going to talk. But she's not going to let us walk down the wrong path—if not for herself, then for Ash. I'm sure she'll point us where we need to go when we get there."

Nox was both relieved and grateful when Amaris's argument came to fruition. Tanith took the lead, guiding them through a valley where the snow continued to melt, giving way to a loud jade river. The footpath became a road before long, allowing them to walk easily along the river.

"It shouldn't be getting warmer," Nox said. She was unable to cling to her relief as anxiety over the anomalous weather replaced whatever she'd been feeling. "We're going north and deeper into the mountains. This isn't natural." Yet the vegetation thickened, dotting the road and mountainside with green tufts of grasses and leafy bushes growing from the rocky crags. The snow continued to melt the higher they climbed, filling each breath with the damp-soil taste of the sunny day after a hard spring rain. Perhaps the weather should have made them happy, but Nox had a point. There was nothing natural about the climate.

Her anxiety thickened with every passing hour, worsened by Tanith's ever-shrinking energy, and she knew she wasn't alone.

Tanith no longer offered obscure riddles. She didn't bother with evasiveness. Their questions for her were met with silence as she stared at the path ahead until they learned to stop speaking to her altogether. Nox attempted to replace her worry over Tanith's moods with a fixation on her aboriou.

"Fjolla!" Nox released a sharp, horrified squeak as they rounded a bend, only for the creature to abandon them, sprinting for the teals and greens of the white-capped rapids. "Goddess—don't!" came her cry as her snow child plunged into the river for its first time. She ran up to the water's edge in time to discover that the beast was not only a competent swimmer but seemed to quite enjoy the chilly waters. The aboriou contented itself with playing among the waters and fish, eating every chance it got until it would eventually rejoin them on the road, shaking frigid droplets from its fur onto the irritable traveling party. Nox purred something about training it to fish for them while she stroked its mane as they turned another corner and froze in their steps.

"Oh my goddess…" Amaris's eyes widened.

The party shared a collective gasp, save for Tanith. Nox looked to Tanith for some reaction, some explanation, but her face remained plastered with an unreadable emotion, though her posture was not one of joy.

It was as if the world had cracked open to reveal cities, mountains, and life itself.

Unfathomably sheer, snow-capped mountains pierced the sky with height, enclosing a valley that seemed nearly as expansive as half the continent itself, stretching as far as the eye could see.

Nox's fingers went to her mouth to stifle her reactions as she struggled to understand. The city filling the valley below was fantastical beyond reason. It was triple Aubade's size, and more beautiful than Gwydir by a factor of ten. Spirals and peaks and glassy, reflective, towering structures and buildings were unlike anything she had ever seen.

"It's stunning," Nox whispered.

"It's beautiful. And it goes on forever," Yazlyn agreed. "Where does it end?"

Where indeed. The city sprawled into valleys and tucked between mountains as far as Nox could see.

Signs of vibrant, thriving life crawled up the mountains on all sides, even dipping into the cracks and valleys between the peaks as it grew. While some structures seemed to be castles and cathedrals of stone, others appeared to have utilized whatever reflective, silvery material had crafted their ship. There were homes and churches and healer's halls and enormous, uniden-tifiable buildings scattered throughout the metropolis. The reflective glass spires of the tall, silvery buildings scattered the sunlight into tens of thousands of sparkling particles as other-worldly rainbows twinkled down over the city.

After days of silence, Tanith finally spoke in a low, sullen voice.

"Welcome to Sulgrave."

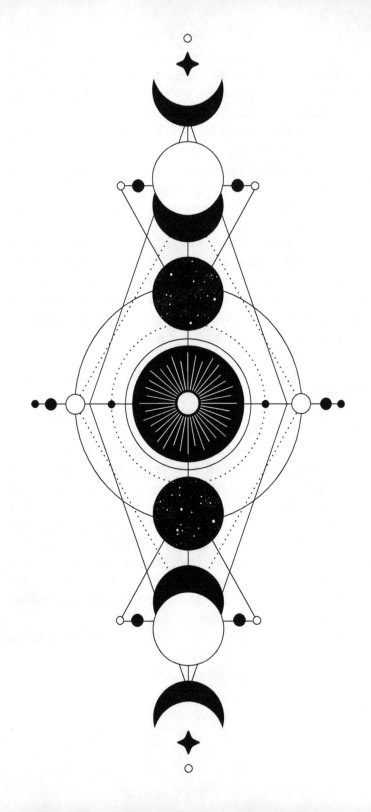

PART III

Heart, Body, and Soul

Seventeen

THE LULL OF SPEECHLESS AWE WAS SHORT-LIVED.

Nox's brows puckered. She tilted her head at the noise that broke her concentration. At first, it almost sounded like a waterfall. It swelled, joining the splashing, rushing rapids until it was louder than the pale, blue-green river beside them. A cloud of dust spurred the military fae into action.

"Someone's coming," Gadriel said. He moved as if to shield Nox, but the newcomers were upon them before they had time to run, to hide, or to make a decision.

Seven white horses and their armed guards thundered down the path to intercept them. Their intimidating silhouette cut sharply against the backdrop of the valley. The sunshine overhead cast a halo effect in the mushroom cloud of dirt behind the arriving fae centurions. Nox took quick stock of the newcomers. The Sulgrave guards shared the gilded undercurrent in their skin that they'd seen only in Tanith, though each appeared to be clad in different colors with a variety of sigils emblazoned on their chests with silver thread. They pulled their steeds into a firm line, blocking any forward progress.

Gadriel took a protective step toward the approaching

armed men and women, but the oncoming fae didn't so much as acknowledge them. Their eyes went first to the snow beast, exchanging a few nervous glances with one another. Their horses whinnied, some balking and chuffing at it as they stopped short of the predator. The scents of dust, of sweat off of horse hides, of Fjolla's wet-dog odor fresh from the river were grounding. The simple, homey scents helped keep Nox's feet firmly in reality as adrenaline pumped through her veins. She was in a foreign land against terrifying mountains and a crew of heavily armed guards. She would keep it together. She would address them. She would explain why she was here.

But the guards were not interested in her. The centurions' collective gaze settled on the small fae over their shoulders. The clattering hooves came to an abrupt stop. A man cleared his throat and issued his booming decree.

The words were firm, and powerful, and intimidating, and Nox did not understand a single word. She'd met travelers from the corners of the continent, but nothing about this language was familiar.

A man in yellow raised his fist, then looked to his comrades. He whispered something to the man who'd spoken first.

He cleared his throat once more. This time, when he spoke, it was in the common tongue.

"Tanith the Red," he said, words cold and booming, "you're wanted for crimes of war, intentional violence resulting in bodily harm and death, and misuses of magic in Territories One, Two, and Five. To your traveling companions: ensure they surrender you peaceably and voluntarily now to be judged by the Comte Council, or we are obligated to bring you to trial by force."

"What?" Ash demanded.

Tanith held him back. "Don't," she urged the reever.

"Hold on," Nox said, moving around Gadriel. Tanith grabbed for her arm as if to stop her, which drew a warning reaction from the centurions. "If you could give us a

198

moment…I'm sure we're a strange sight. The aboriou is with us and poses no threat. The winged fae are from Gwydir. My companions here, Amaris and Ash, come from Uaimh Reev. My name is Nox, and I'm the sitting monarch for the continent's thrones. I seek an audience with your comtes and asylum for Tanith as my ambassador while on your soil."

She didn't miss the proud uptick of a smirk on Gadriel's mouth.

The center-most guard made another uncertain noise as though something were stuck in his throat as he eyed the assorted party. Fjolla shifted her weight, baring her teeth. Nox began to soothe her beast, shushing it from its threatening stance.

Eventually, the Sulgrave man spoke again. "I don't have the authority to grant Tanith asylum."

Nox remained firm. "Then who can I speak with about this?"

A woman in purple asked, "You said you're…royalty?"

Once again, the centurions exchanged uncertain looks. Nox straightened her posture and stood with queenly poise.

The woman said, "We can escort you and your crew to the Diplomatic Hall so you may make your petition. For now, Tanith will need to come with us."

Nox offered a single nod. As she stepped forward, Fjolla mirrored her movements.

The man in yellow frowned. "Um—your beast…"

Nox's eyes flashed between the guard and her pet. "It stays with me."

She heard Amaris's stifled laugh and caught the poorly controlled expressions Gadriel and Yazlyn wore regarding the snow creature. It was possible that the winged fae were as irritated with the queen's acquisition of the beast as the Sulgrave centurions appeared to be. While everyone else's eyes were trained on the aboriou, Ash continued looking between Tanith and the men.

"Tanith—" he whispered her name.

199

She kept her chin forward, unwilling to meet his inquiring eyes.

Nox understood her sullen spirits, her evasive answers, her unwillingness to speak all at once. She'd assumed Tanith's reservedness was something of a general personality trait of the Sulgrave people, never considering that Tanith herself was the anomaly. It was with staggered clattering of toppled dominos that each of the party members reflected on Tanith's oddities and how her peculiarities fit within her role within Sulgrave society. They had not been wrong to find her a strange, murderous zealot.

"What will happen to Tanith?" Nox asked.

"She'll be taken into custody. The rest is not your concern."

"It is my concern," Nox insisted. She shot a warning look at Ash, locking his amber eyes long enough to ensure that he would not do something he'd regret. His eyes tightened as he returned the look. Nox turned to the man at the center and made a motion with her hand. "Escort us to your council. We've traveled a long way and have much to discuss."

Quiet murmurs in the native Sulgrave tongue accompanied their questioning glances. Their body language told a story so clear that she didn't need to share their language to understand the message.

First, the centurions had only anticipated Tanith's resurgence in their lands. That much Nox had gathered. They seemed properly surprised and troubled at who—and what—had met them on the road, though enough time had passed since their arrival that the guards appeared to be adjusting their plans accordingly. They'd been given orders to return with Tanith, not with a motley company of southerners.

Nox held her chin high, though she knew she did not currently look the part of a powerful, regal queen. She had not bathed in weeks. She and the others all held their bundled cloaks and awkwardly shaped sacks of supplies beneath their arms. Her hair remained unbound and her full lips made a firm line as she waited for their response.

She settled into a calm self-assuredness, refusing to avert her gaze. They could either take them to their council, or they could all stay with the arms crossed in the road until they died from their stalemate. And they'd come too far for Nox to let them fail now.

"Fine," said the woman in purple. "Come with us."

The horses brayed as their riders pulled on their reins, turning them sharply to face the city. They kept their mounts at a steady walking pace as Nox and the others walked behind them.

There was a familiar discomfort that came with being somewhere you didn't belong.

She knew Amaris felt it every time she walked into a room. She knew the Raascot fae had spent enough time south of the border under the curse to at least grow to understand and navigate displacement. She, on the other hand, had made a career out of forcing others to recognize that no matter who she met, no matter their title, no matter who was paying, she was the one with the power.

She would fake her way through the unknowable.

She would be the first person in more than a thousand years to establish a political relationship with Sulgrave.

She would not fail.

Amaris squeezed her arm once as they descended into the city below, but everyone remained stiff, shoulders back, chins high so as not to betray signs of weakness, even if the centurions were not looking their way.

With a defeated huff, Nox thought it unfortunate that their lives were at stake, because dammit if the view wasn't spectacular.

Small, violet flowers began to dot the green grass next to the river, soon accompanied by snowdrops, bluebells, the silvery twists of trees, and peculiar magenta blossoms that grew in lovely bunches as they continued their descent, ears popping as their elevation dropped. She craned to look up at the sharp, frosted mountains, amazed by the entirely separate micro-climate the city had from the frigid alpine heights or the straits behind them.

If they were thrown into prison along with Tanith, she'd die without being able to ask how Sulgrave had managed to control a nation's weather. If the goddess was benevolent, things might still go their way.

Either way, their fate was fast approaching.

The moment they left the mountain pass and stepped foot into the proper city, it became impossible to keep up her charade of disinterested importance. Nox openly gaped at the beautiful architecture, the immaculate landscaping, the peculiar materials used to craft their buildings, and the clean, well-dressed residents in their strange garb and impeccable postures that made her acutely aware of how truly grimy they must look.

Citizens paused to look, many covering their mouths, some pointing with surprise.

She supposed they were right to be shocked.

The citizens of Sulgrave all appeared to have the ethereal, angular beauty of pure fae. All wore radiant, fashionable silks and sharply tailored apparel with no need for jackets. Nox and her party, on the other hand, were an amalgamation of demi-fae, of Raascot fae, of whatever the hell Amaris was, of disheveled, unruly attire, and they were walking down the streets of a civilized metropolis with the fabled, bloodthirsty aboriou.

Goddess, she hated every step.

This was nothing like drawing every eye in the lounge as she took proud steps across the salon. These were not appreciative murmurs. Something about the walk among scrutinizing eyes of civilians made every step seem so much longer, farther, and more challenging than their trek through blowing and drifting snow.

Nox looked at the sun. If she'd marked its movements correctly, they'd been following the guards for nearly two hours. And because she was no prisoner, she spoke freely. "How much longer?"

"We're here," replied the woman in purple.

The stone buildings parted to reveal unusual buildings of metal, glass, and curious reflective materials. Nox recognized their destination as a spire that had been visible from their initial outlook of the city. She thought of the tallest tower in Castle Gwydir, then visualized stacking three more atop it as she tilted her head back to absorb the building's enormity. The light caught against the building's solid walls of glass, reflecting painfully as if she were staring into the sun itself.

"How tall do you think it is?" she marveled.

Beside her, Amaris shrugged. "Does it matter? A mountain's a mountain."

The central guard made a face after an uncomfortable pause. "What would you like us to do with…"

Nox made a face while she examined Fjolla. On the one hand, she'd only known the beast for a few days and would already prefer to go back to the ship and sleep beside it rather than have it taken from her. Still, she had enough wisdom to gather that an unsupervised aboriou would cause carnage and devastation if left alone in the stables.

Gadriel gave her a tired look that indicated he wished they'd banish the beast to the straits and be done with it, but Nox's mood was entirely absurd in regards to her new monster. Nox suggested that she bring the aboriou into the building, which was received about as well as she'd expected. Yazlyn and Gadriel looked every bit as irritated as the guards on horseback.

The general took it upon himself to approach the man, hands raised to reveal that he carried no weapons and offered no threat. If anyone was going to put himself in harm's way first, it would be the winged fae. His voice was too low for the others to hear him as he spoke to whoever appeared to be leading their guard.

"My name is Gadriel. Nox, who you've met, is the ruling queen of both Raascot and Farehold. I'm here as her general. Please forgive us, as the crossing was especially taxing. If you could make accommodations for her pet, as well as locate lodging for your visiting compatriots from the continent so that we could move forward with diplomatic relations, the continent would see it as a magnanimous favor."

Nox didn't appreciate him usurping her requests, but she was low on bargaining chips.

She watched as the winged fae and the central guard exchanged a few more words before the Sulgrave man issued a few orders to the men and women around him. She tapped her foot impatiently for several irritating minutes before someone with bestiary expertise was summoned and was confident that he'd be able to lead the snow monster back to his secured stables. It was with both reluctance and an abundance of reassurance on the honor of the diplomatic accord that Fjolla was harnessed and led away from Nox's side through a number of persuasive sausages and offerings of treats.

The time had come to enter the Diplomatic Hall. At least, the time had come for everyone save for Tanith.

Ash made a hasty attempt to physically intervene as the guards reached for Tanith's arm, but Nox cut him off. She attempted the same argument she'd made on the road, raising her voice slightly. "She's with me as my ambassador—"

"I understand," hedged the guard, "and you are free to raise the issue when you meet with the comtes, Your... Highness. However, while she resides on Sulgrave soil, she needs to be held in protective custody for the safety of our own citizens."

"It's fine," Tanith said quietly. "Go with them. Don't worry about me." Tanith unsnapped her red cloak and handed it to Ash before offering herself to the guards. Her eyes remained downcast. They didn't shackle her as she complied, but the escort of seven armed guards for one small fae seemed excessive. They'd made it to Sulgrave, and the reality seemed more like a dissociative episode than a true achievement. The buildings, the people, even the climate were utterly alien. Watching Tanith escorted out by the authorities was simply the cherry atop their bizarre, tiring, problematic destruction pie.

They weren't given the time to process their emotions before they were ushered into the building. Natural light flooded the atrium. Tall, broad-leaf plants had been potted and brought inside to decorate the foyer. The landing floor was enormous and more or less empty, save for the handsome fae who awaited them.

"Welcome," he said, though he did not stand, nor did he bow.

The attendants in the Diplomatic Hall neither dressed nor acted like castle servants. They seemed to be greeted by a concierge of sorts sitting behind an anomalous horseshoe-shaped desk. Behind the seated attendant was a wall of curious flowers fabricated from delicate metals. The concierge offered them escorts to their rooms on a shared hall.

Rather than requiring them to climb the countless stairs it would have taken to get to the wing of bedchambers, they were instructed by their escort to step onto a silvery, rectangular plait that had been rigged with a lever and pulley system to slowly assist in their ascension. The only one who didn't seem to be inspecting the intricate runes that connected the platform with its cords was Ash, as his mind was undoubtedly an untamed sea of conflicting emotions.

The residential floor of the Diplomatic Hall had a large, common sitting area filled with colorful books, floor-to-ceiling windows, and a number of soft blankets draped over the backs of the seating options. A thickly cushioned sofa and matching loveseats and armchairs offered quite the comfortable station. A well-stocked liquor cabinet with a number of glasses and garnishes made the common room all the more inviting.

Down the corridor were a number of rooms, each assigned to a party member. Yazlyn was the first to break free from whatever spell the others had befallen. The sergeant disappeared into the bedroom she'd been offered while the others seemed to hesitate in their doorways. A moment later, she heard Yazlyn's bright, loud combination of disbelief and excitement as she marveled at the oddities scattered throughout her suite.

Nox poked her head out of her room, following the fae's exclamations until she discovered Yazlyn's bedchamber.

"Look at this!" the sergeant gestured.

Nox crossed to where Yazlyn was tapping incessantly a silvery orb that rested on her desk. Each time she touched it, a noise broke forth. She would touch it again and the noise would cease, as if her fingertip controlled a symphony. She touched it once more and let the music flood the room, filling her chambers with an orchestra contained within the small, silver orb. She touched it a final time, and the string and wind instruments and the vocalist carrying its melody halted on their very note, the final sound dissipating in the air as it faded into silence.

"Try it."

Nox lowered her hand carefully to the orb. She felt nothing as she rested her fingertip against metal, but the moment she made contact, the music resumed on the same note, as if the band had been waiting on bated breath with their fingers playing the role of conductor.

The orb was enchanting, but it was not the only noteworthy thing in the bedchambers.

The rooms' walls were composed not of stone but of glass. Nox pressed her entire body against the solid windows latticed with interlinking metal that ran from the top to bottom of the room. The entirety of the city sprawled, every rooftop, street, and astoundingly sharp mountain viewable between the diamond sections of glass. Perhaps when she made it back to Gwydir, she'd see about commissioning a wall like this in the castle.

"What's that?" Nox asked, looking to where Yazlyn was busy running her hands along a stone rectangle that had been pushed against the wall with a seam running along its edge.

"It opens," Yazlyn marveled. She popped the door to the strange, stone box. Nox joined her to wonder at the change in temperature and pressure. Nox nudged the door open to reveal corked bottles of water and cold white wine, still frosty as if the snow itself had been captured and contained within the box. A number of chilled foods sat in the box, fresh and ready for consumption. She closed the door again and began to examine the runes etched into the lid of the box. Yazlyn returned to the desk to resume tapping her orb, but Nox had more inspecting to do. She examined the sphere's base to find another clever ringlet of runes wove themselves around the silvery circle.

"Are you leaving?" Yazlyn asked.

"Carry on. I want to see if my room has anything interesting."

Her suite was substantially larger, which was both unnecessary and wonderfully indulgent. It had many elements familiar to any chamber on the continent. Its bed was lovely, with an exceedingly comfortable mattress. The bathing room's water was able to switch from cool to hot with a speed and ease she'd never encountered. She had an ice box in her room as well and had just begun to examine the contents when a voice spoke.

Nox jolted upward as it sounded as though a man was in her room.

"Your Highness?"

"Hello?" she answered, looking about the room for the voice's owner.

Nox stood and followed the sound to a silver lily on her doorframe. The flower was hollow in the center, and the stem of the flower curved against the door, plummeting down into the floor below. She'd mistaken it for an elaborate decoration when she'd entered the room, now recognizing it as a matching counterpart to the bouquet that had been at the desk when she'd entered the hall. As she approached the flower, she was immediately able to discern its clever design for the communication device it was.

"Your Highness," the voice repeated, echoing through the shaft of the flower. "I was told to inquire as to whether or not you'd like eyes on your beast."

Her eyebrows lifted as she looked into the small, silver funnel near the door. "You want to show me Fjolla?"

The man hidden at the other end of the piece hesitated. "The creature—Fjolla—we've set up visuals and can have someone stop by your rooms to deliver them if you'd like."

"Yes! Yes, of course." Nox didn't understand what was being offered to her, but it seemed within her best interest to accept. A few minutes later, an armed woman arrived at her door holding a mirror. She lifted the ornate object to Nox and informed her that she could see the beast, just as it could see her. Using the mirror, Nox would be able to monitor its well-being from the comfort her rooms. She thanked the strange woman and closed the door behind her, clutching at her mirror.

Fjolla was safe. They'd made it into rooms beyond imagination. And it was time at long last to take advantage of the spelled waterspouts and wash the road from her body. She stripped off a week's worth of grit and filth as the tub filled. She winced as she submerged her bare toes in the scalding tub, then took her time adapting to the piping hot waters.

The soaps and water in Sulgrave smelled nothing like the bubbles of the continent.

She tested them all, finding perfumes and lotions and lathers with delicate scents of garden herbs and fragrant tea. She lathered her scalp and rinsed herself thoroughly of the sweat, grime, and exhaustion of their travel.

Nox sank beneath the water of her bath, absorbing green tea and jasmine through every pore. She blew a few bubbles while fully submerged, then broke free from the hot water.

This was luxury.

Nox got up from the bath and left puddles of soapy water at her feet as she fetched chilled wine from the icebox and the enchanted mirror from the desk. She returned to the bath waters, clutching the bottleneck with one hand and waggling her fingers at Fjolla with the other.

She took two deep gulps of chilled wine, then rested her head against the back of her tub, fully relaxing for the first time in weeks. Her mind thought of her companions, hoping they'd also been able to scrub the road from their bodies. She wished comfortable beds and warm waters for Amaris, whom she promised herself she'd check on shortly. She thought of their first kiss and the continents they'd conquered to arrive here together. Her thoughts began to drift to idle memories of jewels and flowers and gifts in Henares. She recalled the first time she threw her axe. A tug of sadness threatened her newfound peace as she thought of Malik. She wished he could experience musical orbs and ice boxes and tea soaps. She hoped he was safe and well and maintaining his sanity while he oversaw the duke.

She'd never been tempted to sleep in water before, but the weeks on the road combined with the warmth and relaxation of the pleasant perfumes calmed her into a nearly comatose state. Before she realized what had happened, she'd drifted off to sleep.

Malik.

She fought the urge to pinch herself to a waking state. She was in no mood to dream-walk, as the use of this power had never been particularly restful. Something about her emotional state hadn't prepared her for a conversation with Malik. She couldn't relax on a sunny, summer day near a pond. She didn't want to shake off the taxing journey or her confusing arrival in a foreign land. What she truly craved was the rest of a deep and dreamless sleep.

He sat fishing on the small lake beside a friendly-faced older gentleman and had not yet noticed her presence from where he sat on the grassy bank. She kicked herself for allowing her final thought before drifting off to sleep to be a specific person, knowing she'd done this to herself. Before she could take any action to wake herself, Malik had spotted her on the shore.

He jumped up excitedly, saying something to the man beside him. He was waving to her and shouting while she grimaced.

"Nox, come and meet my father!"

He jogged from his spot on the far side of the pond and was at her side in an instant, snatching her hand as he dragged her toward the shore. Despite the dream-like state, she did not feel rested. Her body and mind still felt terribly, terribly tired.

"Malik—"

"He's going to love you."

She hated herself for saying it, but she didn't have the energy to play along. "Malik, he's not real."

The reever regarded her carefully. She had always found the way his sunlight hit his hair to be so angelic, but she didn't have the space in her heart to appreciate his features tonight. His mouth moved to one side. The bird songs and the chirping insects seem to lull as he found lucidity. "We're dreaming again?"

Nox tried to smile, but she was too weak to enjoy the bright, blue day before her. She was annoyed by the happy woodland creatures and their rustling. She attempted to filter the sounds of the singing birds into silence and sighed with relief as their chirps gradually faded. "I'm sorry. I'm just so tired. I would love to meet your father someday, but for now, do you think he'll forgive us if we step to the side?"

His answering frown didn't end with his downturned mouth. His eyes, shoulders, and aura slumped against her words. "Are you okay?"

She nodded. "I didn't intend to dream-walk. I didn't even intend to sleep. But now that I'm here, I should tell you that I made it to Sulgrave. How are things at the castle?"

"Wait, wait. You're in unseen lands and you want to talk about Aubade? Trust me, nothing worth mentioning has happened. My job mostly means minimizing the number of explicit songs the duke sings around the attendants. Just as I predicted: everyone hates him."

"They don't hate you, though," she said with a soft smile.

"No, thank the goddess. Otherwise, the servants would revolt. If the people of Aubade were forced to interact with him, assassination would be imminent." He chuckled to himself, then looked at her with bright earnestness. He tucked a lock of hair behind her ear, and she pinked at the touch.

"Enough of him," he said. "I haven't heard from you in weeks. I'm not trying to sound particularly needy, but goddess, you've had me worried. What was it like crossing the Frozen Straits? Tell me about the people, Sulgrave, the city, the snow. Leave nothing out."

She sighed, wishing he could sense that her exhaustion permeated beyond her very bones. It wasn't a tiredness of the body but a deep need in the mind. "I honestly don't know. We've barely arrived. I took a bath immediately and was so exhausted from the road that I'm quite certain I'm asleep in the water as we speak. Everything is strange here. There's so much glass. It isn't just windows but entire buildings made of glass. Spelled objects seem to be a commonplace part of everyday life."

"You're in the bath? Are you at a risk of drowning?"

She shook her head, neither appreciative nor amused by his concern. "I'm not drugged, Malik. I'd wake up if I gagged on water."

His green eyes weren't unfriendly, but neither were they warm. Something was amiss with his demeanor as he regarded her. "Is there anything you can tell me about Sulgrave?"

She realized that yes, there was quite a lot he didn't know. Nox attempted to keep the weariness from her voice, as her exhaustion wasn't his fault. He'd dreamt of such adventures, and it would be selfish to deny him such tales just because she was tired. So instead, she spoke of the crossing and its misery. She fixated on the northern lights, the aboriou—her new favored pet—glossing over the true soul-shattering despair and hardship of the journey itself. She was able to describe very little regarding the city itself or the people thus far, though she knew the civilians of Sulgrave were as different from them as the pale, fair humans of Farehold were from the bronze, beautiful fae of Raascot.

"Oh, and Tanith is some enemy of the nation. I'll let you know what we find out about that, but it turns out, we weren't the only ones who found her villainous. Frankly, I'm embarrassed we ever assumed this was an issue of Sulgrave's culture rather than consider that perhaps we've harbored a lunatic. It turns out she's peculiar and murderous in the broad senses of the words. She's in custody right now."

His eyebrows lifted. "She's a criminal?"

"A pretty serious one, from the sounds of it."

"Is there anything you can do about it?"

Nox shrugged, truly at a loss for an answer. They were on the same warm, summery pond she'd visited before. She didn't want to discuss their endeavors. She curled up on the grass and muttered something or other about Tanith being their ambassador and how desperately she wanted to sleep. When she looked to the opposite shore, Malik's father had vanished completely as though he'd never been integral to the fabric of the dream.

She hoped that falling asleep within a dream would reward her with the most restful sleep of her life. That was all she wanted for herself.

"Will you hold me?" she asked.

"No more talking for now?"

"No more talking for now."

Malik picked her up slightly, shifting her head onto his chest. She listened to its steady beat and basked in the summer sun. For now, she was warm, she was loved, and everything was exactly as it should be.

Eighteen

THE BATHWATER WAS COLD WHEN NOX OPENED HER EYES.
The bubbles had long since popped and left her in the
murky remnants of what had been weeks of travel without
bathing. Disgusted, Nox drained her bath and poured a
fresh, quick pot of water to scrub her hair a second time.
This dip was only a few moments long, and soon she was
digging through the closets to see what sort of attire had
been provided for guests. Unfortunately, her options were
limited to a white shift dress meant to tie for all body shapes
and sizes; a thick, comfortable robe; or the filthy things in
which she'd arrived.

Nox opted for the cozy robe and allowed her wet hair to
hang in damp tendrils as they dripped in pools onto the robe's
back and shoulders. She raked her hair into a braid, procuring
the enchanted emerald ribbon from deep within her bag to tie
it off. She then inspected the room thoroughly for all of the
features that differentiated it from things she'd found so familiar on the continent. While beds and comfortable blankets
were a universal requirement, there were other touches that
she'd need to find a way to implement in Gwydir. A silver
pitcher had been engraved in such a way so as to keep the water

within it cool at all times. A lovely, two-tiered glass contraption appeared to boil water whenever one pressed the rune resting at its top, should the bedroom's guest want tea without the inconvenience of leaving their room. Unfortunately, the room had no books, though it did have writing paper, featherless quills made of metal, and fresh ink.

Nox tapped on the silver lily near her door and waited to see if a speaker would answer. After a pause, she dared to call down the flower. "Hello?"

Within a moment, a voice responded. "Your Highness? Yes, how can I help you?"

She would have to make a trip down to inquire about the implementation of such a marvelous bouquet of communicative flowers in her own castles once she had the chance.

She asked, "How might one find a fresh set of clothes?"

"They're already en route, Your Highness. A number of new garments will be made available for you and those in your party within the hour."

She made an appreciative face but realized the concierge could not see her expression. "Oh, thank you. And please, my name is Nox."

"Referring to you as such would be a breach of protocol, Your Highness. Don't hesitate to call for me if you have any further questions."

Not waiting for her clothes, she decided to wander out into the hall in her robe to see what her friends had discovered. Amaris had been assigned three rooms away from her own, but it was Gadriel who she hoped to find. If he'd been as tired as she was, he would perhaps also be napping. Fortunately, he answered the door after the second light rap of her knuckles.

He had also bathed but left his road-weary tunic and clothes on the floor, returning only to his black pants.

"Let me put on a shirt."

She chuckled. "Don't bother on my account. They're sending fresh clothes as we speak."

His brows perked. Nox let herself into his room and

gestured to the flower on the wall before briefly describing their functionality and how she'd communicated with the fae at the front desk. As she spoke, his eyes grew tense.

He lowered his voice to a whisper when he responded. "If we can talk to them, there's no reason for us to believe they can't hear whatever is being said in our rooms."

She looked at the silver lily for a long moment, then nodded.

She went to the desk in the corner of his room. Nox produced the ink and paper from the desk, grabbing the metallic quill they'd provided. She began to write a message when he snatched the utensil from her hand. Nox's mouth parted in a silent protest, but before she had time to speak, she saw where his finger pointed. Three delicate runes had been scratched into the side of the quill, nearly imperceptible to the naked eye. He had to twist it in the light for the indentations to catch.

The brief exchange was already telling them more than enough about their current occupancy in Sulgrave. Nox realized she'd even invited a two-way mirror into her bedroom and made a mental note to rotate it to face the corner as soon as she returned to her quarters. Nox held up a finger to indicate that she'd return and departed the general's room. She crept down the hall in bare feet and knocked softly on Amaris's door. When the reever didn't answer, she quietly urged the door open to find the pale girl asleep, dead to the world. Nox smiled enviously at the depth of her sleep as she began pillaging Amaris's belongings for the black enchanted quill. Nox still possessed its counterpart, and if she gave Amaris's component to Gadriel, they'd be able to communicate without any interference from Sulgrave.

She found it among the few earthly objects Amaris possessed still stashed in a bag that the girl had taken from Aubade. In addition to the quill, the bag had a few more dried pieces of fruit, her furry hat and mittens, a lifetime supply of greenstrike blood in a satchel, and for some reason, the reever had pocketed the cuff that had gripped Fjolla's leg with spikes still covered in the beast's dried blood. Nox returned the bag and its contents to where she'd found it and slid the quill under the collar of her robe. As she began to exit the room, Amaris stirred. Nox had paused on the balls of her feet, not wanting to disturb the reever as she rubbed at her eyes, then settled into a deeper, stone-like sleep. An urge—something like a full-body sigh—overcame her. She couldn't help herself. She took the few steps to the bed and brushed a loose kiss on the sleeping girl's temple before turning and easing the door closed behind her.

Nox returned to the general and handed him the quill. He nodded his understanding. Nox waved a goodbye and returned to her own bedchamber to write to him.

Why do you think they're monitoring us?

The general's answering words were a beautiful cursive. His letters looped and joined, slanting to the side in an elegant calligraphy. She'd always liked her handwriting but didn't care for how careless it looked next to his.

It could be innocent. We're foreign parties claiming royal lineage and harboring a fugitive. It's best to prepare for the worst, but I don't know that we need to immediately assume sinister intent. I would do the same if they were under my roof and I possessed such capabilities.

Nox tapped her black quill to the paper a few times as she thought of her next question. She had gone to his room to discuss their plans. It would be so much easier to achieve with a verbal conversation than through exchanged sentences on a page, but it was certainly better than nothing. She opted for a numbered list of her thoughts to help her organize all she'd wished to discuss.

1. *Tanith is in prison.*

2. *Sulgrave is allowing the missions of powerful mercenaries to the continent. We need to figure out the role of the church in Sulgrave society so we know if this is a religious matter or a greater political issue.*

3. *Do we have any hope of establishing diplomatic relations?*

It took a while for any ink to blot itself onto the paper she held, though she assumed the general was carefully choosing his words before he responded. When his slanted script began to plot onto the page, he was answering in the same, numerical fashion in which she'd posed her initial topics for conversation.

1. *Maybe Tanith deserves to be in prison. Let's table that issue until we know more.*

2. *My parents made the pilgrimage across the straits and have lived in Sulgrave for the last two hundred years. They'll be excellent resources in understanding culture and society in the mountains.*

3. *There's no harm in trying, though keep in mind that you will not be winning over one ruler. A comte is appointed to each of Sulgrave's seven territories. The city itself is split into three, from what I understand. The outlying territories populate the valleys and mountains around the city. Your pitch for diplomacy will need to have a wide appeal. Are you hoping to open trade or just establish relations?*

Nox didn't have to think for too long before she wrote back. She didn't mind that her handwriting was more of a cramped scrawl. Perhaps if she were alive and well centuries from now, she would have the practice necessary to also have lovely script.

1. *Don't be insensitive. You weren't in Raascot when she saved all of Gwydir. She's on our side and has rescued not only us but our people on multiple occasions. We're not tabling it.*

2. *Great. Let me know how we can move forward with communications.*

3. *My personal goal was to get them to stop sending murderous hoarders of world-ending monsters. Anything else is a pleasant treat.*

Their communication was cut short as a knock at her door indicated that someone had arrived with clothing options. She thanked the delivery person, then examined her spoils. She had been provided with a rather telling array of dresses, all in two very distinct color schemes. Some dresses were the blacks and bronzes of Raascot, and others were the golds and reds of Farehold. Her memory drifted to the guards who had greeted them, all clad in different colors. She supposed they were dressed to represent the territories of Sulgrave.

Nox selected a black, silken dress with long, bell-like sleeves. A cluster of bronze, embroidered stars seemed to trail down the arms, congregating in starburst constellations at the bottom hem of her sleeve. She could hear a sound from down the hall and could only guess that, if the other girls had been presented with selections anything like her own, it was either Amaris or Yazlyn protesting about their dresses.

She was not surprised to learn that Amaris had refused her

dresses. It was, however, surprising to learn that Yazlyn had not been offered a gown in the first place. Instead, she was in a quite lovely black-on-black combination of flowy, high-waisted silk pants and a long-sleeved, cropped silk shirt that had been slit down the back in such a way so as to allow for her wings. Gadriel's shirt had also been fitted for his wings, though his contained panels meant to be fastened on the top and the bottom rather than Yazlyn's slits. Amaris had tried to get the attendant to give her Yazlyn's other things, but the reever was far too small to fit into any of the curvy, winged fae's clothing options. Eventually, she was fitted into similarly high-waisted pants and a rather daringly cut matching bronze top. It was more revealing than Amaris typically wore, but she was satisfied to have been offered pants.

Nox wasn't the only one trying to conceal her surprise when Ash emerged in black. His mother had been from Farehold, and he'd been the least adaptive to life north of the border. Noting their expressions, he made some argument about how crimson would have clashed with his hair.

Amaris's mouth twisted into a smile as she regarded Nox. "Is that a bow in your braid?"

Nox pulled at her braid self-consciously, unraveling it with her fingers. It didn't look terribly regal to have an emerald ribbon clash against the elegant black of her gown. She pocketed the ribbon, sliding into the slit along her thigh. She could always tie her hair back later.

"I wasn't telling you to take it out," Amaris apologized.

"It's okay," she said quickly. "Emerald isn't my color."

Amaris looked at her, eyes heavy with questions. "You always wear black. I was just surprised. I'll find you a black ribbon to tie your hair back. I'm sure they're easy enough to come by."

A black ribbon certainly would have been preferable, Nox thought, though markedly less effective than the charmed bit of armor she'd been gifted in Gwydir.

They were a sea of bronze and black as their attendant

led them from their rooms and returned to the ascension panel as the pulley system carried them to the top of the Diplomatic Hall. Unlike Castle Gwydir's windowless war room, the top-floor meeting room was composed entirely of glass, with nothing in this space apart from an enormous oval table, chairs, and fae dressed in vibrant colors.

She and her party appeared to be the last to arrive.

As she eyed the room, their color-coordinated outfits suddenly made perfect sense.

She scanned the room, eyeing who she could assume were the seven Comtes of Sulgrave. Bright, clean light poured in from all sides, banishing shadows, illuminating every minute expression. She recognized the colors and sigils from the seven centurions who'd met them on the road, which led her to believe each territory had a respective guard present.

The attendant who'd escorted them announced the names and territories of each comte. The moment she realized introductions were commencing, she shifted into a long-quiet part of her mind. Names, features, personalities, and first impressions were vital. She hung on every word, looking into the eyes of each comte as they were announced.

Territory One was represented by a man introduced as Alastair in a navy-blue suit with a silver sword embroidered over his shoulder. There was a smugness to his presence, as if he was the sort of man who knew he was powerful or handsome or whatever it was he thought so highly of himself, and expected everyone else to acknowledge it.

Surya of Territory Two was wearing a crushed velvet dress of dark, stormy gray with a silver sun stitched across the chest. While she was beautiful, she showed the most age as peppery hair cascaded over her shoulder. Most astonishingly, she had the large, white feathered wings of the seraphim only known to tales that fanned behind her with enormous, intimidating expanse. Nox's eyes stayed on her for a moment too long while she attempted to gauge the woman's temperature, but she was met with a cool, calculating indifference.

She liked the man from Territory Three instantly. Though he was agelessly fae, there was a grandfatherliness to the way his eyes crinkled as he smiled at her. In attire different from the wealthy display of the first two territories, Three wore a rather simple green shirt and dark pants with an elaborate silver tree stitched into the arm, all belonging to a gentle-looking man called Elswyth. She returned a secret smile before regarding the next comte.

Kasar of Territory Four was a proud-looking man in mustard with a lion emblazoned across the entirety of the front of his suit, the beast coming together seamlessly in the buttoned separation of his top. He grunted a greeting, which made him the first to speak.

Nox was admittedly startled when she looked at the woman from Territory Five, though she did her best to keep her expression neutral. *Your heart is spoken for, twice over,* scolded the voice in her head. Ryu was the woman's name, and her stunning, sharp features were unlike any Nox had seen. Her hair had been curiously cut, with one side the shorter, sharper cut than was fashionable even of men, cropped close to her scalp on one side, while the other side spilled over her ears and onto her shoulder. Ryu wore a deep amethyst shirt and pants not unlike the ones sported by Amaris and Yazlyn, with a small, winged wyvern embla-zoned across her shirt.

Six dipped his chin as the name Chloris was called. He was in turquoise and wore rose sigils on the draping, cloth panels that Nox had only seen on the continent's bishops. There was a lack to Chloris that she found neither good nor bad, almost as if the man were not present at all.

The final person at the table was a shrewd-looking woman with a cat-like face in crimson red from Territory Seven named Dhamir. A single line of silver-stitched hearts traced the space from her neckline, over her shoulder, down her arm, and ending at her wrist.

Nox's time at the Selkie had been like years spent in the

theater. She'd learned how to be whoever, and whatever, was needed for the occasion. She understood how to read a room, sense an energy, and react accordingly. She could play the naive maiden when it benefitted her, but she had learned early of the allure of authority and dominance.

Perhaps she should feel disadvantaged by the cultural barrier, but people were people wherever one went. Though Tanith had been the only person she'd met from Sulgrave, she knew men. She recognized their appreciative glances and understood what made them tick. The women at the table might be of a gamble, but she suspected that they'd be more willing to respect a display of competency than any other winsome air she might select. While the names and colors and scents and sights had been a blur, she had honed the skill of active listening. After all, she had learned, men liked to talk. Each time a name had been given, she'd notched it in her mind like a small witness mark engraved on a tree.

Nox led her party to their seats the moment the attendant was finished with announcements. The table had been seated in such a way so that each comte sat on the far side of the oval table, leaving the near side empty for their arrival. She took the center seat but stood at its back as she made announcements of her own. Gadriel and Amaris had elected to stand on either side of her, with the sergeant on the general's side and Ash on the reever's side.

"I'm Nox, heir to both Raascot and Farehold, daughter of King Ceres and Princess Daphne. On my right is my general and his sergeant, Gadriel and Yazlyn of Raascot. On my left, you'll find Amaris, born from the goddess and trained as a reever, and Ash, also of Uaimh Reev. We're here to hold an audience with whoever can help us with the Sulgrave threat plaguing the continent."

"Sulgrave threat?" repeated the crimson woman from Territory Seven, silvery sigil catching on the light as she tilted in interest.

Nox had been ready to elaborate when the man from

Territory One interrupted. Irritation spiked through her as she looked at the man in navy blue. She'd been right to dislike him. He flicked a finger toward Gadriel and Yazlyn as he spoke. "Surya, weren't there winged asylum seekers who entered your territory a few centuries back?"

Gadriel leaned forward.

Surya arched a brow. "The seraphim in Territory Two have the accommodations necessary for the needs of the winged fae. They've been exemplary residents. They weren't so much asylum seekers as they were expatriates."

The man in turquoise mused at this, fully ignoring the newcomers. "I can see the appeal of wanting to repatriate to Sulgrave from their backwater continent."

Nox fought the urge to wrinkle her nose. She kept her expression smooth.

The man in navy blue spoke again. He leaned forward and cocked a single eyebrow. "Why are we to believe your claim to the throne? Our sources had last informed us that a human called Moirai and a fae named Ceres rested comfortably between the north and south."

This time, she didn't hide her smile. Yes, her claims were lofty. Perhaps it was her announcement that she sat on both thrones, her claim of a demi-goddess on her left, or her statement that Sulgrave was a problematic force on the continent. They could doubt all they liked. She was a force of nature and knew they weren't prepared for her.

"Well, Alastair," she began, summoning the first notch in her memory as she leveled an unimpressed gaze. "Why don't I make you a bargain? For every question of mine you answer, I'll respond to one of yours. I think you'll agree that it's less pressing that I justify my heritage than it is that someone be held accountable for why assassins from Sulgrave have been sent to murder tens of thousands of citizens of the continent."

There was another uncomfortable pause as the room exchanged looks and murmurs in their language. While they whispered to each other, she kept a face of unrattled patience, appreciating the many windows of the room and the overlook they had of the city below. Homes and shops and churches and buildings colored her vision, cut by trees and stretches of green or the jades and blues of rivers. The setting sun lit the city on fire, turning each window into shades of copper and gold.

The winged woman from Two in her dark gray velvet dress was the first to raise a finger. She switched back to the common tongue. Surya asked, "Would you elaborate on this...*threat*...on the continent and why you believe Sulgrave is responsible?"

"They're traveling with a known criminal," Alastair said. "Are we going to trust any message from Tanith the Red and her retinue?"

Perhaps if this were the war room, those at Nox's side would jump in freely. In the unfamiliar Diplomatic Hall, no one knew precisely how to address decorum. In an effort not to undermine Nox's authority, the crew stayed relatively quiet as they turned their heads toward her.

Yes, she knew how to handle men like Alastair, and that was to not handle him at all.

She addressed Surya as if the irritant in navy blue had never spoken.

"Certainly," Nox said. "Nearly one thousand of our military forces were killed when a Sulgrave fae bound mud demons to herself. She invaded an encampment in the night. A month later, more than seven thousand were abducted from their beds and dragged into the lake in Yelagin in the middle of the night by nakki—water spirits. A few short weeks ago, Castle Aubade was invaded by ghouls bound to a singular purpose on a night that the late Queen Moirai had intended to be a gathering of dignitaries."

"And," came the shrewd voice of the woman in crimson from Territory Seven, "how do you know that this has anything to do with Sulgrave?"

Nox's lip twitched. "Because we neutralized the threat

in Raascot. Tanith, whom you've called Tanith the Red, has been in our custody for months. If she hadn't been secured, she would have killed numerous others. As our ward, she's gone from our captive to our ambassador. She was dangerous and violent. She came to Raascot to see us perish, and now she's risked her life to escort us back to Sulgrave so that we might mend what's broken. Not only has she confirmed that she came on a skiff of five from your kingdom, but we've since seen her ability to bind beasts in a way that no one on the continent has ever done before."

The comtes stirred at Tanith's name, which set Nox on a delicate tightrope. She had to be careful not to reveal too much as to their relationship. She could appear neither too attached nor detached from the young fae if she wanted to navigate the choppy waters of negotiating her eventual release.

Ash spoke without being addressed, much to Nox's irritation. "Tanith is here as Nox's emissary. We seek her sanctuary while on Sulgrave ground."

His final word was sharper than the rest, as if Amaris had covertly harmed him from underneath the table, forcing his voice to catch. He did not speak again.

The woman in amethyst, Ryu, asked, "So the rumors are true? You did not return Tanith the Red to us as a prisoner but as your ally?"

Nox leveled her gaze, remembering her name just as clearly as the other six at the table. "Yes, Ryu. She arrived in Raascot as no friend of the continent. I've come to find her to be an honorable person misguided by cruel direction. It's what we've crossed the straits to address."

Nox left it there. The comte's feelings of Tanith weren't the only wildcard. She didn't know the role of the church in Sulgrave and had no urge to make enemies were she to find that the speaker was the ultimate authority in the mountains. If she kept her statements vague, she could potentially exonerate Tanith without betraying their need for careful, diplomatic negotiation of the situation. Ryu had watched her response with a cocked brow, but he did not react further.

Nox skimmed the faces in the room to see if she could gauge who favored her and who met her with suspicion. She had one enemy for certain, and it was the man from Territory One. The only friend she was sure she had at the table was the man in green called Elswyth. The women, however, remained challenging to read.

Alastair scoffed as he looked at his fellow diplomats. The silver sword that had embroidered onto his dark-blue suit seemed to indicate less about his ability as a protector and more of his inclination to battle. He spoke to the room again.

"She's asked her questions of Sulgrave, and we're supposed to take her on good faith? You read the report regarding the state in which they arrived. They were half-starved and accompanied by a predator. Now they've come to our council with accusations?"

Ryu steepled her fingers. "They made the crossing, Alastair. Who among us can say the same? If anything, their survival is a testament to their tenacity and abilities. It is no idle crossing."

The woman in gray frowned, her white, angelic wings flaring slightly behind her with her irritation. "Why would zealots from the south be any less intent on crossing than extremists from Sulgrave—if that's what's being accused? Why are we to believe that Sulgrave is sending powerful assassins and ignore the possibility that the continent has equipped clever manipulators to undermine our millennia of peace?"

The twitches in the faces of Elswyth of Three and Ryu of Five confirmed Nox's suspicions. They were the closest thing she had at the table to allies, and she would be wise to foster these relations. The seraphim from Territory Two seemed less promising with every moment that passed, while the man with the lion's emblem from Four continued to maintain his indiscernible haze of irritation—for better or for worse, she couldn't tell.

On her right, Gadriel made a small flick of his hand. It would have been imperceptible from the others at the table, but she felt quite sure that he was asking her permission to speak. Nox lifted her voice again to introduce him.

"Gadriel has served as Raascot's general for me and for my father, King Ceres, before me. I trust his instincts and would like to give him an opportunity for an audience with you now."

She impressed herself sometimes as she glided through her greatest acting role of all time: pretending to be royal. This particular display was no more taxing than feigning captivated interest toward a merchant patron at the Selkie who found his methods of tax evasion remarkably fascinating, though this performance was far more enjoyable. They had no way of knowing she was of lowly upbringing and ignoble profession.

If she did say so herself, Nox was nailing the part.

Gadriel leaned onto his forearms and spoke with centuries of authority. He was no stranger to commanding a room, and nothing about his tone invited doubt. "If the question is Nox's claim to the throne, we'd be happy to procure any evidence within our means while in Sulgrave. If you'd prefer to cross the Frozen Straits and venture to the continent for your confirmation, you'd also glean whatever you needed to know and we encourage you to do so. In the meantime, I propose we address the issue at hand. Is there any reason to either confirm or deny that parties within Sulgrave's church have been charged with violent missions?"

He'd worded his question well, which didn't shock her. She'd tried on multiple occasions to hand him the crown, and may try again if she found it too heavy for her head. He was a natural. If applicable, Sulgrave's comtes could certainly shoot down his question with declarations of peace. Otherwise, they'd be forced to confront realities of church-appointed missionaries.

Chloris of Six began speaking to the others in his mother tongue. Alastair, then Dhamir of Seven, responded.

The man in mustard from Territory Four slammed his fist against the table. He returned to the common tongue. His voice had a loud, gravely quality, like pebbles crunching underfoot. There was a gruff, trustworthiness to the sound.

"When will someone hold the church accountable?" he boomed. "It cannot continue to operate outside of the authority of the seven territories. How are we supposed to police citizens of a church that transcend the identities of Sulgrave as they don't answer to us or our centurions but only to the goddess and their speaker? You know as well as I that the Reds are a violent menace."

She knew with certainty that Kasar was a friend. The lion's heart emblazoned on his chest was one for his people, not for the church. A few at the table stiffened uncomfortably at his outburst, but it was clear from their postures that this was not the first time he'd reacted as such. The agitation Nox had sensed had never been directed toward her, she concluded. If anything, perhaps their arrival had justified long-brewing anger among the lions from Territory Four.

"Kasar," the crimson woman from Territory Seven cautioned, "do be careful not to confuse the All Mother with the parties of the church."

Nox gnawed on the cautionary sentence as if it were a difficult piece of toffee. Dhamir's curiously worded sentence tipped her hand toward the goddess yet away from the church. Nox felt the shift in the room as she began to feel that she had more allies than enemies at the table.

"Surya?" Gadriel spoke to the white-winged fae. "Would you put me in touch with those who came from the continent?"

Surya's face creased slightly. "What is your intent with them?"

Everyone held a collective breath while they waited to see what Gadriel would reveal.

He shook his head quickly. "None, save that it would be

228

beneficial to hear from someone who can empathize with our kingdom and has adapted to life in Sulgrave."

Alastair made a sound. "A question for a question, you'd said. You're here with wild claims, miss. Not only do you purport yourself to be queen of the southern lands, but you've brought a human and been so bold as to say she is the fruit of the goddess."

A tendon in Gadriel's arms flexed. "I would caution you on how you address the queen of the southern continent, sir."

Amaris made a curious face as she eyed the man, pressing him further. "And?" the ivory reever asked.

"If you think your blasphemy—"

"Choose your next words carefully," Gadriel cautioned in a low growl.

Shit. Nox had never expected it would be Gadriel who might derail their diplomatic meeting. She cast a worried look first to Amaris, who kept her challenging gaze on Alastair, then to Yazlyn, who shook her head helplessly.

It was Ryu who came to their rescue. She stood, rapping her knuckles against the table to gain everyone's attention as she announced the meeting had reached its conclusion, with the intention of meeting again in three days after each comte had the opportunity to speak with their respective advisors. There were questions to collect, understandings to reach, and rationale necessary before they might hope for forward progress.

Something about the narrowed eyes and grumbles from at least two of the comtes let Nox know that Ryu did not possess the authority to hold or conclude meetings alone but that they did not have the ammunition necessary to contradict her proposal to end their gathering. Amaris looked at Ryu, hoping the woman could read the unspoken gratitude on her face.

Nox gestured for the others to stay back, allowing the comtes to filter out of the room first.

Ryu of Territory Five was the last comte to exit. She lifted a hand to halt Nox and the others. She cast a glance over her shoulders to ensure that they weren't moving before slipping a note to Yazlyn, who was nearest to her in the corner. Ryu then strode down the corridor to join the others as if nothing had happened.

The moment the door closed, Yazlyn unfolded her note.

"What does it say?" Nox asked.

It was a time and an address.

Yazlyn's forehead creased as she looked at the paper. "Do we go?"

Nox took a stilling breath. "I think we have to."

Nineteen

Y OU THERE. I KNOW YOU," CAME A LOW, MALE GROWL
across the hall.

Tanith didn't bother to look. "No, you don't," she said.

"Yeah, I've seen your face," the man insisted. He kicked
the bar for her attention, then cursed beneath his breath as
the rune-etched gate sent a bolt through him. He insisted,
"I've seen your posters. Damn, whoever hauled you in must
be living pretty. I'd heard you'd escaped the kingdom. I've
never seen a bounty that high. So? How did they do it? How
did you get caught?"

She continued to face the flat, dim wall.

He kicked the bar again, so she said, "I returned on my
own."

He made a disappointed grunt before his silhouette disappeared from her peripherals.

Tanith the Red. War criminal. Misuser of magic.
Murderer.

She closed her eyes and tilted her chin toward the ceiling,
resting her head on the cold wall of her cell. The prison was
filled with fae, yet the smell of unwashed bodies overpowered
any hope for the faint perfumes of herbs and flowers. Perhaps

it was best that the guard had been the ones to apprehend her. It had been a toss-up whether the law or the church would take her into custody first. The guard meant cold prison cells shared with civilians, long trials, and months in prison before her assured execution. It wasn't ideal, but there was a small comfort in knowing that her family and mentors would be proud that she'd been a martyr for the cause in more ways than one, even if it was a cause she no longer believed in. At least, not the way she used to.

Had the church found her, it could have gone one of two ways. Their elimination would have been swift and thorough, which would be painless. It would, however, come with the shame of public denouncement, should they choose to kill her for failing her southern mission.

And that was the ideal outcome.

There was always the chance that the church would not kill her. Perhaps they would have tried to reintegrate her, which would force her to tell them she no longer shared their convictions. She knew the sort of retraining camps that awaited attempted defectors, and she'd choose a filthy prison cell over reeducation any day.

A ripple of noise moved through the prison. It was the metallic scrape and clatter on stone. It was the sounds of teeth ripping into dinner. It was the scuff of boots. The slot to her cell clanged open and closed while a tray was shoved into her little room, but she didn't bother to open her eyes. When she'd thought of Sulgrave food, it hadn't been the sort of things served to inmates awaiting execution. This wasn't the last meal she wanted from her country. These weren't the final thoughts she wanted of her people.

Her people.

An uncomfortable heat knotted her throat as her closed lids became swollen with tears she refused to let fall. Her people were a queen of the southern kingdoms, a handful of reevers, and a couple of winged fae. Her people lived in Castle Gwydir, hailed from Uaimh Reev, were raised in Farehold, had worked in Priory, had served in the south. Her people were orphans, they were military, they were warriors. Her people were kind, came from backgrounds and led lives as varied as her own. Her people were surely meeting with the comtes now and discussing diplomatic solutions to address the church.

The church and government had been clashing forces for years. The comtes would undoubtedly be grateful for just cause to move against the Reds at long last. And if her people needed her to testify against the Reds so the comtes could oversee their accountability, she would. She'd make enemies of the church and government alike and bring shame to everyone who'd known her, if her last action on the All Mother's lighted kingdom brought pride to her people.

And then there was her person.

Strong arms that wouldn't hold her again. Amber eyes that wouldn't twinkle as he laughed, a mouth that wouldn't smile as he looked at her, a hand that wouldn't guide her through her final moments on the earth. She used her thumb to twist the ring on her finger, spinning it idly as she thought of the man who'd gifted it and the heart that had changed hers.

She hadn't said goodbye, because she knew she couldn't. She wouldn't have been able to look him in the eyes and keep her resolve. She certainly couldn't have told him what fate awaited her in Sulgrave, or he would have fought her every step of the way to keep her from leading them north. So maybe it had been kind to keep the truth from him, or maybe it had been selfish to cherish the time that had remained. Because from the moment Nox had told her that their next move was to venture to Sulgrave, she knew precisely how her story would end.

Tanith wasn't afraid to die. She'd been ready for a long, long time.

At least now, she had the honor of knowing she'd done something truly worthwhile with the end of her life. It wouldn't atone for all she'd done, but it was one final act of goodness she could put into the world. There was justice in the chill in the air, the repulsive meals, the sweat and dirt and filth, despite the criminals and the miserable days that stretched ahead. It wasn't the ending she wanted, but it was the right one.

And in that, she found the smallest edges of comfort. In her final moments, she could be proud of herself. And that was worth something.

Twenty

H OW ARE WE SUPPOSED TO MAKE SENSE OF THIS ADDRESS?"
Yazlyn asked, turning the piece of paper and its combination of numbers and letters over. Two hours had passed
since their meeting had concluded as they congregated in
Nox's bedroom. The others were briefed on not speaking
any sensitive information aloud, but there was plenty to say
without letting on to their plan.

"We could ask the concierge how to find it," Ash suggested.

Everyone looked at him with the sort of silencing,
deadpan stare that kept him from chiming in again.

"Get your cloaks," Nox responded. "This is something
we learn on our feet. Yaz, go flirt with the man and ask for
the best alehouse in walking distance."

Yazlyn made a gagging noise. "Flirt with a man?"

"I'll do it," Amaris said. She met them at the front door a
few minutes later.

"You're braver than the military," Yazlyn said solemnly,
thanking Amaris for her service upon her return.

"I wasn't very good at it." Amaris grimaced. "I think he
just gave me an address to get me to leave him alone." Nox
made some comment about sending a girl to do a woman's job.

They exited the Diplomatic Hall, armed with both a fake address for a popular tavern, and the slipped note from Ryu. Their cloaks had proved useless, as it seemed just as warm at night as it had been during the day. A few words were exchanged as to whether or not it might be possible for an entire valley to be enchanted, though the arguments that had erupted from such a question had been fruitless and decidedly irritating.

"For fuck's sake, ask for directions," came Amaris's irritated command after hours of what felt like aimless wandering.

"We're trying to be clandestine," Yazlyn said, squinting at the tiny slip of paper for the millionth time as if it might reveal a new, important clue.

"We don't need to ask for directions," Gadriel insisted.

"I've got this one," Nox said. She left the others in the shadows between a tailor shop and confectionary as she approached a fae man who'd been attempting to steady himself outside of a tavern. He was pretty in the way that all fae were lovely, though something about his slender build and youthful face made her think he might not deserve deception, but alas, he was a victim of the wrong place at the right time.

"Hi." She laced her voice with disarming, honey-sweet warmth. "I was hoping you could help me?"

The man's eyes widened to such a great width that she was certain the whites of his eyes were visible to even her lurking audience. She touched her hair bashfully, careful not to reveal that they were rounded, human ears. She hoped it was peak entertainment, as none of them had truly had the opportunity to see her at work. Only Ash had been subjected to the brilliance of her charm, and if he hadn't had his wits about him, their encounter could have ended very differently.

Seduction was both art and science. There was a subtlety to forwardness that, if done correctly, would make the man feel like he'd led their dance all along. Nox eyed the man as if he were a fascinating puzzle she couldn't wait to understand. She touched his arm lightly as she spoke.

"You need help?" he asked, matching her use of the common tongue. He straightened his spine, doing his best to look taller than he was. Nox had never had a preference for height or build, though; she hadn't thought she'd like a single man in the goddess's lighted kingdom before she'd met Malik.

She struck an airy, purring tone as she spoke to the stranger. "I'm so silly; I've gotten completely turned around. My aunt is in Territory Five, but I was here visiting a friend tonight and I'm afraid I've had too many glasses of wine. Would you point me in the right direction?"

"We're halfway between Three and Four now," he said. "I...you...um...you're not from here."

Genius, this one.

"Alas, I'm woefully southern. My family expatriated decades ago, and it took me a long time to work up the courage to come to your beautiful mountains."

She knew that, as fae, he was far less susceptible to the succubi charms than a human man might have been, but he was male, nonetheless. He dragged his eyes over her a little too slowly. "Ma'am, I'm from Four. These streets can get really confusing. Do you know how the territories are laid out? Between the valleys? Let me escort you."

He was too drunk to be escorting anyone, but as Nox assessed the situation, she determined he'd had one too many drinks to notice the others following in the shadows. And no, she had no idea what he meant by valleys and layouts.

"I'm so lucky I found such a gentleman," she said, giving his arm a squeeze. She kept her hands on his bicep, clinging to his arm as the bewildered man led them down the street.

"It's quite the walk," he said, working his tone up to a mixture of concern and chivalry. "It will take us more than an hour. Would you like me to call us a ride? There are horses—"

"No, no," Nox insisted. She rested her head briefly on

his shoulder, scrunching her nose against the distillery scent rolling off him. "I've always loved the fresh air. Walking at night is so nice, don't you think? It's like the world is full of secrets. So, tell a girl. What should I know about Sulgrave?"

"Well," he stammered, "what do you want to know?"

How to infiltrate the church, stop the Reds, and keep my aboriou safe, she thought.

"What food must I try?" she asked. And once he began talking, he didn't stop. His drunken words stuck together as he became the ultimate tour guide, explaining shops, stories, histories, meals, taverns, and even a rather tawdry bit of gossip regarding Kasar from Territory Four. Nox kept her chuckle to herself, though she was liking the idea of Kasar as an ally more and more with every moment that passed.

An hour was quite the walk indeed, but she couldn't guarantee that the others would keep up if horses or carriages were summoned. She'd see how she could use the hour of companionship to her advantage.

She continued prodding him for information, but she ensured it was a fair trade. The gentleman got every bit as much from the evening as she did, ego swelling with every step. Nox stroked her fingers along his arm as she asked him of Sulgrave. She gained as much knowledge as she could about the various territories, laughing away her ignorance as a result of the wine whenever he'd made a curious face. She'd pressed her breasts into his arm when he'd insisted on what Territory she lived in, but the trick worked like a charm, as all thoughts tumbled right out of his head. He was kind, and the manipulation was unfair, but she was quite certain he'd leave the night with only pleasant memories of helping a pretty, lost maiden.

"Let me walk you to your doorstep. You know, to make sure you get in safe," he said when they reached the border between Four and Five.

She kissed his cheek and told him to call upon her at her inn when they were both sober, so they might have a proper date. She'd shooed him away with the gentle insistence that no man should know where a lady lays her head at night but that if their date went well, he might just escort her home soon. He left grinning to himself as she was able to navigate her way through the alleys before her friends caught up.

It was with a combination of jeers and claps on the back that the other four rejoined her.

"And that's how it's done," she said.

"She pulled something similar to get us from Priory into Aubade," Ash said.

"That's right!" Nox exclaimed. "Ah, noble Sir Vescus, our hero."

"Mmm." Yazlyn pursed her lips. "Good to know our queen is infamous for her deceit."

They estimated that it had taken them three full hours on foot. The night was cool, their stomachs were empty, and nerves were high as they approached the address Ryu had given them. The outside of the building was littered with flowers, many of which seemed to be in intentional shades of violet. The yard surrounding the estate was well manicured and pristinely kept. They stopped outside the estate with skepticism and admiration, five pairs of feet planted on the street as they waited for either something important or readied themselves to make a terrible mistake.

"Well, no time like the present," Yazlyn said, leading the charge. She knocked on the door.

An attendant in purple answered the door and expressed that they were both welcomed and expected. Nox trailed behind, admiring the inside of the home, appreciating that it was every bit as tasteful as the exterior, neither gaudy nor ostentatious. The attendant took their cloaks.

They stepped into the sitting room where Ryu awaited them. She had changed out of her diplomatic purple attire into more leisurely clothes, though she remained in a shirt and pants unlike the other women of the council, who had opted for dresses. The attendants in her home wore mixed clothing, with some wearing the telltale amethyst of Territory Five and others in practical attire for their station and position.

Nox was both surprised and relieved that her judgment had been correct, as in the living room, they were met by the two men Nox had presumed to be friends: Elswyth of Three, who remained in his simple green clothes, and the proud Kasar of Territory Four, still in his mustard suit.

Ryu ushered everyone in and had them served drinks as they sat around the table, ready for dinner.

"So!" Ryu's voice was cheerful. "At long last, we have a just cause to stop the church."

✦

The evening was bizarre, to say the least.

Nox had always liked spice. The ability to try new meals, flavors, and delicacies had been her favorite thing about living in Priory. Though there were familiar elements here and there, Sulgrave's food was delicious, and utterly new. Every sharp bite, every savory melt, every sweet combination was new. Even the utensils proved a challenge to navigate as she and the others were served curious tools for their meals. The Sulgrave fae did their best to turn inattentive eyes to the ways Nox and her companions struggled with their food and how to utilize their equipment before Ryu had whispered for soup spoons to be distributed amongst her guests.

While they ate, they wasted no time getting into the weeds.

Kasar's list of complaints regarding the church would have reached from the Sulgrave's highest mountain top to its lowest valley. The tirade of churning pebbles was interesting, if not entirely helpful. The other two comtes looked as if they'd heard his speech many times, but Kasar was thrilled to have a new group to whom he could recount his distaste for the Speaker and their iron grasp that transcended territory, fae, magic, and country. Nox had only met a few people who had lived in total rejection of the All Mother, but it was rare to come across thorough nonbelievers in a world so filled with magic. If she was honest with herself, she didn't know where she fell in the line between faith and disbelief.

Elswyth was Kasar's opposite in many ways. If the comte from Territory Four had the voice of rocks, then Elswyth was that of new leaves rustling together on a spring breeze. He was most interested in Amaris and asked her a number of questions specific to the path and conception of a demigoddess. Nox wasn't sure if she was grateful or irritated at how Gadriel repositioned himself in the room to lean against the wall beside the reever when she was being interrogated, though Amaris hadn't seemed to mind. Nox supposed she was glad that Amaris had a powerful ally, though she'd be the first to intervene if his hostility got them into any trouble. In the meantime, Nox listened curiously as Amaris answered Elswyth's questions, every bit as interested in the responses as he was. Amaris, it seemed, found it far less relevant than her identity as a reever.

Regardless of all else, Territory Four was interested first and foremost in peace. It seemed that Elswyth had no problem with the conventional church or the All Mother but took issue with the Greens and their collections, the Reds with their violence, and the Speaker behind it all had become problematic over the last fifty or so years. As the church in Sulgrave had been emboldened with its recent Speaker—a fae woman who had lived for three hundred years, though who had risen to the rank of Speaker in only the last century—so had its monetary and military arm of the church. For the first time in more than a thousand years, Sulgrave was changing, he said, and it was not a change for the better.

"And? What of you?" Elswyth cupped his chin and looked at Gadriel.

The general didn't move from the wall. "What of me?"

"Why did you truly ask after the dark-winged fae in Territory Two?"

Kasar barked a laugh. "He speaks cryptically, but I promise

you, you're among friends. A man and a woman who share your description have been helping us for some time, ever since we suspected that the problem was bleeding onto the southern kingdoms. We invited them tonight."

"Tonight?" Gadriel shot a look down the hall as if they might be in the next room. He cleared his throat. "They're my parents. How did they get involved with this operation?"

"Your parents!" Kasar slapped his knee. "You do have more in common with that old winged bastard than just your black feathers, don't you? Yes, I can see your mother in you too."

Ryu rubbed the back of her neck. "You'll have to forgive Kasar. He's rude, but harmless. Your parents are lovely. To be honest, we were the ones who pursued them. Joel and Allua have been exceptionally helpful. There have been rumors of Reds migrating to the continent for nearly one hundred years, but they were never said to do more than reconnaissance. It was challenging enough for someone to make the crossing both ways, but once they proved it could be done... Joel and his wife helped us piece together what was really going on in the south."

Kasar scoffed. "I'd let the Reds take the southern kingdoms if the damned Speaker would leave Sulgrave alone, but she manages to meddle with anyone and anything that gets in her way."

Nox wasn't thrilled at the idea that he'd throw Raascot and Farehold to the wolves, but his statement brought a more pressing question. "What abilities does she possess?"

Ryu answered, "No one really knows, and that's more than a little peculiar. Whatever power she has, it's been enough to create incredible conviction in her followers."

Gadriel spoke again. "You said my parents were meant to be here tonight."

Kasar grunted. "They make it to most of our little get-togethers. Just imagine, the one time they get caught up, their own son happens to be in your sitting room. Life is funny that way."

"I'll need their address."

Ryu spoke then. She had the voice of someone with a military background, and the posture to underscore Nox's assumption. Though the woman was neither scarred nor clad in armor, something in the way she leaned on her opened knees radiated readiness for combatant.

"The Speaker wants power," Ryu said. The others in the room had their time to speak, and now they looked to their host in Territory Five. "The church here set itself up for manipulation by appointing a sole Speaker. Speakers are typically gentle extensions of the mother, settling matters that pertain solely to the church. She slipped in like a snake, and by the time we sensed something was wrong, she'd already amassed loyalists."

Yazlyn cocked an eyebrow. She propped an elbow over the back of her chair and leaned backward. "You've suspected that a Speaker's arrival might lead Sulgrave to this disaster?"

Ryu eyed her slowly. Nox turned to see if they were waiting for Yazlyn to continue speaking, then suppressed a smirk as she understood. Yazlyn was beautiful, to be sure. Her hazel eyes were sharp, her lips made for cursing...and for other things, though Nox had put those days behind her. Her chestnut hair was particularly prominent against the black of her silks. Nox had sensed that Ryu might have similar proclivities from the moment she'd met the fae. When the Sulgrave woman from Territory Five answered, it was only to Yazlyn.

"Do you know why each of Sulgrave's seven territories is ruled by its own comte?"

Yazlyn did not bat an eye. She was not intimidated by the leveled gaze. "The little we know about Sulgrave is undoubtedly by design. So when I tell you no, I don't know much of your politics, I expect you'll appreciate this is not an answer of willful ignorance."

Ryu's mouth twitched. She amended her question. "Why might seven territories avoid appointing a single ruler?"

Gadriel answered, though the question had not been asked of him. His tone was not particularly appreciative of the implied condescension in the woman's question. "Because there is no corruption like unchecked power."

She nodded. "Precisely. The Speaker has achieved what we've spent thousands of years avoiding. The church in Sulgrave has found a way to circumvent checks and balances by speaking for the All Mother in a way that's been irrefutable to its believers, regardless of their territory. This brings me to your ambassador."

"Tanith?" It was the first thing Ash had said all night. Everyone's eyes flicked briefly to him before they returned to Nox and her exchange with Ryu.

Nox nodded. "We know Tanith is what the Sulgrave church calls a Red. The southern kingdoms also have a sword arm of the church. The reevers. They're purpose is for…what is it you do?" Nox gestured to the reevers at her side.

Amaris said, "Magical balance. Reevers are trained in combat, though many of us possess no magical ability. Our only charge is to intervene when magics are being misused to give their user an unfair advantage. The reevers are a centuries-old organization who seem to do the opposite of what the Reds have been charged with accomplishing."

Once Amaris was finished speaking, Nox continued her explanation of the Sulgrave fae in the gully. "We captured Tanith when she'd bound dozens of mud demons and attacked our military. It was a massacre. We were ready to let her rot for several weeks. She was a murderer under the worst-case scenario, and a lunatic in the best."

"But you consider her a friend?" Elswyth asked.

Nox said, "The more we spoke to her and got to know her, it became clear that she was crazy, yes, but due to the beliefs instilled in her."

"She's not crazy," Ash defended. "She has strong beliefs. They're misguided, but she's grown. She's not the person she was when we met her."

Nox addressed the room. "Tanith is a good person. She's loyal to a fault and was manipulated by someone who took advantage of that loyalty. She has killed, and she's not absolved of those crimes. However, I have no reason to believe that she's malevolent. When we were met on the road, we were read her crimes of violence, death, and something about magic? What do you know of this?"

They exchanged looks, but it was Kasar who spoke.

"Tanith has been quite a menace for years. The Reds and their crimes against magic have been difficult to prove, but Tanith was more public with her displays. She helped us build our case, to be honest."

Yazlyn echoed what they were all thinking. "Crimes against magic?"

Kasar nodded. "Unnatural powers. Blood magics. Abilities that don't belong to her. They're forbidden for a reason."

Nox thought of the scholar's hushed words as he'd looked in on Tanith's sickly form in Castle Gwydir. She said, "As they kill their user, correct?"

The others looked at Nox with mixed expressions.

"The things they do require the blood, the life, even the heart of the user. Dabbling in blood magic is a mission of either murder or suicide. Often both."

Gadriel redirected the topic. "What do we know of Surya in Territory Two?"

Ryu said, "Surya is not our known enemy, but I would be careful before I thought to count her a friend. The seraphim in Territory Two are the only populace located on a mountainside. They've used their wings to build themselves a sanctuary at a rather inconvenient elevation for the rest of us."

Elswyth mused at that. "It's not their fault. If I were born with wings, I'd also want to remove myself from the problems of the world."

Ryu eyed the others, her gaze snagging on Yazlyn once more. Their eyes held for too long before she resumed her scanning. Nox was ready to suggest they get a room when the comte engaged her directly. "The believers will meet in three days' time. Kasar and I aren't exactly welcome in the sanctuary. Elswyth has made himself appear intentionally neutral to both the church and its opposition for good reason. But for the rest of us, we've made our skepticism…"

The lion-hearted man finished the thought. "They know we're on to them."

Ryu nodded. "You could attend a service and see what happens for yourself."

Elswyth's face bundled apologetically. "It'll have to be you, Nox. The others would draw too much attention."

They weren't wrong, and Nox knew it. Amidst the dark locks common to Sulgrave, Ash's red hair was as outstanding as Amaris's silvery locks. The winged fae were impossible to go unnoticed anywhere outside of Raascot, unless they could magically glamour their feathers to match the white seraphim of Territory Two. Nox's hair was dark enough to allow her to pass for the common features of the Sulgrave fae, even if her skin tone would be challenging to conceal. The comtes seemed confident that if she kept her head down, she could avoid detection.

The others knew Nox didn't go unnoticed anywhere.

Amaris spoke for the second time in the night. "Tanith claims she was one of several sent south on a suicide mission for some cause in the name of magical purity. Our concern is what her team of five accomplished, and how easy it would be to wipe out the continent if anyone else made it south."

Elswyth exhaled. "Magical purity?"

Ash confirmed the statement. "She had claimed it's the thing that stands between the continent and unity."

Deep parallel lines ran between Elswyth's brows as they furrowed. "I think you might be fixating on the wrong part of Tanith's charge. Purity is problematic, sure, but it's the idea of unity that should be worrying you."

"Unity?" Nox reiterated.

He nodded carefully. "Consider the implications of

what that mission would mean for Sulgrave, Farehold, and Raascot."

Nox watched as Amaris's eyes dropped from the comte of Territory Four, scanning the other Sulgrave faces in the room. Their eyes were shades of chocolates and blacks flecked with ambers, teas, and woods. No one had deeper answers for her regarding why Tanith was sent to the southern continent, but it was agreed that the church was expressing an arm of violence for their mission. They had begun to discuss potential plans for infiltrating the church when a knock came at the door.

It was clear from the way the servant breathed her name that the woman at the door had not been invited. The woman stepped into the entry and found her way into the sitting room where everyone had been tensely waiting. Dhamir was no longer wearing the crimson attire she'd had in the gathering. She wore all-black attire meant to disguise her among the shadows of the night. A silvery broach of the embroidered heart of Territory Seven still clutched her black cloak, though she unclamped it as she entered the room. Her shrewd face was as unreadable now as it had been at the meeting. She eyed the Raascot and Farehold crew for a moment before her knit eyebrows turned to her Sulgrave councilmen.

"Are we here to discuss the way the Speaker is damning the All Mother with her corruption of the church?"

Twenty-One

A RE YOU BUSY?" CAME A QUIET KNOCK AT HER BEDROOM
door.

Nox looked up from her place on the bed, breaking her
attention away from the page where she and Gadriel had
debriefed their thoughts on the night's events. An unassum-
ing, reddish fae light gleamed on her bedside table, as if a
piece of the fire from the hearth had been safely captured and
lit her page just enough for her to legibly write her messages
back and forth. The reddish light cast soft shadows on Amaris
as she stood in the doorway.

Nox set down her quill and pushed her parchment to
the bedside table. "There is nothing that would make me
too busy to see you," she said. She beckoned for Amaris to
approach and read the letter over her shoulder, rather than
risk the listening ears of the concierge.

Gadriel had expressed his discomfort over Nox attending
the church service alone, but they agreed that, in lieu of a
better option, having eyes and ears within the sanctuary was
crucial. Dhamir of Territory Seven was a regular attender.
Their meeting at Ryu's home had concluded with the
promise that Dhamir would meet Nox in three nights' time

outside the Diplomatic Hall and escort her into the sanctuary, helping her to navigate seating, practices, and the best way to remain concealed.

Amaris nodded her understanding, but the motion was not entirely reassuring. There was something staticky about the reever's energy. Nox couldn't quite put her finger on it, but Amaris seemed on edge, somehow. She opened her mouth to ask if everything was okay, but Amaris spoke first.

"You have one of these things too," she said, touching the silver orb, allowing the room to swell with lutes, fiddles, violins, and cellos. There was a foreign greenery to the music that swelled from her box, so unfamiliar from the music of the continent. It was wild and built deliciously, giving a flavor to every passing thought and feeling.

"Maybe they'll let us bring the music home with us," Nox said, but levity escaped her. She frowned at the young woman. For once, Amaris didn't look silver, the way that blue fae lights, broad daylight, or vibrant moonbeams had always made her appear. Tonight, she was a candle, a lovely glimmer in the calming dark, washed in the fireplace's reddish glow. "Is everything all right?"

Amaris's answering nod was unconvincing.

The reever kept a distance, with at least two arm's lengths between them as she took a seat on the edge of a large, soft mattress. A nervousness scratched at Nox, despite the calming, orchestral lull of string instruments. She wasn't sure what caused Amaris to keep her legs dangling off the side of the bed or her eyes downcast. Amaris twisted the fabric of her silken, bronze shirt with both hands.

"Something's on my mind," Amaris said.

"I can tell," Nox responded.

"When we were on the ship our first night, I had a dream…"

Ah yes, the dream.

In an instant, she understood the nervousness for what it was. There was something between them that had existed for a long, long time. Something they'd fought for, that they'd dreamed of, that they'd never had the chance to fully embrace.

But there were no dragons this time. There were no iron bars, or the unbearable weight of learning something that had taken ages to unpack. There was no curse. And for once, they were not asleep.

Nox reached across the bed to slip her fingers into Amaris's and waited a stretch of time until lilac eyes met her own. The moment stretched into a minute. Each second that passed bore a heaviness within its intensity. Nox's eyes scarcely blinked as they carried unspoken meaning. She never wanted Amaris to feel pressure, but she needed the reever to remain doubtless of what she wanted or where she stood.

"It was no dream," was all Nox said.

Amaris's lower lip puckered. Her chest rose and fell with a quick emotion as she felt herself melting under the large, dark eyes of Nox's unrelenting gaze. She needed to remove her hand. She was supposed to lean away and break the tension, but Nox didn't.

Amaris was uncomfortable, as all new things are uncomfortable. She could go back to her room. She could sketch monsters, or take a bath, or tuck herself beneath her covers, but she didn't.

She raised one shoulder slightly as she acknowledged the active sphere. "The music is lovely."

Nox tilted her head ever so slightly. Black, unbound hair cascaded down her back and shoulder. "Yes, we've said as much. Is that what you want to talk about? The music?"

It was lovely. It was wild and foreign and taut with the same tension she felt now. But no, that wasn't what she'd come here to say, to do, to feel.

Amaris's throat bobbed as she attempted a swallow, but it took two tries for her to chase whatever words and emotions meant to bubble up from her throat before they were buried in her belly. She had always been the shyer of the two, and tonight was no exception. She lowered her eyes under the intensity of Nox's burning gaze, then held her breath as she raised her face once more to find that Nox had never looked away.

Nox was bold, yes. But Amaris had been the one who'd come here tonight.

There was an increase in tempo in the music that carried throughout the room as the song found its rhythm.

She battled for courage, saying, "We've never..."

Amaris allowed her eyes to trace up the hand that rested on hers. She followed the outline of Nox's arm, past the bend in her elbow, over her shoulder and directly onto the face that would not look away. It took more bravery to hold this stare than it had to dive beneath the beseul, to battle the ag'dru-rath, to escape the university, or to outlast the mad king. This was the kind of fear she didn't want to escape.

The conversation they'd had in their dreamscapes had been beautiful. They'd been in their underthings, holding one another while they felt no shame, no embarrassment, only transparency of their lives and their paths and their loves. It had been so easy to talk while one slept. Discussing their dalliances and pressing their mouths together as fingers clutched at fabric had come as easily as breathing.

The presence of flesh and breath and life was terrifying.

Amaris's mouth parted and she found only four words. As her lips quivered and her eyes blinked, her eyebrows knit with such conflicting emotion that the only sentence she could muster was "I don't know how."

It was enough.

"I do," Nox replied, voice an ache and a prayer.

And as the music played and the fire crackled and popped behind its glass, a new movement joined the night. Nox hooked her hand beneath Amaris's elbow to urge her to the bed's center. The reever followed the nudge, allowing herself to cross the invisible barrier she'd created when she'd sat. Her heart thundered in response, not with the rapid fear she'd felt

251

with her enemies. It wasn't even the hummingbird's thundering of the fiery passion she'd felt with the general. Her pulse was slow and loud as it pounded, each thud formative, rhythmic, and methodical as it molded her.

"Amaris," Nox said, tucking her hair behind her ear. She left her hand on Amaris as she asked, "I want this so badly. I want all of this—you and me. Is this what *you* want?"

There was a strain to her question, a tension, a moment that could have been terror. Amaris blinked against the question, against Nox's posture of uncertainty, against the shock and surprise that she'd even have to ask. Nox was normally so self-assured, so strong. She knew what to do, she knew the right thing. She was their queen, their source of strength, their cornerstone. But this moment, Amaris felt the weight as Nox placed the power in her hands. Her heart was Amaris's to break or hold.

"More than anything," Amaris promised.

There had never been three sweeter words in the common tongue.

Nox's hand found its place in a familiar notch it had known in her dreams as her knuckle curled beneath Amaris's chin. Her fingers trembled, if only slightly. Dark hair brushed against Amaris's shoulders and exposed collarbone as she leaned in close. Amaris flattened her hand against Nox's back, all space between them vanishing. This was it. She didn't want this to be a dream. She didn't want someone to shake her awake, or an interruption to break in, or for their night to end. She didn't want Nox to have any doubts that she was here for every drop of love and affection and longing that had been shared and unspoken in their years.

This wasn't about a prayer or a destiny or any predisposition that may have drawn them to one another. This was about two women who had loved each other inexplicably since they were brought into this world, and who had neither the courage nor the opportunity to truly take ownership of their feelings. This was about the countless moments their eyes had grazed, the thousands of times their hands had brushed, the moons they'd lain awake wondering if the other was also thinking of them. This was about the nights they'd wished the other had been there to hold them close. This was about the clutch and tug deep in the powerful space below their stomachs, as poignant as the tether around their hearts.

When Nox lowered her mouth as she'd done so many times in dreams, their hot, mingled breath of cinnamon and plum, juniper and snow was Amaris's last conscious thought before the night took on a mind of its own.

This wasn't the drizzle of affection. This wasn't a flash flood of infatuation. This was the river that forged valleys and carved mountains. This was the groundwater itself, the magic that had created the world. The music from the spelled object sang its support as its violins scored her rush of emotion in an intense, rhythmic strum. The deep cellos exploded with the accompanying base as they harmonized the melody with clear, eager violins.

Amaris was peerless in battle. She'd spent years in combat training. But nothing could have prepared her for Nox's leg as it tucked beneath Amaris's knee in a sweeping motion, both rolling until Nox planted a hand on either side of her, Amaris landing firmly on her back. Her head hit the pillow and her neck arched back as she gasped toward the headboard. She closed her eyes, groaning against the haze of kiss, of touch, as Nox's mouth moved from her cheek to chin, her throat, her collarbone, dragging lips and teeth and tongue over each space.

Oh, goddess. She'd experienced elements of this pleasure in dreams, but reality was so much sharper. If Nox's dream walking had been the prick of a needle, then the real thing was the puncture of a pointed sword.

Nox dragged her mouth south as she traced her way down Amaris's stomach, pushing the golden tunic up beyond her navel, then her sternum. Amaris began to lift her shirt, but Nox's hand shot up with a flick, grabbing her wrist, stopping Amaris before she had the chance to move.

Amaris had nothing clever to say. She had no thoughts. Only gasps, only want.

Nox's smile flicked in a wicked glimmer of teeth. A full-body blush spread through every part of Amaris, cooking her with its heat. This was the feeling, the moment, the very thing she craved. She'd spent so much of her life scraping to feel powerful and heard and capable that the release of being dominated soaked into every fiber of her being. Here, she didn't need to be in control. She didn't need to worry or stress or fear or be ready.

She could let go.

Amaris surrendered to the pin of her hands, allowing the queen to continue her trail of teeth, mouth, tongue, and kisses that traced down the space between her breasts, her abdomen, her navel with slowness and intentionality. Each movement sent shivers down her spine. She wanted more. She wanted it faster. She wanted it now. The want became an ache as Nox stopped.

"Sit up."

Amaris obeyed.

"Lift your hands."

She inhaled sharply but didn't look away as she raised her hands above her head, allowing Nox to tug the silken bronze tunic that had been tailored for her over her head. She'd been bare breasted beneath the top, and a hand flew to cover any trace of vulnerability on instinct.

Nox moved her hands away and eyed her again. She stopped, and she waited.

Between shallow sips of breath, Amaris nodded her wordless, eager consent.

Yes. Yes, yes, yes.

Nerves, urgency, and yearning consumed her as she gave herself over. Nox slid her hands down Amaris's arms, landing on her thin wrists as she guided her onto her back.

"Lie down," Nox murmured against her throat, sending every inch of Amaris's skin into the chill of gooseflesh.

Nox could have spent the night exploring every inch of Amaris from the tip of her head to her toes. This was too precious to rush. She savored every gasp, each small sound and all the delicious squirms that betrayed Amaris's pleasure. Every noise, every buck of the hip, every hint at how badly Amaris wanted this only fueled her, heightening Nox's thrill and the wet slick of desire.

Amaris's moans were music, every bit as beautiful as the cadence of the violins. This would be no quick release. She wanted to see it in the urgency of the way Amaris ground her hips, the silent plea she was making for Nox's mouth to go further and further beyond the barrier of what little clothing remained.

Her mouth traced farther south, over her pants at first. Moisture soaked through the silken material of Amaris's pants as Nox kissed along her inner thigh. She smiled to herself, luxuriating in each wonderful victory. She kissed down the sensitive parts of one leg, taunting with her nearness and the fabric's barrier. Her other hand ran along the opposite leg, thumb tracing farther north as the string instruments continued to pick up their tempo. She pressed a hand into Amaris's hips to keep her pinned to the bed as they rolled, grinding with the steady up and down of ocean waves. When Nox tucked her fingertips into the waist-high lip of her pants, Amaris lifted her hips from the mattress without any further encouragement.

"Please," she breathed.

"Patience." Nox clucked her tongue.

She tossed the bronze pants into a silken crumple on the floor, then sat back on her knees and began to remove her own clothing, lifting her black silken dress over her head. This was further than they'd ever gone, more than she'd let herself hope. Now she needed the hot touch of skin on skin more than words could say.

Amaris ran a hand down the length of her own body, slipping it between her legs as if guiding Nox south. Nox bit her lip, holding in the chuckle as she slipped her palm over Amaris's, interlacing their fingers as she forced her hand back to the pinned place beside her head. Amaris tightened her grip with bruising strength, holding her hand as her mouth returned to Amaris's abdomen, leaving several wet, taunting kisses as she worked her way to two pale, perfect breasts.

She released her hand to drag her fingertips along the small curvature of Amaris's breast to where it converged in her tender, sensitive pink peak. She sucked lightly, lifting her eyes to watch what made the reever moan, what caused her sharp inhalations, and what made her back truly arch, from testing her teeth on the perfect, pebbled nipple to working her hand over the opposite breast. The music continued to sing as a third party in the room. The fiddles rang high and bright, an intense counter-harmony as the song beyond them swelled, keeping time to their pleasure. She let out a low, appreciative breath at the body below her, murmuring over the firelight and how it created daring lines as it painted itself down their naked bodies.

The beautiful bend of shadows, the delectable cut of light...for the love of the goddess...this. This was art.

"Kiss me," came Amaris's breathless plea.

Nox's lips were on hers in an instant, mouths, tongues, breaths intertwined. She grabbed onto Nox, tracing lines with her fingertips down her back. Her mouth remained locked in the kiss as she felt a hand travel south. Three soft fingers grazed down the length of her sex, exploring the sensitive entrance before they returned to its top where her nerves bundled in fireworks of pleasure.

Fuck, she cursed in her head. At least, she'd thought it had been in her head. From Nox's single, sensual laugh, there was a chance she'd lost control over what escaped her mouth. She couldn't be held responsible for anything she said or did when this felt fucking divine.

Those three fingers continued to move, gently massaging

the surface area at the apex of her thighs. She couldn't maintain the kiss, too breathless, too enraptured to keep the rhythm of teeth and tongues. She dug the crown of her head into the pillow as she moved off the sheets. Nox rested her forehead on the soft place where Amaris's neck and shoulder met as her hand continued to work.

Goddess, don't stop. Please, don't stop.

"Not yet," Nox said, circular strokes stopping as she cupped her palm over Amaris's sex.

If you're reading my thoughts, then you're cruel for stopping. Her eyes shot open to see why she'd ceased. Nox withdrew her hands in a dark denial, nearly in time with the break in the music. The orchestra from the rhythmic sphere had drawn itself back in a tempting allure as the verse teased the approach of the second bridge.

Amaris's mouth opened in protest at the climax she'd been denied, but she recognized the expression on Nox's face.

She was having too much fun.

Nox flipped her hair to one side, pushing it out of the way as she proceeded to drag wet lines down the center of the reever's pale skin. Amaris watched the motion as each kiss brought her lower, and closer, and lower, and closer. A small curse bubbled past her lips as her anticipation built.

And then, it happened.

As gentle as a landing butterfly, Nox brushed her mouth against the soaked, petal-soft center. Like a lover's kiss, she began slowly, tenderly. Amaris released a shuddering exhalation more telling than any words she could have spoken.

"I know," came Nox's reply, using the rumbles of her low, sultry voice as vibrations against the reever. Nox ran her hands along the strong, pale legs and flattened her thighs against the bed. Amaris relaxed into the vulnerable position, opening completely before her. The reever's eyes remained closed, so she didn't see the way Nox popped her index and middle finger of the right hand into her mouth. Frosted lashes fluttered open as Nox slid her fingers in, entire body bucking against the penetration.

"Fuck." Her word came out in a pant.

Nox continued slowly edging the tips of her fingers inside of the reever. It was as if the orchestra played only for them. The song's bridge raked them with anticipation as the swelling chorus of the rapidly timed, haunting symphony and its pulsing base lurked just around the corner.

Nox groaned as a familiar glow of heart and soul and lust and love burned within, succubus powers awakening. They swelled within her chest, creating a shimmer as she vibrated with energy. Decadent power, stronger than liquor and sweeter than honey, tingled every part of her from the inside out. She knew if she were to look in the mirror now, her skin would radiate the light of life itself. Her glossy hair would be the iridescent rainbow shine of slick, dark oil. Beauty and power were nothing compared to the very breath that turned to light on her tongue as love poured through her.

She watched Amaris's face as her hand and mouth worked, relishing the arch of her neck, her body, her back, savoring the tightening of her eyes as Nox urged her fingers in and out. Heat and flesh and nectar flooded her mouth, dripping down her chin. She was so grateful for the fire behind them, casting the low, beautiful glow of the sweat pooling in the ivory navel and shimmering on their bodies. She didn't want to miss a moment of this.

Above her, the snowy reever was lost to the world. She clutched the sheets at her side, eyes clenched tightly, each breath a shaky, dizzying pant. Nox's mouth worked the sensitive apex, suction and pressure all at once as her fingers beckoned forward, timing one movement with the other. She breathed sex and joy and life itself into Amaris, overcome as she watched the shimmer drip from the tip of her tongue and sparkle as it filled Amaris.

The jolt of power was electric.

Amaris sat up, crying out in pleasure, in desperation. Nox

would have paused if the reever hadn't dug her fingers into Nox's hair, balling them into fists as she begged for more. Once more, Nox snatched the wrists in her left hand and held them tightly as her mouth continued to work and her right hand flexed in its rhythmic motion to the music that filled the bedchamber. The room was aglow with supernatural light, with power, with pleasure, with music.

Amaris tugged her wrists from the hand that held them only once before succumbing to dopamine, to serotonin, to Nox as she tumbled back onto the pillow. Taut muscles refused to relax as her hips increased their rhythmic grind. Nox knew this moment. She understood the rhythm, the clench, the desperate need as she brought her closer and closer to climax. The moment between gasps increased to shallow pants until there was no sound of inhalation or exhalation.

Nox pulled her mouth away but kept her hand moving, rhythm unbroken. "Don't hold your breath," came her low, sultry command, words spoken against sensitive skin.

"But—" Amaris's protestation was scarcely more than a gasp.

"Breathe through it." Nox's mouth returned with a vengeance.

She knew enough not to break her stride. This time, she allowed Amaris's hands to grip her hair in their final moments while her right hand pumped and her tongue moved in its consistent, relentless wet circles of pressure. Nox said a silent prayer to the music, hoping it would never end. The endlessness of the gorgeous cadence of swelling instruments had been five minutes, then ten, then fifteen as the concert had wrapped around them in an unfamiliar and wild, never-ending song. She needed the timing of the orchestra as much as she needed her own movements. The hypnotic rapture of the instruments was their third in the bed, an active participant in their love.

Pleasure-soaked innermost walls tightened around her fingers, keeping time with the pulse of her heart as it joined the body's other telltale signs. Holding her breath may have brought Amaris to the precipice quicker, but each deep, steady breath raking through her would ensure an even more powerful, an even more all-encompassing, life-changing explosion.

So close. Goddess, you're so close. Purring against her sex, Nox said, "Come for me."

She held tight, refusing to let go, continuing to work through the moment until time itself froze. Amaris tensed in a noiseless arch, poised off the bed for one second, then two, then three, neither breathing nor moving as the music's climax sang out with the primal urgency of the violins and the high-pitched screams of the string instruments.

This was it.

Amaris remained there, trapped on the peak before release a moment longer. And when she shattered, it was into ten million pieces.

The climax shook her entire body, its epicenter at her womanhood emanating not outward, like those that had destroyed the castle and the ice and the world around it, but from within. Shining light pulsed through her as the song collapsed into the relief of its conclusion.

Nox's mouth continued to move throughout the first centralized shockwave. She removed her fingers after the second wave, and her mouth relinquished by the time the third began to rake Amaris's body. Nox wiped her bottom lip with her thumb, then popped it into her mouth. She knew her hair was a tangle of sweat and sex. And as she looked down at the woman made of snow, she knew with certainty she'd never known true joy before this moment.

Amaris was almost too tired to raise her head but was glad she did.

The firelight created a hellish halo of fire against Nox's blackened silhouette, lending itself to the full-body shudder Amaris felt. She groaned as she watched Nox suck on her glistening, wet fingers, then crawl over her, hovering just above her mouth. When they kissed, she tasted sex on her lips.

Nox rolled onto the pillow beside her. Amaris blinked, then blinked again. She sucked in a breath. "Holy fuck, you're beautiful."

"You're not so bad yourself," Nox purred.

"I mean..." Amaris didn't know how to explain the ethereal light behind Nox's eyes, god-like luster to her skin, the plum, exquisite curves of her hips, her breasts, her lips. She'd thought of Nox's tanned skin as bronze in the past, but now it truly sparkled and shone as if filled with metallic, coppery flecks of power. Amaris twitched again, aftershocks still seizing her, but she couldn't look away, drunk on Nox's incandescence.

Nox bit her lip, which was a sight too much.

She wanted more. She pulled Nox close, love and sweat and plums on her mouth. She mimicked what had felt so good to herself on her bed or in the tub countless times before, wetting her fingers before exploring Nox's body. She let herself appreciate the glorious, supple fullness of the raven queen's breasts. A sound escaped her lips as she appreciated the way Nox responded to the graze of her nipples. She wanted to remain in this haze and to know how Nox tasted.

"What do you think you're doing?"

Amaris disregarded her, too busy mapping every inch of the beautiful body before her in a way that she hadn't even allowed in her daydreams. She sucked gently on her earlobes. She kissed her eyes and nose and mouth before grazing her teeth along the side of her neck. She ran both hands simultaneously up the curves that moved from Nox's hips to her breasts, loving the sensation of soft, warm skin, of curves, of fullness. As she looked down at the woman beneath her, something in Nox's expression changed. Her dark eyes twinkled, a wicked flame crackling behind them.

Amaris quirked a brow, struck by the ache of curiosity. She leaned into the sensation as Nox dragged her nails from Amaris's temple to the crown of her hair, pushing loose strands away, freeing them from her face. Amaris sucked in a breath as her scalp tightened. Nox twisted a hand into hair, holding it up and away from her face as she knotted it in a fist at the back of her head in a tight, controlling grip.

"No, go lower."

The heat of a familiar blush crept from her neck and cheeks as she leaned into the rough pull of her hair. The authority pushed on an unexplainable hold between her ability to breathe and swallow. Her stomach knotted. A throb of pleasure shot through her as she lowered her mouth obediently, watching Nox's face as she awaited her next command.

"Relax your tongue. Good girl."

She could have screamed. Her entire body reacted to the hypnotic power of those two words. Her spine tingled, moaning against the glorious spark of strength and power. She'd heard them on only one other set of lips before this. She continued in slow, relaxed devotion. A palm slid up Nox's side, fingers digging into her hips. Nox grabbed her wandering hand and clutched it to her chest. She did not close her eyes and arch her back to the ceiling as Amaris had but kept her sights fixed on the reever who worshipped at her throne with every sensual kiss and lick.

With a low, sensuous command, Nox said, "Keep your circles slow. There you go. Steady. Consistent pressure."

She knew she'd succeeded instantly as erotic pleasure flowed into her mouth. She lapped it whole, unwilling and unable to suppress the appreciative moan as she drank deeply from the cup, more powerful than wine, more precious than gold. Nox's body flexed, her thighs buckling upward, pinning Amaris to her as her toes curled. Nox's other hand joined the first in her hair, grabbing closer to the scalp as it pulled.

"Don't stop," she inhaled sharply. "Don't slow down."

Never, she promised with her consistent, relentless licks.

Their eyes connected, and she could have died a happy woman seeing Nox's brows bunched, lips parted, face twisted in longing, in greed, in ecstasy. She would drown between the water of her spit and the ocean of Nox's natural flavors before she'd stop. Lakes of their pleasure pooled beneath her on the sheets.

Just as her jaw began to tire, Nox's other hand twisted into her hair. Her voice broke on her plea. "Don't stop! Goddess, don't stop. Keep going."

The desperation in Nox's voice might as well have been a magic spell.

She summoned whatever stamina she possessed and devoured her whole, crying out in pride and joy and victory when Nox buckled beneath her. Amaris's natural instinct was to raise her head, but Nox clamped her face down and her tongue continued its movements through the second flex of her hips, releasing only once she'd felt the third tremble.

"Holy fucking shit," Nox gasped, still clenching against waves of surprise and pleasure and utter goddess-damned joy. "Oh my goddess." She looked at Amaris in disbelief.

Amaris didn't have words. She couldn't even curse. The moment was too perfect. Nothing she could say would suffice. She couldn't believe someone so perfect, someone so beautiful, was here with her. If every sculpture in the world had tried, they would fail to capture Nox's essence. Neither painter nor poet could re-create what she saw. No religion, no tonic could match what she was feeling.

Nox's hands untangled in Amaris's hair as she continued to rock with her miscellaneously timed tremors. Amaris rested her head against the girl's inner thigh, grinning in pride at her accomplishment.

Nox finally extended her hands. "Get up here."

When Amaris crawled up the bed, she was met with the intimacy of tangled arms and legs over hips as they held one another. Their naked, sweat-soaked bodies melded into one as they faded into each other, their heart rates slowing until they matched pace and their tired kisses brushing against cheeks and necks. The intensity of their passion gave way to the deeper afterglow of something truer and deeper than the lust that had ached between them.

"I love you," Amaris murmured, eyelids heavy as she began to drift off to sleep.

"And I, you. Then, and now, and always."

Twenty-Two

Nox's eyes opened. It had been so perfect. Too good to be true. She was sure she must be dreaming... and yet.

It had been real. This was real. They were real.

Morning light filtered in through the diamond cuts of glass, casting tiny rainbows on the wall, the bed, on the naked, milky-white body beside her. She wiggled her fingers to touch the light, watching it dance, admiring the way it refracted against Amaris's silver strands while she slumbered.

Everything was perfect.

The fire had died in the night and now rested in a quiet pile of charcoal behind the glass. The music box still sang. Rather than the wild emeralds and night skies that had been conjured by the string instruments the night before, a gentle woodwind was singing a melody as soft as falling snow, as if understanding the quiet, early hour.

She was tempted to pinch herself. Nothing this wonderful had ever happened in her life. She ran a feather-soft touch down Amaris's shoulder, settling on the curve where her back and her hip indented. The reever scrunched her face like a sleeping cat, stretching and yawning as she lulled herself into alertness.

Nox stiffened against an acute, nauseating fear.

There was something she hadn't considered—a nightmare that could break this beautiful moment, smashing it to the ground and watching it scatter. She faced the distinct possibility that Amaris would open her eyes, look at the bed, at the crumpled sheets, at the night they'd shared, and show the crestfallen signs of regret.

Her mouth dried as she struggled to steady her heartbeat. Amaris squinted against the early light, fighting the waking world. Nox held her breath while the reever blinked awake. She tilted her face upward. When her lilac eyes met Nox, her rosy lips curved into a perfect smile.

Relief. Joy. Elation.

The love she felt was every bit as consuming as the pleasure they'd shared. She floated away on the feeling. Without understanding why, tears spiked against the inner corners of her eyes. Her heart squeezed as she looked into Amaris's face. "I can't believe you're real."

Pink cheeks, sleepy yawns, happy smiles met her in return. Amaris attempted to hide her face in the tangle of hands and sheets. Nox stopped her escape, pulling her into her arms.

"We're real."

They weren't a hope, or a feeling, or a prayer. No king would drag them from their beds. No queen would lock them between bars. They were puzzle pieces, the beauty of the spaces between things that made the world whole, crafted by the goddess as the only things that fit together in a world of chaos.

Amaris snatched Nox's hand from her cheek, bringing it to her mouth and brushing a kiss to her knuckles. "This is perfect."

"The only thing that could make it more perfect is—"

"Tea and cinnamon buns?"

If Nox hadn't already been suspicious that the concierge was listening in on their conversations, this would have convinced her. The voice in the metallic lily on Nox's wall asked if breakfast should be sent up to her, and she'd called back from the bed to send breakfast for two. If he'd heard them talking, then he'd also heard the show of his life.

Lucky man.

After thirty or so minutes, she'd answered the door barely clutching a sheet to her outline as she'd accepted the tray of fruits and rice and pastries and eggs from a flustered attendant. She winked at him, which sent him into a poorly concealed sputtering, blushing panic—one she enjoyed entirely too much. She closed the door and crawled back to bed with their food.

They remained happy and bare as they picked at the meal, sharing memories, jokes, and stories. Nox had a few anecdotes about Malik that earned a few chucked fruits, devolving into laughter until she retreated in apology. Amaris attempted to conjure equally horrifying facts about Gadriel, but unfortunately Nox could not be rattled. She merely grinned at Amaris's attempts.

"Okay." Nox lowered her voice conspiratorially. "The general doesn't seem to be someone who likes to share his toys. Am I going to have to liberate you from a dungeon anytime soon?"

Amaris spoke through a mouthful of sticky bun. "You're the queen. I'm pretty sure you get the final say."

"No, Snowflake." Nox ran her fingers along the reever's arm. "You get the final say. You belong to no one."

Nox had never known Amaris to articulate her emotions well, but throwing food was surely the lowest form of communication. She chuckled as she snatched half of the sticky bun out of the air. "Keep being a brat and I'll have reason to punish you later."

"Like you did last night?"

"Oh, sweet girl, did you think that was punishment?"

Amaris turned a cherry-red shade that Nox wasn't entirely sure she'd seen before. Perhaps she would have, if the night they'd shared hadn't been awash with the low, burgundy glow of dying firelight.

"What if," Amaris said slowly, "we stay here?"

"In Sulgrave?" Nox asked.

"In this moment. Surrounded by breakfast foods, nude in silken sheets, with each other. What if we don't liberate prisoners or thwart corrupt churches or save a continent?"

"That reevers' oath looking a little weaker these days, hmm?"

Amaris nuzzled into her. "You seem to have that effect on people."

"Perhaps," Nox sighed as she got to her feet, shrugging into a robe while Amaris redressed. "But you aren't people. You're…you."

Nox walked Amaris to her bedroom door, stopping her with her hand on the knob before setting her free. She tucked a single knuckle beneath Amaris's chin, nudging her face upward for a goodbye kiss every bit as deep and as passionate as the one they'd shared the night before. Amaris disappeared behind the door with mussed, white hair and pink, flustered cheeks.

Nox returned to her room and waited for the door to click before she melted. Back to the door, she slid to the floor, heart erupting into bonfires and fireworks and lightning bolts at once. She grinned to herself, burying her head in her hands as she covered her smile. It took a while for Nox to ground herself, stepping down from the cloud on which she floated, but eventually she got to her feet and began to ready herself for the day.

Still humming from their night together, she decided to make the most of her buzz. She couldn't very well cross the perils of the Frozen Straits to stay inside her room. Their midnight walks to secret meetings scarcely counted as the proper tour, and if they were going to see distant, fabled lands, then dammit, they'd better explore.

Yazlyn seemed to have the same idea, as she'd been knocking on everyone's doors for the better part of twenty minutes.

"Just wait," Nox called while stepping into a dress. "Go find a book."

Yazlyn growled something back about how if she'd wanted

to read, she could have stayed in Gwydir, but she seemed to leave them alone until the others were ready. By the time Nox emerged, Amaris and Gadriel had already joined the sergeant in the common area.

Their mission was grave, yes, but there was a levity about the crew. It was impossible not to feel some excitement about the unseen lands. Few had made the crossing, and even fewer had come from the continent only to go back again. So little was known about Sulgrave that they were making history just by being among its people.

"You look like you have a plan," Nox said, creating friction between her palms as she rubbed them together.

Amaris patted the place beside her. Their arms interlaced the moment she plopped onto the cushions.

"We do," Yazlyn answered for the group. "Is Ash coming out, or do I need to drag him by the ears?"

"I think he's still sour," Yazlyn said. She cast a meaningful look out the glass wall as if tossing her attention to wherever Tanith was being kept.

"I don't care how he's feeling. It's not every day people get to visit Sulgrave. He's coming. Now if I—"

"I'll get him," Amaris volunteered.

✦

"Ash?" Amaris rapped her knuckles lightly against the door. She waited a few beats before letting herself in. Still buoyant from the night before, she smiled as she asked, "We're headed into the city. Are you almost ready?"

She found him sitting in the corner chair so rigid and uncomfortable that it appeared to exist for decorative purposes rather than for functionality.

"I'm not really in the mood to go out."

An empathetic spasm clenched her belly as looked at him. He'd always been such a smartass. He was clever, sharp, tenacious, and kind. This conflicted, brooding persona was something new entirely.

She twisted her mouth, remembering how she'd felt the night she'd thought she'd lost the reevers in the forest. She'd been willing to do anything to get them back and keep the ones she'd loved close.

Her soft steps padded against the floor as the black satin shoes they'd provided with a thin leather sole scarcely made a sound.

"Ash, look at me."

His jaw remained clenched in some effort at stoicism, but she knew him well enough to see how his amber eyes struggled to hold back emotion.

"We're going to get her out. Tanith is one of us. Why don't you come with us and get a lay of the land? Consider it a reconnaissance dispatch. You can better help Tanith if you understand her people, her city, and maybe even figure out where the hell they keep the dungeons. How's that sound?"

His chest rose and fell in a quick huff. "It sounds like you're trying to coax a child to put on its shoes."

But it worked. Ash got dressed, joined the others, and exactly fifteen minutes into their trek into the city, Amaris began to wish she'd left him at the Diplomatic Hall. The concierge had supplied them with the local currency as a diplomatic grace, given Nox's royal status.

"Must be nice," Yazlyn remarked.

"Thank you." Nox beamed, fanning herself with the bills. "It *is* nice."

Navy-blue flags emblazoned with silver swords dotted the streets nearest the Diplomatic Hall, should they have had any doubt that they were in Territory One. Most shopkeepers were shocked to see the bewildering presence of a foreigner. Some faces were painted with distrust upon meeting the motley crew, while others sparkled with amusement. A stop into a tea shop and a short conversation about the most popular item resulted in a lovely sweet, caffeinated drink that had the thickness of milk but was as green as spring grass. Gadriel loved it, but Amaris claimed it tasted like hot algae.

They emptied their wallet on unfamiliar sweets, drinks, and delicacies, until the woman serving their drinks crossed to their table.

"If you don't like the tea," she said, "I can get you a coffee concentrate."

They ordered one tiny cup of dark liquid for the table, which was met with mixed results. It was too bitter, too dark, too sour, too different. Yazlyn, however, sipped at the mud-dark liquid then looked up at them with the eyes of someone who'd found religion. She asked if she could leave with ten more, and the woman cautioned that it should only be consumed in the morning, as it would keep you awake all day.

"It's official," Yazlyn announced. "I'm moving to Sulgrave."

The immense alpine cliffs filled them with renewed awe and muttered remarks every time they stepped out of a shop and returned to the streets. Raascot was mountainous. Gwydir was famous for its mines of labradorite-filled mountains. Uaimh Reev was built into a granite mountain. But these snowy, needle-like spindles were unlike anything Amaris had ever seen.

"Do you think you could summit them?" Nox asked between bites, clutching a skewer of fried dough in a syrupy sweet and savory sauce. She looked between the Raascot fae and the mountain peaks.

"Honestly?" Gadriel rubbed at his chin while examining the conquest. "If they're as high as I think they are, we'd have a layer of ice on our wings before reaching the zenith."

She popped the last one into her mouth, then swallowed and asked, "How can you gauge their height from here?"

He gestured to a mountain. A tiny strip of silver indicated its runoff. It tumbled from the ledge like a bride's veil, disappearing in a mist somewhere near the center of the cliff with no pool at its base. A clean, cool breeze tufted the mist to one side in the distance, bringing with it the scent of melting snow.

"Can we do something other than eat?" Ash asked. His personal rain cloud dampened every murmur of admiration, every new, exciting find, every spectacular sight.

They took a break from warm drinks and delicious snacks to gather as much information as they could about Sulgrave. The seven territories, as it turned out, branched into the valleys between mountains, with the exception of territories One and Seven, which served as the heart at the center of Sulgrave. Tiny specks of hillside cabins dotted a few of the green, sparsely populated valleys, which may or may not have been unincorporated mountain towns or small villages. Nox promised to sketch the layout for their records, and they made a few loose promises to ask around and collect intelligence on the elusive kingdom before they returned home to Gwydir to update their maps.

The mountains broke only for the accompanying territories that had branched into the valleys surrounding the primary city. They assumed that there were outlying mountain towns or small villages that didn't identify with a proper territory, but their assumptions were mere conjecture based on the vastness of Sulgrave. It seemed impossible that all of its residents could fit neatly into seven nearby territories.

"How do we go about getting more information without looking suspicious?" Gadriel asked.

"I think ignorance is our best defense," Amaris said.

"Or Nox can flirt it out of them," Yazlyn added.

Afternoon became evening. The sun dipped between peaks, casting a lavender glow over the valley. The diners turned to observe them as they entered, some dropping their utensils to their plates as conversation halted. Nox, in her queenliest voice, greeted the room with a beaming smile as their friends from the south, then plopped confidently down at the only empty table. When the nervous server asked them what they wanted to eat, Nox spoke for the table when she decided that this was a night made for drinking.

Drinks were served in small, clear sipping glasses. Yazlyn

shot hers back and grinned appreciatively as it had gone down like juice. She asked for another round before the others had even tasted theirs. Several shots later, the party was having the time of their lives. They lamented that Malik and Zaccai couldn't be there to experience this with them. They shared embellished stories of terrifying crows, of castle invasions, of armies of the undead.

Warmth bloomed from Amaris's belly to her cheeks. Her fingertips tingled as she reveled in the night. She leaned into Gadriel, who draped his arm around her in return. And maybe the world was dangerous, and fragile, and uncertain. Maybe things never looked the way you thought they might. But at least for now, everything was pretty fucking perfect.

Perhaps it was the booze-colored glasses casting a rosy haze over the evening, but it seemed to Amaris that even Ash had shed his storm cloud as they finished their dinner and drinks and stumbled back to the Diplomatic Hall as a full, happily buzzed crew.

Amaris tumbled into Nox's bed, and the women fell asleep tangled in one another with smiles on their faces and liquor on their breath.

Sleep came on soft, loving arms and left with cruel, violent ice picks.

"Ow," Amaris grumbled, squinting against the first signs of morning light. She clutched at her temples as a fearsome headache shook her.

"I think I'm going to be sick," Nox said.

Amaris's eyes remained closed as she slapped at the bed uselessly, offering a flailing, pitiful hand for comfort when Nox got up to sprint to the washroom. She opened her mouth to ask if Nox needed help, but her stomach roiled in return.

After a few healing tonics and a particularly long bath, they were ready to take on the new day.

Amaris passed through the common room on the way to her own bed chambers and found Yazlyn passed out on a chair. A cloudy memory of the sergeant having a fit and refusing to go to bed itched the place behind her ears. Amaris shook her awake and was met with a string of curses, mussed hair, and a puddle of drool.

"Can you bring me tea?" Yazlyn mumbled, burying her head into the chair once more.

"Sure, I'll—"

"No, wait." Yazlyn held up a single finger. "What was that bitter brown stuff? The strong one. Bring me that. Bring me fifteen of them."

The day stretched on. A few of them wandered into the city to eat or to take walks in staggered intervals, but there would be no more collective outings. Yazlyn left the Hall for a few hours when Ryu had called upon her to invite her to lunch. When the others asked if it had been a matter of planning, she'd told them to mind their business.

Just before dinner, Amaris realized she hadn't seen Ash since the fourth bell.

"I'm sure he's exploring," Yazlyn said, but she sounded unconvinced.

"Or he's trying to find where they're holding Tanith," Amaris responded. Everyone quieted at the thought. When he returned that night, it was with the solemn expression of someone in no mood to talk.

And so life continued much the same for the next two days, doing the best they could to establish normalcy, save for Tanith's absence. Every time Ash attempted to bring her up, he was given a stilling look and urged to write down his thoughts, as they never knew who might be listening. Amaris had seen Ash through a variety of life's highs and lows, but she had no idea what to do with his ever growing discontent. She understood as best she could, but there was nothing they could do except wait until the agreed-upon church meeting.

Gadriel, who'd rarely spoken of his parents in the time Amaris had known him, carried on with his aloof attitude. He made the same face that others made toward Ash whenever someone tried to mention his parents. Though she didn't understand his motives, she trusted his lead and was glad to ignore plans for conquering the world as long as Gadriel continued to bring back treats when he found them.

Yazlyn would go off in search of the bitter drink that made Amaris's nose wrinkle and stay gone for far too long before returning with a grin on her face and evasive lines about how ladies don't kiss and tell. They learned all they could about the city and its layout, and Amaris helped with their maps. Nox stole away when she could to visit Fjolla in the zoology stables, ensuring she was well cared for, and delivering a combination of sausages, soothing pats, and promises that she wouldn't be there much longer.

Then as all things do, their fun came to an end.

Twenty-Three

NOX STRETCHED HER HAND TO THE ACCOMPANYING pillow and traced her fingers along where she wished Amaris would have been. She'd awoken alone. It had been three days since they'd made love, and the dopamine from their entanglement still quirked her lips into a smile. She hadn't bathed the morning after. She'd clung to the sweat, the taste, the smells of juniper and fresh snow as if it had been a perfume.

The time had come for Nox to do what they'd set sail to achieve.

Tonight, she would go to church. She grimaced at the thought as she looked at herself in the washroom mirror, making a pained expression as she raked her fingers through her snarls. If she was going to sit in a sanctuary, she should probably do so without looking like a sexual deviant.

Nox scrubbed herself clean and debated what to do with her hair. She reached into the pocket of her robe and fingered the emerald ribbon. On the one hand, it would be wise to tie up her hair with the protective armor. On the other, she'd need to leave her hair unbound in order to cover her rounded ears. And hair was perhaps the least of her worries.

She exited the washroom and tapped on the silver lily fastened to her doorframe. "Hello?"

"May I help you, Your Highness?" the lily responded.

"I'd like to attend a church service tonight, but I'm unclear as to proper temple attire in Sulgrave. I'd appreciate your advice."

The lily confidently informed her that any of her clothing options would be fine, as it was only church members with assigned stations who wore distinct colors and garb. She supposed if the ribbon would draw too much attention, then carrying Chandra was certainly out of the question. With a heavy sigh, she apologized to her axe, then selected a solid black dress with long sleeves and headed for the common room. She found Gadriel and Amaris sitting closely beside one another as they examined a spread of loose papers.

"You're ready," Gadriel said, lifting his brows in surprise.

"I am," she responded. "Where are the others?"

"They're..." Gadriel's voice dropped off as he carefully selected his words. "On a walk."

Amaris scrawled, *They're scouting the area around the church,* on a piece of paper and turned it around, holding it up for Nox to see.

She sucked in a lip. She struck a casual voice, not interested in overselling her showmanship as she said, "I really wish you two would honor the All Mother with me, but I'll say prayers for you both."

"What can I say?" Gadriel smirked. "I'd have to meet the goddess in the flesh. That would make me a believer."

Nox flipped him a vulgar gesture while Amaris jabbed him in the ribs with a sharp elbow. He devolved into laughter while she turned a violent shade of ruby. Nox left the pair to their plotting and returned to her room to do some note-taking of her own, draining the fog of thoughts from her mind as they spilled onto paper. She used the magic quill, reiterating her plan to her general.

My mission is to be able to re-create the layout, should we need to access the church again. Try to get a head count for staff, guards, and others on the premises. Make mental notes of any important verbiage or standout words. Do not engage.

Gadriel wrote back:

Correct. Do not engage. This is reconnaissance, that's all. You're in good hands. I trust Ash. Amaris and I will find my parents and we'll both converge with information.

She tapped the quill against the page, then decided against voicing her concerns. She did trust Ash. They'd crossed the continent together. They were friends. He'd been a voice of reason when she'd needed it time after time. He was going through something right now, but he was a reever, and Gadriel was right. She was in good hands.

The clock ticked on. The sun moved. Her nerves heightened. She paced in the common room as she counted the achingly slow seconds. She'd just forced herself to settle onto a chair and flip through a picture book when the metallic door to the platform opened and she turned to see a frazzled-looking sergeant. Several curls spilled free from Yazlyn's single braid as if she'd been fussing with her hair. She swallowed hard but said nothing.

Nox's eyes flared. "Well?"

The fae brought a hand to her brow. "Don't be mad."

Nox's chest tightened. The words settled in her stomach like stones. "What happened?"

"I may have lost Ash."

Maybe Nox should have been angry. Perhaps she should have felt hot, or cold, or scared, but the only emotion that found her was confusion. The space between her brows created two clean lines as they pinched. She tilted her head.

Ash was a combat-ready adult, not an untrained puppy.

Yazlyn was not his parent. And lastly, he couldn't possibly get lost in a city where the Diplomatic Hall was such a towering landmark.

As if anticipating her puzzlement, Yazlyn said, "We went to the church. We were both there, and then I turned, and he was gone. I can't know for sure but...I think he left to go find Tanith."

Nox had closed her book entirely. She unfolded her legs from where they'd been tucked beneath her, planting them on the floor as she turned toward the still-anxious sergeant. "So, he's looking for the location of the jail?"

"Not exactly."

Nox rose to her feet. "Spit it out, Yaz."

She scrunched her face in reluctance, preemptively squinting against blowback. "He went into the church."

The air in Nox's lungs evaporated. "He *what*?"

"I think he's looking to see if there's a way the church can exonerate her."

Her eyes darkened. "He wouldn't."

"I don't think he'd compromise our investigation. He's not a fool, but—"

"But he's in love," Nox finished through gritted teeth.

✦

Nox created a game called *Has There Ever Been a More Boring Moment?*

While she sat in the pew, aching from the need to do something—*anything*—else, she conjured a few contenders. She hadn't particularly enjoyed a few of the lessons in Farleigh, especially when they'd forced her to do multiplication tables. She'd found her travel to Yelagin monotonous, as much of the southern kingdom looked very much the same. Many patrons at the Selkie were dull and droned on relentlessly, causing her eyes to glaze as she'd feigned interest.

They were boring, sure.

But it was nothing compared to the mind-numbing tediousness and displeasure of sitting in the back of a three-hour church service, partially concealed behind a pillar so that she wouldn't draw attention. She'd take rage and heartbreak over the impulse of wanting to claw your own eyes out rather than listen to the Blessed Obediences read a single time more, both in the native Sulgrave language, then in the common tongue.

She wasn't sure what she had been expecting.

Sulgrave had been so unique contrasted against all of her lived experiences that she'd really managed to convince herself that religion wouldn't be miserably dull. There hadn't even been singing.

If it weren't for the glass ceiling that revealed the changing clouds and shifting light as evening fell into the early parts of night, she would have had no sense for how much time had truly passed. It had been a fortunate distraction. She saw one cloud that looked like a dragon. Another reminded her quite a bit of Fjolla. Three rows up, a small fae child seemed to point at the same puffy configuration she'd spotted before being shushed by its mother.

Fae lights flickered and glowed as the sun disappeared altogether, providing the only illumination apart from the twinkling dots of stars overhead.

Maybe she'd be able to spot a few constellations if she looked hard enough. She'd never studied astronomy, but if she were in this seat for the rest of her life the way she expected, she'd have time to memorize the shapes and placements of every celestial body and sketch them later. Hell, by the time the service ended, she could probably teach her own astronomy course in the scholar's wing.

She'd long since scanned the crowd and found a few white-winged seraphim, but there were no signs of Ash. She'd even lost hope that she'd catch a glimpse of the Speaker. She noted a few individuals clad in green or gray as they denoted the monetary and service arms of the church, but she spied no one in red.

She hadn't realized she'd been clenching her jaw until the bishop began saying something that made it sound like the service was coming to a close. Relief loosened every muscle. Those around her stood and she expected to be dismissed, but instead, the dreary man in white and gold announced that it was time for everyone to break into small groups to discuss the message and receive the blessing from the All Mother.

For fuck's sake.

Her eyes flashed to Dhamir. The woman had led her to the church and whispered hushed instructions about best practices but had then quickly split off, with the comte from Territory Seven sitting a few rows ahead of her. Nox agreed it would have certainly been conspicuous if the comte were to have arrived with the foreign dignitary. Dhamir jerked her chin to the door with the smallest motion. Was she saying Nox should leave?

She furrowed her brow, and Dhamir's eyes tightened in return.

Yes. Better than birthday sex or Yule presents or chocolates on her pillow: she was being set free from this goddess-awful lesson in torture. She could go.

She hesitated for the barest of moments before obliging. After sitting through nearly four boring hours, now in smaller group settings would perhaps have been the first opportunity to talk to true believers. It may have been the one interesting, helpful thing. She wasn't entirely sure why the comte woman felt she should leave, but she buttoned her cloak and donned her hood. Other churchgoers filtered into smaller gatherings and filed down the corridors to offshoots from the sanctuary. She did her best to stay near the believers around her as if following them to the group before turning for the door.

Nox took a few steps toward the large front doors when a hand stopped her.

"Well, hello there. You're new." The voice spoke in the common tongue in mollifying quiet, but the words were neither soothing nor kind. This was the placating tone of a butcher urging a cow into the slaughterhouse.

Dread speared through her.

Nox turned slowly on her heel and stifled a gasp at what she saw. The woman before her wore gray, but this was no Gray Matron. She would have taken Agnes's presence any day over the eerie face smiling back at her. All of the fae had sharp canines and pointed ears that this woman possessed, but there was something distinctly terrifying in her eyes. Her irises seemed too large even for the fair folk. In fact, they appeared to contain no white at all.

Nox flashed her most charming smile. "Yes, I'm just visiting. It was a beautiful service, but I'd best be off."

The woman tsked quickly as she hooked an arm around Nox's elbow and led her away from the door. Nox locked eyes with Dhamir one last time as she turned toward the hall and recognized the unmistakable expression of alarm.

No. No, no.

Nox stopped in her tracks. She was no passive woman concerned with politeness. She would not be intimidated. "Unfortunately, my friends are expecting me, and I'm already running quite late. Thank you so much for trying to include me."

"I insist."

The woman slipped her hand from the sleeve of Nox's elbow to the skin of her wrist. Nox's eyes shot wide, lips parting in a silent scream as her arm went limp, numbness and tingling beginning at the stranger's hand and crawling from wrist to shoulder, as if she had fallen asleep on their limb. She tried to jerk her hand from the woman's grasp but had no control, no sensation, no power over her arm.

By the time she found her voice to cry out, the tingling had worked its way over her neck and into her mouth, slowly paralyzing everything it touched.

Her heart skidded painfully. Tears pricked at her lids as panic overtook her. What if it reached her lungs? Her brain?

She was powerless as the woman hurried her into a side room before her feet gave out. She couldn't feel them. She couldn't feel anything.

A loud click told her the door had been shut and locked behind them. The happy sounds of churchgoers vanished in an instant, smothered by some dampening power.

From her place on the floor, Nox could move only her eyes.

They were not alone.

The woman in gray yanked Nox into a hard-backed chair, grunting against her dead weight, but Nox was no longer interested in her abductor.

Inhale. Pull it together. Exhale.

Nox couldn't let herself panic. If she was going to make it out alive, she had to get her breathing. She had to calm her mind. She had to focus on the true threat in the room.

Familiarity rose like bile in the back of her throat. The room didn't smell like vanilla. There wasn't a golden curl in sight. But there was an eerie similarity, an energetic signature, a vileness she would have recognized anywhere. Nox had seen one other woman in her life who'd been emeralds and sapphires and pride personified. She'd been taken by the woman, she'd been manipulated by her, and she'd watched her die. This was not Millicent, but it may as well have been.

"Who are you?" she tried to ask. What came out instead was akin to a gargle.

The woman before her was a peacock personified. The tall, slender fae woman was in the blues, greens, and purples known only to the proud bird, all with a crushed shimmer as the colors melded together. Unlike the dark eyes common to the people of Sulgrave, hers were a piercing sapphire. Though her skin retained the gilded undertone of the Sulgrave people, there was a curiousness to her hair. It was as dark as Nox's at the roots, but by the time it reached her collarbone, it began to bleed into a pale, colorless silver. Perhaps she'd spelled her looks to take on distinguishing features, but the final effect gave Nox the sort of chill achieved only by poisonous snakes.

This woman was a predator.

The peacock dismissed the gray-clad servant, which would either be really good or really bad. She wasn't sure if she wanted to be alone with this stranger, but the servant was no better.

The moment the woman left, Nox's finger twitched, if only slightly. An uncomfortable tingle became a fierce burn as blood returned to her hand. She attempted to clench her jaw against the budding pain but couldn't.

"I want to thank you for returning a member of my faithful," the peacock began. Her voice shared the musical lilt that Nox had grown to recognize in Sulgrave, but the tone was off, as if the woman's song were sung in a minor key. Each word stuck to the one before it. "I hadn't expected Tanith's return, but you've patched her up nicely."

Nox's entire hand twitched. She watched the woman's face, ensuring that she wasn't watching the subtle gesture as Nox worked the blood through her palm and forced a fist. Her tongue moved inside her mouth, then her lips. She wiggled her toes inside her shoes. Perhaps she couldn't stand yet, but feeling was returning quickly. When it did, she wasn't sure if she should try for the door handle or charge the woman.

If she was going to buy herself time, she had to try her voice again. She bit down on the bait dangled before her and asked, "You knowingly sent your Red to die?"

The woman flashed a dismissive hand, each fingernail painted with the same crushed-jewel cobalts, emeralds, and amethysts of her dress. Her blue-green shoulders rolled dramatically with her response. "Don't be ignorant. She went voluntarily. Unity is a beautiful, noble cause, wouldn't you say, Your Highness? A queen who, if I'm not mistaken, brought two kingdoms under one banner."

Nox rolled her foot, testing its weight. She kept her movements subtle, ensuring they drew no attention. "I'm bringing peace to kingdoms on the precipice of war. Can you say the same?"

It was antagonistic, but rage might be what she needed to keep the woman's focus off of her hands and feet. She flexed her forearms beneath her sleeve, then her biceps. Soon, she'd be mobile.

"The continent has lacked a firm hand for a long, long time. I intend to do your people a great favor in helping them see the light of the All Mother by bringing us together." She took a testing step toward the edge of the room as she inspected her nails.

Nox flexed her calves, then her thighs. A minute longer and she could be on her feet. "And how's that?"

The peacock's smile was too wide, too toothy, her sharpened canines gleaming wickedly as she grinned. "Imagine this, Southern Queen: a little bird tells me that not only have the southern kingdoms converged from two threats into one but that their new ruler had arrived in my mountains? My valley? It was almost too good to be true. How much more amazing was it, then, to find her sitting in the back of my church?"

Silence.

The peacock's eyes narrowed. "The goddess desires this. Can't you see her hand? She wrapped you in a bow and delivered you to me. The All Mother is truly good, and unity is her will."

Nox hedged. "What should I call you?"

The Speaker arched a brow. "You should call me by title, Your Highness, as I will yours."

"I am the queen of Raascot and Farehold, and my name is Nox. Give me your name, Speaker."

Amusement sparkled behind her eyes. Her lips twitched in a feline smile. "Daifa is my name, though no one has referred to me with such informality in a century."

"From one leader to another, it seems only right."

Daifa's large, blue eyes glimmered with an electric

intensity. "Perhaps time will tell what we become to one another, Nox."

Nox knew she was supposed to feel fear, or dread, or some shock of realization, but none of those emotions felt quite right. Her lower lip raised in an unimpressed scrunch. She had known for a while that she was talking to the Speaker. Somehow, the confirmation spoiled the thrill. Calm settled over her as the same strength that had carried her through years at the Selkie bubbled to the front. She said, "You wanted your Reds to clear the path for you to take control in Farehold and Raascot? How original: a leader is hungry for power. I have to say, I'm disappointed in your lack of imagination."

The skin around the Speaker's eyes tightened. Her nostrils flared, if only slightly. The taunt may have cost her, but Nox was proud her words had hit their mark. The Speaker remained silent as she allowed the disrespect to ripple through her.

Nox engaged her core, then relaxed it. This could be it. She might be able to stand. But if she got to her feet and collapsed, she would spoil her only chance at escape. She needed to know for sure. Biding her time, she asked, "Your information...it came from Tanith?"

She wasn't sure what she'd expected, but it certainly wasn't the self-satisfied smirk that twisted Daifa's lips. The Speaker said, "This? Oh, no. The comtes and their laws have Tanith under particularly close guard, though they won't be able to hold her for much longer. She does not answer to their laws."

Her heart thudded. If she didn't hear it from Tanith...

"You underestimate my faithful."

"Shouldn't they be the All Mother's faithful?"

Daifa positively sparkled. "I was made aware of your arrival the moment you entered the city. Imagine my surprise when it was one of your compatriots who sought me out?"

No. No, not Ash. It was impossible. She was lying.

Nox didn't need to hear any more. If she didn't go now, she never would. She twisted quickly, lunging for the door with every drop of strength. Her limbs were lead-heavy, but she could move. But the moment she reached the door...

She missed the handle. Confused, she tried again. Acidic panic stained the back of her throat as adrenaline pulsed through her. She grasped and failed, fingers glancing off the space around the door as though it had been shielded.

Again, then again. Nothing. She tried banging her fists against the door, but they would not connect. Her hands fell to her side as she realized with horrifying certainty that she would not be escaping. She swallowed down the knot in her throat and turned to see Daifa's light, airy amusement.

"Do you know how I was discovered as Speaker?"

Nox straightened her spine and lifted her chin. She leveled her most royal gaze and banished her fear as she asked, "The position opened up and you were the bitchiest?"

The Speaker clicked her tongue with several short, dismissive staccatos. While their eyes remained unbroken, the Speaker raised a hand and made a short, flicking motion with her wrist.

Nox's eyes began to widen as visions populated before her eyes. The blood drained from her, and with it all hope. "No."

The Speaker's smile grew. "Oh, yes."

Twenty–Four

Y AZLYN WAS ABOUT TO LOSE HER MIND.
She'd counted all of the bricks on the nearby wall.
She'd plucked the tiny bits of grass between cobblestones.
She'd looked for everything red. She'd played a game where,
if she saw three birds in ten minutes, she won. There was
no prize.

Hours had gone by, and she'd run out of things to seek.
She was cold. There were no stray cats to call or even stones
to skip across the alley. She tried numbering stars for a short
while, but the fae lights that illuminated the many streets of
Sulgrave dulled them, stealing their shimmer. She wished
Ryu could have waited with her, but a high-profile comte
would have stood out like a sore thumb. She'd have to make
do with remembering the way Ryu had been leaning on
the pillar outside of the Diplomatic Hall before their lunch.
She'd busy herself with remembering the way their knees had
brushed beneath the table, or how Ryu's hand had lingered
over her own just long enough to establish that there was no
mistaking the nature of their shared meal.

She decided against letting her fantasies drift to the
comte. The woman was *too* effective of a distraction, and if

she bungled the mission because she was busy wondering how Ryu tasted, she'd blow her shot at a second date. She returned her eyes to the front of the sanctuary.

"I swear to the goddess, Nox, if you don't come out in the next ten minutes, I'm going to burst into the church and drag you out by your ears," she mumbled.

She swore it again ten minutes later. And ten minutes after that.

Relief dumped over her like a bucket of water when the doors burst open. The streets filled with noise as happy churchgoers left the sanctuary in their mix of finery and everyday attire, with the occasional vocational costumes of green, red, or gray. Yazlyn flattened herself into the shadows between buildings as she searched the crowd.

Their meeting place had been previously agreed upon. Nox should be on her way to this very alley any second. But as the crowd thinned and only a few stragglers remained, wandering out of the temple at their own leisurely pace, she'd seen no sign of the young queen.

"Where the hell are you?" she asked, peering through the shadows.

Something crimson caught her eye.

Dhamir. She would know where Nox was. She'd escorted her into the church, after all. If anyone would have answers as to what the hell was taking so long, it would be her.

Dhamir hadn't seen her. Yazlyn didn't exactly want to give away her hiding place, but she also wasn't willing to spend another four hours in the dark without answers. She squinted at the figure in the shadows until she realized the comte was looking for something. The woman was scanning the shadows as if she knew to expect someone.

Yazlyn perked. She took her chance. "Psst," Yazlyn hissed, feeling equal parts childish and desperate. It worked. The woman looked around, hearing the noise and searching for its source. Yazlyn repeated the signal a second time, drawing the comte toward the proper shadow. When she was close enough, Yazlyn beckoned her with waving arms. Dhamir's eyes widened as she turned and hurried for the winged fae. She entered the pool of darkness, concealing them both from the overhanging lights.

"Where's Nox?" came Yazlyn's hushed demand.

She watched the woman's face for answers until movement caught her eye. The comte was wringing her hands. Was she scared?

"I don't know." Dhamir shook her head. "She was escorted out of the sanctuary. Who do you have with you?"

Yazlyn blinked through her surprise. This was supposed to be a simple church service. She had no backup. There had been no need. Ash had vanished on some stupid mission to find Tanith. Gadriel and Amaris somewhere among the seraphim of Territory Two. If Nox was unaccounted for, she was truly alone.

"I..." She shook her head, helplessness seeping through her realization. She didn't know what to say. She didn't know what questions to ask. She was military-trained but relied heavily on her squadron. In Raascot, she had allies, she had the advantage of fighting on her home soil, she had reinforcements. She understood the enemy, the battle, and her role within it.

But this was not Raascot. She felt terribly small amidst the looming mountains, peaks that seemed to swell as she shrank. She had no one.

"How bad is this?"

The woman shot an anxious look over her shoulder, and Yazlyn followed her gaze, hoping no one had spotted them. She was still searching the space over the comte's shoulder when the woman said, "I'm so sorry." She pressed a hand into Yazlyn as a jolt of power shot from her palm. Stars exploded before Yazlyn's eyes as she crashed into the cobblestones, spasming against the volts electrifying her very bones. The hot, metallic tang of blood filled her mouth as she bit into her tongue. Yazlyn struggled to keep her eyes open enough to see the frown carved into Dhamir's face as she bent over her. She extended her palm once more to the sergeant's cheek. Yazlyn heard two final words before the world went black.

"It's bad."

Twenty–Five

T HE WORLD WOBBLED SLIGHTLY AS AMARIS LOOKED OVER
the ledge. She wasn't sure if it was the thin, sharp air
making it harder to breathe or if the heights were making her
dizzy. Then there was the third, secret option that gravity was
about to yank her from the cliff and send her plummeting to
her death, in which case she was being wise and discerning
by being scared shitless of Territory Two.

"What's the matter, witchling? You look pale." With a
crooked smile, Gadriel amended, "Pale, even for you."

She sucked in a breath. "Bunch of birds, roosting at the
top of the world…"

His brows shot skyward as he laughed. "You've never
been afraid of heights when we're flying."

"Because you're holding me! Now I'm just supposed
to…" She peered over the edge again. "Not die."

He extended a hand.

"So help me, All Mother and gods of old alike, if you
push me, I will murder you."

Gadriel slipped his arm around her waist, securing her to
him as they continued down the narrow path. On their left,
the world fell off, leaving the city below as scarcely more than

pinpricks at an infinite distance. Smears of green cut between mountains, some containing densely populated territories, others taken by the wilderness. On their right, the ornate, opulent homes of Territory Two had been built directly into the ledge, with scarcely more than a footpath running between them. Silver flags with white angel wings proudly marked their district, which seemed like overkill to Amaris, as it was literally impossible for this territory to belong to anyone else. And though she hadn't been exposed to every territory, damn, did it appear that the seraphim had money. As she eyed Sulgrave's sheer, snow-capped peaks, she thought of Uaimh Reev and how its mountain run seemed like little more than a jog up and down a sloping hill in comparison. The reevers' path had been meant for walking. This, however, had a crumbling, precarious trail that ran from the valley to the territory, should a flightless fae need to visit winged friends, but the steep, neglected steps sent a very clear message: Territory Two is for the winged.

She unclenched her fists, relaxing into his firm hold. There was only one person in the goddess's lighted kingdom who could have truly made her feel safe, and he'd succeeded.

They continued down the path. The homes were interspersed with things that were probably tea shops and libraries and tailor shops made specifically for seraphim, though some of them were at the sort of odd angles that reminded Amaris of nestling barn swallows.

If she was being honest, heights were only half of her anxiety.

She was in an unfamiliar kingdom, on the side of a mountain, surrounded by dove-winged fae, and she was moments away from meeting Gadriel's parents. It didn't help that he also seemed nervous, though excited, to be reunited with his mother and father.

Amaris redirected her attention to stained-glass windows, to curious foliage, to the trees that burst forth from the spaces between rocks, roots nourished by little more than hopes and dreams. The breeze of Sulgrave's curious eternal spring kissed her cheeks, carrying sunlight and snow and pine on its wind.

"Wait here a moment, will you?" Gadriel asked.

She didn't have time to protest before he left her holding on to a shrub as he spoke with the other fae. Gadriel nodded as a woman pointed her finger farther down the road.

"Any luck?" Amaris asked when he returned, fastening her to his side once more.

"It seems Joel and Allua are somewhat reclusive."

"You call your parents by their first names? Is that common?"

He squeezed her hip. "They're at the far end of the territory, but that's all I can get out of anyone. We'll find them. I'm sure they stand out."

She'd opened her mouth to comment on how she knew what it was like to draw unwanted eyes, but she snapped it shut as he shifted his arm, draping it over her shoulders. He'd had so few opportunities to be publicly affectionate. It was the sort of moment she wanted to savor.

The tension sloughed from his shoulders. His chest puffed. His smile was contagious as they approached.

Even still, Amaris wasn't quite sure if she was ready for the encounter. After all, she hadn't known what outfit paired best with "Hi, I fought the queen's ag'drurath with your son, helped him repair his wings at the university, and have been in a rather intimidating romantic entanglement with him ever since, in addition to having a lifelong relationship with the new queen of the southern kingdoms. Nice to meet you. I'm Amaris."

"Gad." She winced as they crept up on the far cliff. "We're running out of territory."

He agreed, and they abandoned the path for the nearest shop. An aromatic cloud of heat and fragrance and flavors washed over her as they stepped up to the woman behind the counter. The shopkeeper was excited to see them, immediately commenting on Gadriel's raven wings. She claimed that Allua was one of her favorite customers. She began to excitedly point out the eyes and nose he and his mother shared, marveling as if lost in some happy memory while she absently twisted a pearl brooch on her dress. The shopkeeper provided exact instructions to the home, including a description of its exterior from the times she'd made deliveries. They departed with smiling gratitude and set on their way.

Thick with nerves, she asked, "Is there anything I should know about your parents?"

The general was amused at her tone. Not many things made Amaris anxious. "Nothing that you can't handle. They're clever people. My father was military. My mother, as you know, was related to our late king, so she's a bit more..."

"Fancy?"

"Polite," he supplied. "I've been told my dad could be my twin. He can be strict, but that's just how he is. Corporal punishment wasn't unusual in our household."

Her lip curled. "That's horrible."

He cocked an eyebrow. "You certainly seem to enjoy it."

She tried to shake off his arm, but he merely slipped it down her lower back, resuming its hold on her waist as they continued their walk. "My mother can be cold, but she's the smartest person I've ever met, human or fae. She also makes a lovely apple pie. She'll like you. You're quick, resourceful, and can be devilishly charming even though you like to do your best to be a brat. Even if you can't cook."

"How do you know I can't cook?"

"I'll bite," he said. "Can you?"

She would have pushed him off the ledge if it wouldn't have done a disservice to them both. Changing the subject, she asked the question that had been on her mind ever since she realized that arriving in Sulgrave might mean meeting his family. "Have you brought a girl home to meet your parents before?"

He chuckled. "Ceres and I were too focused on getting into trouble in our earlier days for any of our partnerships to be more than dalliances."

"Have you…been in love?"

"Sure." He shrugged. "I've had love in my life. But not the way you're asking. I focused on my military career. Meanwhile, Ceres met Daphne. You know how that turned out."

"Sure, sure. Madness, children, ruin. The natural order of things."

She was pleased her jest landed as he bit back his smile.

They stopped in front of a two-story home in the final oranges of daylight. Unlike many others, this one was not embedded into the mountain but backed up against the cliff itself. It had a front yard of sorts, one with a horseshoe of manicured evergreen shrubs protecting its privacy, but the back appeared to end in tandem with the mountain, perched on the edge of the abyss.

Amaris tried to recall what normal people did when they met someone new.

She'd met prospective buyers at the orphanage. She'd met reevers at the keep. She'd met royals. She seemed to be lacking a blueprint for the exchange one might have in an event such as this, though she suspected a handshake was in order.

She trailed slightly behind Gadriel, waiting as he knocked twice, then watched the door.

After a long pause, he took a step backward to absorb the home with different eyes. They were losing the daylight, yet the tall, latticed windows showed no glow from candles or fae lights. Gadriel knocked again before trying the knob. It was unsurprisingly locked, but locks of man or magic had never stopped him before. He put his hand on the door, and the dual bolts clicked open with satisfying clanks. She could tell the house was empty before the door had even finished swinging on its hinges.

"Hello?" he called into the quiet, rapidly darkening space.

Amaris had no hope of an answering response and was quite sure Gadriel felt the same. She stepped into the room, noting its evidence of abandonment. The fireplace was completely clean. There weren't even ashes to indicate logs had recently been near the hearth. Amaris shut the door behind them as Gadriel wandered more deeply into the house. He began opening cabinets, doors, and examining shelves. There were no fresh foods or things that required preservation in the house. The vases were empty, with no decorative flowers or bouquets on the table or the mantle.

It looked as if Joel and Allua had known they'd be gone for some time.

Gadriel murmured something about searching upstairs while Amaris continued to examine the ground level. She listened to the creak of his weight as he finished mounting the stairs and disappeared down the hall, then set to work. It was clear that his parents kept an immaculate living space, but the barest layer of dust had settled on the table and counter. She ran a finger along the space and pulled it up to find it gray with a fine layer of dirt.

Amaris knew enough of altitude from her time at the keep to know that dust gathered far slower at high elevations. She frowned at the gray smudge on her fingertip and surmised that they had to have been gone for weeks. But why?

She continued to inspect the shelves, eyeing the books, the decorative trinkets, and even a lovely painting of two terribly beautiful Raascot fae holding a plump baby boy with dark little wings. One vined plant on the bookshelf had been allowed to die, its leaves withered and brown. Amaris crossed over to the mantle to see Raascot's crest, carved in the glassy obsidian set against a bronze placard next to a small portrait of Gadriel in his attire as general. Either side of the mantle was framed with a vertical tapestry in the greens, browns, and yellows of a wooded glen at sunset. One side was emblazoned with a soldier, while the other marked with the dark shape of a crow. Her eyes skated across the mantle until she landed on something that wasn't meant to be there. Against the vase intended for a floral arrangement rested a small, handwritten note.

Amaris picked it up.

"Gad?" she called up the stairs.

The house remained quiet. She strained her ears to listen for his footsteps as he moved between rooms. She called his name again.

From the top of the stairs, he called, "Did you find something?"

"Here." She extended the small piece of paper to the general. He padded down the steps and read the single sentence aloud.

"*We've gone to find her.*"

Amaris tucked her fingers beneath her arms for warmth as the chilly, mountain night settled through the house. "What does it mean?"

"I have no idea."

✦

Consciousness slipped in and out of Yazlyn's grasp.

Her head throbbed. Her tongue felt swollen and raw. She smacked her mouth, trying to summon enough saliva to clear the residual tang of blood. She was tired. She was disoriented. But something told her this was not the time to sleep.

The sensation of waking slowly visited her like a hesitant old friend. It tapped at her eyelids and knocked on her skull until she answered. When she raised her head, the bitter face of an irate, dark-haired queen was the first sight to meet her eyes.

"You couldn't at least pretend to be happy to see me?" Yazlyn asked. She flinched at the throbbing pain from biting on her tongue. The last thing she remembered was a crowd, a church, a comte…

Ah, fuck. Dhamir.

Strapped to a chair, Nox was still glaring at her from a few arm's lengths away. Her ankles were bound to the chair's legs, and her hands appeared to be fastened behind her, forcing her shoulders back and her chest uncomfortably forward. Sneering, she said, "You had to get yourself captured."

"And what good have you been?" Yazlyn retorted. "What

useful powers do you have? Do you want to try to fuck our way out of here?"

Nox's eyes narrowed, and Yazlyn winced. She hadn't meant to be so cruel, but her head was throbbing, and she scarcely understood her surroundings.

"Like yours are so great?" Nox bit. "Go ahead, Yazlyn, call the ice. See what good that does us."

The sensation she'd mistaken for the gentle fingers of consciousness turned out to be a pounding migraine. She closed her eyes against the dull overhead light and said, "That bitch from Territory Seven? Not a friend."

Nox released a short, agitated breath. "That's disappointing."

"How'd you get yourself tied up?"

There was a long pause before the queen answered, "The Speaker."

Yazlyn forced her eyes open. "You met her? What can she do?"

Nox shook her head, her voice raw with rage. "She has Amaris."

Yazlyn's face fell. She would have shaken her head if the thought of moving her neck from side to side didn't make her want to throw up. "No, she doesn't."

"Yes, she does."

Goddess, she was too sick for this. She needed a healing tonic. She needed Nox to shut the fuck up and trust her. Her brows stitched as she doubled down. "That's not possible. She left the city hours before the church service. Amaris and Gadriel are on top of a mountain right now."

"I don't care where they're supposed to be. I saw her."

Maybe she had hit her head harder than she thought when Dhamir had taken her down. She frowned. "You saw Amaris? Here?"

Rage flashed through Nox. "They dragged her in through the front doors as church was letting out. The people just stood there. You did nothing."

She debated whether or not it would be helpful to tell

Nox she'd gone insane. Madness ran in her family, after all. She decided against it, struggling to find patience in spite of the relentless throb between her temples. "No, she wasn't. I was outside the sanctuary the entire time, watched the service end. I saw everyone leave. I had eyes on the building from the moment the doors first opened to when the last attendant exited the sanctuary. Amaris wasn't here."

Nox's anger swelled to a roar. "Yes, she was, you stupid, useless fae! You were supposed to guard the church. You were supposed to be my backup. You did nothing when they dragged her in by her hair. What was the point of you being outside if you were going to leave us up the damn creek without a paddle when I needed you!"

"Could you speak quietly? I have this goddess-awful—"

"No!" Nox practically screamed. "I most certainly will not speak quietly."

"Whoa, hold on. I know you're mad, but you're way out of line." Yazlyn tugged against her own restraints, groaning at how they'd bound her wings. She felt them strain against the ropes that twisted uncomfortably against her feathers.

"I'm the motherfucking queen. I'm never *out of line*."

"You're a royal pain in my ass is what you are," Yazlyn grumbled, testing her restraints once more.

"You did nothing! They dragged her in—"

With exasperation, she barked, "No, Nox, they didn't."

"How can you be serious? How can you—"

"Shut the fuck up while I figure something out," Yazlyn said dismissively. She ignored Nox entirely while struggling against her bindings. She did attempt to summon ice, but there wasn't even moisture in the room for her to freeze. She couldn't manipulate that which didn't exist. She disregarded the irritable stream of curses and insults while she assessed their surroundings.

The stone walls and rockwork told her they were inside the church. Their room was square and windowless, which wasn't a promising sign. A small hanging light dangled from the ceiling. The room was otherwise empty. There was nothing that could be used for escape or weaponry. If there was a solution, it wasn't locked in here with them. But perhaps if someone else opened the door…

"Have they visited you yet? Has anyone checked in on you?"

"Don't talk to me."

"Oh my goddess, Nox. Are you going to help get us out of here?"

Nox's nostrils flared. "No. No one has checked on me."

"They have to soon. When they do, ask for water. If I can get some moisture in the room, I can potentially cut us free."

"Oh, now you'll make yourself useful?" Nox practically spat.

"You bitter asshole, I didn't—" Her word was sliced through the middle as a thought struck her. "I didn't…I didn't do anything or see anything because there was nothing to see. But I'm hearing you say that you saw it."

"I can't believe I slept with you."

Yazlyn's jaw dropped on its hinges. She slammed her mouth shut, doing her best to keep from rolling her eyes as she worked through the information at her feet. "Shut the fuck up and listen to me. It didn't happen. None of it happened…" She paused as she tested the words. "But you saw it happen."

Nox continued her relentless, blaming glare from across the room. The overhead light cast shadows on her face, making her under-eyes look bruised with her fury. Yazlyn's mind continued clicking through gears as she played the words over and over again, tuning Nox's anger out completely. The lightbulb of her realization went off as visibly as if it had been the one hanging above them on the ceiling.

"That's it."

Nox's voice was still thick with disgust as she reiterated, "What's it?"

"That's it. You saw it happen."

Exasperated, Nox panted, "For the love of—"

"She plants memories."

A pause. A beat. A breath.

There was a flicker behind Nox's eyes. Yazlyn watched the information soak in. She watched Nox turn it over in her mind, watched her work through the steps, watched her struggle against the words until she tilted her chin up to look at Yazlyn once more.

"What?"

"The Speaker. She plants memories. You saw Amaris dragged into the church, right? You are convinced of something that did not happen. Look at your emotional response, Nox. Look at what believing this is doing to you. It would turn you against me, right? It would fuck you up. Make you feel hopeless. Make you think—"

She shook her loose, dark hair. "I don't…"

"Think about it. Not only that, but after thousands of years of peace in Sulgrave, all of a sudden, this woman ascended to the highest rank and has created an army of zealots hell-bent on some power trip. She managed to convince everyone that she was the Tree of Life made flesh. How could she do that? How could anyone achieve that?"

"If they…" Nox still chewed on the information, unable to complete her thoughts.

"Because she planted a memory that convinced all of Sulgrave this was the truth." Levity filled her. She chuckled against the insanity of it all. "What a wicked power. Goddess, Zaccai really should have had a ward made for you. Also, hang on, can we go back to what you said? You're very rude. I'm a great lay."

Nox's forehead creased as her frown deepened. "How do we use this knowledge to our advantage if we're to face her? How do we move forward and differentiate reality from planted memories?"

Yazlyn straightened her shoulders. "Say you're sorry."

"Yaz."

"Apologize for being a bitch and admit I'm good in bed."

"Yazlyn!"

"Fine, then just the apology will do."

Yazlyn watched the battle as Nox fought her smirk. The sergeant knew she was a lot of things, but she prided herself in her unmatched ability to dissolve tension.

Nox's sigh was a long, loud, exaggerated exhalation. "I'm sorry for accusing you of being useless."

"And...?"

"And you're pretty good in bed."

"Only pretty good?" Yazlyn gaped as if she'd been slapped. "That's the worst thing you've said all day." A new thought struck her. Horror twisted her stomach. Her lips pulled back from her teeth in disgust as she asked, "Wait... Nox, why is your hair unbound?"

"What?"

"Why would you wear it down? Why aren't you wearing the ribbon?"

"It's...it's in my pocket."

If Yazlyn had possessed any strength whatsoever, she would have ripped herself free from her bindings to kick the queen in the shin. "What good is it going to do you in your pocket? For the love of all things green and god, you dumb piece of shit—"

"Hey, I'm your queen."

But Yazlyn disregarded the interjection as she finished, "—how are we supposed to keep you alive if you won't do the barest—"

Nox's frustration burned. "Can we focus on one thing at a time? Help me understand something. Why wouldn't she plant any memories in your mind as well? If it's such a useful tool for manipulation..."

The high, metallic jangle of the turning doorknob forced Yazlyn's mouth to snap shut. They were plunged into immediate silence as they watched the door open as someone slipped in, then secured the door behind them. A woman in gray with all-black eyes regarded them. Her gaze flitted between the pair. She was keeping something clasped behind her back, but what, Yazlyn couldn't tell.

Not bothering with the formalities of introduction, the woman asked, "Where are your remaining companions?"

Companions.

Yazlyn would have visibly relaxed if it wouldn't have given them away. She stared at Nox, watching the information click behind her eyes as the woman pluralized the word and Nox realized Yazlyn had to be telling the truth. If they'd truly had Amaris, then the only member of the party they'd lack would have been Gadriel, as Ash had gone directly to the church and Tanith was locked away in a dungeon. Everyone else was accounted for.

"What do you mean?" Nox asked, voice neutral.

The woman procured a small, silver lily. "No one has been to their chambers in the Diplomatic Hall in hours. I refuse to believe they're on a pleasure walk through the city, and I know they wouldn't go anywhere without letting their queen know. Now, where are your companions?"

"Have you checked under your bed? The worst monsters are often closer than you think."

Twenty-Six

THE PAIN ON HER FACE MAY AS WELL HAVE BEEN A KNIFE IN his gut, slowly twisting as he bled out on the floor.

"Why would you do this?" Tanith asked, voice choked with more emotion than Ash had ever heard her use. He pulled out of the hug, his face falling as he watched her. He couldn't have left her to rot in a row of dark cells like the other prisoners, locked away in various states of filth. She hadn't even been able to bathe after their trek across the straits. Burgundy smudges belied her sleeplessness. The gingers and jasmines of her inherent fae perfume mingled with the unwashed smell of sweat and oil. Her red tunic was smudged with grime, but he had no doubt that if she stayed in here, things would only get much, much worse. He'd run to her from the gate the moment the guard had opened it, but this had not been the reception he'd expected. He looked over his shoulder to ensure the disinterested guard remained at the still-ajar entrance to the prison.

Ash relaxed the hold he had on her. "I'm here to get you out."

Her short hair brushed against his chin as she shook her head and pushed out of the embrace. The dim light cast shadows, exacerbating her hurt. Tanith took two steps back, leaving a chilly emptiness where her body had been pressed into his only a moment before. His stomach twisted. A cold sweat spiked over his forehead. Everything was too loud and too quiet at once. The other prisoners banged on the bars, shouting for the guard's attention, overwhelming Ash as he stared at the one who said nothing at all.

"Tanith," came his quiet plea, "I'm here to help you."

Her answer came out with cold defiance. "This isn't help, Ash. This is betrayal."

"Tanith—"

"Shouldn't a reever know better?" She wouldn't meet his eyes.

He suppressed a flinch at the implication. "You said yourself, the reevers and the Reds"

"Someone else does the thinking for both of us," she whispered. "And you're proving them right if you believed for a moment this was a wise choice."

He pressed his lips into a frustrated line to hold in everything he wanted to say, knowing nothing was good enough. He didn't know how to make her understand. He was here for her. He hadn't betrayed anyone. He'd fixed things. He'd saved her. He'd simply entered the church, approached the nearest attendant, and asked who he could speak with about Tanith.

He'd known the others wouldn't be happy with him taking matters into his own hands, but he had to try.

The attendant had been quick to run his request up a chain of command until he found someone else who shared his goal. The woman who'd emerged from the back of the sanctuary looked like someone with power—someone who could get things done. She had agreed that Tanith deserved exoneration and was eager to speak about the terms of the girl's ambassadorship in the southern kingdoms with his companions. It was perfect. He'd accomplished everything he'd needed to so easily. He'd get Tanith free, and he knew the young queen was just as eager for knowledge and information. Even the timing seemed perfect, as Nox would be in attendance later that very evening.

Everyone was a winner.

"Should I go speak with Nox?" Ash had asked.

The woman had waved a manicured hand, jeweled nails catching in the light as she did. "I'll send word to the Diplomatic Hall for your queen and companions. I can have you escorted to see Tanith now. Would you like that?"

She'd snapped her fingers and a guard had appeared at his side. It had been the easiest rescue mission ever recorded. And yet here Tanith was, disappointment dripping from her every pore.

She averted her eyes as she seethed. "I did all of the things of which I'm accused. You had no right to make a deal with the church."

He walked a tightrope between irritation and pleading. His arms had ached to hold her. He'd wanted them to crash into one another with relief and gratitude. He'd imagined the stolen kisses before he liberated her from her dungeon.

He reined in his errant frustrations. Their moment would still happen. He needed her to understand that everything had been accomplished by the book. "The church agreed with me that you should be exonerated. The guards would never have let me into the dungeons to get you—"

She scoffed, and the sound may as well have been sandpaper against his raw heart. "Half of the council is in the church's back pocket, Ash. The guards have little say in what goes on around here."

"You don't understand. Nox wants to meet with the church. Everyone is getting what they want out of this. It's—"

"You cannot come to my country and tell me I'm the one who doesn't understand."

She pressed her back into the wall of her cell and slid to the floor.

No, this was all wrong. She shouldn't be sitting. They

should be on their feet. They should be climbing the stairs, bursting into the fresh air, walking toward the Diplomatic Hall to celebrate their victory.

He extended a hand to her. "Tanith, let's go."

Her face disappeared as she hid it in her hands. "I'm not going anywhere with you."

"Tanith! I'm here to free you."

Bit by bit, her eyes lifted from her hands, locking onto his. The Frozen Straits would have been warmer than defeat in her voice as she said, "You have no idea what you've done."

The blood drained from his face. He wasn't entirely sure he was still breathing. He couldn't even shake his head in rebuttal.

Nothing made sense. Tanith had been a true believer from the moment he'd met her. If anything, she should have been overjoyed that he'd collaborated with the church she'd loved so deeply and to which she'd dedicated her life. Her faith aside, he had known with some certainty that she cared for him. Perhaps she'd never love him as he'd come to love her, but he refused to believe she was this cold.

The door to the row of cells opened as the guards returned. A man stood at the edge of her iron bars and gestured for them. "Let's go."

Tanith stood, not looking at Ash. She walked directly to the guard. "I'm not going with him."

The disinterested shrug told Ash that this sort of decision was above the man's pay grade. When he balked, the guard gave him a less-than-friendly tug toward the door. He stumbled backward, eyes fixed on Tanith only to see that she wouldn't even meet his parting gaze as he was dragged from her.

He was going to throw up.

He mouthed her name, wanting to shout it, wanting to scream, wanting to scoop her into his arms and carry her from the cells, but he'd been rendered utterly useless. Prisoners continued their shouts and clanging tin cups against iron bars as he passed. The sound ebbed as they ascended the steps, leaving the jail and everyone it held behind.

Mere minutes ago, everything had made so much sense. He had proposed a helpful meeting between the church and his crew from the southern kingdoms. In exchange, he would be reunited with Tanith and help to facilitate her pardon. He couldn't wait on Nox to intervene. Days had gone by, and she'd made no progress on Tanith's release, even though she'd endangered her own life to save all of them not once but twice. She had only returned to Sulgrave because of Nox and Gadriel and their agendas. Why hadn't they advocated for her? Where was their accountability?

They should have been hand in hand as they stepped into the cool mountain air. They should have been walking toward the Diplomatic Hall where he'd draw her a hot bath filled with bubbles. He'd have strawberries and aromatic teas and hot buns and all sorts of nice food sent up from the kitchen while she reclined in bed in a clean, fluffy robe.

And maybe his daydreams were why he hadn't heard the footsteps scuff the landing behind them. Perhaps he was too fraught with the night's outcome to catch the moving shadow, to hear the whir of a weapon, to brace himself for impact as stars exploded in his eyes and a high, popping noise rang between his ears. He scraped his hands and bruised his knees against the stone as he fell, grunting against the impact as the night bobbed into and out of view.

He had to stand. He had to get up. He had to...

Two sets of hands manhandled him, yanking him from the ground as he clung to the edges of consciousness. Saliva turned to cotton in his mouth. He was being taken somewhere...dragged...he had to open his eyes...he needed to...

The world went black.

Was he awake? He couldn't be sure. He took in a breath through his nose and picked up on something familiar—something friendly. Fruit? A spice, maybe?

He continued to breathe through his nose. He should open his eyes, but, fuck his head was pounding. He wouldn't be able to hear anything if the ringing in his ears didn't subside. He didn't seem to be moving anymore, but he'd have to open his eyes to be sure, which he had no desire to do, knowing that he'd be assaulted by light.

Maybe if he could open his mouth, he'd be able to ask for a healing tonic.

But ask who? What had happened? Had he been attacked?

With a slow, rallying breath, he opened his eyes. He groaned against his headache, his nausea, his terribly dry mouth. Goddess, he needed a glass of water. Maybe if he...

He couldn't move his hands.

He tried again, but nothing. Ash's eyes flew open as he tried to understand why he couldn't move. He was in a room. He was not alone, though he couldn't waste his time on other dungeon prisoners just yet. First he had to figure out what the hell had happened. He was in a chair. His wrists chafed against rough rope as he tugged. With a failed kick and a helpless struggle, he found his ankles had been similarly bound.

He looked up at long last, ready to ask the other prisoners for answers, when the two other faces came into sharp focus. Nox and Yazlyn stared at him, grimacing and glaring as he tried and failed to free himself from his bindings. It took only a moment to see the ties around the sergeant's wings and the knots that secured Nox to her chair before he fully understood how royally fucked they were.

Yazlyn was the first to speak.

"Is anyone in our crew not completely useless?"

Twenty–Seven

A MARIS MAY NOT ENJOY TOEING THE EDGE OF TERRITORY Two's cliffs, but she could get used to a house like this. She'd been an orphan in linens, a reever in leathers, a jester in Moirai's court, whoever the hell she wanted to be in Gwydir, but her current high silk pants and cropped shirt felt perfectly suited for the sort of life she could picture in a house this fine.

They'd lit a few candles in the sitting room. He'd carried firewood in from the chopped pile that had rested outside of the house, lighting a small fire to keep her warm while she waited. She'd settled onto a chaise and busied herself study- ing the stitched detail of a forest tapestry while he wandered around the empty home. As the hour had grown late enough to cast a blackness amidst the house, the whirring of wind from the valley below rattled their windows.

"Do we leave?" she asked, looking out the window. She wasn't looking forward to their plunge off the ledge, and something about doing it at night made it exponentially worse. She wanted to be able to see the ground speeding toward her so she could make her peace with the All Mother before she died.

"Come here," he said. "Let me show you what I found upstairs."

"More notes?" she asked. Whatever it was, it had to be better than going back to the Diplomatic Hall to receive a secondhand church sermon. The others might be stuck soaking in religious lessons, but if she was lucky, she could delay thoughts of bishops and Blessed Obediences and solemn sanctuaries for another night. The steps creaked underfoot as she followed him up the stairs.

He opened the first door on the second floor but did not step inside. It stood to reason that it belonged to his parents, and apparently it did not contain anything worth exploring.

From there, they entered the second of three rooms. Amaris's eyes popped at the most wonderful personal study she'd ever seen. An intricately carved desk stacked with leaves of parchment, neat rows of ink in crystal pots, and an elaborate array of feather quills faced the night-dark windows. She could only imagine the dizzying view of the valley one might have from the desk during the day. Two of the four walls were composed of solid bookshelves, so overflowing with leather-bound texts and tomes that piles had begun to form on the bedside tables and stacked on the floor. Mirrors, now-dead plants, and trinkets had decorated the study, all illuminated by a dim, reddish fae light mounted to the wall.

"Your parents are...studious." Amaris said.

"Feel free to raid their collection before you leave."

"They won't notice?"

He chuckled. "Oh, they'll definitely notice. But I challenge them to do anything about it from this side of the straits."

They exited the study, and Gadriel led them to the door at the end of the hall, which opened to another bedroom. He gestured for Amaris to lead the way, and she obliged.

He got to work stoking a fire on the hearth while she looked around. It was a nice guest room, she supposed. It was decorated quite differently from the other bedchamber, with a markedly more masculine energy, as this one had a large four-poster bed with black sheets and an equally inky duvet. It had a weapons rack, which seemed a bit odd for a guest bedroom, but who was she to judge.

As the kindling caught and bit into the logs, just enough light filled the room for Amaris to understand what she was seeing. She'd given in to her curiosity and cracked open the wardrobe to find an arrangement of men's clothes, from tunics and pants to slotted fighting leathers.

A small, strangulating knot snagged in her throat as she realized they'd prepared a bedroom for their son. She felt the nostalgia for a life unlived as she marveled at what it might be like to be loved by parents, but it was hard to miss something that had never existed. As she stared at the neatly hung clothes, she knew she would never understand the feeling of coming home to a happy father and worried mother fussing over your favorite dish or how much weight you'd gained or lost. She'd never have tearful goodbyes with relatives before departing on a long journey. She'd never arrive in a foreign land only to find that her parents had stocked and decorated and created a space just for her on the off chance that one day, she might join them.

"It's yours."

His shadow grew against the wall as he stood from his place by the fire. His mouth quirked in a partial smile as he sat on the dark sheets of the bed. He extended his arm in an all too familiar gesture. It had become the international, intuitively known signal that said *Come here, Amaris.*

She stepped toward him, and he wrapped an arm around her, looking down into her face.

"I'm sorry they weren't here."

His crooked smile softened as he pressed his mouth into her hair. "I'm not."

She turned away from the pressure of his mouth and searched his eyes. "You didn't want to see them?"

He shrugged as he pulled her closer. "They're fine; they're just away. Which leaves us with an entirely empty house…"

"Gad," she said with the sort of fidgeting surprise that came from feeling like one was about to be caught. He crushed her against the hard wall of his body, and a familiar heat crawled up her neck. The depths of her belly curled, spreading to somewhere deeper. She was glad for the lateness of the hour, as only the dull red of the fire cast telling shadows on the otherwise traitorous heat that pinked her. "We can't," she said quickly. "It's your parents' house."

"Do you know what I learned?" he asked, ignoring her statement entirely.

She tried to swallow, feeling incredibly small while enveloped in his arms. She tried to take a backward step to look at him more fully, but she backed into the closed wardrobe door, preventing the oncoming, inevitable squirm. When she spoke, it came out more hushed than she'd intended. "What?"

"That I owe our queen a word of thanks. She did me a favor."

She nearly choked. Her heart leapt into her throat. "Excuse me?"

"I told you," he said, his words vibrating through her. "Your first time should be more gentle than anything I could offer you. Your second time, however…"

Her toes curled in her shoes. The room's four walls closed in on her as the terrifying offer of something new, something forbidden filled the air. She could scarcely distinguish her emotions from fear and excitement, but she wasn't entirely convinced the two could be separated. She managed to spit out a question. "You mean…Nox?"

He slipped a firm hand between Amaris and the wooden door, flexing his fingers against the small of her lower back. His teeth glinted with decided wickedness. "I could smell it on you."

Her heart stopped beating.

They were alone and sheltered for the first time in a long

time. They had complete privacy. And most importantly, the general had set a boundary the first time he'd told her no. But she'd given her maidenhood to someone else—to her perfect other. It had been the sort of joining no human or fae could ever understand. He wasn't holding a blushing virgin any longer.

She was safe with Nox, mind, body, and soul.

But Gadriel was something wild and dangerous.

Her head spun before she realized she hadn't been breathing.

"And now," he said, "I have you to myself."

One arm continued to hold her as he reached a hand over his head and grabbed the back of his tunic, pulling it off in an easy motion, revealing muscled, coppery skin. Her heart skipped a beat, then a second, then picked up at triple the speed to make up for its missing pulse. She swallowed as she looked at the delineation of his chest, the curve of his broad shoulders, and the lines that rippled down his stomach, shadowed in the dim crimson of the firelight. Her eyes snagged where his pants ended, two lines of indentation like arrows pointing to the forbidden parts of him she'd tasted only once.

She'd never been good at dealing with her feelings. On the one hand, she'd spent years in training and could disarm almost any man on the continent. She would meet monsters and demons and creatures of darkness with sword lofted and chin high. She had slain the queen of Farehold and broken the curse on the border. Yet with the general...

The hand that discarded his shirt landed on her hip. Her awareness went to his touch as if each of his fingertips was a hot coal raking an achingly slow, intentional line of flame toward her inner thigh. She made a weak attempt to wriggle free, but he pinned her in an instant, sending her into a panicked state of fight, flight, or freeze.

Did she want him?

Oh, goddess, yes. She wanted him more than air. More

than life. But she could not be told what to do. She was a runner. She was a fighter.

A small piece of training clinked into place. He'd pin her every time she squirmed. He'd relish in her heated cheeks, in her sputtering inability to speak, in her short, shallow breaths. He'd pay no mind to a turned face, to a twist away, or the feeble words born of panic, over shyness, over newness.

Gadriel had spent a long time instilling a word in her that she could use to render him powerless if she truly wished. Amaris knew she was one breath away from stopping him in his tracks, beyond any shadow of a doubt.

Snowbird.

He'd made her repeat it. He'd reiterated it. He'd ensured time and time again that she had it, should she need it. And she tore it to shreds as his hand crawled toward the apex of her thighs, because no matter how much her mind clouded, no matter how much cortisol pumped through her, warming her inside and out, no matter what she thought or felt, she knew she wanted this. She wanted him.

Their eyes met for the briefest of moments, just long enough for the pulse of exchange. It wasn't in Amaris to submit. She wanted to be bested by someone worthy. And if she was going to move, it had to be now.

She was ready for battle. And he was ready to win the war.

She dropped to one knee, twisting as she attempted to worm away through tuck and roll. She was fast, but he was so much faster. She hadn't even hit the floor before he pinned her chest to the wardrobe mid-descent. Her hands were trapped against the wall of wood, rendered useless as he pressed his weight into her from behind. A single hand slipped up her front, free to roam her stomach, her sternum, her hips as it pleased.

She struggled beneath his weight, feeling the heat of his breath on her cheek. She gritted back a grin, every bit as enraptured as she was enraged, and she was not ready to lose. His teeth grazed down the sensitive exterior of her ear before pulling her lobe into his mouth. The small sound that escaped her lips encouraged him, forcing the air from her lungs as he crushed into her. The hand between Amaris and the wardrobe slipped beneath her top, feeling for her breast beneath the cropped silk of her shirt. Her gasps of protest and pressing hands were mere signs of encouragement to the predatory male.

A rough hand slipped beneath the hem of her pants. She sucked in a breath as she pressed her cheek into the cool wood of the wardrobe. Gadriel's hand hovered an inch above her sex. This time when she twisted, he used the motion against her, flipping her so that she faced him.

She remained still and defiant as he planted four firm fingers on the side of her neck, a thumb forcing her chin up to look him in the eye.

With a low growl, he said, "You've made your choices, and I won't share. You've belonged to your queen since long before we met, and you'll remain hers. But now, I own you. Do you understand?"

The blood rushed from her brain to other, far more important places with such intensity that she was quite sure she might black out. Yes, yes, an eternity of yeses. She was the queen's and the general's from now until the end of time. She didn't want anyone or anything else. She wanted this insanity, this madness—whatever this was, it was hers.

She attempted to nod, but he stopped her. His hand cupped her throat so that his thumb and forefinger pressed down on her jugular. The gentle decompression made her blood swim.

"Say it."

His hand tightened around her throat. She couldn't help the sneer, the flash of anger, of ecstasy, of pure warrior's combat as she refused to reply.

"Say it," he repeated.

Desire and defiance dripped from her as she said, "I'm yours."

He looked terrifying and gentle all at once as he replied,

"I treasure what's mine." His hands tightened against the soft flesh of her cheeks. "Hold it close, repeat it like a prayer, and remember how I care for you, because I'm about to fuck you like I hate you."

That was what it took for her soul to leave her body.

She heard the shred of fabric before she understood the lightning flash of her tunic being ripped from her. The sound she made could have been heard throughout Territory Two as she turned against his hands, ready to counter his movements. For months, he'd stopped her advances. For months she'd tried and failed to lure him into exactly this moment.

The message was clear. This was not her choice; it was his.

She expected him to angle for the pants at her hips, but instead, his voice was a low, steady command.

"Put your wrists together."

Her eyes glinted. "Make me."

He bit into his lip with the sort of wicked smile that told her he'd been hoping she'd say that. She reveled in it, knowing that in addition to loving her mind, her body, her spirit, he loved meeting an equal in battle.

He'd had his fun. She used his distraction against him, dropping to the ground and throwing her weight downward. It wasn't enough to break his hold, but the plunge of her motion sent him tumbling over her into the armoire. He had to release her long enough for her to scramble to her feet and run for the bedroom door. She threw it open and sprinted with three bounding leaps down the hall before she gasped against the backward motion. He hooked one arm around her waist and the other tight against the roots of her hair, yanking her head back.

He had made the mistake of leaving her hands free. She threw both of them over her head, grabbing his hair in her fists and using the leverage to launch herself upward. It was the countermotion she needed to bring her feet down hard against his instep. He snarled as she managed to liberate herself for a fraction of a second, but her victory was short-lived.

He slammed her into the corridor wall, his fae speed providing just enough time for his left hand to cushion the blow before her skull smacked into stone.

"Are you ready to listen?" he asked, forearm under her chin, pressing down on her throat as his opposite hand continued to cradle the back of her head.

You wish.

She wasn't sure if she'd ever been filled with such a wicked glee.

Amaris brought her knee up toward his manhood, which he barely countered. He reacted with a genuine start, which was precisely what she needed. She used the distraction to throw a punch, but her hook contained her fatal flaw. He snatched her hand out of the air, and she understood the gravity of her error. Once he had her wrist in his control, he was able to flip her into the wall, face, chest, and belly pressed into the cold stones. She knew better than to make such a novice mistake. He could break her arm if he tweaked the pressure in the slightest.

She grunted with exertion as she tried to remember how to get out of such a vulnerable hold, but he didn't seem winded in the least. He had her arm in such a tight twist that she couldn't find the countermovements she'd need to free herself. With a twist and push, he led her back into the bedroom.

He used a foot to kick the shredded piece of her tunic up from the floor, catching it from the air in a single swipe without ever needing to free her hands. He'd twisted her hands together before she even realized what was happening. The fabric had looped against her pale wrists, creating a perfect knot in the center. The soft, silken material made for the perfect manacle. A thrill shot through her when she used her modicum of freedom to turn and look up at him. She'd seen Gadriel's eyes hundreds if not thousands of times before, yet she'd only seen the hazy outlines of the primal look he wore now. The raw exposure of his desire, his strength, had been so carefully shielded for so long.

She tugged at the restraints, but her brows met in the middle when she failed to understand their binding. She opened her mouth to say something but was cut short by Gadriel as he swept her off her feet, setting her lengthwise on the bed while she continued to pull against the knot that had secured her hands. She had training in knots. There had to be some piece of training, some lesson, something important on how to escape, how to unravel…but her brain was too foggy with excitement, shrouded in her haze of desire as she bumped against a blank wall where lessons of manacles and ties might be.

There had to be something. If she couldn't free her wrists, what was available to her?

A wicked delight sparkled behind his eyes as he saw her growing helplessness. He thought he'd won.

She steeled herself as she checked her knees to see if she could drive one up into the general, only to find he had preemptively spread his stance to pin her legs wide. Her knees, thighs, and feet had become utterly useless as they stretched under his posturing. His back, his broad shoulders, his wings blocked out all but the smallest glint of red glow as they backlit the general's outline.

He released a dark chuckle, mirroring something like appreciation as he stilled her in her half-turn. Her back and shoulders pressed into his abdomen as she wriggled once more beneath him. Her resulting cry was a mingle of panic and pleasure. Hot, wet excitement flooded her.

She brought her legs up in a defensive maneuver to deflect him as he tugged at the hem of her pants, but he caught her knees and pinned them downward, tugging them free to reveal her bare, snow-white skin. She seized the moment it took from her to yank her bottoms free from her ankles to drive a hard kick, but he was on her in an instant.

"Go ahead. Fight me," he dared.

She did not disappoint. Amaris moved quickly, using the restraints that held her upper body as leverage as she flattened her knees against her chest, flexing her feet against the general to push away. She'd barely created enough room between her body and his for her bare thighs to wrap around his head as she motioned to flip him. She'd partially succeeded as the general rotated with her movement, but now he had her on her stomach. This time when he pinned her, he began to drag kisses down her back.

She went limp against the delicious heat of his mouth on her skin.

"Do you yield?" came the rumble of his question against her back, a smile in his voice against her flesh as he kissed her shoulders, then her neck, bringing his mouth to her ear to hear her response.

Yes, yes, yes, she thought, but she was too proud to say the words.

A rough tear of fabric from over her shoulder could only be the removal of his pants. She wanted to see this. She struggled upward, twisting against the binds as her wrists chafed. One hand stilled her forearms as his mouth was in her ear.

"Shh, you'll hurt yourself. I should be the only one hurting you."

For fuck's sake, this man was going to be the death of her. And oh, what a glorious way to die. Amaris hated herself for how her moan betrayed her.

"What do you want, witchling?"

Her back arched with anticipation. Goddess, it killed her to admit it. "You, demon. I want you."

She heard the sound of spit and didn't know how she understood its implication. He had licked his palm and used his saliva to wet his cock. Her feet kicked uselessly against his body weight as he pressed into her, one hand on her hips, the other stilling her hands. His legs weighed against her own. The hand that had chastised her wrists slipped down slowly as it found its spot on her throat. In that moment she felt the tip of his hard cock tease her entrance. Her spine chilled as she bucked against him. Another desperate moan to feel him, to have him, to be owned by him.

"Ask nicely," he practically purred.

She'd dreamed of this moment. She'd wondered what it would be like to be beneath the full weight of his body, enveloped in the scents of sweat and sex and black cherry and pepper, lost to strength and power and lust. She'd fantasized about the width and breadth of his manhood. But she'd sooner die than admit it.

When the tip teased her soaked entrance, she released a loud, sharp gasp. She tried to force her hips backward, to shove herself into him, to bring him closer, but her attempts failed.

"No, no," he chided quietly. "Tell me what you want."

"Fuck you."

"I plan to." His hand crawled up from her back to her mouth, but not to silence her. "Now, tell me."

"Don't make me say it." She buried her face in her pillow.

"It's like you don't know me at all," came his low tease. She tried again to wiggle herself into him, but he tightened his grip on her hips, denying her what she craved.

She was proud, but her ego slipped behind the louder needs aching within her. "I want you," she said, and she meant it. "I want this."

"Good girl," he breathed, edging his tip inside.

She gasped again as he worked his way inside of her, relaxing his weight onto her back, crushing her beneath him as he filled her. She knew he felt every curve, every sharp inhalation, every twitch and movement and arch of her back as he waited for her to adjust to him, to accept him, to let him all the way in.

She wanted more.

She tried to press her ass into his hips as he inched himself in farther. His fingertips ran along her lip, then slipped into her mouth as she gladly sucked them in. His low groan of response was music to her ears, releasing a new flood of pleasure. She tried wiggling again but couldn't quite reach his hips. It was with wide eyes that she realized he was not yet all the way in.

"Not yet," he chastised quietly.

But she knew exactly what she wanted. She rocked her hips again. "Please," she begged, need forcing the arch in her back.

"You think you're ready?"

"Yes." Her greed consumed her. "I'm ready."

"Scream for me, witchling."

When he slid himself in the remaining distance, it was a hot knife through butter. She clenched down on his shaft and reveled in the groan that escaped his lips. His first few movements were excruciatingly slow. So gentle, so tantalizing, that it set off an alarm bell within her. Amaris knew enough to recognize the calm before a storm.

Gadriel's hand remained over her throat, as if feeling the vibration of every breath, every moan, every sound. He moved in tandem with her body, responding to every tantalizing movement, but it wasn't enough. She begged, and he did not disappoint.

He unleashed himself.

Lightning shot through her, curling her toes, flexing her calves, her ass, her back, her neck. She hadn't known she was capable of the free, high cries that tore from her throat, but her wild, loud animal sounds kept time with each rhythmic slam. She wouldn't be surprised if all of the pious churchgoers and the Speaker herself could hear her.

"You better not be holding out on me," he growled.

The general raised up onto his knees as he dug his fingers into her hips. Starbursts exploded within her vision as her eyes rolled into the back of her head. She was her own chorus of desperate, greedy noises for him to go deeper, faster, harder. The slap of flesh, the pound of power, the utter surrender sent her deeper and deeper into a cloud of ecstasy.

The music they made was more prominent than the wind from the valley below or the crackle of the fire. She was pretty sure the mountain itself could crumble and she would neither hear nor care. She hadn't thought she could get any louder, move with any more urgency, until the high, sharp sting of a slap sent her bucking. She turned just enough to see the distinct red welt of all five fingers against her skin. Her entire body clenched in reaction, including the deepest parts of her, tightening against him in a way that clamped down and never wanted to let go. With clenched teeth, he brought his hand down again, then a third time.

Pain and pleasure curled, twisted, and hooked within her. She let go completely as they began to swell, building into something powerful, something incredible, something that she couldn't have held back even if she tried. She tried to tell him between her gasps and pants. She opened her mouth, but all that came out was "I'm…I'm—"

The world shattered as she screamed.

She collapsed onto the bed, a shell of a woman with his cock still inside of her.

She wouldn't have even known what had happened had the crack of wood and the high, bell-like jangle of millions of pieces of glass begun to snow down around them. This was no inward pulse and glow but the destructive epicenter that rocked the home's very foundation.

Gadriel's protective wings shielded them from stray shards, and she knew she should be grateful, or afraid, or apologize, or feel *anything*, but she continued to soak in the pleasurable aftershocks, shutting out the consequences as she reveled in the heat of her victory. She'd crumpled from her rigid, passionate, tensed pleasure to the relaxed, deadened figure of someone fully satisfied.

She mumbled something that she'd meant to be an acknowledgment of what she'd done to the home, but she wasn't confident that she'd said anything intelligible. Sulgrave's protective bubble was little more than a cooling chill; soothing, if anything, in the wake of her passion.

"I'm taking that as a compliment." He smiled.

He moved her onto her back more gently this time, her

hands bound as she stared up at him. The crimson glow from the dying fire provided barely the outline she needed to see him above her as he rotated her from her stomach to her back, still fully inside her. She unleashed a gasp in surprise.

"Sensitive, little reever?"

Once more, she meant to say something. Maybe his name, perhaps an agreement, a word, but she managed only a sleepy, amicable sound. He drew out with the idle, teasing laziness of someone who held all of the cards. She moaned as he pulled out of her entirely, eyes closed as she continued to buckle beneath him, still feeling the evidence of his presence within her.

He kissed her mouth with more tenderness than she'd expected. The red from the fire gave him a devilish glow as it backlit his wings, his hair, his arms and legs, warming them despite the cool air from the broken window, which hadn't deterred him in the slightest. He grazed her mouth with his lips in a soft kiss. Rough, calloused hands dragged along the lines of her body, meeting where he'd used her shredded cloth to tie her wrists. She was surprised to feel their weight release as her binds were freed. Her hand went unconsciously to the reddened part around her tender flesh, rubbing where the fabric had held.

"Are you done with me?" she asked.

She had meant for the question to be playful. She'd finished, but she knew enough of sex to know the general had not. She remained drunk on her climax and enjoying the total looseness of her limbs as her muscles had gone to gelatin, but there was a heaviness to her question that she hadn't fully intended.

He lowered himself onto the space beside her, then slipped his arm around her back, cradling her against his chest.

For a moment, time felt like glass. It was as fragile and delicate as the windows she'd broken. She held her breath as she waited, listening to the diamond dust of shattered glass pushed along the floor by the breeze. Bits of her heart chiseled and broke at the prolonged silence, joining the wreckage on the ground.

It was something of a poisonous habit she'd learned from years of being the girl put in the pantry on market day that she'd struggled to develop her voice when she was in pain. Uaimh Reev had helped her to uncover her fists and steel when she needed strength, but the small, cracked part of her retreated further into itself when it felt moments like these. She was not for him. She was to be set aside, reserved, used only for special occasions. She was fine china or precious teacups, rarely utilized, always kept behind the display case. Nox was the queen. Fine china was meant only for royalty.

"Do you want us to be done?"

His question was as heavy with double meaning as hers had been. Gadriel wasn't asking about sex. He knew that her heart was no empty land, free for flags and stakes to be claimed.

She couldn't look at him. "No."

With a gentle tug, he had her face close to his. He repeated his question from earlier in the night. "Then tell me what it is that you want."

Her laugh was a singular, humorless thing. It was barely more than a quick puff of air as she closed her eyes. "I want it all," she said. "I want love. I want adventure. I want lust, and passion, and family and battle. I want my past and my future. I want to fall asleep in your arms just as much as I want to wake up in hers. I don't know if that's fair to you. I don't want you to regret—"

"Regret?" His question cut her tirade at the knees. "With you? How could you even suggest such a thing?"

Her shoulders rolled inward as if to protect herself.

There was no jest to his voice. It was a low, sincere rush of words. "You want it all?"

He flexed his hold and she melted into his arms. She wanted him. She wanted to feel him inside of her. She wanted to be with him. She wanted to fall asleep next to him. She wanted to belong to him. She wanted the world.

"Yes." Her chin quivered.

With the low murmur of a lover, he said, "Tell me."

"I want you."

He moved over her once more, but this time was different. He brushed a kiss against her cheek, holding himself above her as he said, "And I, you. I've wanted you from the moment I met you. Not just your body. I want your mind, your heart—you. I want all of the parts of you, and only you."

He lowered his forehead to hers as he slipped himself inside of her, their jagged intakes of pleasured breath a melody and harmony in unison. Her sensitivity from her first climax made her clutch her soaked, internal walls against him even more tightly. Her legs lifted from where they'd been pinned against the bed by his powerful thighs, wrapping around his lower back to secure him against her.

"Don't close your eyes," he said.

She opened them obediently and was bowled over by the intimacy. This wasn't the aggressive game they'd enjoyed or the dangerous fucking that had shattered windows. He wasn't just looking at her but allowed her to look into him as well. He was showing her his heart.

She bit down on her lip as he coaxed a moan from her throat.

"Don't hold back on me."

"The window—"

"Let all of Sulgrave know I'm yours and you're mine."

Amaris bit her lip as her eyes searched for his once more. His dark lashes fluttered open, filling her with a rush of dopamine as his gaze bore into her. Their eye contact remained unbroken through his strong, steady motions. Every flex of a muscle, every pump, every breath pulsed through her. She felt him tighten, and he lowered his face to bury beneath her neck. He released one wrist, and his free hand tangled in her hair, yanking her head back until she let out a yelp. He bit his sharpened canines into the tender space between her neck and shoulders as he tensed against his climax. She clutched

327

him tighter, holding his body to her own as every hot pump released in shuttering convulsions within her. Every throb was a new, incredible depth of pleasure and intimacy as she felt him empty himself within her.

"If you get me pregnant," she warned.

"You'll what?"

She narrowed her eyes. "I'll kill you."

"I'd quite like to see you try, but you know it will only turn me on." He pushed a kiss into her shoulder. "Will you trust me if I tell you I've already taken care of it? I would sooner die than put someone I love at risk. Well, no risk except for the welts I'm going to leave if you continue to struggle."

Her impish smirk was unmistakable as her hips arched against his, waiting for his eyes to meet her own. When they did, they weren't the tired, conquered shell of a man she'd hope to find. Instead, his blackened eyes twinkled down at her.

"You think we're done? That's cute, witchling. I told you that when I had my way with you, it would take us all night. But I was wrong. I think it will take us much, much longer. One might even say forever."

"Forever?"

"We're just getting started."

PART IV

What Cannot Be Trusted

Twenty–Eight

BY MORNING, AMARIS UNDERSTOOD WHAT IT FELT LIKE TO be a bone-dry husk wasting away in the desert—one that had died with a smile on its face. She was exhausted, she was drained, and she was completely and utterly satisfied.

She could barely open her eyes, but when she did, it was to look at the pale, perfectly healed circle around her wrists that had been red and raw only a few hours before.

The general hadn't been exaggerating. The fabric that had chafed her wrists had been round one of the binds, fingers, positions, and gags that had kept her in knots. She supposed she understood why he'd felt compelled to wait for a gentle, loving departure of her maidenhood. He didn't consider his proclivities fit for a first encounter.

But he was gentle. Just not in the way she'd expected.

After they'd finished for the second, third, fourth time that night, the loving way in which he'd unwrapped her from the bedpost and kissed her wrists had been so tender, so caring. He'd fetched her water, used a warm cloth to clean her, and retrieved the healing tonics from the pantry. She'd winced at first against the sting as he'd dribbled it over her chafed skin, then melted into him as he ran a gentle thumb over the wound, healing it completely. He held her in his arms long after the welts, the bruises, and the pain had subsided. Thoughts of a kitten in a sunbeam lulled her to sleep as she curled up against the general's warmth, falling into a whole and perfect sleep in the safety of his embrace.

Amaris wanted this for the rest of her life. She wanted it all.

Her gaze drifted from her wrist to the bronze hand contrasted against it as it held her, and the wings draped over them as they'd slept, sheltering them from errant gusts from the valley below. She hadn't meant to make a sound, but she couldn't keep the soft, contented sigh to herself.

Dark lashes fluttered open as he woke. He brushed a kiss against her cheek. "How did you sleep?"

"Like the dead." She wanted to drift off on the cloud of sleep once more, but she remembered the destruction they'd caused when she noticed how his feathers rustled against the wind. "The window."

"I'll board it before we go. I'll leave a note."

She buried her head in the pillow. "You're such a good son."

"I hope your queen shares," he said, running a hand along her mussed hair, "because I'm not letting you go."

"She's your queen." Amaris kept her face in the pillow, words muffled by its feathers. "I'm a reever. I serve no master."

That earned an honest, happy laugh. "I beg to differ."

Amaris lifted her head from the pillow to glare at him. And as much as she wanted to curl into a ball and sleep for three more days, she knew it was time to get going.

By the morning's end they'd left the house, using a makeshift board to block the elements from soiling Joel and Allua's cliffside home. Amaris had borrowed a few of Allua's things, as her existing clothes were little more than shreds at the bottom of a wastebasket. Allua's shirts weren't quite suited to a body without wings, but her frame had been similar enough that Amaris was able to use a belt to cinch the clothes around her waist. She made a note to add it to the list of things they would owe his parents when they next met.

Amaris emerged from Gadriel's parents' room with a grimace.

He'd been waiting for her, relaxed against the banister like he didn't have a care in the world. "You look great to me."

"I can hear the conversation now. 'Hi, I fucked your son, broke your windows, and stole your clothes.'"

"Technically, I'm the one who fucked you."

They exchanged challenging looks—hers, one of narrowed eyes and distaste, his, a satisfied smirk.

Amaris's stomach rumbled. She'd planned to add food to the list of things she'd pillaged from their pantry, but no food had been left in the house. There was no reason to linger unless they wanted to tempt themselves with another round in the bedchamber. After all, it was already destroyed.

They locked the door behind them as they slipped into the morning light. Few seraphim had left their homes for the morning. In fact...as she looked around...no one seemed to be on the streets. The windows were shuttered. The doors were closed.

"Does it seem a little..."

"Quiet." He finished her thought.

Gadriel had held her hand as they'd wandered down the street in search of tea and breakfast, but her happy glow soon evaporated. There was a hollowness to the feeling, a lack that spoke to a greater threat. She'd felt it on the quiet, lavender first lights of day when Matron Mable had brought her tea in bed so many years ago. She'd felt it when she'd opened her eyes in the dense, southern forests to hear no sound, no breeze, nothing. And she felt it now. Ice prickled from the back of her neck down her spine, spreading outward until it covered her body in gooseflesh. From the look on Gadriel's face, she knew he felt it too.

There were no civilians to be found, save for one.

She could just make out the white wings and bright tunic of a seraphim clad in solid red on the opposite side of the cliff. They stopped, and they waited.

"Maybe it's just a color," she said unconvincingly.

The set of his jaw told her that no, neither of them believed it to be a coincidence. He was too far away for her to see his face, but her heart dropped into her stomach the moment he spotted them.

Gadriel made a casual show of wrapping his arm around her as they turned in the opposite direction. She forced herself to stroll beside him, though she knew his muscles twitched to run every bit as much as hers.

His feet scuffed against the stones as they approached his parents' home. She slipped her fingers into the hand dangling loosely from her shoulder, squeezing him as they drew closer and closer to the ledge. They were going to run out of path unless they made a dash for the house.

A rustle and flutter sounded behind them.

A low, male voice called, "Excuse me?"

Gadriel ignored it entirely, pace quickening. She tightened her grip the moment she understood his trajectory. They were not going to the house. He was headed for the cliff.

One second passed. Then two. This time when the man called out, Amaris dared a glance over her shoulder just in time to see the seraphim's wings beat as he shot into the sky.

"Go!" Gadriel urged, but his tug was unnecessary. She pumped her arms, legs working at a dead sprint as she matched his pace in their sprint toward the cliff's edge. She took a deep breath as if ready to plunge underwater, knowing the time to skid to a halt at the lip had come and gone. She couldn't stop her momentum even if she tried. Amaris scrunched her eyes tightly, choking on her yelp as she pushed off from the rocky edge.

Gadriel's arms were around her. She felt his muscles, his wings, his body, but they weren't pulling up. Why weren't they pulling up? She pried her eyes open, unable to scream as gravity stole her voice. She clawed at him as if trying to climb higher, to clutch him more tightly, to yank him to safety.

Down, down, down they plunged.

The bright, green world opened up before them as it drew closer and closer. Trees and streams and homes went from flecks on the earth to full shape and color as they braced for impact. She closed her eyes again, tucking herself into his chest as she awaited the horrible, bone-breaking crash as she became little more than gore scattered amidst the stones. She could only hope her death would be swift.

Their turn was so sharp it sapped the air from her lungs. Gadriel opened his wings at the last second, carving through the air as they hugged the cliff. She understood the moment she spied the darkened indent of a cave. He shoved her in first and then used his dark wings to cover the exit, hoping it would conceal them. The white wings of the fae from Territory Two would have stuck out like a sore thumb against the rock face, but if they were lucky, Gadriel's would look like a shadow. It was shallow, but it might be just enough to render them invisible from anyone who'd peered down from overhead. Even those who pursued by air might not think to look on the same side from which they'd jumped.

"What happened?" Amaris panted. An hour ago she'd been naked in bed. She'd imagined her morning involving more salted ham and sticky buns and far fewer near-death experiences.

"Something's wrong."

"Obviously," she hissed.

Shouting voices overhead let them know that the seraphim were in pursuit, and there had to be more than one. She could only pray that they'd remain airborne, scanning the earth and skies without spying their alcove.

She closed her eyes and saw herself paging through strategies and possible outcomes as if she were reading a book. Some chapters ended in their discovery. Others in their imprisonment. The worst, in their demise. And though there had been no training on Sulgrave and its politics, she knew enough of stealth to understand that they were in for a long, long wait.

Morning became noon became the final hours of daylight. There'd been no hint of enemy presence for some time, but they'd need the cover of nightfall if they had any hope of making it back to the others undiscovered. The shrill screech of a circling vulture competed against the wind as it whistled through the valley, but neither was as loud as the cramp and grumble of Amaris's stomach.

Adrenaline nullified her hunger the moment they stepped from the cave and plummeted to the valley floor. Gadriel waited until the last possible moment to flare his wings, catching an updraft and beating them powerfully just before they crashed through the canopy of snarled trees.

"Something must have gone wrong with the others," Gadriel said.

"We can't safely make that assumption."

He cast a backward glance as they snuck their way from the tree and flattened themselves against a nearby home. They picked their way through alleys and stayed under the cover of shadow as they crept onward.

"The others could be in the Diplomatic Hall. What if we were being arrested for trespassing? We broke into a locked home. The others might be waiting for us."

He didn't have to say anything for her to know he disagreed. And she didn't blame him. Her logic was thin at best. Though he made his displeasure known, he agreed that they couldn't make any decisions until they knew if their friends were safe.

Through a triumph of stealth and hours of tedious progress, they finally crossed into Territory One. Any hope Amaris had that the whole ordeal had been a misunderstanding vanished the moment the Diplomatic Hall came into view. The grounds were awash with crimson as Reds marched the perimeter.

"We're in trouble," Gadriel said. He pressed Amaris into the wall and used his wings as a dark block against any prying eyes that hoped to spot them in the gloom.

"What if they're in there?"

He exhaled. "If they're in there, we can't help them. It's crawling with guards."

She was aghast. "You want us to leave them?"

"No," he cautioned. "The Hall is exposed on all sides. We can't get in without walking under a flood of fae lights. And if I'm not mistaken..." He took a partial step back and craned his head toward the sky. He cursed. "Look up. Even the skies aren't safe. We'll come up with something, but sometimes plans take patience."

"We're in Sulgrave!" she whispered through her rage. "We have no idea how swiftly they act here. We may not have the luxury of patience."

"Amaris—"

"You only use my true name when you're trying to placate me." She shoved against his chest. The flash of fear in his eyes told her precisely what he thought of her propensity for chaos. He knew he was not her general. He could not pull rank over her or command her to stand down. She had grown nearly predictable in her unwillingness to observe his authority.

"It isn't wise," he urged. "What I want to tell you is—"

"'Want.'" She smiled, repeating the word. "Because you know that whatever it is, I won't listen." She rose to her toes and brushed a kiss against his jaw, then took a single step around his wings, revealing herself to the shadows.

He caught her face and crushed his mouth down on hers before she'd escaped him, enveloping her in a passionate, commanding kiss. He broke the kiss and looked into her eyes. "You are the most frustrating thing the goddess ever created."

"Well, you'll have to take that up with her the next time you see her." Amaris freed herself from the space beneath his wings entirely.

"Wait!" His eyes widened as he wrapped his hand around her forearm. He squeezed it for emphasis. "These are fae. You can't persuade your way in."

"You're absolutely right. But you see," she said as she tapped her temple twice, "I have the power of underestimation on my side."

He shook his head. "You're just going to—"

"Bluff," she finished for him. She took another step away before squeezing his hand. "Wait for me here. I'm certain I'm going to need you very shortly."

The moment she turned her back on Gadriel, her mask of bravery fell. She puffed up her chest as she abandoned the cover of the shadows. She had three seconds until someone saw her, and perhaps ten until they were close enough to read her face. She shoved her nerves, her anxiety, her desperate wish to have Gadriel at her side down as far as she could as she walked confidently into the center of the courtyard.

A guard perked the moment she stepped into view. She hadn't missed the way every guard in her peripherals had stopped moving. She forced a relaxed, amicable smile as she wiggled her fingers in greeting. "Finally. I was convinced I'd gotten lost. I had no idea how large Sulgrave was! Pardon the late hour." She shot a wink and a smile and breezed past the man, carefree and unbothered.

The man in red looked confused and taken aback all at once. Her skin crawled with anxiety as the other guards turned from their stations to watch her walk confidently into the building, but she suppressed the urge to shudder. Instead, she gave an airy, forward-facing smile as she pressed through the doors. The other Reds stiffened, and she knew with some degree of certainty that her plan was working. They'd been waiting for fugitives, not a guest. They'd most certainly been prepared to apprehend her, but if she was to willingly walk into the Diplomatic Hall and make a prison for herself of her own dormitories, maybe less would be required of them and they could all make it home in time for supper.

She caught a final shrug and the swapping of bewildered gazes before the doors swung shut behind her.

It was time to face her next foe: the bewildered concierge, always at the ready with his bouquet of metallic flowers.

"How are you?" Amaris jumped in with a pleasant smile before the man behind the desk had a chance to speak. She offered another friendly wave and forced herself to maintain a fast, even pace as she rounded the desk and headed for the platform. This was the part she'd feared the most. She didn't know how to operate the enchanted platform by herself, but if she ran for the stairs, they'd see her for what she was: a rabbit chased by foxes.

The smile remained plastered on her lips.

If Amaris was being honest, she wasn't entirely sure that she'd ever mastered acting, save for the times she lied quite successfully to herself about her feelings. She'd had little opportunity to develop the skill, as her time in Farleigh was spent either with the matrons or propped up against sacks of potatoes or hidden in closets. She was genuine with Nox, truthful with the men at Uaimh Reev, and honest with Gadriel, even when she wanted to murder him. But there'd been something on the guards' faces—something all the more prominent in the concierge's eyes—that made her think her performance had not been entirely convincing.

One challenge remained.

"How was your night?" she asked the attendant who worked the platform as she forced herself to relax against the wall.

His brows raised in alarm. The man moved his mouth wordlessly a few times before she tilted her head, feigning something between impatience and confusion.

"My room, please?"

He obliged, though he blinked rapidly as he did so. His hands shook a bit as he triggered whatever rune-etched pulleys and levers worked to hoist her up the building's glass wall. She attempted to keep her eyes unfocused as if she were lost in pleasant thought. She could only hope that he wouldn't wonder why she neither looked at him nor made conversation, if she appeared too engrossed by the middle distance of some happy memory.

She tried not to heave an audible sigh of relief when the door to her floor opened to reveal no guards. She'd made it. She was in the clear. She said a cheery good night, and he offered a stilted farewell in return before immediately lowering himself to the ground floor.

She'd been lucky so far, but an uncomfortable tingle in her gut told her that luck was about to run out.

Silence.

The fae lights remained, but the warm glows of fires that had often licked beneath the doors and seams of the frames of her friends' rooms were dark. She knew before checking a single door that no one was here. She may very well have charged headlong into the Diplomatic Hall for nothing. Perhaps this was why they'd been so willing to let her enter. They hadn't been posted to keep anyone in. The guards existed to intercept Amaris's arrival, and she'd strolled willingly into the cage.

It couldn't be for nothing.

A click ticked within her, counting down the seconds as she rushed to her room. She grabbed her bag, knowing it contained everything she'd brought, save for the quill. Amaris slipped into the hall and hurried into Nox's room, which had been left unlocked. The black quill sat on the writing desk, but she could find nothing else of importance in the young queen's room.

Only two things of note remained: the pocket watch and the quill's counterpart.

Yazlyn had been the last one to snatch the compass and had kept it on her person ever since their fight on the straits. The clock within her continued to tick, but the seconds picked up in speed. First double time, then triple. Amaris wasted no time with decorum as she turned the sergeant's room inside out, dumping out her bags, emptying her drawers, and ransacking the wardrobe. She'd nearly given up when she overturned a pair of shoes only to hear a hard, weighted thud. She shook the shoe's contents into her palm and squeezed the precious treasure with tangible relief. Gadriel's room was the next she tried, but it required no searching. The black feather quill rested nearly on his desk for one moment longer before she snatched it and shoved it into her bag.

A distant noise, something like the brush of glass and gears on metal, froze her in her tracks. The platform was rising through to her hall once again, and she wasn't going to wait around to see who was on it. She tore into the hall and sprinted for the stairwell, yanking the door on its hinges just as the platform came to a stop.

She held her breath as she eased the door shut without a sound, praying they'd search the other rooms before they thought to head for the stairs. If she went down, she'd be met by an ocean of guards, a concierge, and plenty of empty space wherein she had no place to hide. If she went up...

The heavy clamor of footsteps was the last thing she heard as she took the stairs three at a time.

So, this is why they make us run that damned mountain, she thought, bounding up, up, and up, covering ground as quickly as her feet could find a flat surface. Her breath came in puffs as she climbed the spiral steps higher and higher.

Goddess, how tall was this building? She'd been sleeping on the fourth floor, she believed, and the meeting with the comtes was on the tenth? The thirteenth? Or had it been the twentieth? Why had she never counted?

If there was one thing she'd learned amidst her innumerable runs up and down that goddess-forsaken mountain, it was that stamina was a state of mind. Her lungs burned, her legs became gelatin, her body screamed at her to pause, but her body had no say over who fell prey to the Sulgrave fae below. She ignored every plea sent from her arms, her chest, her thighs, and calves to stop, and she did not slow until she'd reached its summit.

She exploded onto the roof, erupting through the topmost door with half-crazed intensity, tightly clutching the bag stuffed with precious possessions. The blast of cool air may as well have been a bucket of water. She wanted so badly to stop, to savor it, to let the stitch in her side abet as she caught her breath, but she was not alone.

An enormous pair of ivory wings flared as the Red from Territory Two turned to greet her. His white wings refracted the glow of the fae lights from the streets below, silhouetting him against the night. He'd been perched on the farthest corner, overlooking the city below like a gargoyle made flesh. As he stood, a slow, menacing smile told her what they both knew.

She'd failed.

She was on a roof with no building to jump to. There was nowhere to go. Nowhere to hide. There was nothing, except...

If she'd let herself deliberate for even a second, she may have changed her mind, so she acted on pure, primal survival and ran the only place she could.

The guard cried for her to halt the moment he understood what she was doing, but she was already three long strides into her sprint. She shot across the roof, gasping against the surge of adrenaline, of fear, of every instinct telling her that this was a bad, bad idea. She was tired, she was unarmed, and she had no confidence that she could take a well-rested fae in hand-to-hand combat, so she darted for the opposite corner.

"Stop!" he cried once more.

He was close enough for Amaris to see the whites of his eyes as she reached the ledge. The man extended his arm, his sound a mix of authority and fear as he tried to snatch her from the air.

So, Amaris jumped.

She dove into the empty sky as if plunging into a pool, knowing gravity would take her, knowing that, though Gadriel was on the ground, he'd have mere seconds to react if she had any hope of surviving, knowing that she was a goddess-damned idiot.

As she twisted through the air, she saw the stars.

She'd never truly experienced the sensation of free fall before now. Even when she'd plummet to the earth from their hold against the dragon, she'd been cradled and safe. When Gadriel had attempted to help her unleash her powers from the tower of Castle Gwydir, she hadn't been truly afraid, as she'd known that he'd be there to catch her.

This time was different. Now there was nothing between her and the open, endless air, save for an odd sort of curiosity, as she realized this hadn't been on her list of ways she thought she might die.

She clutched the bag to her body as her torso rotated downward to see the rapidly approaching buildings, fae lights, and cobblestones. Air rushed past her, wiping her hair vertically in a straight white column. The world was cold as earth approached too rapidly, it was happening too fast, everything was moving too quickly. Rough hands grabbed her. She yelped against the sudden jerk as gravity was robbed its earth-bound victim.

She twisted to see Gadriel—but no, it was not the general who had prevented her impact. The seraphim from Territory Two was barely grabbing the fabric of her shirt, desperately struggling to find a tighter hold as his wings beat backward against gravity's downward pull. He'd captured her. A typical tunic would surely have torn, but the thickly knit, reinforced shirt she'd stolen from Allua's closet held fast. The Red grunted as he attempted to contain her, struggling against the sudden shock of weight. His high-value captive would not be gore and bones on the cobbles of the streets below them. He slipped his arm into the panel on her back that had been intended for the release of wings. It provided the perfect slot for him to grip her as he angled for the roof.

She had been snatched out of the empty void of night. The sound of pressure, of cold, of night and angel wings would be the last things she'd hear before the boots and metallic clangs of a prison were sure to follow. She'd gambled, and she'd lost. She'd misjudged either Gadriel's speed or his watchfulness. She'd made a fatal mistake and had no idea how to save herself from the chains and dungeons and interrogations and the impending life in a cell.

Hell, if she was going to die, she may as well go down with a fight.

Amaris shouted as she hit at the guard, though she wasn't sure what she hoped to accomplish, save for a death on her own terms. She battled against him in midair, twisting against the fae's hold.

The fight within her refused to surrender. There was no wisdom to it. No plan. All Amaris felt was the feral compulsion of a trapped animal to free herself. A wild sound tore from her throat as she thrashed from her captor. She scratched for the seraphim's face. The fae dodged her outstretched fingers, and she began to slip from his hold. She dug her nails into his forearm while flailing as he did his best to drag her upward through the air. But she had one last move. She thrust her hand toward him with an incredible shock wave that sent him whirling backward into the night sky. The victory was short-lived. Though the motion freed her from the seraphim, it began simultaneously propelling her toward the cold, solid ground.

In the fractions of seconds that passed between the moment she'd called upon her shock wave and the result it had on the guard, a sideways impact sounded like a crack of thunder as the seraphim rippled before her. His flesh moved almost like that of a mirage as his white wings knocked to the side. A shadow enveloped them. Two birds of prey—the eagle and the albatross—tore at one another in the sky.

Gadriel had come too late. She was falling. Her stomach lurched into her throat as her innermost organs resisted against the earth's pull. Her last sight would be that of stars and the moon and the chill of night air and fae lights and the rapidly accelerating shapes of vertical buildings around her. Part of her was glad she wouldn't be facing the ground for her impact. She tightly shut her eyes, clenched against the imminent death.

If her eyes had been open, she would have seen how he'd propelled himself toward her with nothing to lose. She would have reached for him. Instead, the wind was knocked from her lungs as he slammed into her sidelong, sweeping her into his arms. Her feet smacked the cobblestones painfully as he caught her head and spine just in the instant before she left the world to join the All Mother.

Amaris threw her arms around him and choked on her cry. This wasn't just the thrill of survival or the gratitude of his rescue but of love too raw, too powerful to name. She wanted to scream, to cry, to hold him so tightly that he became a part of her as she let herself absorb the weight of knowing she'd been stolen at the last possible moment from death's talons.

Fate would not cut her thread tonight. Not if Gadriel had anything to say about it.

She braced herself as he tucked in his wings in a barrel roll, not unlike he'd done in their final moments as they'd leapt from the ag'drurath's spine. They'd jumped from the dragon, and he'd wrapped his wings around her to absorb the blow of the canopies and branches so that she might survive the fall. Her heart ached when she thought of the fall and the way he'd tumbled from the dragon's back so she might get away, not expecting her to stay. But she had.

She peeked from where she'd tucked her head against his chest to find they were not alone in their flight. White wings reflected silver in the moonlight as their enemy closed in on them. Gadriel was fast, but their adversary flew unencumbered by the weight of another.

This was a dance she'd seen before.

She'd been a child in Farleigh with her face pressed against the window as she watched a sparrow chase a hawk. Her eyes had widened with curious fascination as, for some reason, the hawk didn't seem to realize its size or strength. It didn't confront the small, brown bird. It was locked in frantic flight as the tiny, fearless common sparrow dove pecked and chased after it. The hawk would tuck, roll, and evade until it had eluded the sparrow. She'd never understood why something so powerful hadn't turned to smite the little bird, until now.

She was in the arms of a hawk, and she knew why he did not turn and fight.

His cargo was too precious.

Gadriel spread his wings again as he maneuvered between buildings, weaving tightly in the hopes that he might lose the seraphim. Her heart lodged in her throat as she scanned the sky, but she caught no other trace of winged pursuers. Perhaps Sulgrave's ground efforts had been deemed sufficient as only one Raascot fae had been unaccounted for.

With a sharp yelp, they plunged for the ground once more.

Gadriel yelled over the rush of wind, "When I tell you to let go, you need to drop."

She gripped him more tightly, shouting, "I don't want to leave you!"

"I need you to trust me."

They burst from the buildings into what would have been hills and a forest and woods in Farehold or Raascot though in the manicured perfection for Sulgrave may have very well been a large park. The enormous, green garden gave way in a downward slope.

"Gad—"

"Now!"

Amaris let go and closed her eyes tightly, tucking in her arms and legs for impact. She hit the ground with a heavy thud. The air was punched from her lungs as she rolled down the grassy hill before skidding to a halt. She struggled to inhale, but she couldn't move, couldn't breathe.

You can't panic, demanded the voice within her. *You've had the wind knocked from you. You need to get up. You need to go.*

She forced her awareness to other parts of her body,

testing for broken bones. The collision with the earth had taken off a thin layer of skin as it bruised her, but she could move. Soil and vegetation and night sky filled her nose as the hot pain of burns and scratches lanced up the forearms, wrists, hands, and cheeks that had rubbed raw as she'd crashed to the earth. She may have remained fixated on her injuries had a thunderous boom not jolted her attention skyward.

The sound that cracked through the air above her as she rolled was unlike anything she'd heard. It was what she imagined a trebuchet breaking into a castle wall might sound like as the very stones fell around her. It was as if the goddess herself had opened the earth to swallow their enemies. The collision as Gadriel had launched himself to take out the pursuant seraphim had produced such a sharp, bone-crunching blow that Amaris held her breath to see if either man had survived.

It was then that she knew she had been wrong.

They were no hawk and sparrow. They weren't even the eagle and albatross she'd imagined. Gadriel was the ag'drurath itself. He was a force of undeniable fury, power, and terror. The tumble was over nearly as soon as it had started. The bash he'd made against the seraphim's skull was such a sickening crunch that she was sure she'd remember it in one thousand nightmares to come. The guard's wings went limp as he fell from the sky like an angel cast from heaven.

But if the seraphim was the angel, she'd spend every day choosing her demon.

Gadriel landed beside her for the slightest of moments. "Are you okay?"

She barely had a chance to nod before he scooped her into his arms and took off into the night.

Amaris clutched her body close to him, tucking her face into the space between his neck and chest as he held her. He was alive. He was unstoppable. And they were together.

The city moved beneath them as they took off into the

night. Every dark beat took them farther from the danger and deeper into the valley. One hand moved to bring her closer, holding her by the back of her neck.

"I've got you," he muttered against her hair.

"I trust you." And she did.

Twenty–Nine

NIGHT AIR WHIRRED PAST THEM AS THEY REMAINED airborne. With any luck, they'd be unable to spot Gadriel's dark wings against the blackened mountain. They were in trouble, but they had allies. If they could make it to Territory Five, they might be able to seek shelter at Ryu's. Amethyst flags emblazoned with wyverns flapped lazily in the wind along the cobblestone streets, telling them they'd arrived on friendly soil. It was a hope that remained tight in their chest until they passed overhead. Her house was as dark as the night around it, but any hope that she'd simply gone to sleep sank the moment Amaris spotted the shattered window and door on its hinges. Two Reds remained posted at the entrance, but Gadriel banked hard and doubled back the way they'd come.

Ryu, with her bravery and strength of character, had made no secret of her discontent. If the comte from Territory Five had been overturned, it was safe to assume that the other public dissenter, the bold, obstinate Kasar, would have been sacked as well.

There was a wisdom in silence, and this was precisely why the gentle, green-clad Elswyth had presented with neutrality for years. They'd said as much in their meetings: someone needed to hide in plain sight. She and Gadriel didn't have to say a word for her to know they were headed to find the comte of Territory Three.

From their time wandering the city on foot and her hours in the common room flipping through available texts, Amaris had come to see Sulgrave as a squid. Territories One and Seven were the engorged head and body. Each tentacle was a green valley branching between the mountains. While there were no signposts overhead to mark each territory, they made an educated guess and thought of the tree that had been embroidered across his chest. Three had to be one of the lesser-populated valleys.

Amaris shivered, but not against the cold. "We need to hurry," she said.

"I know." Gadriel's jaw was set as he dove forward, racing the sun as the first signs of light created a gradient from black to gray. Another hour and they'd be completely exposed.

"There." Amaris thrust an excited finger toward the horizon. Scarcely distinguishable against the shadowed, emerald canopies, fabric rippled. It had to be his flag.

Gadriel plunged into the trees as the first pink signs of dawn broke against the lowest point of the snow-capped mountains. He tucked his wings between trunks as he barely avoided one blow after another as they headed for the flag. Long before they reached it, the red-and-orange crackle of an unattended fire caught her attention at the flag's base.

Amaris had expected them to stop and examine it, but instead, he pulled up sharp, darting above the tree line once more.

"What is a trap?" Amaris rasped.

Gadriel's lips were a flat line. He shook his head, remaining silent as he pulled wide, choosing a safe place among the trees for them to land. They ducked behind the thick trunk of a lichen-covered tree and peered around it to see the campfire in the distance. "I don't know. A sign that says 'Elswyth is here' would defeat the purpose of a signal."

"Well, there's only one way to find out," Amaris said.

"Yes," he agreed. "And you're going to stay here while I do it."

"I most certainly am not."

"It's only fair," he said. "You pulled the last absurd stunt, after all. And I'm quite a bit harder to kill."

"I don't think you give me enough credit."

He sighed. "Then that's my fault, because there should be no doubt in your mind precisely how highly I think of you. And since you hate being told what to do, I command you to wander off, to sneak, to be absolutely reckless until I return."

She would have rolled her eyes had she not seen the worry in his. The fight within her dimmed. "Fine," she agreed. "But don't make me wait long."

Gadriel kept to the ground, approaching the fire on foot. She searched for something she might use, a log, a branch, a rock, should she need it, but the forest floor was empty. She had only her sack and the stray magical objects she'd grabbed, none of which would help her in an emergency. Her finger-nails bit into the meat of her hand while she watched him weave through the forest, silhouetted by the flame as he approached.

She saw something.

A small shape, scarcely more than a mouse in a fae body, darted from its hiding place behind a wayward boulder. Her blood chilled, and she knew Gadriel saw it too. He stopped in his tracks, wings flaring as he readied himself for whatever may come.

The small shape approached. She could scarcely make out the figure against the fire, save for the hurried gestures. Her eyebrows shot skyward when she realized Gadriel had turned to look at her while the new figure spoke. Whoever it was, he was no longer afraid of giving up her position. Her pulse didn't settle until he was at her side once more.

"Well?" came her urgent whisper.

"We were right—it was a signal, and not just for us. He gave me directions to the safe house. We need to hurry. It isn't close."

And he hadn't been lying. Territory Three was already sparsely populated. They flew so deep into the valley that she wasn't sure she'd be able to see Sulgrave's glistening windows and spiraling buildings even if she tried. Any rational person may have assumed they'd overshot the territory altogether and had crossed into no-man's-land, but she trusted Gadriel, and he was on a mission.

He dipped into a grassy alcove just as the mountain began to bend, and there it was. They'd found a rough-hewn shepherd's cabin. Dawn banished the last of its pastels as a harsh sunbeam cut into the valley, illuminating the humble home. She stepped out of his arms but kept her hand in his as they approached the building. She didn't release the breath she'd been holding until the door opened and a familiar shape stepped out to greet them.

"Elswyth," she said, relief flooding her as if they were old friends. Though they were in a foreign kingdom with only three allies, she supposed he was one of her oldest friends in Sulgrave.

"Amaris, Gadriel, come quickly." The comte's face lit as he ushered them in.

And her list of oldest friends expanded from one to three as she found that not only were Ryu and Kasar safe and alive but they were here, already tucked away in the cabin. They broke conversation and looked up with wide, honest relief as she and the general approached. While one side of Ryu's hair remained short-cropped, the opposite side was no longer unbound. It had been intricately braided and pulled away from her face. She was no longer in telltale purples but instead wore black, as did the comte at her side.

Ryu stood. Amaris thought perhaps she'd extend her hand for a shake, but held in her surprise as the comte pulled her into a warm hug, crushing her until her back nearly popped. Amaris thought for the fifth, tenth, millionth time of Tanith and how very peculiar their little friend was. They'd written off her aloof, taciturn personality as a peculiarity of the land beyond the straits. Though Tanith and the comte shared similar features in many ways, from their inky hair and gilded skin to the sharp points of their ears, they couldn't be more different.

The comte finished her squeeze then held her at arm's length to examine her. Searching Amaris's eyes, she asked, "Where are the others?"

"I don't know," Amaris answered honestly. "We left Territory Two yesterday morning believing that everything was fine, but have spent the last twenty-four hours chased by the Reds. I broke into the Diplomatic Hall. It wasn't my finest moment. No one was there."

Gadriel added, "Ash and Yazlyn were meant to keep watch beyond the church while Nox infiltrated the service."

Ryu didn't seem to be looking at them but past them. Her eyes remained trained on the space behind their shoulders as if watching to see if anyone else might appear. Lines carved out a deep frown. "Yazlyn—"

Amaris returned the expression. "Whatever happened at the church—"

"It would appear that none of them came out," Gadriel finished for her.

Perhaps as a reever, she should have been more observant of her surroundings. It wasn't until a creak from the kitchen that she realized they weren't the only ones in the cabin. Any fear she may have felt was quickly alleviated as two more fae entered the sitting space, locked in hushed whispers. Whoever they were, they had not been spying. The pair barely ceased their conversation long enough to acknowledge Gadriel and Amaris. Introductions were made as other dissenters wandered in from behind the cabin, but Amaris had never been great with names.

353

The important details remained: Territories Four and Five had been overthrown in a coup. Nox hadn't emerged from the church. Ash and Yazlyn had been charged with protecting her, and clearly, they had failed. Tanith was in prison.

"What the hell happened?" Amaris asked. They hadn't exactly been welcomed by the council of Sulgrave's seven comtes, but nothing had led them to believe that they'd been on the verge of capture and imprisonment. Their time in the Diplomatic Hall, wandering the streets of Sulgrave, enjoying food, people, and parks had been magical. The joy that lofted their survival from crossing the straits had led them to forget that all magic comes at a price. "What set this off?"

"You did," came Kasar's gruff response. At her horrified look, he made a face. "Not you, specifically, but we've been at a stalemate with these bastards for more than a decade. The church had been overreaching ever since that damned Speaker showed up out of nowhere. They were growing, but they wouldn't have made a power grab like this without a catalyst."

"Nox was only supposed to attend a service," she said, voice low with disbelief. "It was meant to be little more than a benign reconnaissance mission. A boring one, even."

One of the men who had positioned himself behind his lionhearted leader from Territory Four agreed. "The Reds changed when the Speaker arrived. It happened so slowly, we'd become a theocracy without even realizing it. The two who look like you," he gestured to Gadriel, "Joel and Allua, sought out our little resistance movement after word spread that the Speaker wasn't satisfied with ruining Sulgrave. She has every intention of digging her claws into the lower kingdoms as well."

Amaris perked. "Gad, the note!"

Gadriel fished in a breast pocket to procure a small, folded piece of paper. He handed it to Elswyth. The man from Territory Three stared at it for a long moment before sighing.

"I was wondering if something like this might happen." The others watched him expectantly until at last, he said, "They've gone to find the Speaker."

Amaris's face scrunched. "So, they went to the church?"

"No." Elswyth's response was heavy with a somber sort of defeat. "I'm not speaking of the woman called Daifa. Your parents are looking for the real Speaker."

Thirty

NOX WAS SLOW TO RAISE HER FACE TO LOOK AT THE WOMAN who entered. It was the same woman in linens who'd deadened her limbs and sent her collapsing to the floor, and she was not someone Nox was interested in ever seeing again. Still, the scent of bread tugged her chin upward. Her eyes widened, and she shot Yazlyn a silent warning.

Ice.

The sergeant was going to ruin everything for them before they even had a chance to escape, for the moment Yazlyn saw what the woman was holding, she began to practically vibrate with what Nox could only assume was a poorly contained yelp of victory.

The woman, whose eyes appeared to be composed entirely of dilated pupils, was carrying only two things. In the crook of her elbow hung a wicker basket with small pumpernickel loaves. The same hand clutched a glass pitcher of water. Nox looked at the woman long enough to ascertain that the attendant hadn't seen the winged fae's expression. If the sergeant didn't stop wiggling in her chair, their half-baked escape plan would be over before it began.

Before the attendant had the chance to rotate toward

Yazlyn, Nox drew her attention. "Aren't you going to cut us free? So we can eat?"

She plucked a loaf from the basket with a bored expression. "I'll be back momentarily with a cup for the water. Here." She shoved one of the small loaves in Nox's mouth, and she had no choice but to bite down in shock, the coarse, dense bread souring her mouth. She spat it out, and it landed in her lap. The woman shrugged. "Suit yourself."

The woman repeated the gesture, offering bread to Ash and Yazlyn, but both the reever and the fae kept their lips firmly shut. The woman implied that if they starved to death, it would save her some trouble. "Starve, then. You're both expendable. Your queen, however, will have to eat eventually."

The woman exited without fanfare.

"That was ominous," Ash muttered. "I wonder what they have planned for Nox."

"Sex dungeon," Yazlyn said definitively.

Nox would have kicked them both if her ankles had been free. "Be quiet and make yourself useful."

And useful she was. Yazlyn had manipulated ice on the Frozen Straits, but this...this was magic. Nox quieted as she watched the fae call the water to her in frozen, crystalline form, admiring the glassy spire as if it were a vine growing from its soil toward the sun. The pitcher drained slowly as the hardened, rope-like shape wove through the room until it reached Yazlyn's fingers. Once she had a firm grasp on one end of the ice, the rest folded in itself, collapsing into the tight fit still secured behind Yazlyn on the chair. With the power of will alone, she created a blade and cut her hands free. It took a few more moments to cut her feet free where they'd been bound to the chair, and the blade broke more than once. She would quickly reshape it and get back to work.

Yazlyn opted to free Ash next, if only to get a rise out of Nox. She succeeded, and Nox began plotting what she was sure would be a rather satisfying murder. Yazlyn's hands turned a violent shade of red as she struggled to maintain a hold on the frozen weapon, but the ice still yielded to her command. She'd scarcely finished cutting the reever's hands free when the knob's metallic turn sent a jolt of adrenaline through the room.

"Shit," Yazlyn cursed.

"Yaz, the door!" cried Nox at the same time.

Over them both, Ash boomed a command. "Close your eyes!"

The moment the woman slipped inside, Yazlyn slammed it shut, both she and Nox flinching tightly as they spun away and waited for Ash to call his light. The room exploded with such pure, powerful brilliance that they may as well have stood on the sun's surface. Everything moved in slow motion as the woman screamed, blinded by the punishing light. It had been no more than a second between the time Yazlyn closed the door and Ash unleashed his power.

The moment the sunlight vanished, Nox heard a new, sickening sound.

She opened her eyes to see the icicle that gored the attendant. The woman wrapped her hands around the weapon impaling her, gaping with unseeing eyes as she felt from the frozen object to the blood that had already begun to seep from her gut. With a grunt, Yazlyn yanked the icicle out, letting the woman's blood gush freely from the wound. Her lips curled back in a snarl as she spat on the attendant's collapsed body. And in that moment, Nox decided that no, perhaps she would not murder the sergeant after all.

"You did it," Nox said, first to Yazlyn, then to Ash. "Both of you."

"One more for good measure," Yazlyn said before she drove the sharpened tip into the attendant's neck, severing any small hope the woman might have had of being restored. She gurgled, sputtering sticky, red liquid for a final moment, coal-black eyes bulging until the life behind them dimmed. They remained opened but unseeing.

Nox's tone was dry as she said, "Can you cut me loose, or do you want to stab her again?"

"Well, I'd like to continue stabbing, but you're the queen." She used a foot for leverage against the woman's face as she yanked the ice out of her throat, only to gasp and stumble away. "My foot!"

"Oh, damn." Nox wrinkled her nose. "I didn't think I'd have to warn you about that even after her death. Feeling will come back soon. Now, will you hurry?" She shifted her weight in the chair, hopping slightly to reposition herself so that the sergeant would begin hacking at her bindings.

"Hold your horses while I finish Ash," Yazlyn grumbled. The ice blade was no longer clear but was instead part water, part blood. She used it to cut the bindings from the reever's ankles before she freed Nox.

"Okay," Yazlyn said as she reminded them, "the Speaker can plant memories. If all of a sudden you find yourself seeing, believing, or remembering something painful or horrible, I think we're better off assuming absolutely everything is false."

"Or we can just ask you," Nox said as she reached for the handle.

Yazlyn's brows puckered. "Ask me?"

She nodded. "Your collar. If it worked as a shield against perception, I assume you're safe against whatever she attempts."

"Assumption? That's what you're going on as our fearless leader? No." Yazlyn rested her hands on her hips. "If I were protected from all powers of the mind, then Moirai shouldn't have been able to show me her illusion spell."

Ash shrugged. "Your guess is as good as mine—though I'd say that the perception curse, like the power of implanted memories, goes on inside the mind. Moirai's spells happened externally—they were abilities and powers of the sight before you, don't you think? I've never made a ward, nor do I possess one. So, who knows, maybe you're full of false memories. Who's to say."

Nox made a face. "We're out of options. We trust Yazlyn

and her blasted collar, and we hope for the best. I wanted one too for spells like this, but Zaccai said something about rings and shields, and honestly, I didn't fully understand it."

Yazlyn laughed triumphantly. "That's a pretty tall order." Her eyes widened. "Wait, does that mean this damned peppery ring and its siphon have been nullified since I put on the collar? How delightful." Now that her joints weren't chafed and swollen from the Frozen Straits, the ring slid off with ease. She made a show of slipping it off of her finger and shoving it in her pocket.

"Ouch." Nox made a face.

"You said I was bad in bed."

Ash grumbled. "Would you two shut up? Let's get out of here."

✦

Tanith had never felt so cold. Not on the straits, not while standing atop Castle Gwydir and summoning the harpies, not sick and bloodless, and not when she'd been cast into dungeons across the continent. This icy, leaden chill was different.

She kept her eyes straight and her chin level as she entered the all-too-familiar room. She was still unbathed, face and clothes smudged from her cell. She'd spent more hours here than she could ever count. The large space above the church's sanctuary had been where she and the Reds had gathered. After services for the general population had ended and the bishop had dismissed everyone, they'd break into their smaller groups for tasks, lessons, and training. After she'd sworn herself to the Reds, she'd been taught of the groundwater. They'd practiced calling on the great magic that flowed through the world.

Over there in the corner, a dark brown stain remained from where a Red had misjudged his grasp on the power and had boiled his blood when attempting to summon the unfamiliar power of fire. In the center, a woman had tried

360

to manipulate water and had clutched at her throat, coughing and sputtering, drowning on dry land while her peers watched. Even those like Tanith who'd stayed alive long enough to call upon unnatural magics had done so at great risk to their health, knowing that each time might be the last time. Magic was theirs to command. It only cost them their life.

Near the stairs, a small plaque etched with the names of the fallen Reds served as a reminder of their sacrifice. It appeared that they'd already added hers to the list the moment she'd departed for the lower kingdoms. She'd been expected to die.

"Tanith," the man said her name easily. "It's an exceedingly pleasant surprise to have you return to us. Not only did you serve the All Mother in Raascot, but you've done the goddess a great service in bringing the heretics leading the southern kingdoms to our door. I apologize that the guards intercepted you before members of the church were able to receive you and give you the warm welcome you were due. We're all grateful the misunderstanding could be so quickly remedied."

On either side, the room remained dotted with Reds in various states of relaxation and readiness. Very few held physical weapons, as their command of power had been all the magic they'd ever need. This man, however, had been her superior for years. He'd been the one who'd overseen the development of their abilities, and the burials of the fallen. In many ways, he was her father, as she'd left her parents' arms to be embraced by a new family the moment she'd been reborn a Red.

"Of course," she answered coolly. Her hands remained at her sides, and her face lacked expression. "No apology is necessary, sir. The All Mother required more of me, and I answered Her call. I serve Her wish for the continent's unity. Does the Speaker require any assistance with the acquisitions?"

He arched a brow, but she sensed no disapproval. "They're

361

contained at the moment. The queen is the only one she'll keep. There are still a few outstanding issues to be dealt with, but it's nothing we can't handle."

"Let me know how I can help."

"Yes." He steepled his fingers. "I'm quite certain the Speaker will be calling upon you when the time comes to utilize the monarch."

"Certainly. I look forward to the All Mother's good message spreading to the savages in the lower kingdoms. The Speaker has truly blessed us with such a benevolent opportunity." Her lips twitched as she withheld any emotion and asked, "Shall I meet with the captives now?"

"No," he said, relaxing into the wall. "Clean yourself up. You've earned it. You may use the baths in the church's parsonage. There are a number of tunics for the Reds, Greens, and Grays in the armoire. Be ready for the Speaker to seek you out. You are the most knowledgeable regarding the best methods to garner their queen's compliance."

Tanith made a shallow bow. "I'll make myself ready"—she began to walk for the staircase before pausing—"though from what I know of their queen, she's emotionally and relationally motivated. If it's my place, sir, I recommend preserving the spares. They'll be more useful as living incentive than they would be to us dead."

"Consider it noted."

She dipped her head again and started toward the parsonage. The moment she reached the landing, a fellow Red fell into step beside her. It was unclear whether she was being monitored for support or out of skepticism. She'd been escorted from the dungeons in Territory One directly to the church. It was not yet clear to her whether she'd maintained their trust.

"So? Did you do it?" the Red asked.

Tanith recognized the younger male but did not turn her head to greet him, as they were not friends. He was scarcely taller than Tanith and just as lithe. They'd trained together, and he'd volunteered on multiple occasions to cross the straits. He'd struggled to conceal his disappointment when he had not been selected for the southbound mission work.

"Did I do what?" she asked, trying and failing to keep the frost from her voice. Her feet carried her forward on memory, though she felt disconnected from her body with every step that passed.

"The cleansing! If you'd succeeded in cleansing the southern lands, how did you survive?"

If he'd been staring at her too closely, he might have seen the way her eyes tightened before she forced herself to relax. She'd mastered serene, emotionless intonation. Now was no different. "I succeeded. The groundwater was taxing, but you know as much. It calls on the blood, and I was no exception. The goddess saw fit to spare me so that I could bring the southern ambassadors to Sulgrave."

"The goddess is good," he breathed reverently.

"The goddess is good," she echoed.

He paused outside of the door that connected the parsonage to the church. "I'll be back with food and water. I've been instructed to let you know that I'm here if you need anything. You'll be honored for this, Tanith. I wouldn't be surprised if the Speaker wants you to take over to lead the Reds."

"That's quite high praise," she said quietly. "I'll serve however the All Mother requires."

He opened the door for her and bowed deeply before closing it.

Despite his show of reverence, the lock's small clink answered her question. They did not fully trust her. She could open the door if she wanted and was confident they knew as much, but it would be no simple unlocking. Unraveling the wards etched into each of the church's doorways would use more than she cared to expend. After all, she needed to save her strength.

Alone in the room, she took stock of her surroundings.

The parsonage was more lavish than the barracks typically allotted to the Reds. Their minimalist lifestyle was one of restraint. This room reminded her more of the bedchambers at Castle Gwydir than of anything affiliated with the church. The bed was large, and even from where she stood near the doorway, she could tell the pillows were goose down and that the bed would carry her off into a deep, comfortable sleep, should she want it.

The bathing room was composed not of a typical tub or basin owned by common families but had the heated, overhanging bucket dotted with holes so that its water rained down like a hot, cleansing storm. She tested the temperature with her hand before stripping away the clothes she'd worn for weeks. She stepped out of her stiff, filthy things and into the warm rain. The water at her feet ran in shades of grays and browns as weeks of filth and grime washed away. The soap smelled like chamomile, which felt disrespectfully calming given the severity of the circumstance. She would have preferred to scrub with rat poison and arsenic.

Unity.

She wanted to laugh, but the joke was too cruel, too bitter for the sound. She'd witnessed unity. Farehold and Raascot were being stitched together with kindness, with acceptance, and under a banner of love. What could violence and prejudice accomplish that patience and generosity could not?

Unity. That had been the All Mother's will. Tanith had seen unity in action.

She leaned her hands against the walls of the bathing room and let the water beat down on her until the temperature dropped from its intended heat to a lukewarm discomfort. She remained immobilized until the water was an arctic chill, turning her lips blue, pimpling her skin with gooseflesh. She savored the feeling. She didn't know how to stitch together the wound she felt so deeply in her chest. She didn't know how to heal the pain, the fear, the agony she felt. She wasn't sure that she wanted to.

Worldviews were not changed overnight.

She hadn't bound mud demons and slaughtered count-less soldiers only to apologize and join the courts in Gwydir. She'd been marble, taken in by Nox, warmed by Amaris, held by Yazlyn, and chiseled by Ash. Ash was patient and brave, and he understood sacrifice. Malik was the first human she'd ever known, and he had been good and kind. The black-winged fae were powerful, and different, and lived and worked side by side with humans and faelings. They served a queen whose parentage had been something she'd been raised to believe was an abomination. She'd met Nox with disgust, and in return, Nox had been both fair and unyielding.

They'd called, and magic had answered. The All Mother had loved them with as much light and goodness as the pure-blooded fae she'd been trained to defend.

The only one who needed purifying was her.

Tanith wanted to be good.

She breathed through the shivers, through the bone-aching chill, through the need for chattering teeth, both savoring the cold and unwilling to let it best her. She prodded within herself as she examined the desire that consumed her more wholly than any other.

It was an ache formed around a wound like a scab, shield-ing it from ever healing. She didn't want her mother to be angry, and not just because the woman was quick to use the cane, whip, or whatever was on hand if she stepped out of line. If she understood the line, she would never cross it. She was too small to understand the mercurial shifts in mood that would reward her with extra servings at dinner the first night but result in what would earn her the welts of leather and the crack of pain over skin the next, but nothing hurt more than the suffocating feeling of being a disappointment. She'd made the mistake of turning to her father only once, and never again. The man was a devoted husband, which meant he sanctioned his wife's actions, no matter the cause. And if

Tanith spoke ill of her mother by asking her father to intervene, she'd done nothing but double their wrath.

They were the unit. Their child was the outsider, and it was up to her to assimilate.

And so, she tried.

She swallowed hard as her memories shifted to the spotty memories of her childhood. She gripped at them with slippery hands, but they were too dark to see clearly. She thought of their modest stone home in the heart of District Six. She saw a few snatches of moments, like the first time she'd played in the pale, jewel-toned river; the taste of pale plum that their neighbor used to pickle; or the time she caught a snake with her bare hands, unafraid. Those were the happy moments, and they were few.

She did her chores and then worked hard to anticipate her parents' needs, as well. She never spoke back. In fact, she rarely spoke at all. Even when she thought she was doing something good, righteous, or virtuous, she was proven on more than one occasion to have been wrong. Tanith was ten when she understood the problem had to be inborn. The moral compass within her could not be trusted. The only way to know she was on the right path was if the order had come directly from her parents or the church.

Unlike her mother's rules, the church's rules were in writing.

It was there she first saw the way her mother smiled when she did the right thing. Her mother spoke highly of her—the devoted, faithful child of the All Mother that she was. Her praise was a balm, and for the first time, she knew what she was doing was right. While she may never learn what triggered her mother's anger, at least she knew what brought her joy.

The more time she spent at the sanctuary, the fewer bruises she received. She understood peace, both from physical pain and the even more acute mental toil of disapproval's heavy hand.

Her heart relaxed when she thought of the way things had changed.

By thirteen, she no longer walked on eggshells. Worship earned her praise. Devotion brought her serenity. At sixteen, she announced she was dedicating her life to the Reds. Her mother had made her favorite meal that night. They'd both hugged her more tightly than she'd ever felt. Her heart swelled, and she knew beyond the shadow of a doubt that she was doing something right.

Training was a challenge, but it was one at which she excelled.

She understood discipline, commitment, and endurance. She could anticipate needs. She held nothing back as she gave herself over to the rigorous regimen.

The black-and-white categories of good and bad were clear cut amongst the sword arm of the church, and she thrived. She rose from an inductee to scout by the age of eighteen, and by the time she was twenty, she took her first life in a just and noble blood atonement, in the goddess's name. Atonements—necessary acts for those within the church who had violated the Blessed Obediences—were performed without the comte's approval, but they were enacting the will of the All Mother, and that was the only blessing she needed. She'd heard the word civilians used when they spoke of her. *Assassin.* And perhaps she was. She targeted disease within the church and pulled it out by the root so that the body might heal and remain whole. And in this role, she found not only acceptance but worthiness.

The general public knew the broad strokes of the church and its workings, but the small groups that broke out into the Grays, the Greens, and the Reds were given the specifics of the All Mother's will and her actions on the continent. The priestesses in black who served in the temples dotted through-out the mountainous kingdom were separated entirely from the primary church, serving the goddess directly with sole access to the All Mother. While the priestesses offered the goddess whatever she needed in person, the financial, practical, and military arms of the church were her will in the world.

The All Mother deserved perfection. The goddess was perfect, and so should her people be. The goddess was without fault, and so must those who graced her soil be. She was magic, power, and light. It was with heartache that she heard of the wayward, the empty, the cursed who sullied the All Mother's gift of magic.

And when Tanith was in her fifth decade of life, the All Mother was made flesh and came to their sanctuary to show them how they might make the world perfect. There was no higher purpose Tanith could serve than to give her life for the goddess. When she was selected to cross the Frozen Straits, she understood her life's meaning.

Everything was good. Everything was right. Everything made sense.

Until it didn't.

She'd read the texts. She'd visited the temples. She'd learned the stories. Tanith had sat at the feet of the bishops, listening to the word as her mother had read it before bed, and undergone excruciating preparations at the hands of the Reds.

How, then, were the impure able to summon magic? What did her books say about a halfling who had not one power but two? Who ruled a kingdom of fae? Who was kind and clever, and who offered her sanctuary and a chance for redemption without bloodshed?

Who was this man with a human mother who'd called upon an unknown magic and the goddess had answered with the very thing that might save both Tanith and him? How did he demonstrate love, care, sacrifice, and goodness, when those were qualities only of the righteous?

Why were the wicked of the continent who needed to be expunged from the face of the earth the very same who risked their lives, stood up to their fathers, and chose her over their family units, their kingdoms, or any stringent laws of right and wrong?

Her eyes lined with the sharp spike of oncoming tears, saltwater joining the shower's drenching chill, but she fought against them as she remembered her days in Gwydir.

She'd been solemn. She'd been angry. She'd held her head in confusion. She'd softly wept while she prayed, pleading for answers in the quiet shadows of her room in Castle Gwydir, asking to understand. And her prayer was answered.

It had been slow. It had been excruciatingly difficult. It had taken everything within her to battle, dissect, and to eventually accept.

They were not bad. They were not wicked, or lesser, or useless.

They were good.

Nox was queen of the continent—mixed from her very birth. She should have been cast aside, but instead she'd discovered her powers, risen through the shadows, and taken claim of the thrones. The mixed queen of the southern kingdom was kind, clever, and fair. She'd never raised a hand or issued a punishment. She was not unworthy of her title.

Gadriel was the general of mixed troops of men and fae, and he had demonstrated no cruelty in his correction. He allowed his lessers not only to speak to him as equals but looked to them as friends, as family.

And Ash.

Ash, who smelled of autumn's sweet, dying leaves. Ash with his flame-colored hair, his tanned skin, his easy laugh, and the deep wells of honey in his eyes. Ash who had gone toe to toe with her in the courtyard on their first day of unwilling partnership, who'd saved her life, who'd trusted her, who'd set her free. Ash, who'd given her the aquamarine ring she still wore.

Her stomach was a churning eddy of anger. She hated that he'd done the very thing he'd done so many times—he'd put her above everything else. He'd chosen her when he'd battled their way out of the town house in Gwydir. He'd chosen her when they'd saved each other from his father in the dead of the night, and from the invading troops of Aubade who'd stormed the castle. He'd chosen her as he'd protected her against the taxation of her powers, nursing her back to health time and time again. And he'd chosen her in Sulgrave when he'd been so foolish as to make a deal with the church.

Tanith had met goodness. She'd met kindness, sacrifice, and love.

It was through that goodness that she came to understand that there were things love was and things it wasn't. And Sulgrave's church was not good.

The true blight was the hate that had rooted itself in the church, growing like a weed as it wove itself amongst the Reds, the Greens, the Grays, the bishops, and the priestesses. The All Mother gave Speakers in times of great need, and this Speaker had arrived to bring in a cleansing message.

Tanith saw it so clearly now and was sickened by it.

They had been deceived.

Tears flowed freely, carving hot, salted lines down her cheeks as she wept.

She stepped from the water bucket and looked at herself in the reflective silver of the mirror. She'd expected to see bruises or evidence of some damage from her weeks of travel and time in the dungeon, but aside from the gaunt of her cheeks, she looked perfectly fine. The mirror could only reflect one's exterior, after all. It had no way of showing her heart.

She toweled herself off and ran a brush through her hair. She needed to be presentable if she was to take an audience with the Speaker.

Her hair was still cropped at the chin and would dry in its own time in its typical straight fashion. As her mentor had said, there were a number of tunics in various sizes so this housing unit and its facilities would be prepared for any faithful servant who might need them.

She dressed in a clean, red tunic and matching pants, then sat at the end of the bed with her feet resting firmly on the floor, keeping her posture straight. She flattened her palms against her thighs, then closed her eyes and focused on her breathing while she thought.

Her mentor said they had Nox and two others. As Ash had attempted to strike a bargain with the church, she could only imagine he'd been immediately captured. He'd been so naive. So hopeful. So foolish to have traded anything for her release. He should have left her to rot. She deserved it.

Thinking of him quickened her breathing as her temper stirred, so she forced herself to focus on facts alone. None of them had been in the city's prison, which meant they'd been taken by church officials. If she was correct, that meant her companions were being held somewhere within this building.

Nothing would change the past. Her hands were stained as red as the tunic on her back with the countless lives she'd taken in the name of the church and its divine mission. She couldn't be redeemed. She couldn't atone. But perhaps she could ensure her final actions meant something.

Thirty-One

WHO—AND WHAT—WILL WE BE UP AGAINST?" GADRIEL asked.

Amaris looked from him to the other members of the resistance.

"The church and its brainwashed masses." Kasar barked the irritated response as if Gadriel hadn't been listening.

"The church," Gadriel countered coolly, "is an institution. It's an idea. We cannot fight an idea. We need names. We need motivation. We need weaknesses."

The cabin's modest wooden dining table had transformed into the center of their war room. Makeshift maps and hastily sketched blueprints littered the surface.

Ryu tapped her finger against a piece of paper with the lists of comtes and their territories. "Alistair will fight on behalf of the church. His abilities are gruesome. The comte can snap bones at a distance."

Gadriel kept his mouth closed as he sucked in a controlled breath. "So it's safe to say he'll be the first we need to neutralize."

Amaris frowned. "How do we know Alastair will be there?"

Ryu continued to stare at the page. "Comtes rule

democratically. If they wanted us out of power, Kasar and I should have been voted out, yet our homes were sacked. They were looking to drag us in by the ear. They're making their moves, and it all stems from the church. They'll be there."

Elswyth kept his voice calm as he said, "You should know: they'll be making every effort to keep your queen alive."

Gadriel leaned into the table. "Why do you say that?"

The man tapped his chin. "We've heard the same word for some time now. It's been brought up in ceremonies, in songs, in lessons. Unity. You want motive? This Speaker—Daifa—that is her cornerstone. If Nox has brought Farehold and Raascot under one banner, then Sulgrave is one of the only missing pieces to bring Gyrradin to complete harmony—or, whatever bastardized breed of unification is brewing in the mind of that Speaker. I don't think she could do it without Nox."

"Well." Amaris grimaced. "It's a step, anyway. We stand between her and Tarkhany. But the desert is nearly as hostile as the straits. Relations between our kingdoms are almost nonexistent, save for a few rare expatriates. Except…"

"Except what?" Kasar asked gruffly.

Amaris's face fell as she pictured the map as a crimson wave swept over the world. "Except, there's nothing the Reds can't do. Once she truly succeeds here, the rest of the continent will topple like dominos."

"Well, then we'd better not let them get that far," Ryu redirected. "Back to infiltration."

Kasar sneered, though his expression was not directed at anyone in the room. "You said it yourself: the Diplomatic Hall was crawling with guards. They aren't city guards—well, they might be, but they're not operating under orders from their territories. Officially, Sulgrave and its laws have always maintained firm separation from religion, but this is an insurrection led by fanatics."

Amaris chewed on her lip. They were missing too many pieces. "What powers do we know of, aside from Alistair's?"

"I can make things grow," Elswyth said with a smile. "It might not sound particularly useful, but once we're inside, I can create a wall of vines to prevent reinforcements from entering. You'd only need to limit the immediate threat."

Gadriel expressed immense appreciation for Elswyth's power before asking, "Can this…*Daifa*…do anything we should know about?"

"She can do everything under the sun, given that she'll be accompanied by an army of Reds. Their powers are as good as hers, and we know they'll fight to the death," Ryu said bitterly. "As for the other comtes, Surya can fly, but I'm not sure she'll fight. Chloris speaks to water, which will be of little use in the church. Dhamir, though…she's a heart stopper, and I do mean that literally. Don't let her touch you."

Amaris rubbed at her temple. "We still don't know if Dhamir is for us or against us? Even after she came to the meeting?"

"Well, she isn't here, is she?" Kasar asked. "I think it's safe to say she's against us."

After a collective, frustrated noise, Amaris tried her best to ease the strain. "You'd love my abilities if we were facing humans," Amaris said. "But I'm useless against fae. I'm excellent with a sword and bow, however, so if any of you have weapons…"

Elswyth sent for one of his men to run to the shed and get Amaris whatever she needed.

Ryu flicked a finger. "My abilities might not prove very advantageous. I call the weather."

Once more, Gadriel was impressed. "Now there's something I would love to have had on the battlefield."

She deflected his compliment. "But this is no field. The church will shelter any storm I'd hope to summon unless we want to subject ourselves to a tornado. We'd be as vulnerable as our enemies."

Kasar made a sour face. "You think your abilities aren't useful? Try speaking to animals. Where are we going to get anything beyond house cats and city pigeons—unless I want to barge into the church with a herd of horses?"

Amaris seemed to feel a spark the same moment Gadriel did. They shared an excited glance.

"You speak to animals?" Her question was almost a whisper.

Kasar's eyes narrowed with the slightest suspicion. "I do."

"What if I told you we have access to an aboriou?"

The energy in the room changed. The comtes and their accompanying members of the dissent seemed to tense as they looked between the strangers and one another.

"But they're..." Elswyth began, eyes wide.

At the same time, Kasar's mouth hung ajar. "How..."

Ryu looked around excitedly. "Yes! I thought it was fiction! Word rippled through the guards of you arriving with a beast, and it seemed like the sort of rumor only gossipmongers would spread. They said it was being kept in the bestiary. Goddess, I never considered it was possible. None of them knew the name or breed of your monster. But an aboriou!" She finished with a grin, practically glowing as she did.

Kasar was still shaking his head. "They'd see it a mile off. It would be shot down before we could get close enough to use her."

A slow smile spread across Amaris's face as she reached into her bag. She procured a thick, rune-etched shackle. "Not necessarily."

✦

It was a slow, tedious journey from the valley to the church.

Amaris hadn't slept in nearly two days, and with the cortisol no longer pumping through her veins, she slumped against Gadriel as they walked, fighting the urge to sleep where she stood.

"Do you need me to pinch you?"

"Probab—ow!"

He smiled, but the expression was not entirely joyous, and she understood.

All things considered, this was not their worst plan. This was certainly not as poorly hatched as Amaris's intent to walk into Castle Aubade with the reevers and command Moirai to stop attacking the north. It was also a lot better than their half-baked infiltration on the arm of the Duke of Henares. Come to think of it, given her recent march into the Diplomatic Hall, Amaris realized that she only ever pitched one plan. Perhaps it was something she could work on, if they survived.

This time they had three comtes and respective loyalists on their side, a rundown of powers on the opposing parties, and a clear-cut enemy: Daifa.

There was a shared anxiety over what it would do to the faithful once the one they followed was gone, but Gadriel and Amaris remained hopeful. If the comtes were to be believed, Gadriel's parents were searching for the true Speaker. Long ago in Castle Gwydir, Tanith had said that a Speaker was the All Mother made flesh, one who arrived once every millennium or so when the church faced times of strife. If Tanith was right, then there'd never been more need for such a figurehead than now. If Joel and Allua were successful and returned with the All Mother's true Speaker, it may be the only thing that could end further violence.

Her blood stirred as they reached the end of the forest's sheltering safety.

"Wait," Ryu said quietly before they stepped from the trees. "I'll give us some cover."

With a low chuckle, Amaris realized how very wrong Ryu had been to doubt the usefulness of her abilities. The fog she summoned was so thick, they were able to openly sneak from Territory Three to Territory One without detection.

"How far does it extend?" Amaris asked.

"Everywhere," Ryu answered.

The party split as Kasar and Elswyth took the cuff and made their way toward the bestiary, relying on the fog to keep them sheltered. Ryu, Gadriel, and Amaris pressed on for the church. A few scattered reinforcements followed the divided party, all hidden in the dense mist of Ryu's gift.

Her ability was a double-edged sword, however, as it was every bit as blinding for them as it was for those guarding the cathedral. They hugged the walls and stayed as close to each other as possible as they picked their way down the cobblestone streets, scarcely able to see their own hands if extended before them. While it wasn't impossible for clouds to settle in the valley, its sudden presence had doubtlessly put the church's faithful guards on high alert.

"We're close," Ryu whispered.

Gadriel turned to Amaris. "Are you ready?"

"I'm a reever," came her hushed reply. But she knew what he was asking. He was military and had been trained to kill. Amaris was effective in battle, though her training had been tailored toward demons and monsters. She'd taken very few lives in her time. She didn't relish the idea of killing, but she would not falter when it was required of her.

Then they were there. The fog concealed them until it was too late for their opposition. Whatever abilities the Sulgrave fae guarding the church may or may not have possessed, Amaris would never know. She swung her sword with precise intensity, and the razor-sharp blade whirred as it moved through the air, but did not crunch as it sliced through her adversary's skull. The Red sank to the ground noiselessly as Amaris advanced to the next. She heard what she knew to be the swift crack of bone as a neck was snapped nearby, but to the unsuspecting ear, it may have been the crunch of pebbles underfoot.

She looked at the ruby lake at her feet as she took down her third kill and lifted her lower lip curiously. She'd expected to feel something—fear, regret, nausea—but it hadn't been personal. After all, she supposed, all's fair in war and rebellion, or however the saying went.

The infiltration was quick, quiet, and fatal.

Ryu slid into the space behind her, wiping blood from

her hands onto her tunic. One of her men approached from the side. "Lead the others and secure the perimeter," she said. "We're dead if the Reds intervene. Take down as many as you can."

The guards may have felt something was amiss, but they hadn't acted on it, and now it was too late. All they could do was clear the path to the church and infiltrate so that when Kasar arrived with their beast, they met no opposition. Once Elswyth sealed them in, there would be no opportunity for reinforcements.

Get in. Save the queen. Kill the Speaker.

Gadriel stepped through the fog to meet them at the front door. Amaris waited for him to unlock it, but it took less than a second for him to deliver the news. "It's not locked. It's barred."

"Shit."

"How else do we get in?"

Ryu looked from side to side on instinct, as if she might see a new door. "There are several points of entry along the body of the church, but we should go around back. There's a parsonage on the rear of the building that isn't truly a part of the sanctuary. It was built years after the church and is only connected through a narrow hall. If they've had the sense to bar the main doors, then they're probably cutting off the primary exits. Plus, if we're going to break a window, we should do it as far from the sanctuary as possible."

"Lead the way," Amaris said with a nod.

They followed Ryu as she skirted the enormous cathedral until the hall dipped, indicative of a later addition to the building. They worked their way through the connective corridor from the church to the back building meant to house its clergy. They hugged the glass, iron, and stones until they made it to the farthest window.

Gadriel reached a hand over his head and grabbed on to the collar of his tunic. He slipped his shirt off from his back and wrapped it around his fist, then punched through the window. The garment protected his hand and wrist from the jagged edges as he cleared out the space.

"Help me up," Amaris whispered. Gadriel shook his tunic free of glass and slipped it over his head before interlacing his fingers.

"Save some for me," he said before he posted Amaris onto the window ledge. She took the barest of seconds to scan the room, but she couldn't discern much through the stark change in light between the bright white fog and the shadowed room. She swung her legs over the lip, then held on to the windowsill as she lowered herself as quietly as possible onto the parsonage floor. Amaris turned and froze. She was not alone.

In one dizzying breath she shifted from alarm, to confusion, to relief as she looked into the wide eyes of the small crimson figure, hands raised defensively in the far corner of the room. The fae dropped her hands to her side, lips parting noiselessly.

"Amaris."

"Hi, Tanith."

Thirty-Two

Tanith sucked in a breath as she heard a noise. She sniffled deeply, then used her sleeve to wipe the salt water from her face. She looked around the room and her brow furrowed. It had been sunny when she'd arrived. The sky had been blue. The small home's windows had been glazed over with a thick, white cloud as if the very sky had descended upon the city.

The high, bell-like crack of glass sent her scrambling to her feet. A shape—an arm? a piece of cloth?—waved in the window, sending shards to the floor. Tanith's breath came in ragged pulls as she readied herself, though for what, she couldn't tell.

Then a face as pale as the fog around it popped into the window, squinting into the parsonage. Her mouth went dry as shock settled over her. She knew that face. She remained frozen as the familiar shape swung over the ledge and landed with cat-like quiet on the ground below.

"Amaris."

The reever's thickly frosted lashes blinked against the surprise as she said on a breathy exhale, "Hi, Tanith."

Tanith had never been a particularly sentimental person,

but something within her cracked. She gave in to the compulsion and ran to her friend, tears returning as she threw her arms around her. Amaris returned the embrace, slipping her hands against her back and squeezing tightly. It was all Tanith could do to keep the sobs that threatened to take her to her knees. Tanith didn't even look up as the others crawled through the window. If they were with Amaris, then whoever it was, it was fine. It was safe. It was right.

Whatever fate befell her, she was ready. Even if she died today, it would be among friends.

"What happened?" Amaris asked without fully releasing her. Perhaps the demigoddess could feel Tanith's need for the embrace, and her heart broke all over again. She'd felt more loved, wanted, and accepted in her short time in Raascot than she ever had in Sulgrave.

These were her people.

"Ash." She barely choked out the name.

Amaris tucked her in for another hug. She rested a hand on the back of Tanith's head as she released a pained sigh. "He made a deal, didn't he?"

Tanith nodded against her shoulder. "It never should have happened. I know he didn't mean for any of this. He thought he was just setting up a meeting. At least, that's what he told himself. I couldn't even look at him. I just…"

"Shh." Amaris tightened her hug. "We're going to fix this."

And whether or not she believed it was possible, she was willing to try. They untangled from one another and Tanith greeted Gadriel with a nod.

The comte from Territory Five, however, was someone she knew.

"Tanith," Ryu said, testing the name.

"If you're here with them," she said, "then I am your ally, and you are mine."

The comte held her gaze, chin level, for a long, careful moment. With a shallow bow, her olive branch was accepted, and they could begin. A few of Ryu's men noiselessly joined through the windows, landing with muted feet as they crept into the room. Tanith told them all she knew, which wasn't much.

"They're going to come for me," Tanith said.

Gadriel looked at her cautiously. "Are you in trouble?"

"They think I've brought you here for them. If I'm good for anything, let it be this. Use their belief in me to your advantage. I believe I'm meant to meet the Speaker soon."

"Do you know what they want with you?" Ryu asked.

Tanith straightened her shoulders. "I believe it's a commendation. Meeting her is meant to be a high honor. One few receive."

"You haven't met her?" Gadriel's brows lowered.

"She's addressed the masses, but no, I've never spoken with her directly. Only my mentor has."

Amaris touched her arm gently. "We believe the others are in the church."

"They are," Tanith agreed, "but I don't know where. And there's one more piece of information. I can't be certain as to why, but they intend to keep Nox alive."

The resulting ripple of tight lips, of stressed eyes, of flexed postures spoke to the eerie complication of this news. While it was a relief to hear that Nox was alive and unharmed, the Speaker's unknowable intentions couldn't be good.

Tanith perked. To her left, Ryu and Gadriel had also tilted their heads, intently listening. She knew from the look on Amaris's face that the reever had not yet picked up what they'd heard with their sensitive, fae ears.

"Get in the bathing room," Tanith urged.

One of Ryu's men ran to the window and yanked the curtain to hide the evidence of their forced entry as the group sprinted into the next room and eased the door closed behind them. Tanith resumed her calm posture on the bed, closing her eyes once more, the picture of stoicism.

When the door opened, a male voice greeted her. She

recognized the voice as belonging to one of the highest-ranking Reds.

"There's been a disturbance," he said.

She opened her eyes, keeping her expression fully neutrally. He'd interrupted her pious meditation, after all. "And that would be?"

"The southern queen and her compatriots are…missing."

Tanith cocked an idle brow.

"It appears they've broken free. A Gray has been killed. The sanctuary's exits have been barred, so they must be somewhere in the church. We could use your expertise."

She almost asked him why they'd need her, then remembered that she was the only one who'd crossed the straits, accomplished her mission, and lived to tell the tale. Perhaps they hadn't locked the door because they distrusted her but because they feared her. An ember of pride sparked within her as she admitted that yes, they were right. She was powerful.

Tanith stood with casual coolness. "Has the Speaker joined us?"

He offered a curt nod. "She's in the sanctuary. She'll remain under guard until we've neutralized the threat. Once we've contained the southerners, the Speaker will be glad for your intelligence. She's expressed extreme pleasure with you, Tanith. You've made the All Mother very proud."

"I'm glad." Her words lacked feeling, but that was nothing new. The heart was deceitful, and emotions and their volatility were a sign of weakness. She was glad for the practice as he accepted her cool, unfeeling response.

The man departed from the room with a swift bow and Tanith followed him out. The door closed behind him, but whether or not it locked behind her would be of no mind to them. She knew the others would manage just fine. Gadriel had a knack for locks, after all.

Their shadows preceded them, as only a dim fae light lit the hall.

She walked a half step behind the Red as she considered her options.

The current corridor hugged the perimeter behind the sanctuary. Tanith knew there were exactly six doorways before they turned the corner. Five doorways. Now four. She knew that the man beside her was extraordinarily powerful but that his defenses were down. He'd not only mastered access to groundwater but had been able to replenish time after time as one of the few Reds who survived calling on strange magics. She also knew that if she was going to act, she had to be quick. The element of surprise would only be on her side for a moment longer. She fell another step behind and stared at the back of his head.

It was now or never.

She moved with muscle and power. She was speed personified as she leapt onto his back, anchoring herself on his hips as she slipped one hand over his mouth and braced the other against the back of his neck. She called on her lightning the moment he opened his mouth to scream, shoving the crackling, burning bolts down his throat before he had the chance to make a sound. Tanith dropped to the ground as the man evaporated from the inside out. Within a heartbeat, he was scarcely more than dust particles and memories.

She had taken more lives than she'd ever be able to count, but Tanith had never killed a Red. A tremor twitched through her fingertips as she looked at the tiny, smoking remnants that shifted against the stones on an unseen wind. She stumbled into the wall to catch herself before she fell.

Breathe, breathe, dammit!

She'd made her choice long before this moment. But with this nail in the coffin, there was no going back. She straightened her back as she understood the wind. The door behind her had opened. The quiet padding of shoes told her the others had escaped the parsonage. Gadriel, Amaris, and the others were beside her an instant later, standing on the ashes of her former brother-in-arms as if he had never existed.

They looked at her to confirm her readiness. This was her church. These were her grounds. It would be up to her to take the lead. Whatever happened next, she was with them.

✦

Nox's eyes widened. "What was that?"

Yazlyn had sharper ears than either she or Ash. The sergeant shushed them urgently, then flared her wings to create a physical barrier to halt their forward creep. They froze at the sound of an odd popping burst from somewhere around the corner. The silver clatter of bells, the tinkle of snowfall, the noise of something breaking.

Glass. It had to be glass.

She didn't know enough about the church to understand where they were, save that the rectangular building had an enormous, open sanctuary in the center, and corridors of rooms that ran along its edges. If they continued down their hallway, they'd run into whatever had tingled their sense of alarm.

"Go back," Yazlyn whispered. She grabbed Nox's hand and gave it a tug, but Nox didn't want to go back. There was nothing for them that way.

"To what end?" Ash replied. "There are no windows along this hall. There were none in our room. We're entombed in stone."

"There were skylights," Nox whispered.

"What?"

She kept her voice low but urgent. "We have to go farther in, toward the center. In the sanctuary, during the service, I spent the service looking at the skylights. If you could fly us directly upward, we could break through the ceiling."

Yazlyn frowned. "I don't know if I'm strong enough…"

A red pulse of anger rose Nox's voice to a stage whisper. "Our lives are at stake, Yaz. I'm going to need you to believe in yourself."

The women turned to Ash as he wordlessly agreed. They

crept away from the hall and toward the double doors that would let them into the inner sanctum. They held a collective breath as Ash eased the doors open to see pews, a stage, stars overhead, a large, empty space, and…

The hope leeched from Nox just as the blood drained from her face.

A slow, peacock smile spread across an all-too-familiar mouth.

"Well, hello, Your Highness."

Thirty-Three

S HIT," GADRIEL WHISPERED. HE REACHED FOR AMARIS'S ARM
to stop her.

Ryu nodded once. Whatever it was, she'd heard it too.

Amaris cursed her helpless ears.

She waited for them to press forward, to whisper a new
plan, to tell her what had happened, but instead, Gadriel
surprised her by turning fully toward her. He grabbed her
hands as if they were the only two in the hall, as if their
shadowed pocket of corridor was in a bubble of solitude
rather than a cramped space shared by Tanith, the comte
from Territory Five, and her men. There was an expression
in his eyes that made her stomach churn. A sad, upward tilt
to his pinched brows. An earnestness in the way his dark
eyes shone.

"Amaris, whatever happens—"

It was bad, then. Whatever the others had heard, it was
very, very bad.

She shook her head once, setting her jaw. She'd heard this
speech. She'd been the one delivering it when Gadriel had
readied himself to jump across the pit in the Tower of Magics.
She knew it, and she didn't want to hear it.

She returned his burning intensity. With total resolution, she said, "Tell me later."

For the barest of moments, his eyes shone. Then he became a general once more. He turned to the Red. "Tanith, can you dampen us?"

"I'll do more than that," Tanith said. "I'll carry us forward in the space between things."

Of course, she can, Amaris thought. *The gift of going unseen, of walking in the space between things is impossible...unless you're Tanith.*

Gadriel squeezed Amaris's hand once before easing them forward through the door to the innermost room of the church. Amaris swallowed her urge to cry out the moment she saw Nox. Her unbound hair was mussed. Her back was straight, hands in fists at her sides. Her eyes flashed with defiance as she stood in front of Ash and Yazlyn as though she might shield them.

They were not alone.

Excitement turned to fear in Amaris's belly as she soaked in the room. She and the others continued to pick their way forward, undetected, as they walked into the lion's den.

A venomous serpent of a woman stood atop the stone stage. Terrifying, unnatural sapphire eyes remained fixed on Nox. Amaris expected a forked tongue to flicker out between her teeth as she spoke, but the woman was fae. This had to be Daifa—the one they called the Speaker.

Alastair stood at her side, and the sickening feeling soured when she remembered his terrible gift. He could snap his finger and end Nox where she stood. His wasn't the only terrifying power in the room. Her vision swam once she understood just how many Reds had been stationed throughout the sanctuary. A veritable army was at the ready. And sitting primly in the corner was the crimson-clad Dhamir of Territory Seven. As angry as Amaris wanted to be at the treacherous comte, there was something uncomfortable on her face—a worry, a fear—that twisted her features in stark contrast to the haughty smirks worn by Alastair and Daifa alike.

When the Speaker opened her mouth, a bird-like preen echoed off the walls. She tucked a lock of long, dark hair that faded to a pale tip, behind her ear as if she hadn't a care in the world. Eyes still trained on Nox, she said, "How nice of you to join us."

Amaris's fingers settled against the hilt of her sword. She was ready to fight, ready to leap out from the space between things and defend Nox, but her heart stuttered at Nox's oddly chilling smile. The queen of the southern continents relaxed into confidence as she assessed the small, protective crowd. Then to the Speaker, she asked, "Do they know what powers you possess, Daifa?"

Amaris looked back at Gadriel, then at Ryu, who all wore matched masks of confusion.

She turned back to the Speaker in time to see the thinly controlled sneer. Whether with the informal address or the veiled threat, Nox had triggered something within her. The woman's bright, blue eyes burned with cold fire.

Nox took a step toward the stage. She spoke from her diaphragm, smile spreading as she looked first at Dhamir, then Alastair, then the zealous soldiers at the woman's back. "Your Speaker concocts false memories. She plants them like seeds in the mind, and they take root, growing within you like weeds. Did you know this of her? Of course you didn't. It's how she's gotten you to blindly follow her. It's how she's lied her way into the church. It's how she hides in plain sight, even now."

If there had been any sound within their bubble, she may have heard Ryu's sharp inhalation, or the way her men skidded to a halt.

Daifa mirrored Nox's movement, moving closer to the edge of the stage as she squared off against the young queen. A calculating smirk. A smug breath. A sparkle of green-blue nails as she appreciated her own hand, as if too unbothered to look up from her manicure. With bored neutrality, Daifa said, "How interesting to hear from the one who claims to have gained the thrones to both Farehold and Raascot without it ever reaching our ears. Why stop there? Are you Queen of Tarkhany as well? Do you own the Etal Isles? Perhaps you've ventured north to stake your claim as monarch of our mountains. What other tales will you spin for us, so-called Queen of the South?"

Nox met her with cool impassivity.

"I wonder…what might one achieve if they could plant false memories? Perhaps they could place a vision of their coronation? They might convince their followers as to how they were chosen, adorned, anointed—that they were the goddess made flesh. How powerless would her subjects be if they all believed they'd witnessed her ascension with their own eyes?"

The Speaker twitched.

Nox's feigned sympathy. "Such a small power. You can't create. You can't speak to earth or fire or water. The sorry ability is barely a gift at all."

A few uncertain eyes flickered from Nox to regard their Speaker.

Daifa spoke through her teeth. "Your lies don't bother me, false queen. Your words may affect your little white-haired friend, however."

Nox's smile spread. "You don't have Amaris. You have no idea where she is."

Well, she's about to, Amaris thought as her spirits sank.

Emboldened, Nox said, "Your gift for false memory didn't work on me, and neither will your claim as false voice for the All Mother." She gestured but kept her eyes on Daifa. "I don't fault your people, of course. They believe what their minds have told them. They are no lesser or weaker for seeing a sad fae's gift for visions. You are simply all the more evil."

Daifa tensed. Her smile was tight and controlled.

"I tire of her ramblings." The Speaker flicked her hand.

Alistair stood and offered a malicious grin of his own, sharpened teeth glinting in the white light of the heavy cloud that filtered through the foggy windows overhead. He snapped his fingers, and a sickening noise rang out through the sanctuary. A shocked, choked scream mingled with the crack of bone as Nox fell to her knees.

This time when Amaris lunged, Gadriel stopped her. He shot her a warning look. They were close, but not close enough. They had a few steps left before they could be truly effective. Nox was hurt, but she was alive. From the way she cradled her elbow, Amaris knew that Alistair had broken her arm without touching her.

"I need her alive," Daifa cooed, returning to her seat, "but I don't need her mobile. Show her what we do to the blasphemous."

Ash and Yazlyn's cries overlapped. They burst into action in a flurry of dark wings and anger. Ash sprinted headlong for the comte while Yazlyn dove for the man like a bird of prey.

Alistair didn't move, didn't flinch, didn't so much as blink as his enemies advanced. Daifa and her Reds looked on with tired amusement, as if they had far better things to do. Grin widening, the comte from Territory One snapped his fingers once more.

Nothing happened.

Alistair's face changed. His expression flashed with mingled disbelief and confusion as the percussive sound of snaps happened again, then again. In his arrogance, he hadn't bothered to step aside while the sergeant barreled down on him, cracking him in the jaw with her fist as she landed a punishing blow. He stumbled backward and scrambled for his sword, but the sergeant was a vulture who'd already dug her claws in.

Nox remained on the floor with wide, horrified eyes as the battle unfolded.

Amaris gasped. "Tanith, no!"

"Drop our guard!" Gadriel commanded as he spun in

horror to Tanith. They'd realized in overlapping horror what she'd done.

The moment Nox's arm had broken, Tanith had done the only thing she could do. She'd cast protective shields around Nox, Yazlyn, and Ash while keeping the others hidden in the unseen place between things.

She was calling on not one but two stolen powers. Until she obeyed. She dropped their concealment, and the room reacted as the others were fully exposed. Reds scrambled to their feet. Daifa stumbled toward the far wall in a panic.

Gadriel plunged into battle.

Amaris had once heard a tale of a fae who could slow time—she was quite confident that a tale was all it was. There had been no proof beyond the wishful thinking of men who fell in battle, the campfire stories of warriors who dreamed of a way to pick off their enemy without the flurry of war. While no such gift existed in this soiled, unholy chapel, she felt as though she could see everyone as if it moved with the same glacial slowness of the ice that had bobbed down the river in Gwydir. The sounds seemed to come out of the mouths around her lower, deeper, drawn out somehow. The flashes, pains, and shocks were absorbed one at a time, as if everyone were taking turns in their individual steps of this violent dance.

She saw it all.

Three Reds surrounded Daifa, standing down to protect her while the others sprung into action.

Gadriel, Amaris, Ryu, and her men sprinted for the platform.

A flurry of colors, sounds, heats, and chills flashed as powers and swords broke and clashed around them. On Amaris's side, one of Ryu's men exploded into a cloud of crimson mist, only blood and viscera remaining where only moments before he'd stood. A Red cried out as she summoned a blinding ball of flame, but just as soon as the fireball was born, it blinked out. Ryu's sword dripped as the

Red's head landed with a thump and rolled across the stones from her body.

Amaris saw as Dhamir leapt to her feet, but instead of readying to take on the resistance, she stretched her hand for the nearest Red. The man crumpled to the ground at her feet.

One of Alistair's men brought down his sword against Amaris, but she blocked it easily. With his sword deflected and chest exposed, she kicked him violently to the ground. The point of her sword found the space between his ribs as she sank the blade into his chest. He sputtered a final breath as a flash of chestnut curls and the powerful flutter of wings landed beside the body Ryu had decapitated.

Yazlyn called to the hot pool of blood, and the water within it answered. Before Amaris could blink, the sergeant held a horrid, frozen spear of ice and gore. She thrust her razor-sharp weapon toward a Red, but the soldier blocked it with his shield, shattering it into a thousand pieces. Yazlyn spun to reshape it, creating a crimson shield of her own just in time for her ice barrier to absorb a blow from another warrior. Amaris nearly forgot about the battle around her as she gaped at the awe-inspiring, chilling manipulation of ice. Yazlyn was the thing from which legends were born.

The endless stare of amazement had been no more than three seconds, but it had been too long. She'd left herself vulnerable. The whir of metal sliced through the air behind her. She ducked on instinct just in time to miss the surge and a swing of a fae from Territory One. He'd underestimated her agility and didn't have the time to slow his steps as her sword swept over in an arc, embedding itself in the man's throat. She grunted as she jerked the weapon from his flesh, and it was then that she saw Tanith.

The tiny warrior clutched the stone wall for stability with one hand. The other remained extended as she cast her shield over the vulnerable queen. Sweat beaded on Amaris's brow. Her lips were blue. Amaris knew with some certainty that

Tanith had not stopped at shielding Nox. She'd protect as many as she could, for as long as she could. The only thing Amaris could do to help her was to eliminate the threat.

Gadriel was a flash of wings and weapons at her side. She could have sworn he sliced through a burst of light itself as he cut his way to Alistair. He didn't look back at Tanith's struggles as he shouted, "Keep Nox safe!"

The comte from Territory One spun at the sound of the general's voice.

Amaris opened her mouth to cry for him to stop. She knew something horrible long before Gadriel did. Tanith was so busy shielding the most exposed members of the party that she couldn't stretch her shield for him. In the same instant she opened her mouth to scream, her cry for Gadriel was stolen by a grunt as she blocked yet another blow. She threw an elbow and slashed at the fae, sending him sputtering back, but she could see only Gadriel.

In that moment, the world ended. Amaris lunged, and as she did, she was washed with the sights, the sounds, the collective cry as everyone understood. Still on the ground, Nox unleashed a terrible scream. Yazlyn threw herself toward her general. Ash skidded to a halt in his tracks, stolen sword drooping loosely at his side.

No one could stop it.

Alistair snapped his fingers with cold indifference.

For a moment, Gadriel remained frozen in his attack. In the next, he dropped. His body crumpled to the ground. His wings folded limply beneath him as he toppled from the air like a bird shot down with an arrow.

A horrible buzzing filled Amaris's ears, like hornets had been released into her skull and trapped in tightly. "No," she whispered. The battle wasn't over. The fight hadn't ended. She couldn't let herself be distracted. She had to focus. She had to fight. She wanted to scream. She was going to be sick. But she needed to pull herself to the present. She needed to push forward. She was not ready to meet the All Mother.

But she couldn't look away from Gadriel's broken, unmoving body. Something inside her died. And though she knew she needed to move, her heart had fallen onto the stone floor, broken and lifeless alongside her general. She might have stood there forever had the earth's very foundation not shaken.

A thunderous boom shocked her back to life as the enormous double doors cracked open.

Bodies littered the sanctuary, but both sides jerked their heads up to see what had happened. The doors opened to show a soupy white bank of fog, and to everyone else in the room, there was nothing else. The room was taut with friction as they waited. As far as the Reds, the Speaker, and the armies were concerned, no shape emerged. No wind stirred. Amaris was the only one who could see what caused the high, feminine cry, the whip of black hair, what sent Nox to her side as it bowled into her.

Amaris sprinted toward Nox then stopped mid-stride as a loud, wet sound overtook the room. The others blinked in confusion as Alistair's head and shoulders disappeared. Amaris watched with grim satisfaction as a large, white beast tore into his flesh. The others froze and listened to the moist crunch of blood and bone, coupled with a spray of bowels and the shredding of muscles that alerted everyone to the horrible presence of an unseen monster. The comte's legs disappeared with a chomp, and nothing of the man remained.

Fjolla would have been enough to save the day. She'd ended the sorry smear of a fae's life who'd taken down Gadriel. The aboriou's justice had been swift, but it had not been healing. Yet the animal was not alone. The calvary had arrived. Kasar the lion-hearted bounded into the sanctuary with his sword lofted, bellowing all the while as men flanked him on all sides as he controlled the beast that led the way. Ryu and the fighters had taken out as many Reds as they could, but the tide had turned. The enemy was outnumbered ten to one.

The gap to the sanctuary quickly began to sew itself shut as vines grew between the church and the world beyond. The shouts of guards that had been echoing through the mist began to hack and chop at plants that engulfed the cathedral, but each impact of their sword was replaced with two, three, or four more plants of equal girth.

Daifa began shouting from behind her protective circle of guards.

Her words were...bizarre. It wasn't a command. They weren't rallying cries. What was she...

"Fuck."

If she hadn't been in the sanctuary for Nox's grand pronouncement, she would have never known that the Speaker could plant memories. As the woman shouted, Amaris knew Daifa was rewriting history. She was yelling to Kasar alone. And while her words made little sense to Amaris, the comte in mustard slowed to a halt.

Kasar rotated where he stood and stared at Ryu. He adjusted the grip on his sword.

"Kasar..." Ryu took a cautionary step back. Her sword remained lifted, but the other hand was raised in a placated warning.

"Shit, shit, shit," Amaris cursed as she ran from the action. Her time to fight had come and gone. She dove from the platform toward Tanith, putting as much space between herself and the Speaker as possible. Ash reached Tanith the second before Amaris did. She looked at them with dim eyes as she panted, barely clinging to consciousness.

"Hold on," Ash begged.

The comte from Territory Four took three thundering steps toward Ryu with murder scrawled across his face.

"She plants memories!" Ryu shouted. She matched his steps, moving backward as she pleaded with him. "You know you hate her. You know we're allies. You know you don't trust her. Whatever you saw or heard—"

He raised his sword for Ryu, but Yazlyn was a bird of prey.

She plunged from the sky with a hammer-shaped weapon of ice and gore. She struck Kasar over the head with a single, powerful blow before he could reach Ryu. He was neutralized for now, but he would soon awaken with a vengeance. And though she'd saved Ryu, Kasar's unconsciousness had one swift, unintentional consequence. The moment he fell, the invisible force erupted into chaos. Another Red disappeared beneath the crunch of teeth. The fighter's fresh, crimson blood dripped from a floating, invisible nothing.

It turned and ran for Nox.

"Fjolla?" Nox called into the commotion, still gripping the shattered bone of her arm.

Amaris cried out for Nox's attention, but the queen remained fixed on her monster.

Fjolla's ankle brace had reawoken the anger and pain the beast had spent so much time fleeing on the straits. While Amaris could see it well enough to stay out of its way, the Reds were helpless as she tore through their ranks.

Nox's fingers dug into the aboriou's fur as she felt for its back, swinging herself onto it with her good arm as if it were a great, unseen horse. "Fjolla, go!"

The aboriou was not a tame beast, and this had never been something they'd practiced. Between the heat of battle and the urgency of Nox's kick, perhaps Fjolla sensed that life and death hung in the boundary. The queen intended to urge her beast toward Amaris, but Fjolla turned for the vines that had threaded themselves thickly over the door.

"Come on." Amaris shoved the other reever as Ash scooped Tanith into his arms. They took off after Nox, flailing until she was able to knot her fist in fur. Amaris gripped onto whatever parts of the aboriou she could as its great claws shredded at the vines that had contained them.

"Yazlyn, come on!" Amaris's cry was half command, half plea, but the sergeant remained at Ryu's side. A pillar of flame surrounded them both just as Fjolla gouged through the thickly woven vines. In one instant they were trapped amidst the slain, and in the next, they plunged into the mist beyond. The vines closed around them instantly, sealing Yazlyn, Ryu, and Gadriel's fallen body behind them.

"We have to go back!" Amaris cried.

Fjolla knocked past the guards, sending anyone who tried to stop them onto their backsides.

"I can't make her do anything," Nox replied, voice wavering. She grunted as she adjusted her hold, and Amaris realized that she was clinging to the unseen with only one good arm. She hooked an arm around Nox and tucked the queen against her, alleviating as much pressure as she could as the church disappeared behind them.

The aboriou ran with the same wild, urgent terror that had possessed her on the straits. The beast sprinted as fast as it could, taking it and the four that clung to her fur like ticks as far from the church as possible.

Fjolla remained unseen to all but Amaris. Between the beast's invisibility and the density of the fog, they were flying blind in every sense of the word. The aboriou crashed into a number of buildings until she found the jade river and began sprinting down the road that would carry them out of Territory One and into the valley.

"Fjolla, stop," Nox begged, near tears.

Fjolla did not obey. She was hurt, panicked, and crazed.

"She's going to go back to the ice." Ash's voice was loud, realizing the beast was carrying them down the road that would lead them to the straits. They had no shelter, no medicine, and no supplies. Nox's arm had been cracked in two, and Tanith was barely clinging to consciousness. If they were abandoned on the Frozen Straits, they'd never survive.

"I can do it," Tanith rasped through a ragged breath.

"No!" Ash yelled at her as he clutched her more tightly, but she did not listen.

Her small fingers wove between the thick tufts of unseen aboriou fur. Her face was planted deeply in Fjolla's side. What could be seen of Tanith's hands between the invisible strands of hair began to glow a familiar shade of blue as she bound the beast to herself. Fjolla stopped running immediately.

"Where do we go?" Nox was trying to sound strong, but tears from both pain and fear were staining her face.

"I know a place." Tanith's words sounded like she was speaking through deep under water. She was little more than a phantom as she called on yet another power. Her body went limp, eyes closed, but her hand remained open and flexed to let them know she was alive. She guided the aboriou through the mist, keeping Fjolla under her bindings while Ash wiped the sweat-soaked hair helplessly away from her face. Amaris was doing her best to secure Nox to the beast, as the queen's broken arm provided little ability to maintain the necessary hold on her pet.

They stayed silent as Tanith and Fjolla guided them through the fog. Ash shot a panicked look time and time again as if hoping Nox or Amaris would do something, but they were as helpless as he. Still, Fjolla stayed calm and intentional with her steps as she had taken them out of the city and above the dense fog bank. They were carried up a mountainside, following a trail that seemed to be leading them away from the territories and into a narrow valley.

Though they were no longer in the cloud, the blackened night made it impossible to see. If there was a moon, it was hidden behind a mountain peak. They were alone in the ink, able to discern little more than the ground below them and a few arm's lengths in front.

"Tanith," Ash entreated. "Tanith, you can let go of Fjolla. Stay with us."

She didn't respond. Whether her silence was from inability or an effort to save what remained of her strength, she concentrated on guiding the aboriou until they were deep within the valley. They rounded a sharp, sudden bend that had been invisible from the narrow trail only moments before. An outcropping of rock had shielded it from view as Fjolla plodded into the tight crevice. They came to a stop in front of a stone door lit by a pale, silver fae light.

"Can you hold her?" Tanith asked Nox, sliding off of the beast and slumped against Ash arms. It was the first time she'd spoken in a long, long time.

A hand flew to Nox's mouth. She stifled a shared gasp as Tanith's chalky, deathly pallor became clear to everyone. She took a single step away from the reever before she collapsed. Ash caught her before she hit the boulder.

Just then, the stone door opened up before them, and a beautiful woman in an elegant black dress stepped out.

"What brings you to the temple of the All Mother?"

Thirty-Four

THEY WERE SAFE. AND PERHAPS AMARIS SHOULD HAVE FELT gratitude. But she didn't.

She stepped outside and tilted her face toward the cold, glimmering stars that shone through the breaks between clouds. They'd disappear once more as the weather continued churning overhead, as if the sky itself was not sure whether or not a storm would come or go. She understood, as she felt the same.

She looked into the night sky and thought of how she'd crossed the continent under the cover of darkness in Gadriel's arms. It was at night he'd held her, he'd filled her, he'd made her feel so whole, so loved, so safe. She'd met him under the moonlight.

And it was the daylight that stole him from her.

"Amaris?" As a man, Ash was not allowed within the sacred space. He'd been resting his back and head against the sheer, jagged stones that concealed their narrow passageway and anxiously picking at his skin. He'd been sitting alone in the dark for hours on the mountainside before anyone had come to give him an update.

Ah, she'd almost forgotten why she'd exited the temple in the first place before he'd spoken.

"Here." Amaris attempted to hand Ash a glass of water and a blanket. Her word was clipped and angry. He had not killed Gadriel with his hand, but he may as well have. His deal with the church had ruined everything.

"I've looked around a bit," he said. "We're completely sheltered in this chasm. No one could find us unless they knew exactly where to look. We..." His voice drifted when he realized she wasn't looking at him. He didn't apologize. He couldn't. "How is she?"

Amaris sighed and took a knee in front of him, setting the glass of water beside him as she draped the blanket over his lap. Her posture did not match her message. "She's going to be okay."

"How? Did they have greenstrike—"

"No." She shook her head, then turned to leave. "Drink your water. I need to go sit with Nox."

"Wait." He grabbed for her hand. "Nox did this? She helped Tanith?"

Fury burned within her as she resisted the urge to slap him away.

"She did it once with Malik." Ash got to his feet, tugging at Amaris's hand again to gain her attention. "He'd been crushed by a spider, and she brought him back from the brink of death. She'd given him of her own life. It was remarkable. But then..."

"But then she fell terribly ill, herself? Yes." Amaris spat out the word, anger growing. "She fell on her sword for Tanith. Now we've traded a lifeless Sulgrave girl for a comatose queen because of her damned kiss of life. We've lost Gadriel. Nox is on death's door. Get some sleep." She shook her hand free as she turned away from him.

"No, listen, Ayla!" Ash took a quick step to cut off her progress. "She got better. She saved Malik, and Nox got better without tonics or a healer—you can make her better."

Her rage flickered. Disgust paused as puzzlement bunched her brows. "What?"

Ash continued to nod, perhaps as desperate for a sliver of good news as she was. "Yes. She fell ill after she'd saved him from certain death from the spider, and Malik and I searched for a healer. It took us days to find one and bring her back, but the healer told us there was nothing she could do. She didn't need tonics or medicine or the power the healer could offer her. The woman told us to just…stay with her. Malik simply held her hand and sat with her, and she got better!" His words tumbled out excitedly, each word punctuated and colliding like stones falling down the side of the cliff. "It was affection? Love? It's because of what she is—it's how she gives and takes life, it's—"

"Oh my goddess." Amaris's mouth dropped open. She turned from him and ran back into the temple, leaving Ash silhouetted against the doorway. How could she have been so stupid?

Amaris had been in a sacred temple once before, but this mountain escape was a world apart in more ways than one. This was not the airy, white marble of the Temple of the All Mother that had filled her with awe in the southern kingdom. This temple was narrow, rough-hewn, and seemed like an organic provision that the mountain itself had relinquished onto the All Mother, rather than something crafted by man or fae. It was as if this space had been born a temple from the earth itself. As with before, a twisted, knotted tree rose out of the center. This one was not the thick, expansive canopy she'd seen in Farehold. This mystical tree was a vertical curl that wrapped and wound its way like an enormous vine as it sought the light far above the mountain crevices. Silvery leaves clung intermittently to its sparse branches, and the tree emitted a light that seemed to generate in and of itself. In so many ways, it was exactly like the tree she'd seen before—the one the priestess had called Yggdrasil. In other ways, this was entirely foreign, beautiful and new.

It was not a space for running, but she was the demigoddess. They could fight her on her right to race through the temple. Fae lights twinkled, blurring into dots and lines as she passed. Her feet were too loud on the temple floor as she rounded the tree and dashed into the room where Nox lay unconscious.

Tanith and the priestess were somewhere else—maybe it was the sort of thing she should have cared about, but she didn't. The faint glow of a single fae light cast haunting shadows in Nox's room, but even in the dark, Nox's sweaty, shaky illness was clear. She looked precisely as Tanith had only hours before. But this time, Amaris could help.

She crawled up onto the bed indelicately and tucked her arms behind Nox's head and back, crushing the queen's limp form against her. Her lip quivered as she brushed a kiss into her hair. Tears she'd refused to cry dribbled from her, splotching onto Nox's skin. She burrowed her face in the cloud of black hair and made a quiet, desperate promise.

"I will hold you until my arms fall off, Nox. I'm not letting you go."

✦

Nox had visited dreams. She had never visited a nightmare.

She looked at the world around her and knew with sticky, sinking certainty that she'd descended into hell. The trauma of seeing Tanith die was too much, and perhaps that's why she'd come here. Looking at the girl wither away reminded her of how Malik had looked at her with a smile, blood trickling out of the corner of his mouth as he congratulated her for bringing the demon down with him. Nox had screamed, she'd cried, and then she'd done the only thing she could imagine. She gave.

Tanith would be healthy and whole if she hadn't scarified all she was to save Nox and the others. And as they had settled her onto a humble bed in the back of the temple, Nox knew she'd lost too much. Once more, Nox had lowered her lips to another—not to take, but to give. She had touched her mouth to Tanith's and caught death's final, rattling breath in her mouth. She'd called to the life within her and pushed everything she could spare into the girl who'd been her enemy, her captive, her friend, her savior.

Nox had known what would happen. She would only have moments before the darkness took her. So as she'd collapsed to the floor, Nox had used her last moment to set her intentions. She'd had one chance to get it right. And with that, one name alone rippled through her mind as she'd drifted off on the dark waters of unconsciousness.

Daifa.

Nox had seen forests before. She'd seen oaks and pines and birches and palms. These russet trees, however, were like nothing she'd ever imagined. Painted against the steels and pewters of a stormy sky, trees reached toward the heavens as if to touch the All Mother herself. Nox had seen watercolors of a redwood forest in a storybook once. She'd asked the matron if trees the size of mountains existed, and the matron had said one of the few honest things Nox had ever heard in Farleigh.

"Just because we haven't seen it doesn't mean it isn't real."

She stood now amidst woods recognizable only from drawings and tales, and she shuddered against the sight. Wet soil filled the air, but there was something else on the wind that she couldn't quite recognize—something she knew enough to fear, even if she couldn't name it. The cold, damp night threatened rain.

A single light caught her eye, pulling her gaze from the trees. A dark, stone manor was set at the fae end of a manicured lawn. A candle burned in an upper window. But as she turned toward the house, she understood the smell. Her heart stopped beating as her attention went to the source. Her gaze traveled down into a blackened shadow as she realized she'd arrived with her back to the edge of a pit. She looked down at clean-picked bones, rotting carcasses, and the body of a freshly slaughtered young man. The gray, amphibious form of a vageth prowled near the pit, though it seemed to pay Nox no mind. The canine-like demon sniffed at the pit and jumped in, grabbing what might have been a human femur before leaping out once more.

Her stomach twisted into knots as she watched the vageth sprint up the lawn, brushing by a woman's shape as it did so. She recognized the arched ears, the black hair, the striking face.

Daifa hadn't noticed her. The Speaker was holding her knees to her chest as she looked down vacantly into the pit.

Nox pushed down her fear. She didn't know what to do, but she reminded herself of how long it had taken Amaris to realize her dreams were being infiltrated. Unless this woman had been specifically warned against Nox's ability, surely, she would only see this as an odd dream, if she remembered it at all. She didn't know what to do now that she'd made it into Daifa's subconscious, but she'd come here on purpose. She had to try something.

Nox would be a part of the dream, and this nightmare had only two roles. Daifa and the dead. She slowly approached the Speaker. Voice low, she asked, "Now that you've caught me, what will you do with me? Do I go in the pit?"

Daifa turned to her slowly, dismissing the question wholly. She scarcely registered Nox's presence. "No," she said, "the pit is for imperfections. The pit is not for you."

The misty evening morphed into raindrops overhead as the sky churned into a deeper, more violent gray. The Speaker got to her feet and began to walk toward the manor, and Nox followed.

"She'll be happy about you," Daifa said. Unlike the arrogant preening Nox had come to know from the woman, she spoke with sullen emptiness. Her words were statements, but the only emotion they held was dejection. "She'll be proud."

Who? She longed to ask, but she knew enough to prevent herself from pushing or doing anything that might upset Daifa into waking. "I'm glad," she said coolly. She continued to follow as the Speaker crossed the threshold and into the manor, and she wished she hadn't. Nox forced herself to swallow against the urge to scream. She was in a house of horrors.

The entire estate was crawling with demons, both real and captured, in canvas upon canvas of unsettling oil paintings. Daifa was unbothered, as a demonic infestation was commonplace. A goblin brushed past her on unnatural footing, each step strained, each breath a wheeze. The sickly, greenish creature tugged at Daifa's dress and looked at her with large, expectant eyes.

"Nothing for me," Daifa said. "Not today."

The creature nodded, then carried on in slow, lumbering footsteps as it cleaned the manor. Nox wasn't sure where to look. She watched the goblin limp away, catching more and more of the ghastly art as she did so. Where castles and homes might have hung portraits of landscapes, families, or monarchs, these walls were filled with hyper-realistic canvases of ag'druraths, beseuls, vageths, and terrors that Nox could neither name, nor did she want to ever see again. This twisted gallery was wasted on her. Amaris would have loved the opportunity to walk through the museum of horrors.

She covered her mouth to stop from yelping in surprise as the vageth ran in from the outdoors. Clods of mud flew from the creature as it left brown, soaking mudprints in its wake.

"No!" a voice scolded angrily from the top of the staircase. "Who let him in with dirty paws! Well, this just won't do."

Nox stumbled back in surprise. She'd come to visit Daifa. She hadn't expected anyone else. But then again, this was Daifa's dream.

A woman with toffee-colored hair stormed down the stairs. She looked so out of place amidst the demons. She had the pale complexion of someone from Farehold but the arched ears and beautiful features of a timeless fae. Her clothes were custard, much like her hair and the stones of Castle Aubade. Though her clothes were beautiful, they were not the stiff, uncomfortable things often worn by nobility. It was jarring to see in this manor, in these woods, in this monstrosity. The woman made a gesture with her fingers, and a series of horrible, crab-like mites emerged from the walls, funneling the mud into their mouths until the floor was spotless once more. Nox suppressed a gag as the monstrous crustaceans returned to their hiding places, no more than stones that lined the walls of the manor.

"I've found it," called Daifa to the buttery-haired fae.

There was something familiar about her, but it was the greasy sort of thought that Nox couldn't quite grip. It was as though they'd met before, if only through a drawing or a story. There was a strength about her beauty that Nox didn't always see in the fae. She had eyes as golden as a royal crown, but there was something cruel and shattered behind them that anchored Nox in the terrible truth that nothing good had ever happened in this place.

The fae perked as she approached. Her face softened with something that may have resembled a cool, distant form of affection. Though the women were roughly the same height and appeared to be more or less the same age, she smiled down at Daifa as if she were a mother loosely embracing a daughter. One hand cupped Daifa's chin. "What have you found, my love?"

"Unity." Daifa spoke only one word as she gestured toward Nox, but the fae with brown-gold hair neither saw nor acknowledged her presence. Nox was a phantom, one only Daifa could see.

"Good," the woman said, still looking into Daifa's sapphire eyes. "Honor your cornerstone." She patted her dismissively on the head before breezing away.

"I'll have to leave," Daifa called after the toffee-colored fae.

The woman stiffened. She turned around slowly. "Leave?"

A dark, tense energy filled the corridor. Nox shivered as if a cold wind had blown in from the outdoors.

"To unify the continent. I cannot stay here."

The woman's expression was terrifying. On someone else, the trembling lip may have looked like she was about to cry. On her, it looked like fire was about to burst from her throat like a terrible dragon. "That's not why—" She stopped herself, flexing and releasing her hands. It seemed as though she was struggling for words. After a long, hostile moment, she asked a cold, monotonous question. "And where would you go?"

Daifa looked over her shoulder at a portrait that did not contain a monster. He did not belong in this house. He was one of two portraits, both of striking, happy fae. One was of a woman with rosy cheeks, pale hair, and eyes as blue as the ocean. Daifa gestured to the portrait of a devilishly handsome fae with black hair, dark eyes, and a tattoo that seemed to be crawling up his back from somewhere hidden beneath his black lapels. He, like Daifa, had distinctly Sulgrave features.

The Farehold fae looked as if she'd been slapped. "You won't find him."

"Wouldn't you want me to?"

Her chin trembled slightly. "You don't understand, Daifa. This is not... You're not meant to leave. You'll stay here. You'll stay here, and you'll be with me, and you'll remain safe. We have everything we need. I have you, and you have me."

Nox clawed at the very fabric of the dream as it tremored with transition. It rippled and shook until they were no longer in the corridor surrounded by portraits. The woman with golden eyes was nowhere to be seen. The rough, red bark of the towering trees surrounded them. The woods were thick with the scents of pine and petrichor. Rain fell heavily, slapping against the forest floor with loud intensity.

"Are you leaving?" Nox shouted after the woman, following the Sulgrave fae with large, unnaturally blue eyes. She was calm. She was empty. She was not yet the cruel, clever peacock who would be the Speaker.

This was no nightmare. These were memories.

Nox stared at the woman breathlessly. Gadriel had done

the same. He returned to a memory time after time. Amaris had shown her Uaimh Reev in one of their dream walks. And Daifa…what did Daifa remember?

The blue-eyed fae looked to her absently. "I have to. This is why I exist."

Nox shielded her face from the rain as she followed. She slipped on roots, struggling to pick her way through the mud and stay on two feet. An unnatural hissing slithered through the pillar-like trees, and she wondered what horrors were in the woods with them. She struggled for a question. Anything that would help her understand. "And…what do we do now that we've found the meaning of your existence?"

Daifa turned her head again and the rain stopped. There hadn't even been the ripple of transition. Everything had snapped into place all at once, scarcely giving Nox time to screech to a halt from where she'd been walking through the forest. They weren't wet. There was no mud on her shoes. They were standing in Sulgrave's cathedral. It was not covered in vines and littered with bodies as it had been after the battle but clean and empty, save for a single bishop and a Red. She had spoken unintelligibly to them and their faces had slackened with reverence. "This." Daifa gestured, a serene tour guide as she took Nox through her memories. The Speaker was taking her on a tour, answering every question with a reciprocal memory.

This was wrong, though Nox couldn't place why.

She dared a test, even if she might regret it. "Daifa, can you give me a glass of water? Here, in this sanctuary?"

Daifa's long, loose hair cascaded down her shoulders, pale tips brushing just beyond her elbows. Her lower lip puckered at the request as if it were illogical.

Nox's gut twisted at her test. Daifa was showcasing memories, yes, but could she not create dreams at all? As dark, as horrible, as unfathomable as much of it had been, there was no imagination. No invention. Nothing that resembled a dream, not really. They had stepped directly from memory

410

into memory, one after the other. She tested the Speaker further, continuing to ask questions.

"Why do you want me alive?"

Daifa's frown was not unkind. "Haven't you been listening?"

Nox returned the down-turned lips. "For unity?"

"For unity."

The repetition was already wearing on her. Nox's mouth twisted to one side. She crossed her arms. She didn't mean to look defensive, but her confusion wrung her ragged. "And why is unity so important?"

"I..." Daifa's thought trailed off. "I don't know."

"What do you mean? It's all you care about."

"Yes."

Nox dared to press harder. "You're motivated to unite the continent, and you're using force and the church to do so. Why? Why send Reds to cleanse Raascot and Farehold? Why usurp so much power in Sulgrave?"

"It's why I exist."

"So I've heard..." It was almost as if Daifa were caught in a loop. This was getting Nox nowhere, but the woman also had seemed entirely unbothered by her presence. Daifa had not been disturbed, nor had she pushed back at a single question. Nox leaned into more current events.

"There was a battle today in the church. Were there survivors?"

"Yes."

"And?" She clenched her muscles against the urge to reveal any frustration. "Where were the captives taken?"

Daifa listened, and the dream rippled until it was the destroyed, blood-stained, vine-covered sanctuary they'd narrowly escaped. Still, she did not—or could not—dream with imagination. They were in yet another memory. They looked down at the sanctuary as it had existed in the moments following Nox's escape with the others.

Gadriel's body remained crumbled on the platform along

with the other corpses that had fallen, but Nox could not bring herself to look at her fallen general. They watched a ghostly, phantom version of the Speaker as she was escorted out of the room by the surviving Reds and into another room. Nox took note of the passages and turns so she could re-create the steps exactly, marking where the Speaker walked as she led them to where Yazlyn, Ryu, and Kasar had been bound and gagged.

"Daifa, listen to me."

The Speaker turned curiously. Even still, in the present day, she was not the woman Nox knew. She had none of the traits, none of the anger, none of the fighting spirit or cockiness or vitriol that Nox had encountered. She tried something new.

"I will tell you what you need for unity. Are you ready to hear?"

She seemed to consider and then made an open gesture with her hands.

"Insist that your hostages remain unbothered. You want my compliance uniting Raascot and Sulgrave? I can help you. But I'll only speak to you if everyone has been unharmed. I will cooperate as long as everyone is healthy and whole. Do you understand?"

"I do desire your cooperation. For—"

"Yes, for unity. You've said as much. One more thing?"

"Yes?"

"What stands between you and unity?" Nox waited on bated breath, hoping for a weakness, a clue, a hint as to what might lead to the Speaker's undoing. She looked into the woman's unnaturally blue eyes for far too long as Daifa considered her. Her lips twitched and her hands flexed at her sides, tendons popping before she relaxed them once more.

"Everything."

Thirty-Five

G ADRIEL HADN'T MOVED IN HOURS.
   This was death. Or, the closest one might come. His
body coursed with chips of ice, sweat, and agony. The ability
to survive did not mean he did not suffer—for suffer, he did.
The sickness and misery coupled with the ache in his heart
at being separated from the ones he'd loved. He'd heard their
screams. Nox, Amaris, Yazlyn had fought, they'd cried, they
believed him dead, and for all the world, he was. This hadn't
been his plan. He'd never intended to fall. But the moment
Alistair had broken his neck, he'd known that staying down
was the only way he could maintain the upper hand. Under
the best of circumstances, healing tonics and safe conditions,
it would have taken him a while to move again. These were
not the best of circumstances.

   The parts of him that enabled him to move, to speak, to
blink, had severed. The horrible, wrenching cry of loss rang
in his ears. He'd listened as they'd escaped, and he'd prayed
that they ran as fast as they could and as far as they could.

   Yazlyn had not done the same. His sergeant, his unhinged
friend, had cried out as she dove for him. She'd stood over
his body. He'd listened to the bloodshed as she continued to

fight alongside Ryu. And he knew that Yazlyn had not made it out of the church.

It was quiet now. It had been quiet for a long, long time.

He was amidst the corpses of the slain. Ryu's men, Kasar's men, Reds, and Alistair's fae from Territory One. The Reds were the hardest to kill, but that made sense. Sulgrave was not a warring nation. Their combat training was decent, but those who held swords had not been battle-ready. The magically inclined, however, were the true threats.

He would have smiled if he could have at the swift vengeance against his attacker. In the sounds, bursts, and chaos that had ensued in the moments after he'd fallen, Alistair had been consumed by what he could only assume had been a very hungry, angry Fjolla. The great, invisible beast had launched herself into the chapel with the same fury and confusion that she'd brought upon them under the night skies of the Frozen Straits, bound to the will of Kasar.

And then the bitch Speaker opened her mouth.

The tide's turn was swift. Everything began to crash around them the moment she invaded Kasar's mind. And so, while he had not planned on dying that way, perhaps it was the best thing that could have happened. He spent his life preaching patience on the restless, and now it was time to put it into practice. Remaining within the church would keep him close to his captured sergeant, and even closer to the Speaker.

His fingers were sticky with blood that did not belong to him. For hours, he'd looked into the unseeing eyes of a fallen Red. The young woman had tried to summon flame, and Ryu had intervened. Her body was several arm's lengths away. She was one of many, but her face would be the one burned into his mind for decades to come if he survived the night.

The unnatural twist of his neck didn't just throb, it screamed at him with each agonizing beat of his heart, but he couldn't move—not yet. Another collector would be coming any minute to drag another corpse from the piles of fallen bodies within the church. Gadriel did his best to ensure that even his chest neither rose nor fell as he took shallow breaths through his nose. If anyone looked too closely, the cold sweat of his clammy skin would betray the life he clung to.

Reds continued pulling the dead out of the sanctuary and into the courtyard, but they did so in shifts. Fortunately, the volunteer forces removing the fallen hadn't stripped the dead of their weapons. He would presumably have been searched and relieved of any valuables before being burned at whatever funeral pyre or thrown in whatever mass pit awaited the bodies, but as it stood, he had several knives, his short sword, and centuries of military training.

The remaining dissenters—namely Yazlyn, Ryu, and an unconscious Kasar—were contained with merciless immediacy. He could only guess at the reason they'd been spared. With Nox missing and Daifa desiring her compliance, hostages and threats seemed like a logical next step.

Doors squeaked. Boots scraped. A quiet grunt. The drag of fabric. The squeak of doors once more.

He'd carefully counted the seconds between each collector, timing the rate at which the sanctuary was cleared of the deceased. There were at least two full minutes between the entry and exit from one Red on to the next as the volunteers took turns tugging corpses out of the cathedral. His next move would be a matter of timing.

After another creak of door hinges and the sound of shoes, he counted to three. If he was going to move, he had to do it now. His body was as stitched on its own as it was going to be. He snapped his neck back into place with an excruciating pop. Bile burned the back of his throat as he fought the urge to cry out. He bit down on his tongue—hard. His vision swam and he lost count of the seconds. Gadriel fell to the floor once more, replicating his splayed position, this time with a markedly less broken neck.

The double doors at the front of the sanctuary opened,

and no light save for the glow of streetlamps filtered in. They were well into the late hours of night now. The time had come to make his move.

A Red grabbed the fallen body of one of Ryu's men. The Red seemed too small for the body she'd tackled, but she gripped the soldier roughly by the shirt and began the arduous process of dragging him off of the stage, down the aisle, past the pews, and out of the double doors. The moment the doors clicked to a close, Gadriel was on his feet. He slipped through the door nearest to the platform—presumably the one the bishop would use to enter and exit the stage for his messages. He just needed to get out of the sanctuary and into any acceptable hiding space as he planned his next move. Gadriel angled his body toward the first door in the hall and pressed his ear to it, ensuring it was empty. The lock posed no trouble, and he had quickly unlatched it and let himself into the room just off the sanctuary.

He'd found a broom closet. He was surrounded by dust pans, buckets, and the astringent scent of cleaning liquids. Patience. It was easier said than done, but he counted the seconds once more until he was certain another collector had come and gone. He knew lone actors rarely executed successful assassination missions, and sloppiness would do him no favor. If he was to eliminate the Speaker, his first priority needed to be locating Yazlyn.

Not a lot had been said in the moments following the brief, horrid battle. He had no indication that they intended to relocate the prisoners. In fact, it hadn't sounded like anyone, Speaker or Reds included, had truly exited the building. This made him a tad more cautious because it implied that all his enemies remained silently under the same roof. It was eerie, particularly given the chapel's suffocating stillness. Though he strained his ears, he heard nothing. No life, no breath, no scuffles or birds or mice.

Gadriel's eyes rapidly adjusted to the shadows of the broom closet, and he understood why the church was so silent. Dampening runes were etched into the frame. Given the insignificance of his current space, he had to guess that such runes had been engraved into every frame in the building. This rendered his ears useless. He'd be just as likely to open a locked door onto Daifa herself as he would to reveal Yazlyn.

But this is why he'd trained. After so much time in darkness, he finally had a reason to live. Not only was there a monarch on the throne who deserved the title, but he'd found someone worth living for.

His violent, clever, brave, beautiful witchling. Once this was all over, he wanted to buy her something exceptionally beautiful. He realized with the odd, passing clarity of someone on the battle who may or may not be facing death that he didn't even know her favorite color. He didn't know if she liked jewelry. He…he had so much to learn about the one who held his heart.

But to survive the night, he had to find his sergeant.

Gadriel eased his way out of the broom closet and began picking along the perimeter. He rounded a corner until he crept up on the foyer. Far beyond the bend of the hall, the double doors at the front of the church creaked open and closed. Footsteps sounded. As a collector came to drag another body, he kept his eyes trained on the small sliver where he could see the front of the sanctuary.

He found what he hadn't even realized he'd been looking for.

Stairs.

From his angle in the hall, he could only see one small section of the entryway, the doors, and a single staircase. To the right of the double doors, the stairwell ran upward. Presumably, the opposite side would have a downward-leaning set of stairs, though he'd have to fully expose himself in the church's open atrium before he could know for certain.

Strategically speaking, the Speaker would most likely be

upstairs. The loft would be easy to secure against enemies entering and ascending from only one chokehold and provided more opportunities for escape as they had window access. Hopefully that meant the inverse was true, and his companions were being kept in the basement.

From the struggling sounds of the feet and the harsh, truncated noises of intermittent dragging, he assumed it was the same small Red fae woman hauling men three times her size across the chapel floor. The moment her grunts gave way to the swinging and clicking of the double doors, he set into motion. Gadriel moved quickly and quietly, relieved to see that he was correct—the stairs on the left did indeed curve downward. He wasted no time curling down the stairwell on the balls of his feet.

A guard was standing at the landing with his back to the stairs, but Gadriel had the man in a chokehold and had rendered him unconscious before he'd even heard the general's approach. As the guard fell, the fae in the center of the room snapped her head up in attention. Sweat, pain, and swollen eyes looked up at him in the dim lighting of the basement.

There she was.

He locked eyes with Yazlyn, who was hanging by her wrists from bindings on the support beams that made her dangle just above where her toes might touch the ground. Rope had been wrapped around her torso to bind her wings tightly to her body, and a strip of cloth gagged her into silence. He rushed for her, but in doing so, he'd failed to secure the room.

The small Red responsible for clearing the sanctuary had followed him down the stairs.

Yazlyn grunted out a harried warning one moment before a whir of metal sounded near his ear. Gadriel leaned out of the blade's path with scarcely an inch between him and the cutting edge of steel.

He grabbed the Red's sword arm, summoning the heat

required to make her cry out in a yelp and drop her weapon. In two brisk strides, Gadriel shoved the Red up against the wall, forearm against her throat and other hand clasped over her mouth.

"Stay silent and I'll let you live."

Her face scrunched into angry defiance, but he shoved his arm harder against her throat. He growled a question that came out as a demand.

"Where are the other hostages?"

The Red raised her hands against his chest, but not in any defensive combat maneuver. He realized his mistake a second too late. He knew better. She was no guard—she was a Red. He may as well have been fighting Tanith. The fae echoed the power he'd wielded against her, mimicking the heat that had made her burn so hot that she'd dropped her sword. The girl's skin was instantly an inferno, causing Gadriel to jerk his hands away and let her drop to the ground as his shirt burned in tatters near his chest, welts already swelling in the single second between her assault and his release.

She landed like a cat on the balls of her feet, crying out in anger as she lunged for him.

Gadriel went for his blade, but she called to the very metal in his hand as it began to melt onto the stones, molten dripping onto his shoes as it pooled on the ground below him. He released the hilt scarcely a second before its metallic lava enveloped his hand. Acting on instinct, he forced a surge of air through the basement, using his mighty wings to knock her from her feet—a power she could not mimic with appendages she did not possess. The moment the Red hit the ground, he was on top of her. His hand balled in her hair and he yanked with such unnatural speed and strength that her neck was broken before she'd even realized she'd smacked the stones. He grunted angrily at the lost potential for information, but his skirmish reminded him of something incredibly valuable: underestimating the Reds would get him, and everyone around him, killed.

"Let's try this again," he said, offering a weak smile at his sergeant before turning his back on her. "Give me a second, Yaz."

She grunted in what could have only been annoyance.

Gadriel crossed the basement, returning to the landing where the first guard he'd neutralized remained on the ground. The general relieved the man of his blade. He used the guard's very sword to slit the unconscious man's throat. There was no dignity in slaying a man in his sleep, but this guard was a Red. The very lives of the southern resistance hung in the balance of their next carefully chosen actions, and he could not spare a Red on battle decorum alone. At least the guard would be able to go peacefully.

Yazlyn made an impatient noise to urge him to hurry. Her feet wiggled as she failed to touch the ground beneath her, writhing uncomfortably from where she hung.

"As if I was going to let you die," Gadriel attempted with a weak chuckle. "You're the closest thing to a sister I'll ever get. Oh, wait, that's not true. Nox is a cousin. I guess that makes you expendable." Gadriel cut the ties from the beams first, catching her before she could tumble completely to the ground. Her arms went as limp as jelly, and for a brief moment he worried that her shoulders had been pulled from their sockets as she'd hung from the beam. Fortunately, her arms appeared to still be working as she began to tear at her gag. He finished cutting her loose, from the cloth around her mouth to the rope binding her wings, before pulling his troop into a quick, emotional hug.

"I thought you died!" Her voice was thick as she looked at him. She then balled her fist and punched him in the shoulder. "Fuck you. As if you could ever replace me."

The general attempted to chuckle, voice hoarse. "Come on, I thought you knew me better than that." He left her to glower while he searched the basement for tricks, traps, or weapons. He wouldn't be caught unaware twice. "Do you know where they've taken the others?"

She did. "The comtes—or, what remains of them—are being corralled into one place. They took Ryu—I mean, they took those who fought with us. The Reds took me down here as Ryu was forced upstairs with the others. I think the Speaker needs to make her move to get everyone on her side. The way they were talking…they weren't trying to conceal anything. They'll be rallying up Surya, Chloris, Elswyth… They're out finding every comte as we speak. Since Daifa can plant memories—"

"We're about to lose every ally we have in this kingdom."

Thirty-Six

N ox's velvety lashes fluttered open. Amaris gagged on her relief. She'd practically drowned Nox in restorative tonic as she'd poured the small brown bottles down her throat, tilting her head back so she'd swallow, even if it had been an exercise in futility regarding her comatose state. She'd begged. She'd kissed. She'd hugged and held and prayed. Even if Ash was right and love would repair the life she'd willingly given, her bones remained fractured, and that was something no amount of affection would heal.

Amaris had fretted. She'd paced. She'd dabbed at the sweat on Nox's face with a clean towel. She'd tugged Nox's tanned arm free from her shirt and wrapped the break, binding it tightly to her body to allow it to set. She wasn't sure how quickly the tonic would work to mend the bone, but the temple had no shortage of the glass bottles, should they require more. She absently hoped it wasn't possible to overdose on healing tonic, though she'd never toyed with administrative dosages. If it was, and she'd killed the love of her life, she'd be sure to march back to Uaimh Reev and make a note to add it to the reevers' texts before committing whatever atrocious crimes against academic negligence her rage could conjure.

"Nox." She squeezed her free hand, chewing her lip, struggling to keep her voice from cracking. "You don't have to talk. You're okay. I'm here."

She didn't want to tell Nox how her eyes had grown dry from her reluctance to blink as she willed her to get better. Amaris had stared for signs of life, studying her lines, her cheeks, her chin, her mouth. She'd watched the rapid movement beneath Nox's closed lids as the raven queen had fallen into dreams. She'd even prayed, for perhaps the first time in her life. Feeling the joy that filled her when her lilac eyes met Nox's dark, sparkling gaze was like drinking a pint of pure sunlight.

Nox tried to speak and Amaris nodded encouragingly.

"What? I'm here, I'm here," she repeated.

"Where's Fjolla?" the queen muttered weakly.

Well, that was new. The medicinal dose of anger inoculated her against her sorrow. "Are you serious? You just committed suicide to save Tanith, and the first thing you ask about is your stupid pet?"

Nox struggled to sit up. "Is she here?"

Amaris's lips parted with disbelief. "She's fine. Your overgrown dog is still invisible to prying eyes, but from the splashing, we can only assume she's having the time of her life catching fish in the river. But, in case you've forgotten, we have more important things going on. What were you thinking?"

"She's still invisible? So the shackle—"

Amaris dropped her hand. "All right, go back to sleep. Give me the pillow—I'm ready for you to go under."

"Wait, wait."

Irritation still plain in her face, Amaris helped her into a reclining position. She didn't bother with gentleness as she yanked Nox forward and propped pillows behind her back. She may have stayed angry for a while longer had Nox not slipped an arm around her back. Just like that, her rage subsided. She breathed into the hug.

"I knew what I was doing," Nox grumbled into her hair.

"Yes, you altruistic bastard. You gave your life for—"

"No," Nox cut her off. "I killed two birds with one stone. I knew I could save Tanith, and I knew from experience that it would render me unconscious. I knew I could visit Daifa in her sleep."

Amaris's mouth became cotton. She released Nox to fully take in her facial expression, scanning the shadows for emotion from a full arm's length away. She leaned apart, tensed against the information. "You went into the Speaker's dreams?"

Nox closed her eyes. "And I thought we were fucked up..."

"What did you see?"

Shadows played on her features as Nox shook her head. "It's hard to say. There was a pit in the earth of dead bodies. Darkness, woods, death, demons...vageth, beseuls, ag'imni... At first I thought it was a nightmare, but...I don't think she's...right."

"Of course she's not right!"

"No, I mean..." Nox twisted her face in a frown. She closed her eyes as she seemed to reflect on what she'd seen. Every sentence drifted off unnaturally as she struggled to piece together her information. "I don't think she's whole. She doesn't seem fully...real."

Amaris blinked several times, squeezing moisture back into her eyes as she struggled to process what Nox was saying. Whether the dimness of the room or the shadows of the fae lights, Nox's face didn't seem to be resting in a natural position. "What?"

Nox continued shaking her head. "I don't know how to explain it. It seems like...she was nothing more than a pretty shell with a singular motive. Another woman in Daifa's dream referred to it as her 'cornerstone,' as if the motive was what she was built around. She doesn't know why she's doing what she's doing. She... I don't know how else to explain it. I don't think she's...real."

"That's…" Amaris allowed her sentence to remain unfinished, realizing whatever she was about to say was rather cruel. She rerouted her wording. "That's not possible. I mean this lovingly, but you sound insane, Nox. It had to have been a nightmare." She fluffed the pillows behind Nox as she pushed her back into a more relaxed position. "I'll excuse it as you recently returning from the brink of death. I still don't forgive you for scaring me like that, by the way."

Nox's expression changed. Her brows lowered, rearranging themselves into anger. "I knew I would be fine." A pregnant pause stretched between them before she mused to herself, "Maybe this is part of what drove Ceres mad. Living in the nightmares of others is not for the faint of heart. But I'm telling you, there's something not whole about her. She doesn't seem like…a person."

"Okay." Amaris considered it carefully. She didn't like Nox's tone of voice. The way her words drifted, the disconnect in her speech, the absence of logic in her words was disconcerting. That said, she trusted Nox. Her hand resumed moving idly against the curtain of raven hair while she sorted through her emotions. "Assuming she isn't real. Assuming it's true—"

"It is true."

"Right. But, if it is, what good does this do us? How can we use this information to our advantage? And perhaps most importantly, what was the motive?"

Nox knew this answer instantly. "Unity. She's singularly obsessed with the idea of unifying the continent. It was rather annoying to hear over and over again, actually, but it's the only thing she thinks about. It's all about unity. It's a damned driving force, as if it's repeated over and over in her mind on a loop. It's part of why I don't think she's a person—not really. She doesn't have other thoughts. It's why Daifa sees keeping me alive as an asset in connecting her to the southern half of Gyrradin. I don't know if it explains why she's been sending martyrs to the continent, other than that fae lineage might be a common denominator in unification. Perhaps she sees a homogenous race of fae coming together more easily."

Amaris looked into the face of the half-fae queen, and trouble clouded her eyes. "So, she's eliminating diversity to bring the continent under a single banner? But the Speaker is taking Sulgrave, Raascot, and Farehold with so much violence. No one will want to unite under a tyrant."

"Unless she can plant the memories necessary to make people see things her way. Getting rid of humans and halflings might just simplify the dissemination of her message. Maybe the magical connection between fae..."

Amaris's mouth scrunched into a tight line. "But why? With Moirai and her curse, she wanted to keep Ceres away from her daughter and prevent their union. It was hateful, but logical. What would Daifa's reason be?"

"That's the thing." Nox sat up again, exuding a mixture of nerves and excitement. The sudden burst of energy forced Amaris to shove her back into a reclining position. Clearly the dark-haired queen was already feeling better, but Amaris didn't want to take any chances. Nox continued humming with animation, using her hands to emphasize her point. "Daifa doesn't know. She truly...doesn't know. I'm telling you, something about her is wrong."

Amaris absorbed the information, reacting as though she'd sucked on something sour. "Is it possible she's been brainwashed? Maybe she's under someone else's enchantment or control?"

"No, it wasn't like that. I almost feel like she was...made this way. I know this sounds crazy, but... What do you know of manifesters?"

✦

Amaris had only met one priestess before, and she'd distinctly recalled wanting to throw her shoe at the elegant woman from Tarkhany. While the priestess had been as beautiful as the night sky and more regal than any queen, she'd spoken in infuriating riddles and nonanswers. Their meeting had occurred months before Amaris would learn that the very priestess from Tarkhany who'd twinkled at her with such curious perception was the surrogate who'd brought her into this world. She hadn't known what to feel, except that the revelation had brought her nothing but torment.

This priestess before her was a different breed entirely.

She was of Sulgrave descent in appearance only. Unlike the stoic, poetic woman who served at the Temple of the All Mother in Farehold, this priestess brimmed with joy. She held none of Tanith's tranquil gravity, nor did she reflect the dynastic power of the comtes. This priestess reminded Amaris of Sister Mable—a faithful woman who always wanted to believe the best in the world. When asked her name, she had deflected to inform Amaris that she was a servant of the All Mother.

"They give up their names when they take their oaths," Nox had whispered.

"How do you know that?" she'd whispered back, albeit less quietly.

In a slightly more normal speaking voice, Nox answered, "When you left for Aubade to seek Moirai, I had to distract myself. Otherwise, I was pretty sure Ash and Zaccai were plotting to kill me for bothering them. They don't find me as charming as you do." She winked. She looked over at Tanith, who had been present for her in-depth research. "I buried myself in theology texts so we could unpack Tanith's brain. I'm pretty much the resident expert on religion now."

Tanith narrowed her eyes from where she'd been listening to their conversation.

"I meant it facetiously, Tanith. No one questions your expertise," Nox amended. She shared a secret, exaggerated expression with Amaris as Tanith returned her attention to the priestess.

"And what a miracle it is," the priestess said quite happily. "We have a queen, a demigoddess, and a Red all under one roof beside the Tree of Life. How fortuitous. I've been blessed by the All Mother with the honor of your company. Now that you're all feeling well and restored, how may I serve?"

They'd sat in a circle at the foot of the tree as the priestess dispersed the modest meals she'd made for everyone. Small packages that appeared to be in green, leaf-like substances contained a packed rice, meat, and vegetable compressed into easily carried triangles. The lap of the black dress that had been an important distinction of her station as priestess had served to hold all of her triangles until she'd handed them out.

Amaris carefully watched how Tanith held the triangle in her hands and bit into the entire thing, consuming the green covering, as if it was a part of the meal. She copied the actions and found the simple meal quite delightful.

"Can you have your cooks in Gwydir make this for us?" Amaris asked.

Nox shrugged at Amaris. "Bold of you to assume we'll ever make it back to Gwydir." She then redirected her attention to the smiling priestess. "What do you know of the Speaker?"

The priestess looked at her quizzically. "Are you asking about the Speaker as a concept, or do you refer to the woman who's currently residing in Sulgrave's church?"

"Well, both, I suppose."

"A Speaker is someone who arrives to aid the people, usually in times of great strife. There hasn't been one in my lifetime, and I'm in my ninth century of servitude. The All Mother makes herself flesh to live and walk among her people, intervening on the behalf of goodness and peace. There have only been a few in recorded history."

"And the one in Sulgrave's church?"

The priestess chewed on her food with some disinterest. "Yes, she is a curiosity, isn't she?"

Much to everyone's surprise, Tanith was the one who prompted the priestess to divulge more. She lowered what

428

remained of her meal and regarded the holy woman. "How would one distinguish a false Speaker from a true Speaker?"

The priestess finished eating before extending a hand upward toward the branches that rose and twisted skyward, weaving their way up the narrow temple's crevice. The extended fingers of her gesture pointed their direction to a small apple that grew on one of the tallest branches, far from the float of their gazes. "By their fruits."

Amaris's eyes traveled up the trunk of the tree, over the knots and limbs and fresh, silvery leaves, to the lone apple. It was a similar, silver-green color to the one that Nox had once thrown at the back of her head. Though these trees were somewhat alike, the produce they bore was exactly the same.

Both literally and theologically, that was the point of bearing fruit.

You spotted a pear tree from a plum by the fruit they produced. The same person could tell one thing from the other, no matter how similar they might appear, by the actions one brought into the world.

Fruit was a term Matron Mable had used on more than one occasion when humming about the love of the All Mother. It was how they'd always known the purity of her intent and wholeness of her faith. The analogy had been simple, if inelegant. If we are all in the All Mother's image, then we, like trees, bear fruit. Our fruits are told not by our beliefs, our good intent, or by the thoughts in our mind. Fruit is only what we bring into the world. Our tales, our hearts, and the veracity of our faith are told by the lives we live, the paths we take, and the way in which we love. We are the consequences of our choices. We are not our beliefs, but our deeds. No matter who you are, or where you are, you are the summation of your actions.

While these trees, like the temples around them and the priestess within them, had been different from stone to stitch, the fruit was the same.

"And"—Amaris looked to the priestess seriously—"do

you believe the Speaker in Sulgrave's church bears the All Mother's fruit?"

The priestess smiled kindly at Amaris. She leaned forward and rested a hand against the reever's pale fingers, engulfing her hand where it rested on her knee. "There is no Speaker in Sulgrave's church."

Nox and Tanith both looked to her in rigid alertness.

Tanith's voice was tight, as if her throat were constricting. She seemed to be controlling incomprehensible emotions as she strained to get through her question. Amaris suspected Tanith had been struggling with her faith for some time, but hearing it from the mouth of a holy servant of the goddess appeared to be a new experience entirely. Tanith asked, "If you don't believe the Speaker in the church is the true Speaker, why wouldn't the priestesses say anything? Why would you stand idly by and allow the people to be deceived?"

The priestess, though fae and with the ageless beauty that had no discernible decade, took on a distinctly maternal expression. The kindness and heaviness on her heart were clear. "You cannot be deceived when you know to look for fruit."

Nox began, "But what if her powers—"

"I know of her powers." The priestess was calm. "I've been as subject to her abilities as the others. I know of the memories she plants, and the minds she's melded. And yet, no matter what seeds she sows or visuals she creates: Are her acts kind? Is she empathetic? Does she desire peace, balance, and help? Is she an agent of justice? Does it matter what she shows the people visually, if she brings pain, violence, and destruction into the world? Does it matter what she calls herself if she's using her title to grab for power?"

A hand went to Tanith's heart as if a physical wound pierced her chest. Her nails scratched against the fabric of her shirt. Her fingers tightened into a fist, as if she were pushing into an injury that throbbed within her rib cage. She closed her eyes, averting her gaze to the side.

Amaris wondered if anything in her life had ever felt quite

like what Tanith was feeling now. She decided that yes, when her life had shattered after Nox had rejected her, chasing her from her bedroom, she'd felt her soul dissolve into sawdust. Nox had been her friend, her family, and, in so many ways, her faith. She'd believed in their connection the way others believed in the goddess. She'd clung to their love the way the faithful whispered prayers. Whatever heartache Tanith was experiencing was the fracture of the very love for the goddess that had sent her over the Frozen Straits in a skiff. It was the passion that had urged her to dedicate herself to the Reds. It was the fervor that had committed her to magical purity, regardless of the bloodshed. She had been ready and willing to die for that love.

"Come, now." The priestess set whatever remained of the food directly onto the temple floor. Scooting on her knees, she was ever the picture of the benevolent grandmother. The gesture was so terribly empathetic, so human. She wrapped her arms around Tanith, and the tiny girl broke, sobbing into the priestess's black gown. The holy woman held her tightly, the way a mother would hold her child.

"Your heart is open, loyal, and good. Your faith is part of what makes you beautiful. Do not mourn your past. Leave it there, where it belongs" She squeezed Tanith more tightly before pulling away. The priestess held her just far enough to wipe her tears away with her thumbs, cupping the girl's face in two comforting palms. "This guilt and shame belong to the deceiver, dear heart. Not the deceived."

Amaris looked away uncomfortably, feeling as though she were invading an intensely private moment. Her heritage and its link to the goddess had no bearing compared with the expression of zeal and piety that Tanith had dedicated with her life, service, and willingness to die. This was not something she should be here for. Amaris hedged, motioning that she and Nox should leave.

"Wait." The priestess looked up, still rocking Tanith. "Are you going to ask about the true Speaker?"

Her breath caught. "You know her?"

"Mmm, something tells me you do too."

"You mean Amaris?" Nox exchanged glances with her as Amaris remembered Tanith once referring to her as an acorn from the Tree of Life.

The priestess shook her head. "No, no. She communicates through her fruit."

"Through her actions," Nox clarified, lowering her brows carefully.

The priestess smiled easily. "Her fruit in the literal and the metaphorical." The woman allowed a hand to drift upward to where a silvery apple dangled from a branch. "They only grow when she has something to say."

Nox blinked once, then again. "What?"

"Her symbol is a tree; her message is fruit." The woman continued rocking Tanith. "A lot gets lost in translation as metaphor. Some is little more than allegory, after all. What a web."

Amaris looked between the women, feeling the same irritation she'd felt at the temple in Priory. "I've only met two priestesses, so forgive me for my impropriety, but everything is too cryptic. Can you speak plainly? Spell things out so there is no miscommunication?"

The priestess sipped the air delicately. "The first apple grew three years prior, then again a few months back. I assume it was in response to the imbalance. The All Mother is good, and she believes in free will. She doesn't interfere in our ways. We're left to our choices and their consequences. She shared her location, but little else. It wasn't until the winged fae came that I knew I was to share her whereabouts. She needs no rescuing, no physical servants, no cage. She is the wind, the forest, the air. At the fullness of time, when some came seeking for her truth, I knew I had been given the knowledge for this reason."

"Did you eat of the fruit?" Nox asked breathlessly.

"I did," the priestess said, "and saw nothing. So, another

grew. The cycle goes on until someone is worthy of receiving the message."

Amaris released a shaky breath. "The winged fae? You told them where to find her?"

The priestess's face remained serene, voice airy as she said, "The goddess's ways are not ours to understand, nor is her timing."

"But why didn't—" Tanith began, then stopped herself.

The priestess released her from the embrace and wiped away her tears. "Ask, child."

Tanith used the back of her hand to wipe what remained. "Why wouldn't the All Mother come? Why would she allow this to happen to us?"

The priestess arched a brow at that. "It isn't free will if she directly intervenes, is it? And whose agenda would she be serving? I believe we're accountable for our own role in peace. We can't wait for someone else to do it for us. Though every few thousand years, things get a little out of hand."

"And this..." Tanith drifted off. "This Speaker... The Reds... Because of me, this is one of the worst times in thousands of years? I've done this."

The priestess cupped her chin. "It's nothing that can't be undone."

Thirty-Seven

Nox's eyes adjusted quickly from the dim temple to the dark, twilight gloom of the hour before dawn. She stepped over the redheaded faeling, ignoring him completely as pebbles crunched underneath. He could catch up. She had things to do.

"What—" Ash roused from the depths of sleep. The blanket fell around him as he jumped to his feet. "Tanith!"

Over her shoulder, Nox heard their embrace. Fine. Tanith could forgive him. She shot them a glance just in time to see their embrace as, little more than half his size, the Sulgrave fae buried her head against his chest.

Ash's relief was palpable. "Thank the goddess you're all right. I can't believe—"

"We don't have time right now." Nox was already leading the march down the mountain pass.

Tanith grabbed his hand and dragged him after the others. "The Speaker lives!" she said quickly. "The real Speaker. The goddess's mouthpiece. The All Mother made flesh. She's real, Ash. She's real."

His amber eyes flashed in the dark like a cat's caught against a yellow glow. "How do you know this? And where is she?"

Nox was on a mission, not to be slowed. The night was cloudy, and very little could be seen aside from the black silhouettes against the dark gray sky. She needed all of the focus she could muster, even if she could spare her ears. Their voices trailed her down the path. "The tree, the fruit...she had sent a vision for the priestesses of where she might be found. Not to us, though; apparently, we aren't the only ones who seek the Speaker. Two winged fae visited the temple a few weeks prior deep in the mountains. If they survived the journey, they could have arrived and returned by now."

"Gadriel's parents," Amaris supplied after the quizzical stretch of silence.

"It's all the proof," Tanith promised. "It's all the proof that the nonbelievers said we didn't have. She's coming to save us."

Amaris looked over her shoulder at Tanith. "I didn't want to question the priestess, but why would she tell two Raascot fae where to find the Speaker? Why would she divulge that information to outsiders? Why did she tell us everything?"

Nox so rarely heard irritation on Tanith's voice, it was almost amusing. She was having a reverent moment, and Amaris was spoiling it. Tanith snapped, "When have you known me, or any of us, to conceal our message? Even in your dungeons and in your chains, did I hide the message of truth from you? It's not the fault of the faithful that the faithless so rarely consult the church. Truth is meant to be shared."

Several steps ahead of them, Nox made an appreciative face as she listened in. Tanith wasn't wrong. Even if she'd been unwilling to talk directly to those of mixed magic in the beginning, she'd been quick to divulge her dispatch, religion, and mission to anyone who would listen. She'd been compliant from her earliest days in their cells.

Amaris spoke to Tanith again. "I had an entirely different experience with a priestess in Farehold. She was not very forthcoming."

Nox called to the group without bothering to turn around. "Ah, yes, I know the answer to this one. That's because they didn't feel it was their place to intervene in your fate. They were worried that if they told you of your purpose, it would influence your actions."

"That's right." Amaris's voice hinged on bitter. "I forgot that you were present for my birth. How lucky for me." Nox continued choosing her steps in the dark but noticed that Ash and Amaris were having a far easier time selecting their footing on the narrow mountain path. Perhaps the reevers' years of trail running had allotted them a sure-footedness that eluded Nox.

Tanith frowned at the exchange of information. "You witnessed her birth?"

"Now's not the time, Tanith." Nox's eyes remained forward.

Ash chastised her quietly. "Hey, Nox, don't be like that."

Amaris offered a grumbling explanation. "Queen Dream Walker here shared a memory with the Tree of Life. The belief that I was the result of some prayer—we only know it because Nox saw it. Well, that, and because the priestess Ceres captured confirmed it… And then the Raascot fae acted on it… Come to think of it, maybe I'm still mad at Gadriel."

Nox stepped on a rock and groaned at the pop as her ankle twisted.

"Whoa!" Amaris caught her before she could fall. "We won't get there any faster if you tumble down the side of the mountain."

"Where are we going?" Ash asked. "Does the Speaker— the real one—have some place in the mountains?"

Nox's annoyance with Ash had not subsided. She snapped "We don't know. It could be a cabin. For all we know she has her own heaven on earth."

"If I were a goddess—" Amaris began.

"You are," Nox said curtly.

"As I was saying, if I were a goddess, I'd make myself quite the palace, and fill it with lovely men and women who were sycophants to my will. And nice things to eat. And beautiful, exotic trees. And…no. We aren't going to her place, wherever it may be. Joel and Allua are on a mission to bring her here. I was just at their home in Territory Two, and there was no sign that they'd been present in weeks. If they've succeeded, then they're going to bring her directly to the church. None of this will end until the fraud is off the throne."

"Wait." Ash tried to get the others to pause, but no one listened. "I don't understand. If we don't know where she is, or if they've succeeded, why are we in a hurry? Why not wait at the temple?"

Nox stopped then. The others crunched to a halt beside her.

"Because our people are in there," she said, turning to Ash. "We left Yazlyn alone. Ryu and Kasar rallied to fight with us, and we abandoned them. Gadriel…"

"Gadriel will be fine," Amaris said.

Nox's features softened. Her chest tightened as she looked into the face of denial. "Amaris, he couldn't have survived. The comte shattered my arm from fifty paces away. When he turned to Gadriel…"

"I thought he died too. I mourned. And then I remembered something: I've also broken Gadriel's neck." A half smile tugged at her as the memory flickered across her face. "He's a sick fuck. He gets off on this game. As long as they didn't swiftly behead the fallen, we have a man on the inside. If I know him, he will already be well on his way to freeing the others, if he hasn't already."

Nox couldn't believe what she was hearing. Her heart stuttered. "He's alive?"

Amaris folded her arms across her chest. "I guarantee it." After a moment, she amended, "Almost."

"Oh my goddess, I thought you weren't speaking about him because you were in shock. I assumed this was denial. He's really alive?"

Amaris chuckled. "He's particularly hard to kill."

"Damn," she whispered, resuming her walk. "Not a bad trait for a general to have."

"So he's said."

Nox resumed her walk, this time quickening her pace, emboldened by the news. Maybe she just needed to create space between herself and the others. Or maybe she was in such a hurry so she could reach the jade rapids and be united with Fjolla. She couldn't decide. But she did miss Fjolla.

Amaris fell several steps behind, keeping step with the others.

Ash's voice was thick with displeasure. "What are we supposed to do with information on the true Speaker? I feel like I've been left out of important planning and discussions. Is anyone going to catch me up?"

There was a smile in Amaris's words as she said, "I guess you shouldn't have been born male. Then maybe you could have come into the temple with us. Sorry, Ash."

"You're hilarious, Ayla."

Tanith chimed in, "I've heard you use this name before when speaking to the demigoddess. Why do you call her that?"

Nox peered over the side of the ledge to ensure that there was no one as far as the eye could see. If normal speaking voices carried down the trail to her ears, she didn't need the enemy catching them on the fault of idle chatter.

The sounds of their feet on the trail continued scraping along the mountain as they spoke. Amaris said, "It means 'oak tree.' It's from my early days at Uaimh Reev, though he's never let me live it down. Ash used to mock me for my footwork when we would spar, as if I were rooted to the ground."

There was nothing but the shuffle of dust and pebbles over rock before Tanith responded. There was a frown in her correction when she said, "No, Ayla means 'the light around the moon.'"

And though she didn't stop to observe their expressions, Nox could hear the wheels turning. She slowed as the path turned around an outcropping of boulders in anticipation of a reaction and was glad when it came.

"Can you two give us a moment?" Amaris asked. Six jogging steps later, she rounded the bend, leaving the other two behind, and was at Nox's side. "Did you hear that?" Amaris asked.

"Mmm, I did, *Ayla*."

Amaris chuckled lightly, her laugh a gentle breath drifting between them. "Nox means 'night,'" she said finally.

Nox stopped walking. The corner of her mouth twitched.

"Odrin once told me..." Amaris began. She twisted the trinket around her neck as she retreated into her memories. "Do you remember why the matrons called me Amaris? They said it meant 'gift from the goddess.' I was a gift to line their pockets. And Odrin said it meant 'child of the moon.'"

Nox leaned into the cliffside, glad for the bend in rocks that offered them privacy from the other two. She took a slow breath as she considered. She slipped her hand into Amaris's. "The matrons weren't wrong."

Amaris's pale brows flattened.

"You were a gift from the goddess. Just not in the way they intended." The urgency she'd felt only moments before ebbed. Her muscles relaxed as she looked at the child of the moon, the gift from the goddess, the light around the moon, the moon itself.

Nox was the night, and Amaris was her perfect other. A cool wind from the valley below tufted ivory locks of hair around Amaris's face as she returned the unbroken gaze. The clouds broke overhead, illuminating their lines as the last pearly lights of night waned. One hand stayed intertwined, while the other pushed a pale strand of hair away from her face, tucking it behind her ear. She leaned in close enough for their lips to brush, exchanging warm breaths of winter and spice. "And what is night without its moon?"

Amaris drank in a breath as their lips touched fully, Nox sucking in her bottom lip, then her top. They were the only ones on the path, on the mountain, in the world. The warm, exploratory kiss was sweet, sensual, and beautiful. With a shift as subtle as a whirl of the wind, their bodies connected. Nox leaned into the sheer mountain at her back, pulling Amaris toward her as she leaned into the rock behind her.

"All I know is"—Amaris breathed between kisses—"I've been a lot of things. I've been a fighter. I've been a fool. But you've always been wise and resilient and goddess-damn strong. I love that I was made for you." She pressed her forehead against the curve of Nox's neck as they cooled, hips still connected, fingers still laced. Nox kept her hold on the back of Amaris's neck, resting her cheek on top of Amaris's head. "You'll thrive, Nox, no matter what happens. The night can, and does, go on without the moon. But the moon without its night is lost."

Thirty–Eight

G ADRIEL PRESSED HIS FINGER TO HIS LIPS. HE SHOULDN'T
have had to demand silence, and yet.

"A two-man mission to take on an army of Reds and the
Speaker?" Yazlyn hissed after Gadriel as he crept up the stairs.
He tensed against the urge to kick her down the stairs. If they
survived this, he needed to get better friends. He walked on
the balls of his feet, keeping every movement light. Silence
was his priority, even if his sergeant seemed determined to
get them caught.

"I just feel like there are easier ways to get me killed," she
whispered.

"So help me," he mouthed, dragging his thumb across
his throat as he threatened murder. Her rolled eyes told him
exactly what she thought of his threats.

He paused just before they'd be visible to anyone who might
be in the foyer and listened for collectors, but no sound came.
Presumably, the bodies had been sufficiently removed from the
sanctuary. Either this was great news, as it meant the church
was empty, or it was terrible news, as it meant the collectors no
longer had a timed task. He supposed he was about to find out.
Regardless, it afforded him the chance to respond.

"She can wait her turn to die. Right now, we get out of here." Gadriel waited a few more beats to ensure no one was coming in through the double doors before they finished ascending the stairs, turning abruptly into the hallway that ran the rectangular perimeter. Yazlyn stayed on his heels, leaving no space between them as they moved with cat-like silence. He intended to lead them back toward the parsonage, hoping they could exit through the same broken window through which he'd entered.

The doors that lined the exterior wall unnerved him, knowing that each was lined with sound-dampening runes. They couldn't all be harmless broom closets. Any one of the rooms might open to reveal an enemy, and as long as their doorways contained dampening runes, he wouldn't hear them until it was too late. They were halfway down the hall when a sound came from the back side of the church. Soft voices and the gentle noises of shoes on stone floated from the very direction they'd been angling.

The reaction was instantaneous. Gadriel didn't have to say anything. Yazlyn turned on a dime without waiting for the order and crouch-sprinted back toward the foyer. They scarcely rounded the corner before the voices had floated into the very hall they'd occupied only moments before. They were temporarily safe in the atrium, but the solution was imperfect. If they remained in the foyer for more than thirty seconds, anyone could enter from the double doors or come down the stairs from the loft. There were too many points of entry.

He looked at Yazlyn and almost wished he hadn't. Her hazel eyes widened with urgency. It was a single, hurried look, a plea; she was a sergeant demanding a plan from her general.

He would not fail her. Leading the way, he crept back into the sanctuary. They hugged the outside wall, staying low enough to dive into the pews should someone enter. When the sounds from the hall began to fill the foyer, he slipped between the pew benches and yanked Yazlyn after him. He would have preferred to be in the reeds of a marsh or the bramble on the edge of an open battlefield rather than hidden in the spaces between the long chapel seats, but any cover was better than none.

"Send everyone! Send them now!" a male voice boomed from an entrance near the back of the sanctuary.

"But, sir, the comtes—"

"The comtes aren't going anywhere. I'll stay with them. If you don't intercept those Raascot bastards before they reach the church—" His sentence stopped as if sliced in half. The silence was so instantaneous that it felt as though his words had been cut with a sword. Gadriel dared to look up to see whoever had owned the voices had disappeared, presumably behind a door with dampening runes.

"Who?" Yazlyn mouthed the word.

Gadriel knew who. It had to be his parents. If Joel and Allua were anywhere near the church, it meant they'd found the Speaker. They also were about to be intercepted by a powerful army of Reds without knowing what hit them. They remained scrunched between the wooden pews, still askew from combat, as he pointed toward glassy ceiling windows reflecting the same early-morning lavender that he'd looked into so many times when he'd stared down at Amaris.

Yazlyn looked up at the pale, lilac sky, then back at him. Her eyes flared meaningfully. It was a yes, a no, a *What the hell are you thinking?*

He couldn't take flight from the cramped space between the pews. They crawled between the wooden benches and emerged into the aisle. He'd barely taken a single step into the sanctuary when a hard blow came from out of nowhere. Gadriel's jaw absorbed the impact of the punch. A burst of flame erupted from the unseen enemy. He swung hard and missed, unable to fight what he couldn't see. He tried again, but Yazlyn was quicker. She called to the water that remained in the ceremonial basin on the platform. She barely had time to meet fire with ice when another strike came.

They were fighting a Red. No amount of ice or punches or reflexes could prepare them against what a soldier willing to die for their faith might procure.

"Come on!" Gadriel grabbed his sergeant's hand and leapt skyward.

He was knocked from the air by a hurricane-force gust. The Red stepped out from behind their unseen barrier as the warrior continued to manipulate air, rendering Gadriel's and Yazlyn's wings utterly useless. They struggled to stay on their feet, wings tucked against their back against the wind as they battled toward the guard. He opened his mouth to shout at Yazlyn to go without him, but the wind stopped.

He continued looking at Yazlyn, but she did not return his gaze. Her attention was fixed elsewhere. He followed her gaze to the Red, now standing motionless, hands outstretched, eyes bulging. He'd been immobilized. Gadriel had been flexed for battle, but his shoulders relaxed as he took a step closer to the enemy. It was just enough to see a blue-white frost crust over the man's skin, crawling over his arms, his neck, his face like ice over a lake.

"You…" He could scarcely articulate his thoughts. She'd frozen the man's very blood where he'd stood.

She panted, hands still raised for a fight. She looked at him with the barest of shrugs. "I thought it couldn't hurt to try."

There was no time to appreciate her handiwork. The church erupted as feet pounded through the corridors. Their combat had given them away. The enemy would be upon them in a second.

"Go!" Gadriel gave her another shove to shake her from the shock of her killing blow.

They took to the sky, covering the space from the chapel's floor to ceiling in a second. He pulled the sword he'd stolen off the basement guard and used the pommel to meet the glass, shattering it around them as they burst from the church's ceiling. He grunted against the exertion. Jagged shards tore at their skin, wings, and clothes as they emerged. The sounds of fractured, falling glass rang out like ten thousand silver bells, alerting everyone in the church to their commotion. By the time the other Reds could turn to see what had happened, they'd be long gone.

They were two eagles on the horizon, shooting as far from the city as they could against the first, purple lights of morning. Gadriel led the way, not quite knowing where he was going but having ascertained the emptiest valleys that tucked themselves within the mountains from his former flights. None of the Reds had been the seraphim of Territory Two. The enemy would not have time to ready arrows or pursue them. They'd be too distracted by the frozen statue of their fellow warrior who'd turned to ice where he'd stood.

✦

"Lovebirds!" Ash jogged up behind them, breaking the girls from their intimate moment. His feet scraped against the trail, Tanith's hands still laced between his fingers. "Did you hear that?"

Amaris pulled away from where her lips had barely parted the lush plum of Nox's mouth and strained her ears. She was still tangled in Nox's arms as she listened, but she had no gift for fae hearing. She followed Ash's outstretched finger as she examined the purpling clouds for a sign.

"There." Tanith this time. She pointed to a nearby peak where the dark shape of two large birds could scarcely be distinguished from the gray of the mountain.

The four strained their eyes at the enormous birds. As black as a crow and as large as an angel.

"It's them." Nox shielded her eyes from the budding morning light as she stared into the clouds. "It has to be

Yaz and Gad." Nox released Amaris completely as she moved toward the ledge.

Amaris looked between them. "How do we get their attention?"

Ash squinted after the airborne fae. "I could use the light—"

Nox practically hissed at him. "She said how do we get *their* attention, not how do we get the attention of the entire kingdom of Sulgrave."

"Let me," Tanith whispered.

"No." Ash tightened his hold on her, eyes darkening. "You just came back from the brink of death. You can't keep calling on the groundwater if it means we're going to lose you."

A moment passed with the party eyeing the large birds and their flight path against the mountain. Amaris looked to her queen, then to the others. She flattened her mouth in a tight line as she considered the options. It was Gadriel. It had to be. "Do it," Amaris said to Tanith.

Nox and Ash tensed beside her.

Amaris was unmoved. "My bag, along with the green-strike blood, is in Elswyth's cabin in Territory Three. We wouldn't have been able to get there last night when we were escaping. It was no good to us when she was already on the brink of death. However, if Tanith uses one small ability now, I can get us to Three and to the blood. It's worth it. Do it." Her face was set. There was no room for argument.

Ash's lips remained parted as if to argue, but no sound was made.

Tanith closed her eyes and...nothing happened.

Three seconds passed as chilly morning wind continued to gust up from the valley. Amaris chafed her arms for warmth as she continued to stare at the lavender clouds.

Come on, come on.

The large, distant birds banked against the wind. She could have pumped her fist into the air and cried as the shapes began to fly toward them. Tanith's grim face was a glimmer of pride.

"What did you do?" Ash demanded.

"It's them." Her voice contained more smugness than any of them had ever heard. "They're coming."

Nox's jaw dropped open. Her eyes were saucers. "You spoke to their minds? You communicated mind to mind?"

Tanith's teeth flashed against the rising morning. She looked neither weary nor ill. Perhaps it had been the brevity of her usage of the power, or maybe it would just take a while for her to show the effects, but Tanith seemed happier than ever. Clinging to Ash's arm, surrounded by companions, and arguably the most powerful, useful individual in the group, Tanith was aglow. Even if the world happened to be falling apart around her, Amaris had never seen her shimmer like this.

The enormous birds swooped low, hugging the mountain on the other side of the valley as it dropped toward the blue-green mountain river. Their shapes stayed near to the ground as they began their ascent, presumably so that their silhouettes wouldn't be spotted against the morning sky by prying eyes. In one heartbeat they were a blur of wings and feathers. Before she could distinguish the faces and features of the fae, they were upon them. A minute later, the Raascot fae had landed on the trail.

Amaris tried to stifle her happy shriek as she threw her arms around Gadriel. The sunlight itself seemed to shine out of his face at his joy over their reunion. At her side, Nox embraced Yazlyn, though perhaps not as warmly as she deserved.

"What do you say?" Yazlyn smiled. "Why don't we just set Sulgrave on fire and go back home to Raascot?"

Tanith crossed her arms, unamused.

"Hey, Tanith." She made an apologetic gesture, though her eyes were still heavily implying that they could set a match to the mountain kingdom and never look back.

"It's good to see you again, Yazlyn." She unfolded her arms, planting her hands on her hips as she allowed herself to smile.

Gadriel had released Amaris and addressed the group.

"I'm so glad you're all right." He hugged Amaris again and then looped Nox into the hug. Nox yelped and began to squirm out of the show of affection, but Gadriel was going to force them all to be loved whether they wanted it or not. Amaris stifled a giggle at the impropriety. This had always been something Amaris had loved about Gadriel. His gravity, his seriousness, his deadliness—none detracted from his ability to experience pure, undiluted joy.

"We're fine." Nox blushed, finally worming out from under his arm. Amaris continued to hold her breath against the chuckle. She'd spent years at Uaimh Reev learning how to love and be loved by family. Nox, on the other hand, still had a ways to go in accepting platonic affection.

He laughed and roughed her hair as if she were his younger sister rather than his queen.

"This is why I promoted Zaccai to general," she grumbled, smoothing out her hair. She shot him a look. "What the hell happened? How did you two get out?"

The light behind his eyes switched from friendly to serious as he gave his report. "I wasn't able to learn much, other than that my parents have been spotted. Yazlyn and I overheard them saying they're dispatching the Reds to intercept two Raascot fae, and since they thought the two of us were already captive, it must be them. This has to be good news. If they're returning to Sulgrave, I assume they found the Speaker."

Nox balked. "If you're telling us we have to fight off one dozen Taniths in order to help Joel and Allua, then we're going to die."

Tanith shook her head quickly. "Please keep in mind, I was selected to travel south to kill you because I was the strongest."

"Oh, great," Nox mused.

"I mean this as a positive," Tanith countered. "Many do not possess the same access to groundwater. And knowing

448

how many Reds fell in the sanctuary, I have to assume only six or seven remain. Their leader will undoubtedly stay with the Speaker. Which means we'll be up against five or six Reds at maximum."

"Just five," Yazlyn slowly corrected. "I killed one more in the church when we were escaping. I just…froze his blood while it was still coursing inside him."

Everyone, including Tanith, regarded the sergeant with perplexed expressions.

Yazlyn explained, "When Amaris was hurt, I helped to cool her blood to slow her wound, but with an execution like this… I've never done anything like it. I'd never even considered it. I don't know what came over me, but one moment he was fighting, and the next moment…"

Tanith was thoroughly impressed. "And you don't feel ill at all? That's an incredible breakthrough in ability, Yazlyn. You might be even more formidable than you realize." She dipped her chin once in respect before continuing. "The other Reds aren't as developed as I am. The best and most capable were sent across the straits tasked to summon and bind the beasts, leaving those who required more training, devotion, and practice behind in Sulgrave. We won't be fighting five Reds with my range of ability, though it would be a mistake to underestimate them."

"Five of them, and six of us," Amaris said.

Nox chewed on her lip. "I think you're better off if you count things five on five. I don't know that my abilities are terribly useful in battle. Unless, of course, people can be killed in their dreams."

Gadriel was the only one who reacted to Nox's attempt at levity. The general went strangely rigid, wings folding tightly behind him. He looked down into Nox's face for any hint of jest, eyes unblinking. "What did you say?"

Her brows gathered. She looked to the others to see that they were just as confused as she was. She returned his stare. "What?"

Gadriel's shoulders and chest had stopped moving, as if he weren't breathing. "Why would you say that?"

Nox took on a defensive posture, moving one foot behind the other. Two straight lines gathered between her brows as they pinched. "When we got to the temple last night, I knew that before I passed out, I had one chance at visiting the Speaker. I didn't know what I hoped to gain, but I walked into Daifa's dream. She seemed oblivious to my presence, so I did my best to ask questions. I tried to tell her to spare your lives. Again, I don't know what it was I hoped to accomplish, but I believe I walked through her memories with her."

Amaris didn't understand why Gadriel was unwilling to relax. There was something vaguely ominous about the way he refused to move. He said, "Ceres tried to enter Moirai's and Daphne's dreams for years. They were warded every hour of the night and day. They were impenetrable. He was never able to attempt any such assassination for the late queen or visit his princess. If you've already been in Daifa's mind, she must not wear any wards against abilities of the mind. Nox, do you know what this could mean?"

Tanith's soft voice wafted from over Amaris's shoulder. "She wouldn't need to ward herself. She's never met opposition before now—nothing has stood in her way before your arrival. Everyone who's attended her services or met her has been instantly won to her side. Now that we know she can show us whatever we need to see in order to believe her, it tracks. It also makes sense why the only people spared from her zeal were those who'd never attended a service." Her tone dropped to barely above a whisper as she breathed her final thoughts on Daifa. "It's the darkest gift I've known."

"Can you visit her again?" Gadriel's voice was still heavy with intensity. The others may as well have been phantoms for all the attention he paid them. "Today, we'll intercept my parents before they reach the Reds. We'll get to Territory

Three for the supplies Amaris and I left behind when we rallied with Elswyth. Later tonight, when the others are sleeping, can you visit Daifa?"

Nox looked at the others as if waiting for someone to laugh or to come to her aid. Everyone was staring at her. "You really think I can kill someone in their dream?"

"I think all of Gyrradin needs you to try."

Thirty–Nine

I'M GOING TO BE HONEST," YAZLYN WHISPERED. "I FEEL LIKE our plans keep getting better."

Amaris chuckled as she thought of how she was already living up to her silent vow. Any plan was better than no plan at all.

Sulgrave's Temple of the All Mother was wedged into a crag between Territories Three and Four. This had advantageously positioned them to pick their way toward the safe house that held Amaris's bag of supplies. Reaching the supplies, however, came with a treacherous obstacle. The day was blessedly overcast—a gift that prevented the harsh shadows and sunlight from giving them away as they crept along the boulders and low conifers that clung to the steep mountainsides.

Their plan to tackle the Reds and get to the supplies was a rather simple military strategy. They would run parallel to the enemy, cutting off their adversary in an inverted "L" shape with the two strongest members blocking the Reds from the front while the others ambushed from the side. The church's assassins left on foot at roughly the same time Gadriel and Yazlyn escaped. Thanks to the Raascot faes' gift for flight, they'd been able to spot several dots of crimson in the distance.

If the Reds had spotted Joel and Allua, then they knew something that Amaris and her retinue did not. It served in their best interest to follow the Reds. And so, they did. They picked their footing carefully, maintaining a distant parallel from the brightly colored red tunics as they continued down the least populated valley. Every so often, they'd lose visual contact of the enemy. Tanith would briefly tap in to whatever ability she needed to reestablish connection, never using the power for more than an instant, lest she feel taxed. The team advanced along the mountainside amidst the scraggly pines undetected.

"I think we got lucky," Gadriel said.

Amaris agreed. Wherever the Reds were taking them, it was far from the populous city center. They continued to tail them as they angled for one of the unaffiliated valleys—a rocky, green space dotted with little more than sheep and the solitary cottages of shepherds.

"Are you okay?" Ash whispered to Tanith.

Amaris paused to hear the answer. Their Sulgrave ally wasn't showing any signs of wear aside from her thinly veiled irritation at his concern. "I'm fine, but you won't be if you keep asking me."

He grumbled. "Forgive me if I don't believe you. You've proven on more than one occasion that you'd rather die than ask for help."

Yazlyn took entirely too much pleasure at the back and forth, and Amaris couldn't blame her. Tanith was sounding more like one of them with every day that passed. She and Yazlyn shared a poorly concealed grin. Whether it was the thrill of impending battle or the excitement at being reunited with the others, things were finally going their way. The only dampener on their spirits seemed to be the clouds overhead, and even that was probably for the best. Amaris looked up at the flat, overcast sky as it churned into deeper shades of gray and prayed that the rain would hold off. The wind answered her prayer, dismissing it as it shook the evergreen branches around them and spat a few wayward droplets onto their path.

"Ash." Tanith looked at him, her features softening. "Thank you."

Ash slowed.

"For caring, I mean," Tanith said. "Thank you."

They didn't have time to appreciate the girl's tonal shift, or the way it had melted over Ash like butter. Amaris looked directly at Gadriel through her cloud of silver-whipped hair. His eyes touched hers before scanning the faces of the others. There would be time for sentimentality after they accomplished what needed to be done.

"Okay," Gadriel cut their chatter short as he assumed the leadership position. "Tanith and I will draw them out."

Ash didn't have the chance to protest as Gadriel anticipated his objections.

"Listen, reever." He squared off with Ash. "It has to be her. No one doubts your skill in close combat. You're a talented asset. But the fact remains: Tanith has the greatest range of abilities, and I'm the most difficult to kill. She and I will go out to meet the Reds by cutting in front of them. When they engage us, you'll attack from the side." He turned to his sergeant. "I'd like you to hang back and see how many you can freeze without being detected. Stay with Nox."

Yazlyn nodded quickly in acknowledgment, her hand touching the hilt of the sword that might not need to taste blood today. Her chestnut curls obscured her vision as she looked at Nox. It was clear that their young queen was experiencing a twist of emotions. Nox mumbled something between irritation and self-pity. Her hatred at being the crew's weakness was no secret.

"Hey," Amaris said quietly. "There are a thousand things you can do that we can't. Let me stab some bad guys while you rule the world."

Nox's berry-dark lips tugged up in a small smile. Her

glossy hair moved unbound in the wind as she slipped her hand into Amaris's and squeezed it gently. Her eyes swirled with the sort of black infinity one saw on a cloudless night. There was an anger in them, a want, and Amaris wished she could say it had to do with her, but she was quite certain that Nox was missing her attachment to her stupid axe or, worse, her goddess-awful pet.

The team held fast.

They'd reached a chokehold in the valley before the Reds, and now was their time to wait. The church's assassins advanced toward the narrow, grassy path between two thick outcroppings of boulders.

"Who knows," Yazlyn whispered from where she hid. She kept her eyes on the ruby specks in the distance as they advanced. "Maybe I'll pick them all off before they even see us coming."

It was clear from Yazlyn's cocky smirk that she had been joking, but Tanith eyed her rather seriously. "There's no reason you couldn't."

Yazlyn frowned. Her hazel eyes searched Tanith for a sign of jest.

Tanith remained serious. "You've been able to manipulate ice for years, but you've never applied it to such ends. Sometimes power is less about your ability and more about your usage."

"But they…" Yazlyn wanted to rebuff, but she couldn't quite wrap her mind around the words she needed.

Gadriel didn't let them get too deeply into the conversation. "I still need to draw their attention forward with me. Even if Yaz picks them off one by one, we can't have them turning to look in our direction and risk exposing Nox." He cast her a glance. "I'm sorry, Nox, but you have kingdoms to serve. Their focus needs to stay forward toward the valley. Once we're fully engaged," he turned to the reevers, "Ash and Amaris will ambush from the side."

"We still don't know where your parents are," Yazlyn said.

"But we know where to head in order to find them," Gadriel replied.

Spatters of red between the pine needles meant the Reds had already rounded the bend and entered the valley. Gadriel turned to Tanith and issued his hushed command. "It's time to go."

Gadriel advanced, but Tanith turned to Ash before she moved. "I'll be fine."

He tried to smile. "I know you will."

"And you?" she asked.

He shrugged. "We've got this."

She returned the smile. "We," she repeated.

Not him. Not her. Not the Raascot fae, or the orphan queen, or the reevers, or the Sulgrave loner. *We.*

The attacking team disappeared between the branches as they stayed low, hidden against broken boulders while the Reds continued on the hard-packed grass below. The others looked at Ash while he watched them go.

"She's stronger than all of us combined, Ash," Amaris whispered.

Half of his mouth quirked up in an insincere attempt at levity. "I tend to surround myself with women who can kick my ass."

Nox's quiet chuckle warmed them. "Good man." The wind whipped a strand of dark hair into her mouth. Nox spit to get the hair from where it had stuck to her tongue.

"Your hair," Yazlyn said suddenly. Amaris tensed at the intense change in mood as the fae's teeth flashed. She'd gone from amicable to feral in a second, and Amaris had no idea why.

Nox looked to the sergeant, and then her hands flew to her glossy black locks. With a panic-stricken face, she plunged her hand into her pocket and procured an emerald ribbon.

Yazlyn's anger did not ebb. She burned with an intensity that set both Amaris and her brother on edge as she snarled. "Look at me." She eyed Nox, voice quiet with a thinly controlled heated emotion. "Were you wearing it when you faced the Hand in the throne room?"

Nox's flicker of emotion wasn't one Amaris understood. Her face tightened. Her mouth twisted. "You have to understand—"

"Why weren't you wearing it when we entered the sanctuary?" Yazlyn demanded, her posture looming closer to the queen.

Nox's angry reply was a rush of defensive whispers. "We'd just gotten free. And it doesn't work on powers of the mind! It would have been useless! I didn't—"

Yazlyn leaned in until her furious glower was mere inches from Nox's. She lowered her voice to a threat. "Listen here, Queen of Raascot," she said in a low, terrible growl. "You had no way of knowing if they'd come at you with power or steel. If I see you take that fucking piece of fabric off one more time, I will hold you down and tie it around your throat until it's as fastened to your skin as my goddess-damned collar. If you don't? Then I'll take your head off myself and make sure Gadriel ascends."

Nox scrambled to her feet and straightened her shoulders. Amaris watched on in horror as her eyes shot to the trees, terrified that the fight would give them away, but the sergeant matched her defensive posture. Nox was scarcely three fingers taller than the fae, but her matching fire made her tower. "That's right," she said with a fiery heat. "I am the Queen of Raascot. And you will back the fuck off, sergeant. You have no right—"

Yazlyn snapped her sentence in half as if it were a twig to be broken. "You will not take it off again. Am I making myself clear?"

Amaris had had enough. She joined the women on her feet and pushed her way between the two, but Yazlyn's unrelenting fury made even Amaris back down. A bewildered trickle dripped down her spine.

"I said," Yazlyn spat, "am I making myself clear?"

Nox stared with ice and anger in her eyes, holding Yazlyn's unblinking glower.

"What the hell is happening?" Amaris demanded.

Yazlyn jabbed a finger toward Nox. "Are you going to tell them what a foolish, selfish, idiotic bastard you've been, or should I?"

"Hey," Amaris said, cutting in as her anger grew. "I don't know what your problem is—"

Yazlyn exhaled loudly. "My problem is that your stupid lover—"

Amaris lifted her blade. The reever held the small knife to the sergeant's throat in the breath of time it had taken anyone else to blink. Her lilac eyes were a dark, terrible shade of purple as she glowered. "Try again without the insults," she snarled at the winged fae.

Yazlyn narrowed her eyes at Amaris, refusing to flinch away from the knife at her jugular. As she spoke, the skin of her throat brushed the razor-sharp edge of Amaris's dagger. "Nox, tell them what you did. Or rather, tell them what you didn't do. Tell them how you left Farehold and Raascot open to being two kingdoms without a queen." Venom dripped from her as she repeated her command. "Tell them."

The storm kicked up around them, matching the rage in her eyes as it howled and whipped around them. Nox still hadn't unclenched her fists or allowed the angry burn of her gaze to waver. When it was clear that no one was coming to save her from confrontation, she raked her strands back with quick, angered fingers and knotted the ribbon in her hair before she met Amaris's gaze.

In the battle between defensiveness and guilt, Nox said, "I was gifted this emerald ribbon in Gwydir. No one who wishes ill intent can harm me while I wear it. At least, with physical weapons."

"Now, Queen Nox, first queen to unite Farehold and Raascot, tell us: have you been wearing the single most precious item in all of Gyrradin?"

Ash spoke for the first time. "I thought she couldn't wear wards—"

"This isn't a ward!" Yazlyn bit. "This has nothing to do with magical abilities. It's charmed for physical harm. Look." Yazlyn moved her sword toward Nox before either of the reevers could defend her. She stabbed down in a killing blow. Yazlyn's thin sword glanced off of Nox as if sliding off of a slick, oiled surface. "It's armor."

Nox raised her arm with full intent of stabbing Yazlyn out of a sheer flurry of temper, but Amaris grabbed Nox's forearm. She whipped to Nox with equal incredulity, intercepting the descent of her blade by gripping her wrist. "You've had armor with you that could have protected you all this time?"

"Amaris—"

"What the hell is wrong with you? Why would you ever take this off? Do you have a death wish?"

"Were you seriously going to stab me?" Yazlyn gaped at the queen.

Nox's snarl was defensive. "Don't you think I'm being beaten up enough?"

"No." Amaris had repositioned herself to stand with Yazlyn. "I don't think you have. Would you have been safe in your fight in Gwydir? Would you have been protected against the aboriou if she hadn't turned out to be a giant, dumb dog? Would your arm have been spared in the cathedral?"

"My arm is fine now—"

"That's not the point!"

Amaris narrowed her eyes. "I'm telling Malik."

Nox's voice pitched into a whine. "Please don't. He'll be so disappointed in me."

"Good!"

Their argument crashed to a halt as Ash shushed them with furious intensity. Cherry curls tumbled over Yazlyn's shoulder as she tilted her ears toward the noise. Amaris swallowed whatever residual feelings she had on the topic and turned to eye the dashes of color between the branches.

They were close.

Amaris shared a nod with Ash before they moved toward the valley.

"Wait," Nox whispered after Amaris somewhat anxiously.

"Don't worry," she said. She'd wanted to stay mad at Nox for her infuriating recklessness, but the concern was clear on her face. Instead, she offered a wink. "I don't need a ribbon to make my way back to you."

She fell into step beside the other reever. It was years at the keep; it was endless hours in the ring; it was the deep, unspeakable bond that blurred between warrior and family that pulled them into synchronicity as they advanced. She strained to see the final flash of crow-feather black as Gadriel and Tanith disappeared from their advanced placement down the trail.

"The storm—" Ash began, nerves frayed as he looked ahead to where Tanith had disappeared.

"Is on our side," Amaris completed. It would cover their tracks. The wind would distract the Reds from the treacherous sound of a misplaced foot or sliding pebble. They stopped along the rocks once they'd reached their attacking position. She shoved the wayward bits of hair from her face before she caught his wrist. "Ash." Amaris's voice was a soft, quick sound. She pressed her back into a rock, knowing they were one small movement away from drawing attention.

His creased brow asked his question for him.

Amaris tightened her hold on his arm. "Would I have been a better fighter if you'd spent our time in the ring stressed over my progress? Stop worrying about Tanith. Give her more credit. She's stronger than all of us. You need to focus on the fight, and on your role in the battle. Pick up your feet, or I'm going to have to start calling you Ayla."

A brief smile barely reached his eyes as he said, "I'm neither tree nor moon."

"What are you, then?"

His smile reached his eyes. "What did the people in Stone call us? The league of guardians? I'm an angel."

"So gallant," she breathed, looking over her shoulder. They were in position. There were only a few seconds between them and the impending battle. "Together?"

His amber eyes were a warm shade of melted honey, comforting her as he met her stare. "You've fought by my side for years, Ayla. You know there's nothing we can't do."

Forty

AMARIS WATCHED ASH BRANDISH HIS BLADE AND GRINNED at how different their lives were. How times had changed since she'd wielded a wooden placeholder while getting her ass kicked at the reev. She'd come so far from looking up at the copper blaze of hair from her back, breathless and miserable on the ring floor. Together, they'd worked, they'd grown, and they were ready for whatever came next.

She looked away from Ash and at the empty space where a dark blotch of wings had been a moment before. Her gaze darted to the valley. The wind stole the air from her lungs as a burst of feathers and a rallying cry led the attack. Tanith and Gadriel sprang into the valley with a shock of force and power.

They moved in sync as they made their way toward the edge of the brush. A bright light muddied her peripherals. The clang of metal. Angry shouts. The grunt of battle. She couldn't look at them again or she'd lose her resolve as they sprang into action. Ash matched her step for step as they darted from the rocks to ambush the Reds from the side.

She burst into the valley, sword aloft, while Tanith wielded her electric power against the enemy with pulverizing force.

Amaris vaulted into the air, bringing her sword down in a powerful arc while a crack of lightning shot through the advancing party. Between Gadriel, Amaris, and Tanith, three Reds had fallen before they'd even registered an enemy presence.

Tanith's cry was high and mighty as her voltage rocked the earth. A single Red thrust her hand into the sky, casting an answering shield over herself and the remaining Reds at her side. Gadriel shot into the air and dove in a rapid movement, bringing his sword down for the front-most Red as Tanith used her power to nullify the shield, ripping its protective force from the center-most Red with a grunt of effort. She tore down the Red's defenses with a gasp of exertion, watching as Gadriel's blade ate through the neck of the leading party member.

Two remained. Amaris's eyes watered as she slashed for another. The Red rebuffed her with a powerful blast, sending her skidding into the dirt. At her side, she heard Ash cry out as the metal heated in his hand. The Red watched his blade drop but was caught unaware by his answering kick. He hadn't lost a beat as he threw himself into hand-to-hand combat.

One of the church's assassins screamed Tanith's name as she cast a shield over all three of her exposed companions. The small Red's shrill cry was a desperate, horrified plea for Tanith to stand down, but she did not. Amaris raised her blade to take down a Red, but before she could even begin to cut into the assassin's flesh, the fae had been frozen into a chipped statue of blood, skin, and ice. Yazlyn had successfully wielded her abilities from the bushes.

They'd won so quickly, so completely, Amaris scarcely had time to process the gore before her. Bodies littered every side. One she'd cut down where he'd stood, one had become a pillar of frigid stone, another evaporated, another Ash had tackled.

One remained.

"Wait!" The Red who had screamed for Tanith threw up a shield for herself alone. It glimmered as it cast a shimmering coverage around her. "Tanith, wait!"

Amaris looked between the two Sulgrave fae. She was smaller than Tanith, with plump cheeks and wide eyes that made Amaris wonder if she'd even reached her eighteenth year of life. Her hands remained outstretched as she trembled, struggling to keep her shield in place.

Amaris looked across the battlefield to Gadriel, who nodded at her to stay at the ready. Ash moved nearer to Tanith, prepared to defend her to the end.

"Nyana." Tanith said the other Red's name, no ire in her voice.

The quiet that followed was the silence that preceded weeping. The unmistakable hollow of pain tore through the gore and death of their small battlefield. The only sound was the exhausted panting of the single Red as she maintained the exertion of her borrowed power.

"Why would you do this?" Nyana asked, her question thick with sorrow. Her eyes scanned the carnage of the fallen men, brimming with a wound too sharp for tears. Her eyes took in the blades of the foes surrounding her. Her face was painted with pain and treachery. While the fae were often ageless, something about Nyana looked particularly young. The ache in her eyes reflected the naivete of one who'd never known betrayal.

Tanith relaxed her posture ever so slightly, eyeing the girl. She kept her chin high. Her hands were no longer raised to call on the groundwater of power, but she had not fully dropped into a position of acceptance. She spoke with authority. Everyone remained poised for action while they watched Tanith anxiously.

"You're on a mission to intercept two Raascot fae escorting a stranger. Do you know who the stranger is, by chance?"

Nyana shook her head, hands still raised as she glimmered with her shield. Her words sounded strangled. "It's not my business to question—"

Tanith's voice was fierce as she stared at the young Red surrounded by her fallen brethren. "It's because they've found the Speaker—the true Speaker. If you and the others had met the Raascot fae on their path, you would have killed the All Mother made flesh. You're on a mission to murder the goddess."

"No." Nyana's eyes were as wide as saucers. Her arms struggled to maintain her borrowed power. "You're lying."

"It is true," Tanith said, face blank as she eyed the girl who'd once been her sister in arms. "The woman residing in the church is a deceiver. She's a wolf in sheep's clothing."

It was too much. The moment became as thick as tar. Nyana's eyes rimmed with silver as tears began to spill over her cheeks. She could have cried for her fallen comrades, or wept over the church's deception, but instead, her grief was the wound of betrayal. It was clear to everyone that Nyana couldn't believe her eyes as she continued to stare at the traitor before her. "Why wouldn't you just talk to us?" she begged, each word punctured with injury. "You've murdered us. You've slaughtered us. We were your brothers and sisters, Tanith. We're your family."

If they hadn't all been carefully watching Tanith's face, they may have missed the tiny, controlled flinch. Tanith was in pain. She kept her voice level as she said, "You know as well as I that none of you would have listened. I would have been dismissed as a heretic. You would have killed me as quickly as I've killed you."

"You don't know—" the Red argued, lips turning blue from blood loss.

"I do, Nyana. It's all we've been trained to do. We don't question. We obey. We murder. We're born of blind obedience in the name of goodness—crafted in submission, bloodshed. You know it's true. You know what we are."

Nyana's forehead dotted with saltwater. The beads began to drip as she fought. The tremble in her arms increased with every passing ragged breath.

Tanith's voice stayed tight as she addressed the girl in the red tunic. "If you don't drop the shield, your use of the stolen power will kill you on its own."

"It's not stolen, it's—"

"It's drawing on your blood. It's blood magic. That's why it wounds us. That's why it's forbidden. What we do is not good. It is not what the goddess intended."

Nyana's face hardened, dismissing Tanith entirely. Her jaw set as she raised her hands even higher in defiance. "If I drop the shield, you'll kill me. I die either way."

Tanith looked to Gadriel and tilted her chin to one side in a way that encouraged him to lower his weapon. The others followed suit. Ash took two careful steps to reposition himself to stand near Tanith. His honey-colored eyes were trained on her as she spoke; she'd been such a force for power, violence, and zeal and yet still maintained this well of compassion for another lost soul.

"I know you have a good heart." Tanith attempted to soothe the Red the way one might speak with an animal whose leg was caught in a trap. "Your faith, like mine, is why we dedicated ourselves to the service of the All Mother. You desire the will of the goddess as much as I do. We can still serve the goddess. The true goddess."

"How can you know the Speaker in the church is false? After all of her miracles? After everything she's done?" Her arms were trembling violently. They were going to give out any second. A distant rumble of thunder told them that the storm was about to turn. A decision had to be made, and it had to be made quickly.

"She plants memories." Tanith spoke with conviction. "The false Speaker is a fae with the power of memory creation. It's one evil power of the mind. Not the power of the goddess. Not the power of creation—but the single, horrifying ability to lie. She's deceived us, Nyana. But it isn't too late to help the true Speaker make her way safely to the church. Peace can be restored. Drop your shield."

"I can't," she rasped, voice hoarse with fear and exhaustion. "Drop it, or you're going to die."

Nyana gritted her teeth, skin graying and clammy as if she were growing more ill by the moment. "If I drop it out of fear of death, I'm a coward."

"If you drop it to help purge the church of its infestation and restore peace, you're a hero."

Amaris held her breath as she watched, and hoped, and prayed.

Their eyes were fixed for a long time, each Sulgrave warrior—defenders of the church and lovers of the All Mother—refusing to avert their gaze. A beat passed, then another. Nyana broke her shield. The flash in her eyes as she shattered the shield should have been the warning they needed to react, but the surge of anger Nyana displayed was too quick, too all-encompassing for response. With every drop of remaining strength, she threw out her hands to summon the swords of the fallen and fling the sharp weapons spiraling with incredible speed toward Tanith.

The high-pitched zing of metal filled the air.

Silver, razors, steel, cries, blood, and pain glistened before the single blink of an eye.

It was over before Amaris knew what had happened.

In the heartbeat it had taken the others to register the shower of blades as they rained down upon the short-haired heretic, Ash had thrown himself into Tanith to cover her with his own body. He'd grunted as he'd slammed his chest against her, his arms wrapping around her protectively. He'd barely had time to make contact before the sharpened, metallic weapons were impaling themselves through his back, his legs, his arm, and his neck.

Gadriel reacted on instinct, diving for Nyana. He took her head from her shoulders with a clean swipe of his sword. The last remaining Red fell unceremoniously to the ground, but it was too late. Her last act had met a mark. The damage had been done.

"No!" Tanith screamed a single, savage plea.

But it was not for Nyana. The sound of her hoarse, anguished scream ate through the valley, crawling up the mountains, carving itself into the rumble of the thunderheads that gathered overhead. She scrambled to get out from under Ash where she'd fallen and put her hands on him, trying to call upon the ability to heal.

Hysteria overtook her as she cried out again, trembling with panic and rage. Her words came out with a rabid intensity. "Someone, get the swords out of him! Get them out! Get them out now!" She began crying, her shoulders shaking with the effort as tears fell freely. Amaris and Gadriel both ran for her. Amaris began attempting to remove the blades from her fallen reever brother while Tanith pressed her hands into the gashes to heal the wounds.

Gadriel had stopped one step away from where the women knelt. He was staring silently at what she either hadn't seen or refused to acknowledge.

The hilt of a single, long dagger embedded itself through Ash's throat. Its crimson, dripping tip protruded through flesh and vertebrae. His amber eyes remained open, though they held no glimmer of life. Blood dripped from the corners of his mouth, running down his cheek and joining the small river of blood where the sword remained embedded. His spinal column had been severed before they'd even known what had happened.

"Tanith." Gadriel slid a hand over her shoulder.

"Get off me!" she screamed with animal intensity, shaking Gadriel's touch away. The wind continued to pick up, whipping her short, dark hair around her face in a violent, angry cloud. The thunder rumbled again, echoing her cries as if she herself was the source of the turbulent, oncoming storm. She bared her teeth as if to lunge at the general's jugular if he came near her again.

Amaris had stopped moving. Her pale fingers were stained red from where she'd removed the weapons from Ash's back, his arm, and his leg. She had stilled above the final hilt, staring down at her friend, her family, her brother, her reever, the first man she'd ever kissed, the sparring partner who'd taught her how to be resilient, how to hold a blade, how to survive in the world. His eyes were no longer honey, nor were they amber. They were empty, unseeing chips of dull brown.

A dark void began to swirl within Amaris. Anguish forced her into petrified silence.

Tanith looked up with furious intensity at the remaining reever, anger gagging her as she yelled for her to continue. "Amaris, get it out! Take it out of him! Take it out so I can heal him!" Her hands were drenched red with his blood from where she'd tried to heal his wounds, but no matter how she called on the ability, nothing happened. It was as if she was possessed. Yet, her powers of healing held no sway here. The body could not stitch together that which no longer lived.

Amaris tried to move. She fell to her knees, looking at the impossible gore with vacant eyes. Her ears rang with the thunder of blood and rumble of storms as she blinked at the impossible sight before her, body chilling with an unnatural cold. She was distantly aware of Tanith's ongoing screams as the Sulgrave girl continued to push on his wounds, begging them to heal. She'd never seen anyone so unhinged. Tanith was a fox, gnawing off its own leg to remove itself from a trap. She was a rabid dog. She was wholly human, and not human at all as denial raked through her with deep, savage claws.

"No, no, no," Tanith cried, groaning against the heft of his weight as she held him to her. His blood pooled against her shirt, her pants, soaking every part of her. "Ash, come back." Her tears flowed freely as she clung to him. She lowered her face to his, resting her forehead against his. "Come back to me."

"Tanith," Gadriel tried again, but she wasn't listening.

Amaris knew Gadriel had seen death. He'd seen battle. She knew he'd been through pain, and loss, and grief. He hovered his hand above her shoulder, then withdrew it as a man who knew that she could not be reached.

Tanith lowered her mouth to his, a sobbing, horrible kiss. His lips were motionless beneath hers. They were not the passion and love of the moments they'd shared. They held no spark, no joy, no tension or desire or movement. They were limp and chilling with every passing moment as the blood leached from him. They would never move again. His mouth would not accept hers. His tongue would not rise to meet her. His hands would not hold her. He was gone.

Her fists balled in his soaked tunic as she kept her lips locked onto his, shoulders shaking with her anguish as the copper of his blood stained her mouth. Amaris stared at Tanith, and she could see the way the girl's heart had cracked, fracturing into two pieces where the organ had been whole only minutes before.

"Goddess, please," she cried out a sobbing prayer. "Please."

The reever wrapped her arms around Tanith's shaking form but didn't try to pull the girl away. Amaris held Tanith as the tiny girl shook with wave after wave of shock, horror, and sorrow. From deep within the trees, Yazlyn and Nox had begun walking toward the noise of her cries.

"I can't," Tanith gasped, crying against Amaris's hold.

Rain drops began to fall. Slow, intermittent droplets of what was sure to be a soaking downpour came down in tiny, wet stones as if even the sky were mourning. The others stood overhead, standing back a few steps as Tanith continued to cry. Amaris held her as the rain increased, drenching the party, their weapons, their clothes, the ground, and the fallen. The rain began to wash the blood away from their hands and faces, cleaning the gore and evidence of death from those who remained.

"We have to go." Yazlyn's quiet voice could barely be heard over the rain.

"We can't leave him," Tanith insisted, but the plea seeped from her voice, dripping onto the ground as it joined the raindrops. "We have to stay with him." Her words were raw and scratchy from her screams before she joined Amaris, echoing the despondent, numb pool of a wound deeper than that which might be made by any sword or blade.

Gadriel knelt beside her and put a firm hand on her shoulder, rain glancing off his hand, his arm, his shoulders as he peered into the grief-stricken face of the fae. She did not shake him off, looking up into the steadying face of the general. He wasn't just a friend, or a warrior; he was a grounding force. He knew of life and death. He knew of pain and loss. Her eyes clung to the steadiness in his face and voice as he stayed still in the downpour. "We won't leave him." She continued looking up at him. Her face slackened with her own helplessness as her eyes slid away from the general's. Her short hair had glued itself against her face and neck in the soaking, cleansing rain. "We'll stay here and give him a proper burial. We won't leave him."

A shock began to settle over Tanith.

"A burial?" She repeated the word without comprehension as another raindrop fell. Amaris began to pull her away, and she allowed herself to be moved. With the help of Nox and Yazlyn, they kept Tanith on her feet while Gadriel began to dig. Amaris joined him, removing the remaining blade from Ash's throat as the rain bathed him of the evidence of his final moments. She closed the unseeing eyes of her friend, her brother, her partner. Amaris knew as she moved Ash and looked into the face that would never again smile that she would put the monster of this memory in a box too tight and too deep to ever feel. She would wrap it in chains and bolt down the edges. She would never allow the lid of this box to reopen.

Ash had been everything to her for years. He was her family, her reever, her lifeline. She had tangled with him, fought with him, and trusted him. She'd once felt her heart crack when she thought she might lose him. He'd been the first man to ever see her naked, and he'd been too level-headed to let her grief get the best of her in her haste for redemption and acceptance. He'd been a cornerstone with which she'd built the foundation of her new life. She had watched his hardened edges soften as he fell for the tiny, murderous ball of fury. She'd watched him grow, defend, and love as his heart wrapped itself around Tanith. Finally, she'd watched him do exactly what she might have expected him to do: she watched him sacrifice himself for what he loved.

They'd been in the valley for over an hour after their friend had left this world to join the All Mother. Mud from his hands to his shoulders, Gadriel returned to where Tanith remained kneeling numbly by Ash's body. He took a knee beside her, looking to her for a nod of acknowledgment.

"Are you ready?"

"Here?" she asked, voice numb.

Gadriel's face twisted empathetically. "We'll send him off with honor."

She shook her head mutely as she turned to the shallow grave that the general had spent thirty minutes digging. She looked up at Gadriel, then down at Ash. "He doesn't belong in Sulgrave. No one can visit him here. He can't rest here."

"We can't—" Gadriel had scarcely begun to argue when Amaris placed a hand on his arm to stop him.

Tanith rested her hand in the middle of Ash's chest and closed her eyes. She squinted her eyes tightly against a loud, painful sob that erupted the moment she summoned her lightning. When he evaporated, the only thing that remained was the ash of his namesake. With a guttural cry, Tanith lowered her face to the pile of dust where her lover had lain, sobbing into the memory of where he'd been only moments before.

She drew in several ragged breaths as the rain began to fall with more intensity around her. The water seemed to pull her into a state of hurried attention, instantly scooping as much of the ash as she could into a pile, hidden beneath her hands to protect it from the wind and rain. Her cries continued, joined by the impending noises of thunder as the storm approached, but Tanith hadn't finished. Through her cries, she called on one final power. It was challenging to see what happened as her hands glowed, but when she pulled her fingers away, all that remained was a rough, golden coin.

Amaris bent beside Tanith and put her arms around the girl as she shook with her sobs, absorbing her tears as she stared at the object Tanith had made. At the bottom of the coin was the half-circle and sunbeams of morning light. The light that had cut through his father's darkness. The light that had saved Tanith, that had stood between her and chaos, that had enveloped her so wholly that it had transformed her from the inside out.

Amaris understood the final power.

"Alchemy," she said quietly. Her word felt so empty. It meant nothing, stolen on the wind as it whipped her hair against her face. Tanith leaned her forehead against the side of Amaris's head, tears losing their volume, though her grief had not ebbed. Her fingers wrapped around the sacred piece of metal as she clutched it to her heart.

Amaris was vaguely aware of the looks exchanged by the Raascot fae, but she couldn't see them. She could only stare at the space where her brother had been as she clutched the one he'd loved. She didn't know what such a coveted power had cost Tanith, but she assumed it didn't matter to the girl. She was so broken, so shattered, that no act of magic could possibly wound her more than the loss from which she'd never fully recover.

The storm raged on, wind and lightning striking chaotically through the gorge as thunder cracked overhead. Tanith felt a fresh wave of anguish as Yazlyn took it upon herself to be the one who broke their mourning. They needed to get to shelter. She turned into Yazlyn's hold, burying her face against the winged fae's shoulder while she cried, tears lost to the wholly cleansing water of the thunderstorm.

Forty-One

D IRT, NEGLECT, AND COLD PRESSED IN AROUND NOX.
Night had fallen in the small, decrepit one-room
shepherd's shelter that had sat empty on the mountainside.
Rotted floorboards caved to sinking dust and the remnants
of a foundation. Crowding inside the shack with the others
felt scarcely better than remaining exposed to the elements
of the mountain's thunderstorm, but it was all they had. She
cast an uncomfortable glance at the single, filthy cot that had
been pushed up against the wall.

Gadriel used his warmth to heat the small space. "You
ready, Nox?"

It was the first time anyone had spoken in hours.

She frowned at the rain pouring in through the chimney
as it sputtered onto what remained of the rotting floor. Yazlyn
moved to close the flue. There would be no fires lit. There
would be no celebrations. There would be no joy.

"No," she said quietly.

His pained expression told her that he understood.
She would never be ready. She sank gingerly onto the cot,
shuddering against the damp muck as it soaked through her
clothes. Her heart was broken. She was soaked to the bone.
She couldn't do what needed to be done.

Nox stared at the moth-eaten pillow. She could only imagine the colony of dust mites thriving in its remnants. "I'm an insomniac even during the best of times. But this…"

Tanith looked up from where she'd been holding her knees against the wall on the far side of the cabin. "I can put you to sleep," she whispered. It was the first time she'd spoken since being torn from Ash's body. Lightning cracked beyond the small, glass window, illuminating the solemn faces within. Rhythmic pounding accompanied the storm beyond. Thunder's loud rumble was only a second behind its silver flash.

Nox didn't know how to talk to Tanith. She had no idea what to think, let alone what to say.

Gadriel moved from where he'd remained against the far wall. "We can't wait for the storm to subside. Yazlyn and I have to use the night to recover what we can of Amaris's supplies from Territory Three. We'll get the greenstrike blood you need." He looked to the last remaining reever, eyes softening as they met the gentle, heartbroken lavender of her gaze. "Amaris, if you stay here and watch over Nox…"

"I won't go anywhere."

Nox fidgeted. She wanted to use her ability to meet Malik near his sunny pond, to have Amaris walk her through the Uaimh Reev, to confer with her general after a battle over apple pie. This was something else entirely. She didn't feel brave. Her people needed her. Everyone needed her, and she was letting fear seep in at the seams. "I don't think I can do this. If I can kill Daifa, doesn't that mean I can also be killed?"

Gadriel took a knee beside the cot. He looked at her for a long time, and from the searching depth of his eyes, she knew he would not lie to her. "Yes. It does."

She swallowed audibly, twisting her shirt between her fingers. She'd never been a coward. Her fear felt so terribly selfish in the wake of the sorrow that flooded their hearts. "I have no resources in there. I won't have Chandra, or armor, or my blasted emerald ribbon. None of you can come with me."

He arched a brow at that. "I don't know if that's true. Ceres could conjure things within his dreams. In theory, you could create any of us."

Amaris spoke from the far side of the room, but there was no joy in her voice. "You visited me in my dream once and you were able to shift my dream into a lakeside cabin in Yelagin. You made that possible."

"Once you do," Gadriel warned, "she may realize she's dreaming. You need to be very intentional with your choices in there."

Nox closed her eyes. She tried to envision herself as someone brave. Someone capable. "Do you think I can imagine an army?"

"Perhaps," he said, "but I think the safest bet is to kill this Speaker before she has the chance to feel afraid. Nightmares often wake people from their dreams. If you can get to her and end this before she's shaken awake by her night terror—"

"Be yourself, Nox," Amaris said softly. "Don't try to be a warrior. Be someone clever. Be someone wise. Be you."

The tendons in Nox's arms flexed as she took a fistful of her shirt. She disregarded Amaris as she turned to the general. Her anxiety matched the storm's crescendo. "But you said yourself: we have no reason to believe this will work."

"We have no reason to believe it won't. Your dreams have had real-world consequences on more than one occasion. We need to try. If this works, you'll be slipping past every possible pitfall, guard, and wall of security between us and the Speaker. You could take her out in the single most covert assassination in history."

"But Ceres never..." Her argument fell to cinders in her mouth. Her breath came in shallow, uneven pulls. She was stalling for time, and they all knew it. Her dark eyes scanned the others in the room, and she hated what she saw. They'd suffered an unspeakable tragedy. Amaris had lost a brother. Tanith had lost the lone lifeline tethering her to this earth. They'd faced something so horrible, so unspeakable that no one could move, breathe, or speak, and yet here she was, refusing to do her part in the battle.

This was the only fight they asked of her.

Gadriel spoke with the calm resolve of an advisor, free from reproach. "Ceres wasn't able to establish relationships or make eye contact with the enemy when we were at war. Moirai never removed her wards. He wasn't given the opportunity. You've met Daifa, you've spoken with her, you've successfully walked through her dreams before. Once Tanith puts you to sleep..." He looked over his shoulder at where Tanith's head bobbed with exhaustion.

A dagger had lodged in Nox as well, though it wasn't one visible to the eye. It was the guilt that came with sitting out from battle, from surviving, from asking anything of those who clung to life in the face of horror. She struggled to discern how much of Tanith's appearance was due to grief and what was a result of her magical drain. Was she drenched from the storm, or was she covered in sweat? Was she shivering from shock and cold, or had blood sickness dragged her down?

"We have to go," Gadriel said quietly, and she knew he was thinking the same thing. They'd lose Tanith if they didn't retrieve Amaris's bag from Territory Three.

Nox's heart, stomach, and throat met in a single, miserable knot. She looked to Amaris and admitted her deepest shame. "I'm scared."

The ancient mattress creaked, a cloud of dust puffing into the air as Amaris sank into the space beside her. She wrapped an arm around her waist. "To be afraid is to be alive. But you're not alone."

Nox looked at the hands that couldn't stop twisting the fabric into anxious knots.

Amaris's voice was kind but firm as she said, "You are the most capable person I've ever met. Before this very minute, I wasn't sure if you had the capacity for fear. You were sold to a brothel and you discovered your powers and created an army. You took this terrible life and you turned it into two kingdoms. You transformed two orphans without homes into lovers with castles across the continent. You crossed the Frozen Straits. You killed Millicent. You have built a family who would die for you out of the dust and ashes you were given. There is nothing you can't do. This is just going to sleep. All we need you to do is dream."

"I'm supposed to be the one who does the comforting," Nox murmured.

"Yes, you are." Amaris smiled, though Nox knew her heart was too fractured for the expression to contain real joy. "To be honest, I'm not sure I'm fully comfortable with this role reversal. When you wake up, I'll give you your title back."

Nox smiled weakly at the joke, but she could feel Amaris's heartache radiating through the shelter. There was no more time to be bought. She turned to lie down on the decrepit remnants of what had once been a wool blanket as she settled onto the cot.

"You're probably going to want to try to unclench," Amaris said. "You look like you're bracing to be slapped."

"This bed is disgusting."

Amaris exhaled a slow, humorless laugh. "But it's the one you get."

"Shh," Nox said, eyes tightly closed as she scrunched her face. "I'm doing my best."

Amaris continued to hold her hand. "I'll be right here. Remember that when you're in there, no matter what you see, or think, or feel, I'm right here, holding your hand. Now, relax, and focus on Daifa."

Nox kept her eyes closed as she listened to the shuffle of feet around the room. Yazlyn's voice was low and unhappy as she asked, "Are you sure you can do this?" After a beat, she said, "Do you have the strength, Tanith? If this is a bad idea…"

"I can do it," came the feeble, whispered response. Nox winced as a chilled hand settled lightly over her forehead. Tanith spread her fingers wide and said one word: "Sleep."

And she did.

PART V

Manifestation

Forty-Two

THE MOMENT HER FEET TOUCHED EARTH, THE WORLD BEGAN to ripple.

She recognized the enormous, red-orange, castle-sized trees, but this time they trembled as if she were looking at the disturbed surface of a pond. The grass around her, along with the scents of soil and carrion wafted in and out as she struggled to find stability. It was nearly nightfall. The dream hadn't even begun, and her fear already threatened its very fabric.

Breathe! You need to calm down.

Nox called on a memory of how her own panic upon hearing the news of the ghouls in Aubade had almost shaken her from Gadriel's dream many months ago. He'd sat across from her while chopping wood in the sunset outside of his country home and warned her to control her emotions while dream walking. He'd looked so serene, so unbothered. Nox took a few soothing breaths.

One by one, the mountain-sized trees snapped into place. The world stabilized as she counted to ten. Five breaths in, and five breaths out. She was ready. After all, it was only a dream.

She turned with aching slowness to survey her surroundings.

Daifa was once again sitting beside a deep pit of soil and decay. She'd been in the same position last time Nox had visited. Her unnaturally large, blue eyes had been staring vacantly at the evidence of death in the dark, deep pit in the same long, manicured yard. The windows of a stone manor were lit with the orange glow of fireplaces and torches in the fading evening light, just as it had been the last time Nox had visited.

Nox wondered if Daifa dreamed of anything else, or if this moment sucked her back time and time again like the dark, horrid sun at the center of her universe.

The false Speaker still hadn't noticed Nox's presence. It gave her a few more moments to unclench her jaw, to relax her shoulders, to anchor her feet. She had come here for a reason. She was not powerless. She would not fail.

Nox held her hand out in front of her and thought to conjure a thin, sharp blade. It bloomed in her hand like an unfurling flower, taking perfect, razor-sharp shape. She shifted the dagger's weight so that her hand was on the hilt and held it behind her back. One quiet step at a time, she began to slowly approach the Speaker.

A sound caught her attention as a vageth bound its way to where the Speaker sat on the earth overlooking the pit. Daifa rested her hand on the amphibious canine as if petting a dog. Nox had recalled the demon's presence from the first dream, but she could never grow used to seeing a vageth like this. Its dark gray skin belonged stretched over a frog, not a canine. It had two large, coal-black eyes, but two smaller eyes dotted the space beneath its primary orbs as if it were an insect. The teeth were not from the mouth of any normal animal but hundreds, if not thousands, of dense, horrifying needles. It was a demon, and yet Daifa stroked it while making soothing noises as if it were a common house pet.

You have a sword. You can do this. You need to focus.

Nox continued urging herself to suck in calming breaths, inhaling through her nose and exhaling through her mouth.

She took a few steps closer to the pit, and Daifa turned her head to regard her. She tightened her grip on the hidden weapon, then made a choice. She decided to speak first, hoping she could keep Daifa at ease by establishing some sense of familiarity. She tried to think of what she'd need to hear if it were her dream.

"We're close to unity," Nox said quietly. She hoped the word struck a comforting chord.

Daifa regarded her absently, eyes scanning Nox from her hair to her feet with lazy disinterest. "She'll be proud," the Speaker murmured. "She'll be glad."

Daifa had said something similar in the last dream.

Her. The toffee-haired fae in the manor. She was the one Daifa hoped to impress.

They were caught in a memory loop Nox had seen once before. She knew that, no, the woman would not be pleased. She would not be happy at all that Daifa would be pressing forward with plans for unification. She didn't want to enter the manor, knowing it crawled with goblins and was plastered with portraits of demons. She couldn't let the dream advance that far. She moved her feet softly, shifting her weight to her toes as she positioned herself closer to Daifa.

Nox fixated on the words she knew the Speaker would want to hear. She'd heard them over and over the last time she'd walked through this memory. "Now that you and I can work together, we can unify the continent. We can unite Farehold, Raascot, and Sulgrave."

Daifa nodded with what may have been considered boredom at the thought. Her hand continued to move against the vageth's slick, taut skin. "That's all I've ever wanted."

Nox nodded gingerly as she took another slow step. She was close now. Three more steps. "I want it too. It's why I brought Farehold and Raascot under one banner. They're one kingdom. All we need now is to assemble Sulgrave."

The Speaker nodded, her voice both present and absent. "That's easy enough. I've already brought Sulgrave together.

The comtes are with me now. When we finish with them, the rest of the continent will follow."

Nox hesitated. "What did you tell the comtes to...unify them?"

Daifa continued to stare into the pit. Her eyes were glazed over as her face pointed toward the rotting, decaying shapes of death, organs, and bodies. Some of the dead looked like they could have been human or fae. Others appeared to be the bones and bloated shapes of monsters. "The gifts of the All Mother, of course. I showed them memories of my manifestation. Once they saw evidence of the miracles, they knew I had to be followed. Some were more persuasive, or violent, than others. One must do what one must do."

A mist dampened Nox's cheek. The rain would begin soon.

"Manifestation," Nox repeated carefully. In two more steps she'd reach Daifa's resting place. "Is that the gift of the Speaker?"

Daifa stroked the vageth at her side and shrugged. "It's the power of the old gods, we all know that. The All Mother was a manifester. She"—Daifa waved her hand toward the house—"is a manifester. All Speakers are manifesters. They arrive with the power of the goddess, and their position is undeniable. It's creation itself."

Nox's heart skipped arrhythmically. If the Farehold fae within was a manifester, did that make her the true Speaker? Nox struggled to remain calm as she pictured the woman who'd conjured horrid crabs from the walls as the person on the church's throne. She swallowed her anxiety and leveled her tone to ask, "So, should she be the real Speaker?"

Daifa raised and lowered her shoulders lightly. "What is 'should'? She won't be interested. Her window of interest has come and gone, and she's contributed in more ways than anyone could ever know to the current state of the continent. She's been in these wilds for a thousand years. She doesn't care for unity. She never sought to fill the shoes required for unification."

"And why do you desire unity?" Nox regretted the question the moment it escaped her lips. She'd already asked this question. She knew the answer.

"It's all I care about," Daifa said with the same empty, hollow voice. It was another nonanswer. This time, she offered more information than the last. She looked up at Nox, sapphire eyes dull against the misty evening. "This was my first memory." She gestured to the pit.

"What?" Nox blinked. A single, large raindrop landed on her cheek. She looked up at the cloudy sky overhead.

"I opened my eyes, and I was here," Daifa said, unfeeling. They were naught but empty, emotionless facts. "I didn't remember my name, but she told me. I didn't remember how I'd gotten here. I knew that I was to be likable and winsome. I knew that I was to be feminine and eloquent. I knew that all I wanted was to bring the world together. I knew it all from the moment I opened my eyes in this pit, without knowing my name. It's strange, don't you think? Or maybe it isn't. Perhaps that's why it's necessary to remember. We make our memories, after all."

Nox's grip slackened on the weapon. It slipped slightly from her hold behind her back. Yes, it was very, very strange. She fought against the urge to make sense of it now. For the moment, all she needed to do was keep Daifa talking. One more step. She asked, "So you come here to relive it?"

Daifa looked amidst the sun-bleached bones and unceremoniously discarded bodies in varied stages of rot. "I return thinking that maybe someday I will remember what came before. Maybe I will recall how I wandered into this forest, or how she found me. But, I am who I am. I know why I exist. Perhaps there is no more."

This was Nox's final step. She could strike now, but it had to be true. Nox had no training with a weapon such as this. If it was only a wounding stab, Daifa would wake up before she could complete the job. Nox imagined the dagger at her back elongating and sharpening into an executioner's axe.

The weight changed as she felt Chandra's heft in her hands. She would need to be able to take off the Speaker's head in one swing.

The vageth perked and looked toward the house as rain began to fall. It was a scattered, gentle rain that didn't immediately send one running. The strange, blue-eyed fae didn't appear to be in any hurry to escape the weather.

Nox was running out of time.

Nox remembered this part of the dream. She knew the rain would drive Daifa inside, along with the canine and its muddy footprints. Daifa began to push herself up from where she'd been sitting, and Nox stiffened. The blue-eyed fae woman with dark hair and distinct, Sulgrave features stood and began to eye her curiously.

"What's behind your back?"

Shit.

Nox cursed herself. Of course, the axe wouldn't be fully concealed as the dagger had been. She'd been a fool to change its shape so quickly. The edges of the world around her began to ripple, but she was quite certain it was from her own emotional response. The redwood trees and looming shadows struggled to become whole and still once more.

Daifa frowned. As she did, the ground wrinkled and wavered.

"Is this a dream?" she asked quietly.

Nox bit her tongue to stifle her reaction. She feigned innocence. There was only one goddess-damned word this woman cared about, and she'd wield it as intently as any weapon. "We are here to discuss unification." She put one foot behind the other, readying herself for the swing of her blade. "Should we go inside to get out of the rain?"

Daifa took a step toward the manor. If she took one or two more, she'd be fully in front of Nox. If her back remained turned, she wouldn't see the axe or have time to wake up before the queen had accomplished what she'd set out to do. Nox's heart rate increased again, and the ripple was her downfall. She attempted several stilling breaths, but Daifa paused once more. "I'm dreaming," she said quietly.

Nox scrunched her face behind Daifa's back. She was the wrong distance now to swing an axe. She'd been encroaching while planning to bury a dagger in the woman's temple. She could still recover from this monumental error. She could still do what needed to be done. With a half-step back, she could swing Chandra in a successful arc.

Instead of heading into the manor, the Speaker rotated to face her. Her face remained blank, save for the idlest of curiosities. "Why would I dream of you?"

Nox breathed out slowly, considering the best way to maintain a sense of calm. "To discuss our next steps. You need to use me for unification. How may I assist you with your vision?"

"No..." Daifa tested the word, eyeing Nox suspiciously. "That's not right." She positioned her body so that one shoulder was to the manor and the other to the pit. She seemed distracted by the weather and lifted her face to the overhead clouds. "If this is a dream, I can make the rain stop, can't I?" Daifa closed her eyes, and the sky dried instantly. "And I can make it light?" She seemed to be turning back the clock as the last lights of twilight grew brighter. The clouds began to part as an orange and red sunset grazed the tops of the enormous redwood forest. "This is what manifestation is really like," Daifa said, almost sadly.

Nox had been wrong. Daifa had the capacity for imagination. And now that she'd discovered it, Nox was quickly losing control of the dream.

"You can achieve unity without manifestation, Daifa. As long as they believe they've seen your miracles, you can still accomplish your cornerstone."

"Cornerstone." Daifa swirled the word in her mouth as if tasting wine. It soured on her tongue. "Now you sound like her." She looked over her shoulder at the large estate. The Speaker tilted her head as if an idea struck her. Daifa made a movement with her hands, and a man appeared.

A fully formed, tall, dark-haired fae man stood before them dressed in black. He looked every bit as real as Nox or the Speaker, from the point of his ears to the gleam in his eye. His shoulders were broad, stature looming, and hair as black as her own. He'd populated the world where, only one moment prior, no one had stood.

The blue-eyed fae smiled with a faint pride at her creation.

Daifa ignored Nox entirely, looking to the man. "I've always wanted to talk to you."

Nox recognized the man from the portrait the last time she'd visited the dream. The man had thick arms, a wide chest, and the curling waves of dark, cropped hair. He was inexplicably handsome and shared many distinct characteristics of the Sulgrave fae. Once more, she spotted the prominent tattoo crawling from his arm to the base of his neck, though she hadn't seen a single tattoo on the streets of Sulgrave. She blinked several times at the strange man, not knowing what to do or what it meant. Did his sudden presence change her plan? Could he turn against her in any way?

He opened his mouth, but dust and wind were on his breath.

Nox understood the problem just as the Speaker did.

Daifa didn't know how he might sound. She'd never been able to imagine his voice, his words, or his personality. All she knew of him was what she had learned from the portrait. Daifa furrowed her brow deeply and stepped close to the man. She touched him to ensure he existed, attention focused fully on the stranger.

"I was hoping I'd find you in Sulgrave," she whispered to the fae man. She ran a hand along his features. "Either you aren't here, or you don't want to be found."

Nox's fear wormed deep within her as she slowly lifted the axe. Daifa was distracted. If she was going to act, it had to be now.

"I've always thought you may have been my father," Daifa cooed, still looking at the man. "She won't talk to me about you, but I look so much like you. You and I—"

Nox summoned all the strength she could muster into her arms and raised the axe to the side, willing it to be the cleanest and sharpest axe in the history of manufacturing. She allowed herself a single, loud grunt for power as she stepped, swinging the axe parallel to the ground. It bit into Daifa's neck, chewing through flesh, muscle, and spine with one single, successful sweep.

It worked.

A loud, high ring like the single toll of a bell rang through the yard as the weapon finished its arc.

The Speaker didn't even have time to register surprise. A red line formed, blossoming into a masterfully executed cut as her head parted from her body, tumbling to the ground and rolling into the pit like little more than a child's ball kicked down a grassy knoll. This ball of nightmares had hair, and teeth, and sapphire eyes, all disappearing beneath the lip of the pit as her head vanished into the depression in the soil. Her body sank against the strange, mute man. He grabbed Daifa's limp, decapitated form to hold her up but did nothing else.

Nox looked around. She'd expected to immediately wake up.

She dropped the axe, and it blinked out of existence.

"Is that…is that it?" She looked to the vageth, then to the strange man. "Is that it? Did I do it?" But no one would be answering her questions.

Nox looked around again with more terror. The burnt-orange bark of the redwoods remained as present and towering as mountains. The lights in the stone manor continued to shine. The vageth continued to prowl along the pit, eyeing the bloodied addition to its collection of carnage.

"Wake up," she whispered to herself, but she did not. She looked to the man clad in black, and he looked back with no true sentience in his eyes. He had been a fiction within a memory—no more real than the queen's wish that they were all safely home in Gwydir with warm beds and happy families. Nox pictured a dagger once more, and this time she attempted to stab herself in the hand, hoping the pain would shake her awake. It did not.

"Wake up, wake up!" She felt her nerves growing. The world began to ripple, and as it did, relief crashed over her. The relief had a calming effect, stilling the world once more. The very alleviation that the dream was ending thwarted her attempts to shock herself out of this nightmare.

"No! Dammit!" Nox pinched herself several times, but any time the world would waver, she couldn't prevent the cool, calming relief that followed. The ripple was reassurance. The ripple was escape. She was caught in a cycle of her very worry and respite, each clutch of comfort soothing her with its efficacy. Nox was trapped in a memory.

She didn't know what to do.

She looked to the man. "Do you know who you are?"

He inclined his chin and opened his hands, allowing what remained of Daifa to crumple downward from where he'd held her.

She had no idea where to go, but she didn't want to stay here amidst the mass grave of monstrosities. The stench of death was stronger than any fresh scent of the forest.

"Should we go inside?"

He began to lead the way, and Nox followed him into the manor. It was clear that he could take basic direction, but she was far from considering this strange, fictitious man an ally. Just as she had been the time before, they were greeted by the goblin that walked by, its spine a tangled hump, its feet irregular sizes and shapes. The goblin didn't seem to notice them as they entered.

The butter-toned Farehold woman came to the stairs to yell about mud, but this time the vageth had not come in with muddy paws. Her memory loop had been disrupted. The sky was dry, and no rain fell. The fae seemed confused as to why she had come to the stairs and turned to go back down the corridor.

Nox began to slowly enter the halls, examining the portraits of horrors, hoping that something would be terrifying enough to jar her from her sleep. She'd never seen such terrifying beasts painted in excruciating, lifelike detail. She peered into the gaping features of a beseul when a sound snagged her attention. She'd lost herself to the demonic images when her attention caught on the strange man. He was near the oil painting that had been commissioned in his likeness, eyeing it curiously. She had no idea how much awareness the created man might have, but she felt decidedly disconcerted that he'd identified himself.

"Can you do something for me?" she asked.

He looked at her with vacant eyes.

"I need you to slap me, over and over. Don't kill me. Don't let me die. I just need you to—"

The fabricated man did not hesitate. He didn't even let her finish her request. Instantaneously, the stranger struck her. She felt the sharp, hot sting of his hand against her face as she stumbled backward against the force of his strike. Her ears popped against the sudden, intense pain. Before she could blink, he had lifted his hand again and struck her once more. Nox fell to her knees as the world around her began to ripple just as she hoped it would. His open hand was coming for her again, and there would be no comfort or relief. The welts were hot and angry as they seared through her skin. The man grabbed her by the front of her shirt to hold her still as he brought another powerful slap against her face. The world trembled from the pain, and this time, she hurt too much to feel relief. He hit her again, and she felt like she was going to lose consciousness. Her jaw ached as if it had been popped out of its socket against the force of his impact. The man raised his hand, and with a final slap, the world dissolved into black.

491

Forty-Three

N OX FOUGHT TO FILL HER LUNGS AS SHE SCRAMBLED FROM her clammy, panicked sleep. It took several ragged pulls for her to recognize the dilapidated shepherd's cottage. A hand went to her rapidly beating heart as she pressed her fingers against her chest, grateful she was still alive. The storm continued to howl beyond.

A dream. It was a dream. She was safe. She slapped a palm to either side of the cot, searching for warmth, for comfort, for the promise that had held her as she'd tumbled beneath the waves of sleep, but Amaris was nowhere to be found. Nox didn't know if her mission had been successful, nor did she know how long she'd been under or why Amaris would leave her. But she wasn't alone in the cabin. Tanith's dark, crumpled silhouette was scarcely discernible on the floor.

Her fingers moved against the still-warm lines where she could almost feel the hot sting of welts from where she'd been struck. She opened and closed her mouth to ensure her jaw was still in its socket. Nox then moved her legs over the side of the bed and knelt on the ground next to Tanith, checking the fae for a pulse. It was faint and erratic, but she was still alive.

"No," Nox said. She muttered into the darkened silence of the dirty shelter, knowing the girl couldn't hear her. "This isn't how you die. You don't survive battles and zealots and Reds and losing the love of your life just to fall to my need for sleep."

Nox tucked her arms beneath Tanith's small frame, one under her knees and the other against her upper back. She grunted against the dead weight as she attempted to get Tanith up to the cot. Tanith was small, but Nox wasn't exactly known for her physical strength. She fretted over the waves of helplessness. She had no innate gift for healing, and no stolen life to offer as she'd once done in Malik's time of need. She didn't know what to do, save for the certainty that Tanith couldn't afford to lose any more body heat against the chill of the ground while so gravely ill. The moment Nox had her lifted, the clatter of something metal hit the floor.

Nox took a knee as she bent to retrieve the object.

Her heart sank as she lifted the thin, golden coin made of ashes and sunlight. With a lump in her throat, Nox slipped it into Tanith's hand. She stroked the hair back from her face, though each of Tanith's strands was wet and stringy with cold sweat.

"Tanith?" The fae was so far gone, there would be no waking her without medical intervention. Nox suspected that even if she had been physically and magically whole, her fractured heart would have prevented her from rousing.

She looked at the dark blotch of soaked, rotted wood where rain had gushed in from the chimney flue. She wished she could light a fire for them to keep warm. Even if it weren't a sodden mess, they still couldn't risk drawing attention to an orange glow against the pitch dark. Nox had no way to fight for them if they were spotted. She had no idea how she was meant to protect Tanith while left alone in this shack.

If Gadriel were here, he would have been able to warm Tanith. But he wasn't. No one was. Not even Amaris, who'd sworn to hold her through the night. She'd need to figure something out if she wanted to keep them alive. She had no idea how long she'd been asleep and how long the Raascot fae had been on their retrieval mission to Territory Three. More pressingly, she needed to know if Amaris had left of her own volition or if something was terribly, terribly wrong. The reever had specifically promised to hold Nox's hand through the entirety of her dream.

"Hold on," Nox whispered to Tanith. It was a useless plea, but she needed the fae to fight.

Nox crossed to the small glass window and pressed her face against the pane. Rain continued pattering against the dust-covered glass, but it was no longer the angry downpour of furious storms. She peered out into the dark, moonless night. The thick, stormy clouds blocked out any hope she might have to monitor the passage of time.

Then…something.

Her breath caught in her throat. She blinked rapidly and then looked around the cabin for evidence she was dreaming. She pinched herself. Nothing happened. She pinched herself even harder, but the world did not ripple.

She was looking at a house that had most certainly not existed before she'd fallen asleep.

Despite the dark night's gloom, she was staring directly at a large structure right outside the shelter's door. It was almost as if their ramshackle cabin was nothing more than a yard shed for a lovely stone home. The sunshine and marmalade glow of warmth and fires illuminated the windows of the home, calling to her where she shivered in her still-damp clothes in the small, filthy shack. She looked over to where Tanith remained unconscious. She needed to go see whether or not this was real or a dream, but if it was real, she didn't want to abandon her gravely ill friend.

This had to be a dream. It was impossible. There was no other option.

Unless…

Nox opened the door to the shepherd's cottage and stood

494

for a long time in the doorway. Droplets soaked her feet, her legs, spat against her face as she stared. She reached a hand into her hair to ensure that the emerald ribbon was still tightly secured to her locks before closing the door behind her and cautiously advancing toward the house. Chilly pellets erupted against her cheeks and soaked her damp clothes. She shuddered against the cold as she reached the front door of the impossible structure.

Nox raised a trembling fist to knock against the door that shouldn't be there. She took in the sleek estate against the downpour and hesitated. Was this wise?

What would a reever do? What choice would a militant Raascot fae make? Would Yazlyn pull out a dagger and try to bury it in her thigh for this?

But they weren't here. Either she was still asleep and this was a dream she could control, or this was real and it was up to her and her alone to make the call. Tanith was dying. She was alone. She needed to do something.

Her knuckles barely made contact with a single, brief rap on the door before it was yanked open. Nox almost stumbled forward from the sudden change. She was hit with a wave of warmth as the soaking, homey heat from the fireplace poured out of the home and hit her on the threshold. Her jaw dropped as she looked into the pair of lavender eyes set in Amaris's shocked, moonlit face.

"You're awake!" she gasped, throwing her arms around Nox. She fumbled through the gesture, hands full with something peculiar.

"What is this?" Nox asked, scarcely able to spit out the words. "Am I awake?"

Amaris turned over her shoulder and shouted, "I'll be right back," into the room. She then grabbed Nox by the hand and dragged her back toward the cabin. They sprinted through the cold downpour once more before reentering the shack. Amaris led the way, kneeling by the cot within a matter of moments. Amaris slid a hand under Tanith's head.

Nox looked between the strange glow of the home that most certainly should not exist and the grimy cot on which Tanith rested. She fidgeted. "Amaris…"

"Can you help me hold her up?"

Nox agreed numbly and kept Tanith's head up, mouth slackened. Amaris unscrewed a small vial and began to empty the contents onto Tanith's tongue. She rubbed on Tanith's throat a few times the way one often might with an animal in order to engage their involuntary muscles and force them to swallow.

"Amaris, what the hell is going on?"

The reever unscrewed a second vial of liquid and began to empty it into Tanith's mouth. She didn't look to Nox as she focused on her task. "It's amazing, Nox. There's no other word for it. You have to see for yourself. If this works, we should be able to bring Tanith back to the house with us. I don't want her to wake up alone."

"Like I did?"

Amaris paused then and reached out her hand, wrapping her fingers around Nox's wrist. "I'm so sorry. When everything happened while you were still asleep. I needed to make sure we were safe. I didn't mean for you to wake up to an empty room." She sucked on a breath before rising from where she'd knelt on the floor to stand in front of Nox. "So? Did you do it?"

Nox ran her teeth across her bottom lip, nibbling it as she considered the question. "I have no idea. Yes, I killed her in the dream, but then…the dream went on. I was still in her memory. I have no way of knowing if it worked. Everything about her—everything about her dreams, her memories, it was all wrong."

Amaris tightened her grip. "You've used that word when describing her several times. I can't imagine what you've seen or what you've felt. Are you okay?"

"Dream walking is…" Nox drifted off.

Amaris's face twisted, her concern deepening. "Why don't we take a break from dream walking for a while?"

Nox knew she was avoiding saying what they were both thinking. Everyone wanted Ceres's madness to be circumstantial. If there was any possibility of hereditary link, or that it had been exacerbated by his powers, no one wished for Nox to be subjected to such a fate.

Tanith made a small noise.

"Tanith?" came Nox's and Amaris's overlapping gasps of concern. Nox was still holding the Sulgrave fae's head up. She watched as Amaris chafed her arms for warmth. Amaris's fingers drifted to Tanith's neck, pressing her middle and index finger into the jugular to check her heart.

She appeared dead to the world, though Amaris said her pulse seemed to be growing stronger.

"Tanith," Amaris continued, "can you move? I'd like to get you somewhere warmer and drier. I just need to make sure you're okay to be moved."

Tanith groaned and her head lolled as she went back under the waves of consciousness.

Amaris was objectively smaller than Nox, but her years of training, hardened muscles, and athletic build gave her an advantage when it came to carrying the weak Sulgrave fae. She clutched Tanith to her chest, cradling her like a doll as Nox opened the door to the shack, then the door to the house. Nox remained in the doorway in a state of utter shock at what she saw. The reever wasted no time crossing the threshold and walking into the middle of the sitting room of the strange home, leaving Nox to gape.

Amaris went directly to the fire. Three other bodies were standing in the living room, instantly alert to their presence. Amaris set Tanith down, and one of the new bodies was moving to put a pillow beneath her head.

Aside from Amaris and Tanith, two fae with brilliant raven wings stood near the fire.

"You're Gadriel's parents," Nox said definitively.

The beautiful fae woman who'd been kneeling to put pillows beneath Tanith's head smiled up at her. Her large, night-dark wings folded neatly behind her. Her face was stamped with an impossible timelessness. She could have been Nox's age, or two thousand years old. The woman offered a small bow as she said, "I believe that would make you our new queen, Nox."

Nox blushed deeply. "If Gadriel is my cousin, that makes you…"

"That's right," Allua said. She tossed aside formalities as she took the three steps it took to envelope Nox in a hug. "I can't tell you how honored I am to have you for a niece." She pulled away and braced Nox's arm. "Please, allow me to introduce my husband." She gestured to Joel. The man could have been Gadriel's brother. He offered a polite, curt bow.

"You look so much like him," Allua said quietly. "Your father, that is. Ceres was my brother. I don't know if Gadriel has told you as much."

Nox swallowed. "I did meet him once, briefly. It wasn't a good experience. I don't want to speak ill of him, but my father was able to see me before he…"

Allua's face fell with a solemn, knowing nod. Over Allua's shoulder, Nox couldn't quite understand Amaris's uncomfortable expression. The reever remained near Tanith's head as she frowned after Nox. She hadn't said or done anything wrong, as far as she knew. She was already in what may as well have been a figment of her imagination. This house shouldn't exist. They shouldn't be here. Nox pulled out of the embrace with skeptical discomfort. She asked, "What is this place?"

"This is Nomy," Allua said quietly, introducing the wispy, lovely figure who'd been standing in the room like a phantom. Nox's eyes had glazed over the impossible figure before now. The woman was an amalgamation of every feature she'd seen on the continent. Her skin was the bronze of Raascot, with the same nose and bone structure she'd recognized from the beautiful Tarkhany priestess. Her hair had the multidimensional whites and golds of Farehold, her eyes the almond shapes of Sulgrave, her irises a rich shade of complex, interwoven amethyst.

Amaris looked to Nox. "She really is the All Mother."

Nox eyed the woman. "Is it true? Do you claim to be the All Mother?"

She returned Nox's look as if gazing from a very far distance. She looked not at Nox but through her. "I make," was all she said.

"Nomy." She tasted the name. "It means 'Creator.'"

Amaris arched a speculative brow, though she said nothing.

"Like I said," Nox amended quietly, "I had time to get deeply into theology when you left for Aubade."

"And etymology?" Amaris whispered back.

"That's almost what it means," Nomy said with a dismissive smile, almost as if she weren't entirely present. She wafted on the same distracted air that Daifa had in her dreams. She said, "But I suppose you're close enough."

"Who gave you that name?" Nox asked.

The glimmer in Nomy's smile met her eyes. Her alertness sharpened at the question. Her nose even crinkled in delight. "You are clever. I admire that. I was made to make and thus was well named." She took a few steps closer to the fire. "Do you like my house, Queen of Raascot? Is there anything you would like?" Her voice was a song so foreign, so strange compared to the lilts and accents of the continent. It was lovely and unusual in a way that sent a chill down Nox's spine.

She cocked her head. "What are you asking me?"

Nomy tilted her face, expression reminiscent of how an animal's ears might twitch while trying to understand the curious ramblings of a human. "I'm asking what I'm asking, of course."

Allua translated. "Would you like any food? Water? Clean clothes?"

Nox found Allua's informality jarring. The fae had left an arm draped on Nox, like a mother holding a child. With her large wings catching the edge of the crackling fire, Nox had been steadily warming from the night's chill. Nox wanted answers. She wanted to understand. She wanted all the wrongs righted. And she would demand all this and more, but, first things first.

"I suppose we haven't eaten…" Nox began slowly. "But I'm more worried about Tanith. What can you do for her?"

Nomy looked to where the small, chalky fae shivered on the settee. Tanith's eyes moved quickly beneath her lids, her dark smear of lashes twitching and tightening as if she were caught in a deadly dream. Nomy said, "I created the medicinal blood she required. Now she rests." The woman gestured absently to a low table beside a sofa where several stacks of clothes rested, neatly folded. Nox hadn't noticed them when she'd first arrived. "There are plenty of rooms upstairs. If there aren't enough beds, let me know, and I will make more."

"I've got her," Joel said quietly. It was the first he'd spoken since Nox had entered the house. Though he looked like Gadriel, his voice was more of a tenor compared to his son's authoritative bass. He bent to lift Tanith easily from the ground and began carrying her up the stairs. With no other clear course of action, Nox stayed on his heels as she followed the pair up the stairs. Amaris grabbed the stack of clothes. From over her shoulder, Nox overheard Amaris's request for hot broth and chamomile teas. She turned her attention away from the reever as she followed the Raascot fae to the first door on the left.

Joel set Tanith gingerly on a bed and immediately stepped away from the fae. He offered a distinctly uncomfortable nod to Nox and Amaris before departing the room. Nox stared after him with no idea how to categorize the man. Her eyes shot to Amaris.

"What the hell?" Nox's question came out in a low, urgent hiss. "What is happening here? What is this place? Am I truly awake?"

She was met with a deadly serious gaze.

"This isn't a dream. I was holding your hand while you

slept, and then something happened. I spotted them in the valley," Amaris began. "There was a strange light through the window, and I saw this group approaching the fallen Reds. I was worried for our safety—for your safety. I didn't have to get very close before I realized who I was seeing—at least, I recognized Gadriel's parents immediately. The All Mother…"

"Why are you calling her that?"

"She's a manifester, Nox. She has the power of creation. And…look at her. She looks like everyone. She's all of us." Amaris tumbled over her words.

"Did she say that? Does she claim to be the goddess?"

Amaris's mouth twisted. "Well, no, but—"

"What of Gadriel and Yazlyn?"

Amaris shook her head once, her hair moving with the motion. "It's why we set up our shelter so close to the cabin. They'll come to look for us here, so we needed to stay close by. All Nomy had to do was imagine it." She punctuated her sentence with the snap of her fingers.

Amaris had flippantly referred to this manifested residence as a shelter, but they were in a home as complete and elegant as any Nox had ever visited. It was Farleigh, it was the Selkie, it was the Duke of Henares's estate, it was Gadriel's country home from his dreams. She was in the loveliest two-story stone house that could have possibly been dreamed into existence. Perhaps that's what made it so lovely, and so eerie. It was a dream fantasy brought to life.

She allowed herself to soak in the extravagant surroundings. The beds were wrapped in a rich, red silk. The carpets were a dense, luxurious crushed velvet. She wasn't sure if Tanith would love the color or hate it. Maybe the Sulgrave girl would never want to see the shades of red again. A fire crackled warmly in the hearth, adding yet another flicker of crimson to the room, illuminating the homey decorations dotting the space. This seemed as if it were a home that had stood for one hundred years, not one that had been imagined while Nox slept.

"How did you get close to them without them killing you?" Nox asked, picturing her little reever as she crept close to two winged warriors and Nomy. Any parents who birthed and raised Gadriel had surely been no pacifists.

"I make a lovely first impression." Amaris shrugged. "I think it was obvious that I'm not local to Sulgrave. Then with my eyes... well, I don't really look like anyone, do I?"

Nox fought the urge to wince at the strange, phantasmal woman. "Except her."

Amaris nodded slowly. "Except her."

It wasn't fully true, nor was it false. Nomy and Amaris didn't share complexion or eye shape. Their hair was composed of variant shades of whites and golds, and their eyes were differentiated purples, but they were distinctly unique amongst their peers. The one thing they had in common was that they belonged nowhere. Tanith had once said that the All Mother was the Tree, and Amaris was only an acorn. Nox saw the Tree in her now.

Amaris sat on the edge of the bed, resting a comforting hand on Tanith's sleeping shape. "She's going to be okay," she said.

Nox looked at Amaris skeptically. "Is she?"

The wounds she'd suffered were so much deeper than the physical or the magical. Greenstrike blood would do nothing for her shattered faith. It would not fill the empty hole that had been carved where her heart should be.

"She made it?" Nox asked quietly. "That blood, I mean. Nomy conjured the greenstrike blood?"

"It's what she does. She makes things." Amaris looked to Tanith's resting form, then up to where Nox stood with her arms crossed. "Why did you ask me about manifesters? After your first walk into Daifa's dream, you asked about manifesters. Why?"

She breathed out slowly, ready for the question. "I don't think Daifa was born. I think she was made. But what's more... I don't think Nomy is the All Mother... or, maybe she is… and feel free to call me a heretic but… I think maybe that's just a name we've given to the rare fae who possess this gift that seems like omnipotence. There's little a manifester can't do. What if it's just a rare power we deify?"

Amaris frowned. "But my birth, and the prayer—"

"Who's to say you weren't manifested? Why couldn't a manifester take interest in things like the prayers of men and fae? Perhaps the existing All Mother, whoever reigns as manifester, uses her Trees as a sort of…point of connectivity. I don't know. I haven't figured it all out—or any of it, for that matter. The books, the research, it's all theory and conjecture and blasphemy at this point. What I know is this: when you left for Aubade, all I did was read. I may not have the answers. I'm no more knowledgeable or more educated than the bishops and priestesses and decades of churchgoers before me. But I didn't go in looking for the confirmation bias of the faithful. The two of you, you look like each other. I kept seeing recurrent themes and…"

A long silence stretched between them. The pops and crackles of the cheery fire mingled with the deep breaths of Tanith's sleepy sounds.

"You do that a lot lately," Amaris said quietly.

"Do what?"

Amaris patted the bed beside her and Nox took a seat, leaning into the reever. "Your sentences, your thoughts. They seem to drift a lot more easily. I'm worried about you."

"I'm just thinking." Nox sucked on her lip as her eyes drifted shut. "It's just me thinking."

Amaris squeezed her hand. "Just don't get so lost in your thoughts that we can't pull you back, okay? You're needed here."

Nox gave her an appraising look. "It's complicated, isn't it?"

Amaris furrowed her brow.

Nox considered her carefully, studying the face she'd spent so many years seeing. "Being everything to someone; it's complicated, isn't it? With you and me, things have changed and grown and evolved so much over our lives. Who we are, our roles… They've changed so many times. Being family, friend, confidante, warrior, queen, assassin, lover, sister… Sometimes it's hard to know who, or what, we are to each other."

"Come now, Your Highness. You were never one for cut and dry," Amaris chided.

"I just mean, it would be a lot easier to argue with you and put you in your place if you were just one thing or the other—"

"Put me in my place?" The reever feigned offense. "But instead, you have to see me as a complete person? The horror."

Nox smiled. "Hush."

"I will do no such thing." After a pause, Amaris asked, "How does it feel?"

Nox tucked a lock of hair behind her ear. "How does what feel?"

Amaris cocked a brow. "To not have all the answers? To not be able to quantify everything? Whether it's her, or this, or me, or us. Do you think you'll make it out alive?"

"You're a brat."

"You're not the first to suggest it."

Tanith made another noise and they both looked toward her. She rolled over in her sleep, which seemed like a good sign. Amaris rose. "I'll bring the broth and tea. You can sit with her if you'd like. See if you can get her into some dry clothes."

Nox had no trouble changing Tanith, whether or not she was queen of southern Gyrradin. Not only was the girl tiny, but Nox had plenty of experience helping others. Between the children at Farleigh, Amaris when she was sick, and girls at the Selkie either too drunk or too high from the poppy dens to take off their boots before bed, she'd helped many an individual out of their day clothes and into clean things. Tanith still had the anemic coloring of something forgotten in the snow; her veins were a visible cluster of pale tree branches beneath her near-translucent skin. But beyond the sickly shades of whites and blues and grays, the barest hints of color returned to her cheeks. Whether or not she'd wanted to survive, it looked as though the fae would live. The damp things had been holding the chill against her skin. Dry clothes would be the next step in helping her feel like a person again, even if it would be a long time before she felt whole.

Nox had finished helping Tanith into dry things when she heard a noise. There was a gasp, a crash, a yelp, and an exchange of voices. Her blood pressure spiked as she ran for any object that might be used as a weapon. She ran for the fireplace and wrapped her hands around the iron poker beside the hearth, feeling her heart in her ears. Nox swallowed against her fear and crept into the hall, angling toward the stairs. She wasn't sure what she could do that a reever, a manifester, and two Raascot fae couldn't handle, but if she was to run and hide, she needed to assess the enemy.

A loud, happy noise came from the baritone of a masculine voice. The gravitational tug yanked her toward the stairs like fate itself was summoning her forward. Nox realized what she was hearing as she stepped out from the hall.

"You're back!"

Gadriel released his mother from a crushing, feathered hug while Yazlyn and Amaris remained locked in animated conversation. With four winged fae and the others crowded into one living room, the space was beginning to feel cramped. She may have been imagining it, but Nox began to feel as if the space had grown to accommodate the company.

Yazlyn turned to her through her smile. "Tanith?"

Yazlyn's smile faded as Nox nodded. Tanith was alive, but that was all she was. No one was ready to discuss what had happened in the valley.

Gadriel seemed to catch himself in the midst of his reunion and spun to Nox. "The dream?"

She swallowed as she took a step from the stairwell, bringing herself further into the common room with the others.

"I think I was successful? But I don't know. She died. I killed her. I just… I have no way of knowing if it worked. I didn't wake up after it happened. It didn't feel right."

"Here," Amaris murmured to Yazlyn, pushing a bowl of soup into her hands. The two disappeared up the stairs in a blur of whispered exchanges.

Nox remained in the living room with Gadriel, his parents, and the utter anomaly called Nomy.

"How did you find her?" Nox asked, looking first to Allua, then to Joel.

Joel mussed his hair like a man of twenty rather than someone centuries older than Gadriel. He shrugged. "Finding her was not difficult. She wanted to be found. Or rather, the All Mother wanted her to be found. It was getting there that was the hard part. She's made returning, however, unnaturally easy. I don't know how to explain it."

Gadriel's forehead remained creased as he looked around the room. "I'm thrilled we've found this ally. She'll be incredibly valuable once we unseat the fraud. But Nox, I'm going to need every detail I've missed. I think the others would benefit from knowing."

She told them everything. She began with their initial meeting with the comtes and the obvious dissent. She shared their clandestine meeting at Ryu's house in Territory Five. She explained how she'd gone into a church service but had not been allowed to leave. If it hadn't been for Yazlyn, she wouldn't have understood the false Speaker's ability. Because she had met and spoken with Daifa, she had been able to visit her in her dreams.

Everyone leaned in as they listened, save for Nomy.

"You remained in her dream after you beheaded her?" Gadriel repeated. He exchanged a brief, concerned look with his mother. Allua and Ceres were siblings. If anyone knew about his dream walking, it would have been her.

"I've said this a few times but… I don't think she was real. I know how that sounds. It's crazy. But I don't think that

Daifa was a whole person." Nox looked to Nomy. "Could you make a person? Could you make an adult fae, right now?"

Nomy eyed her with her dark, purple eyes. They were so much more ominous than Amaris's sharp lilac gaze. She was beautiful and terrifying. Serene and eerie all at once. "I believe I could. I've never tried. Shall I now?"

"No!" came a unified chorus from the room.

Nomy's pale hair spilled over her shoulders as she regarded Nox curiously. "And if someone is different—if they think differently, if they're curiously motivated, if they are created rather than born—are they not real?"

Joel's jaw feathered as he listened—a clenched frustration that reminded Nox all the more deeply of his son. The lines in his forehead were evidence of thought rather than age. The timelessness of his fae body betrayed nothing of his centuries, though a well of complex emotions churned in his dark eyes. "You believe that the Speaker ruling in Sulgrave was created by a manifester?"

Nox had been ready for the question. "I do. After being inside her mind... I do." She said it again, unwilling to elaborate further.

Gadriel looked to his parents, then to Nomy. "Nox has beheaded the false Speaker in her dream walking. Do we have any reason to believe that she would live or die in the real world?"

The room sagged as it shared a collective frown.

"It's so theoretical..." Allua said slowly.

"No," Nomy said with some certainty.

They looked at her.

"You believe this woman was made, rather than born. If this is true, then she cannot be killed, only unmade."

Their collective gazes intensified. Nox asked, "Can you kill an ag'drurath?"

Their lips seemed to part at this, everyone brought to singular thought.

The woman regarded them with distant, ghostly disinterest.

Her eyes shimmered with interwoven stitches of violet and plum as she returned Nox's stare. "Demons are no natural beasts. The dragons will regrow their limbs, the ag'imni will respawn, the ghouls will rise again. Unless they are unmade."

Nox looked at the alabaster fae. "How do you know this?"

Nomy's returning smile was gentle, almost pitying, but Nox was far from mollified.

She would have pressed on, had Gadriel now stood and made a parting gesture.

"Nox, may I speak with you for a moment?"

She cast a skeptical glance at the three who remained around the fire while she followed Gadriel beyond the sitting room and into the kitchen. After a long, uncomfortable pause, Gadriel thought better of it and led them into the damp night air. The storm had depleted, leaving the night and its final hours to cling to a cool mist. He closed the door behind them. "Do you not trust her?"

Nox made a face. "Why did we—"

"Fae hearing. Can't be too careful. Now, you have to clue me in: What is your gut telling you?"

She crossed her arms over her chest. "How do we know this woman is good? Why should she be in power? Just because she has the abilities of a manifester, are we to believe that entitles her to rule Sulgrave?"

She watched Gadriel's expression change from patience to something else entirely. There was a cool stoicism to the way he shook his head as he asked, "What entitles anyone to be in power? What we need isn't to approve of the kingdoms and their ways. We came here to ensure that Raascot and Farehold were no longer being assaulted. If Nomy can unmake Daifa, then do we care how she leads? She seems rather...mellow."

"That she is." Nox was chewing on the inside of her cheek thoughtfully as she looked out over the dark valley. "Have you ever heard any of that? That the demons were made?"

He hadn't. "It doesn't seem far-fetched. They don't bleed

red. We don't know anything of their birth or reproduction. If there is a manifester out there creating monsters—"

"She made Daifa."

He looked at her seriously.

Nox took an intense, hushed step. "Whoever made the demons made Daifa. In the dreams, Daifa was always sitting at this pit. She had once told me the pit was for imperfections. It was filled with the bodies of things that were... almost human, almost fae. There were vageth and goblins and portraits of demons all over the manor. Whoever made Daifa is the mother of monsters, and she is the worst of them all."

His expression faltered. "Are you sure this wasn't a nightmare?"

"I'm sure. These demons were created."

"And Daifa was her final monster?"

Nox thought of the buttery fae whose eyes had gleamed like gilded crowns. She'd marched through the great and terrible manor with power, but she hadn't seemed cruel. "I can only tell you what I saw. It was a memory of a manifester. She didn't seem evil...at least, I don't think so. Nor do I think she wanted to make Daifa evil. I just think...she didn't know how to make anything good. In the memories, it seemed like all she wanted was for Daifa to remain with her." Nox looked toward the indigo blurs of grass and stone beyond the valley. The chilly mountain rush of wet earth and conifers grounded her. She returned her eyes to the general. "If I didn't kill Daifa, what does this mean? Everything was worthless?"

He flexed his hand as if to touch her shoulder, then dropped it to his side. He tucked it into his pocket as sorrow painted across his features. "Not at all. We eliminated her army of Reds." He paused, side-stepping the pain of acknowledging their own loss. "Tanith is alive. We found the true Speaker. My parents are here, though that one may be more of a personal win." The corner of his mouth flicked upward, but it didn't reach his eyes. He continued looking toward the glassy water droplets that clung to tall blades of grass as he said, "You survived the night and attempted something no one has ever attempted. We learned so much."

"I can't stop feeling like you should just be king—"

"I thought we covered this."

Her shoulders slumped. "We did. You're just a natural."

His smile was patient and brotherly all at once. "Give it two hundred years and you'll be a natural too. You haven't had any time to just exist in your role as queen. Between dethroning Moirai and then eliminating the Sulgrave threat, this has been more strain than any one monarch has faced in…well…ever. I can't think of any ruler from the history books who's done anything like what we've accomplished. I don't want to diminish what you're feeling, but you'll go down as Gyrradin's greatest monarch."

"And the most beautiful."

"And the most humble."

Her smile faded as she looked at the closed door that separated them from the kitchen. Once they reentered the house, there'd be no going back. "Nomy is strange. She isn't anchored in reality. But I don't have to trust her. I just need her to be less evil than Daifa. Is that right?"

"If we can remove a blue-eyed fae monster committing genocide in the name of unity and replace her with some silvery manifester whose primary crime is being odd, I think we've done fine. Unless you're looking to make a play for the Sulgrave throne as well."

She almost choked on her cough. "I have never wanted anything less."

"Good. Let's get this over with and get home. We have a continent to save."

Forty-Four

T HE CITY WAS A GHOST TOWN.
Nox kept a brave face as they walked the cobblestone
streets, but she knew the others shared her trepidation and
nausea as they passed shuttered windows and bolted doors.
Silence was far eerier than the battle they'd anticipated as
they'd readied themselves to hack their way to the church.
No resistance met them as they entered Territory One in the
gray, overcast light of mid-morning. They'd expected a small
centurion presence at the very least, but there was nothing.

"Tanith?" Nox kept her voice low. "If the Reds were
vanquished, what powers would the church have at its disposal?"

Tanith remained in a state of broken despondency as she
followed. Her limbs carried her numbly forwarded. She had
never been overly communicative, but there was no questioning the blackened void of her spirits. She hadn't wanted to
get out of bed. She hadn't wanted to follow. She'd done so
nonetheless, forgoing the red tunics and britches for a black
shirt and black pants. It was everyone's first time seeing her
in any other color.

It was the only confirmation Nox needed that this was a
funeral procession.

"Nothing," Tanith answered. "Our leader—their leader, I mean—will still be with the Speaker. The other guards will pose no threat against a manifester. Truly, with Nomy here, I don't know that the rest of us are required. She's the goddess made flesh."

Nox looked at the unruffled woman in a formal, pale gown, glinting in shades of blue and silver. Nomy walked along them as if she had nothing better to do. Nox didn't care for it one bit. Her hair was as long as her navel, hanging in gentle waves around her shoulders and down her back. She seemed like she belonged in a painting, not in the heat of battle.

Tanith's eyes remained glassy and front-facing. Listless and distant, she added, "Their only card is that they hold the comtes. Daifa may ransom them."

Tanith's pain was palpable. She needed their help, and Nox longed to give it, but now was not the time. Healing would have to wait. She reeled in her skepticism of the foggy, so-called manifester. Turning to Nomy, Nox asked, "And? What will you do?"

"Whatever is required," she answered. There was a gauzy quality to the way she spoke, as if each translucent word billowed on an invisible breeze that grated on Nox. When they'd discussed their plans for taking on Daifa, everyone had said with some conviction that Nomy was the only plan they needed. Even her tried-and-true general, lover of plans, enemy to all things spontaneous, stoically agreed that they'd done all they needed to do.

At least they'd answered her questions, to whatever unsatisfying end.

Allua told her that they'd gone to the Temple of the All Mother in Sulgrave nearly one month prior, and the priestess had shared their desire to remove deceit from the church.

"She gave me an apple from the tree," Allua said. The woman fell into step beside her as they navigated Sulgrave's abandoned streets. His parents looked so much like him, from their facial structures and the angelic fold of their feathered wings to the militant rigidity of their postures, but there was a soft familiarity to Allua's features. Something vague and curious that Nox had seen so many times in the mirror. As they were clearly exposed to the elements, the city's emptiness called for silence. Allua kept her voice low. "The priestess said they grow when they're meant to be eaten and that she'd been waiting for me—for anyone—from the moment this one budded."

Nox resisted the urge to mumble something about how she had not been given any such clarity, but then again, she supposed they'd arrived at their respective temples under very different circumstances.

"And then it just took you right to her?" Nox asked.

"It showed me where to find her," Allua confirmed. "Getting there took several weeks. She's been secluded in the mountains for centuries. I don't think we could have reached her without wings. When we finally arrived at her house, she was sitting outside in the garden with a cat on her lap. She didn't even react when we approached. We told her about the false Speaker and that she was needed."

"And?" Nox cast a glance at the floating feather of a woman, then dropped her voice to scarcely more than a whisper. "She shared your goals? You trust her? She's…aloof."

Allua followed her train of thought. The women glanced at the wispy fae composed of little more than clouds, bubbles, and pearls. "She's bizarre, to be sure, but I don't think it's a bad thing. She just seems accustomed to a life without people. To be frank, she doesn't appear to care about our goals. Or anything, really. She seems…indifferent."

"Can anyone exist in this world without an agenda?" Nox murmured. Still discontented, she said, "I wish Fjolla was here."

Allua offered an appreciative sound over the aboriou, but Yazlyn, whom Nox hadn't realized had been listening in, muttered an obscenity about the beast as they came to a stop in front of the cathedral. In the absence of their feet scuffing the stones, the world was utterly silent. Even the wind held its breath as it listened and waited.

"This is it?" Nox's apprehension ballooned. It had been too easy.

Amaris moved into the space beside her. "Well, we're here, aren't we? This has to start somehow. Who wants to do the honors?"

Everyone, save for Nomy, turned to look at the general.

Gadriel made a tight expression as the weight of everyone's expectations settled on his shoulders. He eyed the church. Nox knew it had been the right call before he opened his mouth, but once he did, it was with the deep command of a general as he called to those who hid within the sanctuary. "We've come with the true Speaker. Send Daifa out to meet us. If she is really chosen by the All Mother, then she'll have nothing to fear."

Amaris pinched her arm. "Are you wearing your ribbon?"

"Shut up about the fucking ribbon." Nox flashed where she'd interwoven the protective armor through a discrete braid within her hair.

"I like her," Allua said from over Gadriel's shoulder.

Gadriel chuckled, and Nox wanted to smack them both for their irreverence on the eve of battle. Perhaps looking death in the face and laughing was a family trait. She wondered how much spirit Ceres had before he'd lost himself to his grief. When this was all over, she'd have to ask Allua to tell her all about the man who had fathered her.

"Hey, new Speaker." Yazlyn turned to Nomy. "If they're not coming out, can you just…make them? Can you move it along here?"

A thin, colorless brow arched as Nomy answered, "I don't possess mind control, though I do suppose…" Her mind wandered as she began to make a shape with her hands, as if painting a vision in her mind with her fingers before her. At first, there was nothing, and then all at once, a mountainous creature appeared. In the large space between where they'd stood in the courtyard and the cathedral, an enormous, stone golem towered over them.

Nox stumbled backward, mouth ajar. She wasn't the only one who scrambled out of the nightmarish creature's path. At her side, Amaris gaped with horror-stricken eyes as they craned their necks to look at the stone monster. Tanith tensed as if ready for battle, though how one might fight a monster of boulders, she could not tell.

The manifester was as unbothered as if her creation had been little more than pouring a cup of hot tea and serving it to her guests. She asked the golem pleasantly, "Would you be a dear and go fetch the one they call Daifa?"

Nox's head spun. She grabbed Amaris's arm to steady herself as the beast obeyed. Each of the titan's steps was an earthquake, causing their knees to buckle and the houses around them to tremble as joints and beams ached and rocked with the movement. The cobblestones beneath the creation's feet became craters with each step. The golem reached the front door and didn't attempt for a handle. It crashed through the double doors as if walking through paper. The door disintegrated into splinters and kindling.

"Holy shit!" Yazlyn gulped. She was the first to articulate the whirlwind on everyone's mind. Holy shit indeed. Nox swallowed hard as she watched the cracked wooden puncture for signs of life. The world waited on bated breath. And then, the church answered. Shouts and cries erupted from within the church as the golem advanced. It disappeared into the sanctuary leaving the crashes of destruction in its wake. A high, loud scream pierced the air as sounds wafted from within the sanctuary.

Clouds began to gather overhead with rapid intensity.

"It's Ryu," Gadriel said as he grimaced at the oncoming storm. "She can call the weather."

An angry flash of browns and russets cut through the air as Yazlyn shook her head in vehement denial. "Ryu wouldn't—"

515

"We have to assume that Daifa's turned them all," he growled. "It wouldn't be Ryu's fault if she remembers irrefutable proof of whatever Daifa wants her to see." His voice rose to counter the storm's swell. The twisting winds began to wreak havoc as natural disasters brewed around them. Nox lifted her forearms to shield her eyes from the rain, then cried out as they became cruel, icy pellets. She tried to call for someone to do something, but no one could help. On all sides, the Raascot fae struggled against the gale lashing against their wings. Amaris clung to her arms as they braced against the tempest.

She almost didn't catch Nomy's bored flick of the wrist before the punishing wind and rain vanished. In the blink of an eye, they'd been sheltered. Amaris slackened her hold on Nox's forearm as they righted and stared with wide, disbelieving eyes. The storm's raging sounds were little more than a dying hum behind thick, indestructible walls. Nox's hand twitched against the urge to cover her mouth as she looked out the shelter's front. The wall before them was made of glass so dense and powerful it may have been diamond, allowing them to watch the front of the sanctuary within the safety of their impenetrable fortress.

"Oh my goddess…" Yazlyn ogled in disbelief. The ripple of shocked murmurs and struggling breaths were the only sounds in the inviolable structure.

Nox would have continued staring at the splintered wood, the sanctuary's front, the pounding rain, had a subtle, brown shape not caught her eye. She moved her shoe to the side as she frowned at the curious buds popping up between the cobblestones around them. Soft, conical mushrooms sprouted underfoot. She scarcely had time to register the anomaly before the mushroom at her toes released a tiny puff of clouded air.

Gadriel's eyes widened with a flash of realization. "Elswyth—"

"Hold your breath!" Amaris cried out her warning.

There was a collective intake of air as everyone braced to withstand the poisonous mushrooms. Tanith was quick to act as she searched for an exit—a window, a door, a crack in the structure so they might let in fresh air. She searched for a seam in the walls with the intensity of someone charged with serving and protecting the goddess. Tanith scrambled while others twisted to the manifester with wide, pleading eyes.

With another wave—this one slightly more engaged than the last—Nomy had called countless rodent-like creatures into existence. They appeared as if from nowhere, using their tiny, finger-like paws as they plucked and gnawed and gobbled the mushrooms whole. Nox nearly released the air in her lungs as a fluffy, curious rat looked at her with intelligent eyes. It brushed her shoe with its bristly tail as it cocked its fluffy head to the side.

"You may breathe," said the manifester. Nox looked away from the chubby-cheeked creature and into the deeply amethyst eyes glimmering with something that may have been delight. It was the first true sign that Nomy had the capacity for emotion.

"Shall we?" she asked. She pressed her hand into the diamond-hard front of the shelter to open the door, releasing whatever had remained of the noxious air. The unusual, furry rodents scattered from the shelter as they escaped into Sulgrave's streets. Another act that should have killed or destroyed their resistance effort had been thwarted with near boredom. Their hair was scarcely damp from the storm before they'd been sheltered. The fae's feathers were unruffled. Their blood was free of poison. They were safe. They were fine.

"Nox…" Amaris looked up at her with the lilac gaze that twisted Nox's gut. Amaris didn't need to finish her thought. She looked entirely too much like Nomy, as if they were long-lost relatives.

"I get it," Nox said, eyes unblinking with the reverence that trickled through her. She hated it. She loved it. She may not have understood it, but she embraced it. Nox looked away from Amaris's features and back to Nomy once more. "She...she really must be a goddess."

The storm around them continued to whip, but a new sound joined the destructive howl of winds. Growling, barking, snarling, and the thundering of paws began to run toward them.

"It's Kasar," Gadriel said quickly. "He speaks to animals. He's calling on creatures."

"Fjolla could be with them! Don't hurt them!" Nox's tone changed from disbelief to pleading in an instant. She folded her fists in a prayer before her as she begged for Fjolla's safety.

The alabaster manifester made a curious face as she regarded Nox. She didn't so much as break their gaze before they were surrounded by nets. Dogs, coyotes, cats, foxes, and beasts began to slam into the nets, thrashing their claws wildly for those within the shelter. Nox scanned the nets for evidence of Fjolla, knowing that her aboriou still wore her cuff.

"Surya of Two has flight, but I don't believe she has more. What can Dhamir do?"

Yazlyn narrowed her eyes at the memory of the woman from Seven who'd grabbed her from where she'd been waiting outside of the church. "She can render you unconscious with a touch. Neither Two nor Seven will pose a threat to us from a distance. What of Chloris? From Six?"

They were answered with a horrible sound. Words tumbled out of several sets of mouths at once.

"What is that?"

"Is that a—"

"It can't be."

"He'll kill everyone in the city!"

Froth and debris stole her breath as Nox craned her neck to look up at their certain demise. The water that crashed through the valley was a tidal wave more than six stories tall, devouring everything in its path. Houses, shops, and buildings crumbled as they joined the destructive wave. This was it. This was the end. Nomy began to shut the shelter's opening, but Nox shouted, "The animals! The citizens!"

One beat. Then another.

Nomy twisted her as she made a decision. The earth ripped open as a void to the very core of the world opened up. Everyone stumbled into walls, grabbing for traction, for grip, for support as the very crust of the universe popped and split. Nox scarcely had time to register the gaping maw in front of the church before it swallowed the water wholly, its catastrophic wave disappearing as if through little more than the drain in a washbasin.

"I'm going to be sick," Nox said as she took several staggered steps behind the manifester. Her shoulder blades connected with the back of the shelter before she ran out of the room to retreat. This was true, raw power. This was history in the making, and she had a front-row seat. It was too much.

"My golem should be out any moment with the one they call Daifa," Nomy said calmly. "I will say, this day is more interesting than I thought it would be. It is quite fun, don't you think? To think on one's feet like this?" The purple gems within her eyes glittered as she offered them a rare smile.

No, Nox thought definitively, this was not fun.

The city was in ruins. Beams and stones and the silty wash of destruction pooled around the pit like a beaver dam as the wave's remnants dripped into the void. The bark and howl and thrash of wild animals quieted as the creatures waited in a state of shock. Raindrops slowed overhead. Even the wind was lesser.

"Shall I close it?" Nomy asked. "Or do we toss your false Speaker in?"

Nox's mind whirred as she struggled with what to make of the question. It took a moment for Nomy to make it clear she hadn't truly been asking. She sealed the hole with a flick of her wrist. If it weren't for the sodden wreckage piled in precarious angles, Nox might have been able to convince herself that the street had never changed. As she looked with a clenched jaw, wide eyes, and tense shoulders, she realized the manifester had been telling a joke. This ghostly, eccentric woman had spoken for no other reason than to amuse herself.

Nox knew people. She'd met them all, though they'd come in different shapes and worn various faces over the years. Nomy was not people. She didn't seem cruel. She wasn't enjoying the destruction, but neither did she seem thrilled at their swift and effective counteracts. Everything was one curiosity after another, one vaguely interesting act and its mildly interesting, answering response.

Nomy was true neutral, and Nox had no idea what to make of her.

Something new tore her from her internal battle. Nox spun toward the cracked remnants of the ruined doors. All eyes remained trained on the sanctuary as a stone arm, then head, then body boomed from the church. The golem had returned, dragging a woman out by her long, black hair. Nox recognized the peacock instantly. She was flailing wildly, blue eyes flashing with anger as she hurled obscenities.

"This is the one?" Nomy turned to the others, tilting her head. Lips parted, eyes wide, they could do little more than nod. "Give me a moment," she said.

Nomy left them behind. Amaris slipped her fingers into Nox's. Gadriel's shoulders straightened as he and the other winged fae readied themselves for action. But they could do little more than watch.

Daifa's thrashing stilled as Nomy approached. Her hands went to her roots, clutching the place the golem continued to grip her hair. She went limp as the true Speaker approached. Nomy ran a hand along Daifa's face and murmured something, but she was too far away to be heard.

"What are they saying?" Yazlyn whispered.

"Shh!" came Nox's frenzied command.

Daifa shook her head in rejection of whatever was said,

but much of her spirit had died with whatever was spoken. The Deceiver remained listless as she stared up into the Speaker's disinterested face. Nomy looked at her patiently.

And they waited. And waited. And waited.

"Do we...." Amaris had just begun to ask.

Before she could finish her thought, the comtes slowly emerged from the church. They stood wordlessly as they watched the stone monster clutch their leader. Nomy's gauzy sleeves fell to her elbows as she lifted her hands to acknowledge their presence.

"The Deceiver has something to say to you," she called out to the people. She then motioned to Daifa. "Go ahead."

Daifa shook her head as much as she was able in the beast's stone grasp, lips pursed tightly.

"You won't apologize to the people before you're unmade? Where is the honor in that?"

Daifa hurled an obscenity, and the true Speaker sighed.

"I had hoped for more, though I suppose you cannot be blamed. You were made by one who cannot make things that are good. That is not your fault." She then looked to the comtes, then to the faces peeking out of doors and windows as Sulgrave dared to brave a glimpse of the madness. "Then it is I who will apologize on her behalf. You've been subjected to atrocities in the name of the goddess. The reign of chaos has come to an end."

Nox had expected war. She'd been ready for blood, for death, for loss. She'd been braced for Daifa's insults, her fight, her one, final trick.

Instead, she watched, slack-jawed, as, with an unceremonious twist of Nomy's wrist, Daifa simply unraveled. Nox could hardly believe her eyes as Daifa's hair, limbs, flesh, and bones spun like yarn, twisting into the wind and floating away in ribbons. The streams of blood were not the crimson that flowed through the veins of men and fae but the black, viscous blood of the demons. They spiraled on an invented wind, twisting upward as they disappeared. The final droplets of her spoiled blood disappeared into the sky, and she was gone as if she had never existed.

Nomy smiled serenely as she turned to address the others. "There, it's done."

Nox was speechless, and she was not alone. Tanith, Amaris, and the Raascot fae looked on with dizzying bewilderment. They weren't the only ones struggling to grapple with terms. Just in front of the cracked wooden doors, the comtes were blinking as if rousing from sleep. It was as if scales of Daifa's deception fell from their eyes as her false memories unraveled just as she had. Citizens began to emerge from their homes, all with eyes trained on Nomy.

"That can't be it," Nox whispered.

They were at Nomy's mercy, and Nox wasn't the only one who saw it. Everyone was waiting on the manifester's announcement. Perhaps she'd arrived to turn the continent on its head. Maybe she would create a new kingdom. Nox's fingernails bit into the meat of her hand as she readied herself, knowing that no matter what Nomy said, she and the others were powerless against manifestation. She forced her eyes to remain open. She wouldn't look away as the world came to its end.

Nomy's pale tendrils tufted in the breeze as she looked from one side of the courtyard to the other. She absorbed the wreckage, the ruin, the terrified faces of comtes and civilians alike, and she made her pronouncement. "I will stay today to help you repair what has been lost. Then I will be on my way."

Nox's heart stuttered. "What?"

"Wait." Tanith snapped to action. The others followed as she jogged toward the Speaker. Tanith extended tentative fingers as if to stop the woman, then thought better of touching a goddess. "You aren't staying?"

Nomy's mouth turned down. "Why would I stay?"

Tanith's expression mirrored what Nox felt. Her dark hair bobbed around her shoulders as she shook her head in denial.

Confusion pinched her brows as she implored, "You won't rule? You won't lead the people?"

Nomy tilted her head with a renewed interest. There was no hint of unkindness as she said, "The people don't need leading. They have the message. They have each other. And now, they have freedom. Anyone who comes claiming to rule is a false god or goddess alike. In the All Mother, there is peace. In the All Mother, we reflect her namesake: *all*. Please remember that and tell the generations that follow. You are not accountable for this spurious leader's deception, but I do hope you will recognize weeds sown in your gardens in the future."

Tanith looked like the air had been sucked from her chest. Nox could have kept her eyes fixed on Tanith's crisis of faith, had Ryu not burst through the others as she ran for Yazlyn. "I'm so sorry," she was saying, reaching for Yazlyn.

"It wasn't you." Yazlyn slipped her hand atop Ryu's, nestling into it.

"I wouldn't hurt you. I wouldn't—"

"I know." Their foreheads met as the two shared a long, unspoken moment.

Nox and Amaris exchanged a wide-eyed look that said they would be speaking extensively about the implications of that single touch the instant they had a second to themselves. Nox forced herself to give Yazlyn a modicum of privacy. She looked around to see that Gadriel was already hard at work helping the people. He had joined a shopkeeper who was attempting to lift a pole from where it blocked his door. Another flutter of wings from the far side of the courtyard came from Joel and Allua as they milled about the others, checking for injuries. The other comtes were discussing amongst themselves with rapid intensity.

"What do we do?" Amaris asked, looking for a plan.

"I...I honestly didn't think we'd make it this far," Nox confessed. "I have no idea what to do next." Her words were cut short as Surya of Territory Two stretched her wingspan to their greatest, pearly width. The flash of angelic feathers quieted the courtyard as everyone turned to give her their attention.

"Queen of Raascot and Farehold," she said, her voice trembling slightly. "You... you did this." She gestured to the space around them.

Nox stiffened briefly, feeling a flash of fear that she was being blamed for the destruction that had been brought upon their city. The heads of the others turned from where they'd gone to watch the exchange. Gadriel had released his project and straightened his back while Surya spoke.

The seraphim continued. "You freed Sulgrave from the deception of a false goddess. You..." She was too bewildered to summon the gravity she was attempting. "You crossed the Frozen Straits to bring an end to a terror that we didn't even know we were facing. You battled against authorities who neither wanted nor accepted your help, because you knew we needed it. You liberated us from betrayals of the mind. You brought the All Mother made flesh to us. You..."

Nox struggled through the urge to remain speechless. She fought for the words she needed. "I only sought peace in our lands. I'm glad to have helped Sulgrave, and to know that the rest of the continent is safe from Daifa's threat."

"No," Dhamir of Territory Seven said. "It's so much more than that." She approached Nox and clutched the young queen's hands in her own. Eyes filled with reverence and honor, she tightened her grip as she took a knee, bowing before her.

Dhamir remained on the ground for a long moment, head dipped low as her hands remained in the queen's. Nox wanted to yank the crimson-clad comte to her feet. Her stomach rolled. She opened her mouth to beg Dhamir to get to her feet when a shape in green moved.

Elswyth knelt from where he'd remained by the sanctuary, kneeling in reverence of their savior. Ryu and Kasar were quick to follow from their places in the courtyard, dropping to one knee and lowering their heads in gratitude.

Nox tried to shake her head, to tell them no, to ask them to stop. She stopped breathing altogether as Surya, then Chloris lowered themselves to the damp stones, one earnest knee at a time. Their heads remained bent in reverence while she shot her friends a pleading look. She hoped the Raascot fae might come to her rescue, but Gadriel was the next to kneel before his queen, though he did so with the hint of a grin. Amaris winked as she took a knee, watching as all the people who'd observed from their homes, the streets, and the windows knelt in deference. Yazlyn was the last to move.

"Don't," Nox mouthed. If anyone could throw formality to the wind and be irreverent, it would be Yazlyn. Surely the sergeant would save her from this shocking, mortifying show of respect. Surely Yazlyn would see that she didn't deserve it. Surely *one* person would see how absurd it was to venerate her like this. "Please," she mouthed as she pleaded.

Yazlyn chuckled noiselessly. Nox was the only one who could see the obscene middle finger she flashed as she knelt beside the others.

Nox was alone on her feet in a sea of solemn gratitude. Her heart was in her stomach, her eyes swam, and her soul had left her body and hovered somewhere near the Unclaimed Wilds. She had to be dream walking. Perhaps she'd inhaled the mushroom's poison after all and this was a hallucination. She couldn't speak. She had no idea what to do. Water lined her eyes as she drowned in the sort of honor that, if given a thousand lifetimes, she never would have envisioned for herself. Whatever it was, she was thirty seconds away from emptying the contents of her stomach onto the comte from Territory Seven.

Infinity collapsed in on itself. The moment stretched until the end of time. Then, at long last, Dhamir got to her feet. It was fortunate timing, as Nox realized she'd been holding her breath throughout the entire ordeal and had been on the verge of passing out. She forced herself to draw in a steadying breath through her nose.

Dhamir squeezed her hand one more. "Sulgrave will be indebted to you forever. I know I speak for everyone here when I say that you will always have allies to the north."

Kasar's booming voice carried over the courtyard. "Would you like your monster back?"

His informality was a warm hug. The tension melted from her as she grinned a response. "Yes, very much."

He called to the beast. Fortunately, the aboriou had not been among those that had tangled in the nets. It took a few minutes for Fjolla's paws and her unseen form to gallop through the streets, but she came to a rest in front of them. Amaris and her ever-seeing eyes helped to guide Gadriel's hand to the cuff. Once it fell off, the aboriou immediately nuzzled against Nox with relief from the pain of the cruel, spiked cuff.

Nox's temper flared. "I can't believe you put her back into this torture device."

"We kept her alive by keeping her invisible." Amaris crossed her arms defensively.

"I think," Elswyth's gentle voice began speculatively, "that there is an opening for a comte in Sulgrave. In Alistair's absence, I believe we might be best served with an ambassador to the south. What do you say?"

Oh goddess. She'd been premature in assuming her responsibilities had ended. Nox looked at Elswyth as she considered his question. She was not interested in staying in Sulgrave any longer than necessary and certainly wasn't willing to lose any of her companions to the distant mountain kingdom. She caught the jerk of auburn curls as Yazlyn jutted her head in quick succession to where the Raascot fae stood.

Joel and Allua straightened when they realized Nox was looking at them. She offered a small, hopeful smile. "What say you? Do you intend to remain in Sulgrave?"

Joel put his arm around his wife and kissed her hair. The gesture was so intimate, so loving, that Nox's insides squeezed. She was looking into the loving embrace of her aunt and uncle. This is what family looked like. "What do you say, Allua? Would you like to be a comte?"

She grinned up at her husband. "Our next adventure?"

Surya returned the calm, happy expression. "We're lucky to have you. I'll feel honored to have another winged fae on our council."

There would doubtlessly be much to plan, but Amaris squeezed her hand. "I have to talk to her."

Nox almost asked who but caught the dash of misty white as Nomy milled out of the line of sight like a dandelion puff on the wind.

"Come with me?" Amaris asked.

And so, they approached the Speaker, rounding the corner to find her aimlessly wandering from place to place as she created odds and ends with little more effort than the wiggles of her fingers. She fixed things that were broken, handed out sweets to children, and even grew a tree or two where she felt things could be lovelier. She had said that she'd stay through the day to help them with whatever needed fixing and appeared to be doing just that.

Nox trailed behind as Amaris jogged over to the mystical woman. Nomy turned to regard her with the same idle inquisitiveness. Her eyes trailed over Amaris's white hair, her lavender eyes, and landed on her scar. Amaris asked, "Can I ask you something?"

"Can you?"

Amaris worked to control her frustration. "Did you make me?"

Nomy's expression went from indifference to delight. In an instant, she became sunlight. She laughed with the high, silver tinkling of bells. "Oh, to take credit for such a thing. I do suppose we look like kin. I wonder what other beasts and beings bear a striking resemblance as they spawn from a common source. Continents, countries, churches, tut, tut, tut."

Amaris shot a helpless look at Nox, then back to Nomy.

"There are other manifesters, aren't there? When Daifa was unmade, her blood was black, like a demon's. She was made. I think she was made by whoever has spent the last ten years sending demons through the continent. The influx of creatures…the horrors in the south…it can't be a coincidence."

"Ask your question."

Nox watched the frustration flicker on Amaris's face as she doubled down. "Am I made? Am I manifested, that is?"

Nomy cocked her head with interest. "Were you born?"

She nodded slowly. "So I'm told. I was born to a priestess with whom I share no biology. It's been said…well, I've been told a lot of things. It was suggested I was a prayer made flesh."

"Then the prayer was made. You, however, were born." The woman began to turn away.

"And how could—" Amaris began, eyebrows creasing.

"Hmm?"

She rallied both words and courage. "How could a tree hear a prayer? How could I be made? Are you really a goddess? How could—"

The manifester smiled without her eyes. There was a distant sadness in them. "Do you exist?"

Amaris shook the absurdity from her like a dog flicking water from its fur. "What?"

"I said: Do you exist?"

"I…yes."

"And has neutrality been restored?"

"…it has."

"Then does it matter?" And with that, her conversation was over.

Amaris looked at Nox. "I feel like I should be angry," she said.

"Are you?" Nox asked.

"Maybe a little."

Nox cupped her shoulder. She ran a thumb over the tender place where chest met shoulder as she said, "Then allow yourself to be angry. And tell me all about it in a second. But while we're getting unsatisfying answers from a walking riddle, I have something I need to ask."

She looped an arm around Amaris's waist as she called after the Speaker.

"Nomy?" She lifted her voice so it might carry over the stones. "Where will you go?"

"Wherever is required, when the time is right," she sang without looking back.

"And if you're needed, you'll send more fruit?"

"If only the fruit were mine to claim!" came her laughing reply as she continued on her odd little tasks around the homes and shops, smiling at the people. Children and faithful ran to touch, and she allowed them to grasp her hands. She bent to hug a small child as she breezed along her peculiar journey.

"I feel like I know less now than before we began," Amaris said.

Nox relaxed her head against Amaris's as they watched the womanly tuft of cloud and magic work her miracles. With a shrug, she said, "Maybe that's the point."

Forty–Five

"WHAT A DAY, YOUR MAJESTY." AMARIS CLOSED THE DOOR behind her as she let herself into Nox's room. A laugh bubbled through her. They'd done it. They'd done more than survive. They'd thrived. And Amaris wanted to celebrate.

They were back in the Diplomatic Hall once more. The fears, trials, and turmoil had come to such an intense, crashing halt that it almost felt like it had been a terrible nightmare—one from which they'd collectively awoken. Now they were back in their rooms to receive the gifts, foods, treasures, clothes, and pleasantries being sent to their rooms from every man, woman, child, field mouse, house cat, and earthworm in Sulgrave. It felt that way, anyway, given the suffocating mountain of gratitude. The concierge was kept on his toes as his penance. He spent every moment running between the desk in the atrium and their rooms as he dealt with the onslaught of presents.

"The queen is off duty," Nox replied wryly, waving off the royal greeting. Amaris had caught her just as she stepped from the bathing room in a fluffy robe. A cloud of hot steam silhouetted her as she ran a comb through the wet strands of her long, black hair, which hung nearly to her navel. Amaris raked her eyes over the supple curves and damp tendrils, landing on the emerald ribbon braided into her strands. She'd sworn on Fjolla's life that she'd never go without it again, which had been a worthy enough promise to satisfy Amaris and the others. Her eyes trailed from the ribbon to the tiny puddle on the floor where Nox's hair drip, drip, dripped onto the ground.

"Oh, that's too bad," Amaris said, snapping the door's lock into place behind her with a satisfying clink. Nox arched a brow at the movement. Her hands stilled in her hair. "I thought perhaps..." She took another step closer, then another. Something about returning from the brink of death victorious had fundamentally changed her. There wasn't a trace of shyness as she said, "I could pick up where we left off in the courtyard."

"In the courtyard?" Nox's brows knit together. Her fingers stilled against her damp hair.

Amaris knew exactly what she wanted. She crossed the room, stepping so that Nox's back moved gently into the doorframe that had connected the bedroom to the bathing chamber.

"I haven't paid my proper respects," she said, lips hovering a hair's breadth from the queen's berry-dark mouth. She stood on her toes as she brought her mouth to the queen's. She grazed her lips over Nox's with gentle, exploratory suction as she leaned into the queen's.

Nox let out a soft, appreciative sound. Her eyes fluttered shut as she gave in to the kiss. Amaris curled herself around Nox, the scents and flavors of plums whetting her appetite as her mouth watered. She dragged her mouth from Nox's ear to her jaw, then down her neck, inhaling nutmeg and cinnamon with every breathy kiss.

Goddess, she missed this. Her need to be near Nox had only grown with every passing day since their incredible night before the world fell apart. Amaris wrapped the fingers of one hand against Nox's neck, tilting it so she had better access to the other side. She continued to trace intentional kisses down the exposed parts of Nox's throat. Her free hand began to untangle the rope that secured Nox's robe.

She was too distracted to see the defensive motion coming.

Nox swept the control from her in a fluid, possessive motion. She slammed Amaris backward. Her head bounced against the opposite edge of the doorframe.

All thought of gentleness evaporated.

Nox ripped the shirt up over her head, mouth moving against her lips, her tongue, her neck, her collarbones. Amaris's eyes rolled in ecstasy when Nox cupped her breast, rolling the peaked, ready nipple between her fingers as her kisses continued. One hand balled in Amaris's hair, yanking her hair backward and eliciting a sharp, high cry. She began to take what she wanted, and Amaris writhed for more.

Nox's hand passed over her pale body, following the line of her stomach down to where her pants remained buttoned. Her mouth continued its commanding, rhythmic movements, tongue and lips kissing with abandon while her hand continued to move lower. She dipped her fingers beneath the fabric and moaned into Amaris's skin with appreciation at her warm, wet response. Nox robbed in slow circles with her hand, claiming it for herself. Amaris's groan was lost as the sound was muffled with the greed and possession of another kiss.

"Oh, goddess," Amaris moaned.

Nox smiled, dragging her teeth along the reever's jaw as she began to tug down her pants.

"Wait," Amaris rasped, barely able to choke out the word.

Nox stilled, hand paused, mouth still against her jaw. "Are you okay?" She relaxed the fingers that had pulled the silvery hair to the side.

"Goddess, yes. I'm more than okay." Amaris swallowed as she untangled herself from Nox's hold. "I told you, I wanted to finish what we started in the courtyard."

"But—"

She looked into Nox's bottomless, dark gaze as she slowly lowered herself. Amaris took a hip in each hand, urging Nox to get comfortable against the doorframe as she knelt before her. The warm robe fell with feather softness as it pooled on the space around her feet. "Your Highness."

"Oh." She moaned the word.

✦

Nox leaned back against the doorframe, breath hitching in surprise. Her heart squeezed in time with the throbbing need she felt in deep, curling places. Both of her hands found themselves tangled in Amaris's silver hair, holding it out of her face in tight, authoritative demand as the reever lowered her mouth. Her kisses and licks traced along Nox's inner thighs, teasing her as her hips rocked on instinct.

Amaris let one of her hands trail up the inside of Nox's leg, grazing her entrance. Her hot breath drew closer. She was licking, kissing, tasting, and exploring everywhere except for the very sensitive, center-most place that Nox craved. With a groan, Nox had had enough teasing. She pushed Amaris's mouth against her, raising one leg as she pinned the reever to her. Amaris slipped one finger in, then another while her tongue licked right up the center of the raven queen. Nox released a sharp cry at the sensation, back arching off the frame.

"Don't stop," Nox commanded.

"Just like this?" Amaris asked, her question spoken into the soaked, velvet-soft apex.

"Just like that," she breathed through her gasps. "Fuck."

"You're fucking delicious," Amaris moaned.

"Shut up." Nox panted her response.

Amaris repeated the motion, her fingers working in a rhythmic, steady penetration. Her mouth continued to move against Nox, feeling her hips roll as she rode the reever's face. Amaris didn't stop the appreciative sounds as she lapped at the milk and honey on her tongue. Stars popped behind Nox's eyes at the pleasurable vibration from every moan that rumbled from the reever's throat into her, through her, filling her.

"Don't slow down." Nox's words came out in a rasp. Her back arched even farther from the doorway, body growing rigid as the curling sensation swelled into a line as tight, strong, and powerful as a bowstring. She yanked Amaris's hair as she begged. "Don't stop; oh goddess, don't stop; oh god—"

The warmth that had curled in her stomach grew tighter and tighter. Her entire body clenched. Her grip on Amaris's hair tightened, and the reever made a proud, appreciative noise against the small pain of the yank on her hair. Her fingers continued moving, her mouth relentless as Nox constricted around her fingers. For a perfect, endless second, Nox went fully taut. The world became darkness and diamonds. She had stopped moving, stopped breathing, completely frozen in the final instant before climax.

Goddess, she loved this woman.

Goddess, she loved this mouth.

Goddess, she loved *this.*

Then, she shattered. She cried out, not caring who might hear. She had no control over the burst of volume that tore from deep within her as she broke. She almost collapsed against the doorway, but Amaris hadn't let her move.

Nox's body rocked with the waves of pleasure that crashed over her. She was in free fall over the cliff as the reever continued to ride the wave, eliciting several more clenching aftershocks from the queen until Nox had to yank her mouth away.

Amaris sucked the drops of flesh and plum and sweat-soaked cinnamon off her fingers as she looked up at Nox, who still hadn't removed her hands from where they tangled in the silver strands of her hair. Her eyes were glinting with wicked pleasure.

A single eyebrow arched up as she stared down at her lover. "I hope you're not tired, reever," Nox panted. She looked into her big, lilac eyes, glowing with an oxytocin high as pleasure coursed through her. "Because you're in for a very long night."

✦

Nox's heart sank when she opened her eyes on a warm summer's day. She knew this pond. She knew the happy songs of these birds. She knew how this sunlight created dappled shadows from gently undulating leaves.

She lifted her eyes to the lily-pad green ones that were already staring down into hers. Malik's questions tumbled one after another. "Are you safe? Are you okay? I haven't heard from you—"

"I'm fine." Nox raised a hand. She stopped herself from saying everyone was fine. It was no longer true. This was why she had stones in her belly the moment she saw him. She didn't want to bring him pain. "We're safe. I have a lot to tell you. Amaris is fine. She's asleep beside me as we speak."

His face softened. Malik crushed her in a warm hug. His mouth said, "That's wonderful," but his body said, "I've missed you so goddess-damned much." The way his warmth seeped from his skin into hers, glowed like an inward sun, was a goodness only he could conjure. He, the one who had offered more love in her life than she could scarcely handle. Two reevers and two kingdoms was no small collection of hearts. What was a girl to do?

The inner sunlight worked its charm. She relaxed, if only slightly, as she returned his smile. She wasn't ready to say what needed to be said. She wanted to stay in this happy sanctuary for a minute longer.

"Do you ever see me in your dreams?" she asked. "I don't mean dream walking. I mean, do you ever see a false version of me?"

He left his arm around her as they slowly lowered themselves to the banks. She rested her head on his chest and listened to his steady heartbeat as they basked under the eternal summer sun. "I do. But those dreams have a forgettable quality. They don't feel real. Nothing is lasting or tangible. It's not like this."

Nox matched his breathing. Deeply in, then deeply out. "I don't even know where to start, Malik."

"Then I'll go first. The Duke of Henares is dead."

She rolled onto him, propping herself up so that she could carefully watch his expression. "He's what?"

Malik made a face. "He was gathering wildflowers by the cliffs and tumbled to his death."

"And Farehold—"

"—does not give a shit. The servants were relieved. Moirai was a tyrant, and the duke was an imbecile. They realized something while he served as your puppet king."

"And what's that?"

Malik shrugged from his place on the grass. "That the power of thousands outweighs the power of one. Someone can only remain in power as long as the people allow it. When he died, everyone in the castle decided to just keep living their lives. I was his overseer as his false cousin, so I've stepped into the role to help the people."

Her lips pulled away from her teeth in a slow, true smile. "You're king."

"No, I'm—"

"Malik, you're Farehold's king."

"You're not listening, I—"

She shook her head, eyes sparkling. The sunlight was true now. It burned through her as if this was the first thing in her life that had ever made sense. She looked at him with every drop of intensity she possessed as she said, "It has to be you. You were born to be king."

"Reevers will seek for themselves neither power nor glory."

"You didn't seek this for yourself."

"My oath says I will answer to no king—"

"You *are* the king. You answer to no one."

His face crinkled in denial. He couldn't stop shaking his head while he sought to make her understand. "My vows, the reever's oath—"

Nox crawled onto her knees. She grabbed him with a hand on each of his strong shoulders. Her fingers dug into his thickly muscled arms excitedly as she grinned. "This in no way violates your oath, Malik. The duke was a fool and a placeholding pawn and everyone knew it. They want you. You are benevolent. You are fair. You are a better king than anyone deserves, and there is no one I would rather have on the throne. It has to be you."

"But, Nox..."

Delight bubbled through her as she challenged him to find a single flaw with this plan. It was fate. It was destiny. "What?"

"If I'm in Aubade, and you're in Gwydir..."

Her smile flickered.

It took him a long time to say, "I was supposed to come home to you."

She closed her eyes slowly, lowering herself to the grass and relaxing into him once more. He kept his arms around her. She kept an ear to his now-unsteady breaths while the insects buzzed, and the birds chirped merrily in the canopies surrounding the pond.

"I'm going to say something," Nox began.

"I already don't like it."

"No, hush. I'm going to say two somethings. And at first, you're going to want to protest and argue, but I need you to just listen." She rolled onto her backside, sitting up once more so that she could face him fully. She snatched one large hand between her own.

"I could never give you children."

"I don't—"

"Tut, tut," she said, silencing him. "Not only could we never consummate our relationship in the flesh, but even if I could, I have no desire for a progeny. Children are cute, and sometimes they're sweet, and then they're exhausting. Some women are born for motherhood, and that's beautiful. But I'm not one of them. I'm no mother, nor do I want to be."

"Nox, I don't—"

"I said hush!" She tapped him gently on the tip of his nose. If it had been anyone else, it probably would have infuriated him. Her cool self-assuredness had a calming effect. "I knew you would protest. Now, that's only part of my something. Let me finish."

He furrowed his brows in silent protest. His eyes became a wary shade of emerald as he allowed her to continue.

"I've inherited two thrones with no want or need to continue my lineage on either of them. I'll be queen. I'll be a good one. And when my time has come and gone, good, fair, kind people need to be in power in Aubade and Gwydir. Gadriel is closest in line to the throne after me, and I know he doesn't want the title, but I'm not fully fae. I won't live for thousands of years. He may yet have children. Hell, he may have them with our literal demigoddess someday. Those aren't the kinds of things I know, but I know that Raascot will be cared for. Farehold needs that. Farehold needs certainty, and strength, and compassion. It doesn't need someone making a power grab to subjugate the people. It needs a king who values the downtrodden, someone who sees humanity every-where he looks, someone who wants to feed the poor—"

He sat up, if only to press his palm into his forehead. "You're making it sound like I'm the hero in a children's story."

"You are, Malik," she said with quiet gravity. "You absolutely are."

"And what would I do?" he pressed.

"Well." Nox took hold of her fingers. She pressed on her index, then her middle, then her ring as she listed some of his tasks. "You will protect the throne from those who wish it harm. You will dismantle the bishops who abuse their power and harm others in the church's name. And, you will just talk to me anytime you have questions on leadership. I'm a seasoned monarch now. I'm fairly certain I know everything."

"I don't want to lose you."

"Then don't lose me."

He rubbed at a headache. "This is a lot to think about."

"Too bad. I've decreed it."

He mock-glared. "I answer to no king."

"Then it's spectacular that I wasn't born with a cock, because I'm no king. This is my royal proclamation as the continent's queen. I am confident no one will protest. They love you. I could have Tanith send the harpies as soon as we return."

"Asking Tanith for more? I'm sure Ash will be thrilled."

And there it was. The dread, the stones, the heaviness that had kept her from readiness to see him for so long. She quieted, taking his hand once more. A long quiet stretched between them, filled only by a mourning dove's coos. The leaves moved gently overhead, rubbing together as the forest in his memory gave way to a breeze. The wind touched the surface of the pond ever so slightly, creating the smallest of ripples on the otherwise glass-like pond. There would never be a right time. There would never be a good time. There was no gentle forest, no comforting arms, no safe space that would soften the coming blow.

"Malik, there's something I have to tell you."

Forty-Six

I T WAS TIME TO SAY GOODBYE. NOX AND AMARIS HAD EXPERI-
enced their share of farewells. Each had been cruel, they'd
been traumatic, they'd been violent, they'd been against their
will. It was something else entirely as they readied themselves
to hug the others of their own volition. This goodbye was
their choice, and theirs alone.

And as wonderful as Sulgrave was in Daifa's absence, it
was not their home.

"You don't have to go." Allua kissed her son on his
forehead. It was such a wholesome, parental gesture. Gadriel
made a long-suffering expression as he allowed the gesture. It
was jarring to see the war-hardened general with his parents
in such an intimate way.

"You know I do." He smiled. "That one over there would
be lost without me."

Nox grinned, though the expression did not light her
eyes on the somber occasion. "It's true. He's the real ruler of
Raascot. I'm just the puppet queen."

Allua moved to Nox, and this time it was the queen's turn
to receive a forehead kiss. Her heart sighed at the glimpse of
a life that would never be. This was a kiss from an aunt. This

was family. The woman didn't care for titles. Whether general or queen, son or niece, everyone was worthy of affection. "I don't believe that for a second."

They'd spent a full week in Sulgrave following their final, tumultuous battle outside of the sanctuary. If Nox wasn't with Amaris, she was with her long-lost family members, soaking in every drop of parental affection and attention that the woman had to offer. Joel and Allua had made it abundantly clear that they were proud to have her on the throne. She'd loved hearing stories of Ceres from his childhood. It had been healing to learn all of the things she'd needed to know about when her father had been a good, whole man.

Amaris had also gotten to know Gadriel's parents, though to a far lesser degree. He'd been proud to show her off to them, but Nox's bond with her relatives took precedence. Joel had made it very clear that he approved of his son's choice in partners.

"Keep him in line?" Joel looked to Amaris, clapping her on the back.

"I plan to," she promised. "As a reever, he has no authority over me."

Though no one else noticed, Gadriel gave her a look that let her know she'd pay for that verbiage later. A thrill ran through her. She savored the antagonization and whatever punishment would surely follow.

It wasn't until their final day and announced departure from the mountain kingdom that the comtes revealed they had been concealing a rather magnificent skiff that had made only two voyages across the straits. It was an incredible ship—the likes of which no one in the party had ever seen. They would be traveling in luxury compared to the miserable trip in the tiny tin ship they'd endured on their original crossing. Kasar busied himself overseeing the supplies and barking orders left and right as foods, gifts, and treasures were loaded onto the ship.

"We still have to get these things from the skiff to Gwydir." Nox had looked skeptical.

Kasar made a dismissive noise. "Worry about that once you cross. We'll set your coordinates so you're heading directly southeast, crossing at an angle. It'll put you as close to Gwydir as the straits allow. Then you can send whichever enlisted men who need a good workout to gather your things in the following weeks."

"I'm sure they'll love that," Gadriel muttered.

"Haven't you been looking for a reason to punish Lucas?" Yazlyn asked. Amaris's memory flickered to the hazy fog of rummy and mead and a group of enlisted men who'd gotten under the general's skin when he'd come to fetch her.

Gadriel's spirits floated. "Yes, yes I have."

Amaris looked over her shoulder at the ship to where Tanith had already presumably found the quietest corner, tucking herself into whatever furs and blankets she could find. She'd been the first to board. There was no one in Sulgrave with whom she wished to part. She'd made it clear that nothing remained for her in these mountains apart from heartache. Her life was in Raascot now, even if it was not the world she'd imagined.

"Are we ready?" Nox looked around. The formal goodbyes had been held the night before at a dinner that the council had held in the honor. They'd eaten more than they could handle and drank far too much, but the healing tonics had alleviated any hangovers. Now at their last moments on Sulgrave soil, they only needed to hug the comtes who'd joined their inner circle.

She looked around to where Elswyth was helping Kasar, scanning for the comte from Territory Five. "Where did Yaz go? Wasn't she just here?" Amaris asked.

The boarding process had been tedious, and she wasn't entirely certain whether they'd been preparing the ship for one hour or five. Still, she was surprised the sergeant would risk ducking out this close to departure. Amaris knew enough of Yazlyn's feelings about the cold to know she would sooner die than fly back on her own.

A few moments later, Yaz and the comte emerged from the building, hand in hand. Ryu's face was flushed. Yazlyn's hair was askew. She seemed to realize this as everyone's eyes widened, and she immediately brought her free hand to smooth her auburn curls. They approached Nox, Amaris, and Gadriel and exchanged a look before Yazlyn spoke.

"I'm not going."

Nox blinked several times. "But, Yaz..."

"Sergeant," Gadriel said softly.

"Don't 'sergeant' me," she chided quietly. "You know there's nothing for me in Gwydir." Her eyes flitted briefly to Nox, and then away. Yazlyn hadn't been happy for a long, long time. The military had called her into a life of service, and the road had called the only woman she'd ever truly loved. The queen had never been a replacement for what her heart had needed. The months of their tryst would remain little more than a passionate, angry memory.

The time had come for Yazlyn to choose love over duty.

And maybe that was why, despite what it did to them, despite the roiling emotions, the squeezed hearts, the sinking sensations, no one tried to talk her out of it. The best thing was rarely the easy thing.

Amaris was the first to hug her. "Good for you." She squeezed. "You deserve all the stupid happiness in the world. And maybe to be somewhere that encourages you to drink less."

Yazlyn chuckled into her hair.

"And to think..." Amaris finished her tight hug. "I really hated your guts."

Nox laughed. "Oh yeah." She did her best to keep her smile kind. "Thanks for the reminder. Maybe it'll make your leaving a little easier."

Yazlyn's grin turned impish. "If you think it'll help to pretend you still hate me, I don't care what lies you need to spin. I know I'm the most beloved sergeant in the history of Raascot's military."

Nox was the next to give her a hug. "I'm sorry, for—"

Yazlyn shook her loose. "For fuck's sake, you're always trying to ruin perfectly lovely moments! I don't accept your apologies." She grabbed Nox by both arms. "Raascot is lucky to have you. I'm sure Farehold is too, but I don't care very much about them."

"Yaz." Gadriel said only her name.

Amaris could scarcely look at his expression. She'd never seen sadness in his eyes. Not like this.

Yazlyn lifted her chin, though it quivered. "Don't you dare ruin my reputation by making me cry."

He crushed her into him, and for a moment, they were just friends, just family, just two people who loved the shit out of each other. She held him tightly. He returned the embrace, flexing against the depth of the hug. "You've been my general just as much as you've been my brother. You've ruined my life so many times, so fuck you for that. And you've saved it more times than I can count. Take care of Gwydir, okay? Steal a few almond pastries from Zaccai for me, just to piss him off."

"For you? I'll feed his almond pastries to Fjolla just so I know that, somewhere across the straits, you're laughing."

Yazlyn wiped at her tears with the back of her sleeve. "Goddess damn it, all of you. You're going to make my charcoal run. I'm trying to look tough and cool, and you're ruining it for me. But thank you for taking that stupid beast with you."

"She's not stupid," Nox murmured.

"And," Yazlyn countered, looking at Gadriel, "this is why I'm so glad you're the one who has to deal with Nox. Good luck there."

Ryu looped an arm around Yazlyn's waist. She looked seriously at Nox, Amaris, and Gadriel as the comte said, "I promise to make life exceedingly difficult for her."

They grinned at that, but Gad was the only one to speak. "That's all we ask."

"Yazlyn?" Nox looked at her uncertainly. The sergeant

wiped at her eyes again, watching with curious, glassy eyes as Nox dug in her bag. She procured a black, feathered quill. "You should have this. I own its counterpart. Stay in touch with Allua so Sulgrave and Raascot have a line of communication between kingdoms. And, so that…you know…you can check in sometimes."

Yazlyn's choked laugh was half sob, half joy as she vowed to send only dirty drawings.

And then their time had come.

The three boarded the large ship and waved goodbye to everyone who stood on the docks. Tanith did not emerge as they pushed back from the dock. Three comtes and three Raascot fae waved at them. Nox waved back until she was nearly knocked from her feet by Fjolla. Though they'd been assured that plenty of meat had been packed to satiate the animal, Fjolla was also more than capable of burrowing through the ice and hunting as she had for her entire lifespan before encountering them.

The enchanted mechanisms of the ship required no effort on their part as it pushed away from the docks. They continued waving until Sulgrave and their loved ones were little more than dots. Eventually, Nox, Amaris, and Gadriel ventured below the deck into the warm, insulated cabin where Tanith stayed quietly huddled. They'd gained allies, memories, an encounter with a goddess, and a place etched in history among the most intrepid of heroes. They should be happy.

But Nox knew that regardless of what they'd accomplished, they'd lost more than they'd ever be able to express.

Nox could see it in Tanith's every cell. Pain radiated off of her, yet she refused to speak. She didn't even look at them as she bundled the furs tightly to her chest, as if attempting to plug the bleeding from a physical wound. If the blades had pierced her instead, a physical pain may have been excruciating, but it was so much easier to admit "my body is in agony" than "my heart is broken." She knew that Tanith would see

Ash's absence spread over everything, as if it were the sky itself. The most acute pains are those of lives unlived, and Ash and Tanith had been robbed of the touches, the kisses, the passions, and the stories they could have told together.

Nox knew loss. She knew tragedy. She knew that grief could be a dull gnaw, a sharp bite, a soft brush, or the complete amputation of part of oneself. And so she vowed to be whatever Tanith needed—whether to punch through her anger, to leave her alone, or someone to share tears with.

Nox's gaze flitted to Amaris.

The moonlit love of her life would mourn the brother she'd lost. Ash had been among the only family she'd ever had in this world. Gadriel would surely miss his parents. Nox would fondly remember the comfort she'd felt in faithlessness, before she'd seen true power, before she'd understood and believed in the All Mother. She'd miss her life when she had the freedom of anonymity, the recklessness of being no one, the liberty in being able to become whoever, or whatever, she wanted back before she'd had a name, a title, and a purpose. They would leave so much behind in Sulgrave, but all that mattered was what was before them.

There was something she believed at her core.

The future was no straight line. It was a winding valley, and every new bend and corner contained within it an entirely new and surprising landscape. They had wounds to heal not just in their hearts but in their kingdoms, their people, and their lands. If the pain could shape them in ways that made their journey beautiful, then it would not be wasted.

Epilogue

N OX STRETCHED HER HANDS TO RECEIVE HER BABY, BUT THE aboriou had other plans. Her stark white fur was all the more beautiful against Gwydir's blue-black stones, as if she'd brought a piece of winter and its most precious creations home with her.

"Get that thing out of the castle," Gadriel grumbled as Fjolla jogged up and down the stones of Gwydir's throne room carrying her favorite, enormous femur bone in her jaws. The general made a face while picking what seemed to be an endless supply of white animal hairs from his black fighting leathers. Her gigantic paws and the clip-clop of her nails on the labradorite were a sacrilegious sound in what had served for hundreds of years as such a solemn, royal space.

"I don't know, I think she's pretty cute." Zaccai smiled and opened his arms for the creature. Nox supposed she could accept her aboriou giving the bone that had once belonged to a stag to the spymaster. She was glad they got along.

Fjolla nuzzled up to him. He plucked the femur from her maw and tossed it to where Nox was sitting—rather unlady-like—on the petrified throne. Rather than facing forward, she had draped her legs over one side and her hair over the other. Her glossy black locks dangled loosely over the arm, save for the tiny braid that had been carefully, secretly interwoven with the emerald ribbon, never to part. The aboriou gave her a sloppy, upside-down kiss before running for the bone large enough that it must have belonged to a nearby elk. Amaris grabbed the bone just before Fjolla could reach it and tossed it toward Zaccai. The mighty white beast continued playing fetch with the commander and the reever while Nox smiled from her place on the spindly, wooden throne.

"The throne room is the only room big enough to play inside!" Amaris protested with a grin, which received narrowed eyes from Gadriel. She ignored him rather intentionally as she caught the bone once more.

"Can I help you, General?" Nox leaned to the side so one hip remained planted on the seat that was meant to hold her entire bottom, one hand propped itself against the armrest, her fist plopped against her cheek. She'd spent so long avoiding the throne room for the power of its memories. She'd felt like an imposter against the enormity of her new title and the importance of the space. Now, when she looked at the gray-white driftwood colors of the spindly throne of what had surely been the mighty roots of a once-great tree, she didn't see a mad king. She didn't see the past, or the responsibilities, or the weight. She only saw opportunities for how the world might be better simply by who sat upon its hallowed seat.

"You know we have the entire castle grounds to play with your monster. The throne room is supposed to be a sacred place."

Nox smirked. "I don't care much for what people are supposed to do." She knew the others could tell from the way she treated the ancient throne like a lounging chaise that she believed every word of what she'd said.

Gadriel fought the disarming urge to chuckle at that, and she knew she'd won the exchange. He sighed as he watched the Queen of Raascot as she kicked her feet up over the arm of the chair, but his heart wasn't in it. She was an unconventional monarch, but she'd done more good for the world in her short time than Ceres had in centuries. She knew Gadriel felt lucky to serve as her general, as he frequently told her as much. "I'm actually here to borrow Amaris, if you think you can spare her."

Amaris tossed the bone again, leaving the aboriou to play with the commander. She wiped her hands on her pants before slouching onto the arm of the throne where Nox was resting. Her lavender eyes twinkled as she winked at the raven. "What do you say, Your Majesty? Can you spare me for the night?"

"Come here." Nox extended her hands outward and Amaris slid into the space beside her in the seat. She slid thin, soft fingers into Amaris's silver hair and pushed a kiss into her temple, smiling against the smell of juniper. "I need to pay Malik a visit. You kids have fun."

Amaris took her time returning the kiss. Nox knew she'd never tire of juniper and snow on her tongue. When their lips parted, Amaris touched her forehead to Nox's. "Don't say hi to him for me. I don't want to come up in your weird dreams."

Gadriel extended his arm and Amaris jogged from the throne, blowing a kiss over her shoulder at the queen. Nox caught it in the air and put it against her lips as she watched the two walk out of the throne room. Amaris rested her head on the general's shoulder as they made their way to the door.

"Don't shatter any more windows!" Nox shouted after them. She was going to have to commission a glass-free cabin in the woods for the obnoxious pairing unless Amaris figured out how to stop creating natural disasters every time the general swept her off her feet.

Amaris threw her middle finger up over her shoulder. Nox's nose wrinkled with her smile as the double doors swung to a close behind them.

Zaccai raised his head from where he'd been ruffling the fur around the aboriou's ears. "Are you going to go check on her today, or should I? Maybe she'll want to come out and play with Fjolla?"

She was glad for Zaccai's empathy. The others were kind. They cared. But the commander seemed to be the only other person in the castle who carried Tanith's burden on his shoulders the way she did.

"No," Nox sighed, heart heavy at the thought. "I've got it. Thank you."

The commander gave her a sad half smile at that before returning his attention to the furry creature. He led the once-fabled beast of lore out of the throne room, presumably toward the yard where Fjolla could splash and fetch near the river. She made a few nipping motions toward the bone as the enormous doors swung to a close behind it.

Quiet pressed in from all sides.

The throne room felt so much different when it was empty. She refused to feel haunted by its ghosts. Perhaps the continent was blood-stained, but its future didn't have to be. She would be a fair, thoughtful queen. She would rule with a loving and open heart. She'd unite the kingdoms in ways that the continent hadn't attempted since the last fae queen of Farehold had pursued when she'd sat upon the throne. And with Malik serving as Protector of the Realm in the south, the continent had never been closer to peace.

Dream walking was an imperfect solution to the distance that separated them, but she could think of no one else more worthy of the crown. He deserved every good thing and wanted that same goodness for the people. He'd even moved his parents into the castle, finally able to shower them with the gifts and appreciation they deserved in spades. However much she missed him, he felt the longing ten times over. And though it hurt her to know their arrangement caused him pain, she knew that some bones had to break to heal properly.

Nox dragged her fingers along the labradorite rocks, heart sinking as she looked at the aurora borealis caught in every stone. She thought of their night under the northern lights.

She thought of the last time they'd all been happy and whole. And she knew there would be joy, there would be jokes, that life would go on, but that the castle would never again be filled with the wit or sarcasm of Yazlyn's irreverence.

Nox withdrew her fingers from the dim shimmer that connected her so vividly to her memories. She wished Yazlyn had returned with them, though she knew she had no right to the emotion. The winged fae always had the perfect, disarming smart-ass remark to bring levity to any situation. Yazlyn had been a person, not placeholder for Nox to work through her own complicated emotions. The sergeant—one who had an entirely new title and identity now separate from Raascot and its military—deserved so much better than what Nox could ever offer her. It was her own selfishness that still wanted those crumbs, the part of her that wished she could hold all the threads with loose hands and never worry about how or why they'd unraveled in the first place.

Grief was strange like that.

And maybe that was what hurt. It twisted and stung to know Nox had never been good to her, even though she deserved every drop of love, happiness, and adoration the world had to offer. Somewhere across the howling winds and endless ice, she was undoubtedly bringing comedic relief not only to Territory Five but to anyone lucky enough to be around her. For a time, Nox had been so fortunate as to call her a friend, a lover, and a confidante. Ryu was blessed to have such a beautiful, snarky addition to her life.

Part of growth was realizing the times you deserved the role of villain in other people's stories.

She moved with slow, sad steps as she walked the corridor. This was her home now. She felt it in her bones. Entering the midnight-hued kingdom had been like knitting together a piece of her heart she hadn't realized she was missing. She savored every step on the stones, each high glass window, every wooden pillar, every lantern, rug, curtain, and corridor.

So why did she feel this way?

She pushed through the double doors to the kitchen without even realizing where her feet were carrying her. She scanned the bottles lining the shelves before a green bottle with a faded, paper label caught her eye.

It was just past the three o'clock bell after lunch, which was probably late enough for a drink. The snow had finally begun to melt, and after their arduous winter, spring's arrival was reason enough to celebrate. She poured herself a generous glass of red wine from the green bottle that rested beside the tray of fruits, filling two elaborately gilded floral pieces of stemware. Nox pushed the door to the kitchen open with her hip as she set off to find the one with whom she intended to share her wine.

She knew precisely where she was going, but melancholy slowed her tracks today.

Nox took her time wandering down the corridors and paused outside the room that had belonged to Malik. Maybe she'd sleep in this bed tonight while she visited him in his dreams, hoping they'd be on the sunny banks of his favorite fishing pond once more. The room no longer smelled like him, but it would be his for as long as he wanted it.

Ash's room carried a different sort of silence.

The emptiness of this room would be one they'd never be able to fill.

She was quite certain that as long as she ruled in Gwydir, no one would sleep in this bed.

Nox took a slow, calming breath as she left the corridor of chambers and made her way to the training yard where she knew she'd find Tanith. She leaned against the door to the courtyard and watched the Sulgrave fae quietly as she stood in the middle of the ring, stretching and contorting herself with slow, intentional control. A warm spring breeze ruffled the purple flowers blossoming on the vines. The plants hadn't cared about the season. They crawled across the walls and brought color to the courtyard, snow or shine. Their purple was the primary splotch of color, as Tanith wore black. Once she'd taken off her red tunic in Sulgrave, she'd never again donned the color.

"Do you have time for a drink?" Nox called softly.

Tanith opened her eyes and slowly brought herself to a comfortable resting position. She extended her hand for the stemware. Nox caught the tiny aquamarine stone on the fae's thin fingers as her hand wrapped around the base of the glass. It was the only piece of jewelry she wore, save for the small, gilded coin on a thin chain that rested near her heart. It would forever remain etched with the sun's rays—sunshine on the darkest days.

Tanith's sorrow was a third presence in the room. It was a ghost that would live in this castle for a long, long time. Nox took a seat on the ground beside the fae, tucking her feet beneath herself. Wine was typically meant for sipping, but Tanith took three deep gulps before coming up for air. Less than a quarter of the dark liquid remained in her glass. She stared down into its crimson pool while Nox searched for the right words.

"Are you okay?" Nox asked carefully. It was a question she rarely asked, because she knew the answer.

Tanith's smile was wry and humorless. Only half of her mouth responded to the motion. "I'm not," she answered honestly.

"You know, we don't expect anything of you. You don't have to fight. You don't have to serve. You will be welcome here to stretch in the courtyard, eat pies in the dining room, read romance novels, go shopping with Amaris and me, and live your life. You saved Gwydir. We owe you our lives. Even if you hadn't…you're part of our family, Tanith."

The Sulgrave fae hadn't looked up from where her gaze remained fixed in the purplish liquid that remained at the bottom of her goblet.

"I've always had a purpose," she finally said. "I've always served."

Nox attempted to give her knee a comforting squeeze.

"Your worth has nothing to do with what you can offer us. We're lucky to have you."

Tanith met her eyes then. The quiver of her chin was so slight that Nox might not have noticed it at all if she hadn't been watching for exactly this emotion.

"I thought about becoming a reever," Tanith said slowly.

This surprised Nox. Her eyebrows moved up and she used the excuse of her wine to conceal her mouth from any words that she might regret.

The Sulgrave fae had carried on before Nox could voice any opinion. "Ash loved being a reever. His father was consumed by the reever's mission. For a while, it seemed like the next logical step for me. At first, I thought maybe it would be what he would have wanted. But if..."

Nox could sense the impending negation. She straightened, leaning forward as she waited for the fae to complete her thought.

"If?" Nox promoted.

The girl shook her short, dark hair. It moved seamlessly around her chin against the motion. "But," Tanith continued, chewing on the sentence, "even if the reevers are good and just and serve the continent well, I don't think I can become a Red again, even if it is under another banner. I don't want to go to Uaimh Reev. I don't want a new master."

"Then you won't have one. You belong to yourself."

Tanith looked down into her glass. "I do want to continue the work."

"And what work is that?"

She drained what remained of her wine. It had been a generous pour, and the Sulgrave girl was already so small. "The reevers have spent so much time in Raascot trying to understand the infestation. Even if the Reds were to blame for binding the creatures and coordinating their attacks, I'm not satisfied that eliminating the Speaker and ending their suicide missions goes deep enough. There's more to the monsters in Gyrradin than anyone has learned. That spider you faced with Ash and Malik? He said they've never heard or read of any monster like it. It shouldn't exist. These beasts of the land, their numbers, their influx... I think it's what drove Elil insane."

"Are you talking about the manifester?" Nox asked quietly. They'd discussed the one who'd created Daifa a few times, but the conversation was little more than theoretical. Nomy had implied that there was more than one, but Nox didn't know what to do with that information. She considered the theologian's words once more, wondering what it would mean to be a fae born with the ability to create. And if she couldn't change it, then perhaps it didn't matter.

"There weren't always demons," Tanith said finally. "The oldest records tell stories of kings and queens and wolves and bears and snakes and deer and fish, but mentions of things like the vageth, beseul, and ag'drurath didn't begin emerging until over a thousand years ago. I'd like to find out why. The real reason."

This time, Nox let the perplexing emotion rearrange her expression. "You want to find out how the beasts came into being? You'd like to become a historian?"

She handed her glass back to Nox and began to stand. "Elil was on to something. He was a bastard and his son deserved better. I'm glad he's dead." Her voice fell off as she side-stepped mentioning Ash with any more specificity. The Sulgrave girl took a moment to keep the emotion out of her words before continuing. "I'll stay in Gwydir, if you'll have me."

They walked away from the ring slowly, enjoying the gentle rustle of the violet flowers.

It didn't seem relevant, she supposed. If Tanith wanted to throw herself into whatever tomes or research or projects that might distract her, that was precisely what she should do. If she could find any solace in diversions from thinking about her reever or feeling Ash's absence, then any project she chose would be supported by the others. Nox began to lead them out of the courtyard. "Of course. You're welcome to the castle, the rooms, the library, and anything you need for your research. You don't even have to ask. You're one of us."

"I…" Tanith looked away distantly, mind lost to a memory. Her eyes seemed unfocused on a gently moving violet flower on the vine. Her voice had dropped when she spoke. "I might need to meet with a healer."

Nox's brows folded in concern. "Are you unwell?"

A thin hand fluttered to her stomach briefly, then flexed as she released it to her side. Her eyes remained on the distant, trembling flower in the courtyard as she finished her question. "I'll be fine. Please, could you send someone to my rooms?"

"Of course."

Her eyes drifted to the fae's stomach once more before she forced them away. Whatever it was Tanith asked of her, she was not ready to speak of it. She couldn't allow her mind to wander to tragedies or speculations. For now, all that mattered was that Tanith was safe, accepted, and had a home within Gwydir. Nothing else mattered.

The Sulgrave girl dipped her chin as she departed for unknown parts of the castle. Nox continued to sip at her wine, carrying Tanith's empty glass back to the kitchen. She certainly hadn't expected that the murderous little creature who'd once been so enraptured by the corrupt church to become their friend. Tanith had been a ball of zeal and prejudice when she'd been captured on the cliffsides of the gully, but she'd paid for her crimes time and time again. She'd fought for them. She'd rescued them. She'd eliminated the remaining Reds, putting their lives before her own on more than one occasion. Between her faith, her country, her people, and the man she'd grown to love, she'd lost more than any of them.

Tanith deserved good things. She deserved freedom from her pain, however she chose to find it.

Everything was different, and perhaps that was the wound that wouldn't heal.

Maybe Nox didn't know how to experience peace. Her

life had been spent in stages of anticipation and survival. Now the continent was united—a word that brought a wry smile to Nox's mouth as the thought skirted through her mind. Daifa, damn her, would have loved that knowledge.

She was safe. Raascot had loved and welcomed her with open arms. Amaris would never be dragged from her grasp again. The Selkie had been shut down, never to reopen. The curse was broken. The threats were quelled. She was living in the very prayer she'd never dared to whisper. She had immeasurably more than she could have ever asked for or imagined. Nox was the queen of the united north and south, with more love and ease in her life than any one person deserved to experience.

After ditching the empty glasses, she joined Zaccai on the lawn where Fjolla practically knocked her to her bottom with her frenzied excitement. The great white beast buried her face against Nox's belly, and she felt the odd tug in her heart begin to ebb. Maybe that was the thing about spending your life in a state of survival. Unlearning the constant need to exist in fight-or-flight was just as challenging as staying afloat had been.

The secret to life might not be about making a great impact, since changing the course of the continent certainly hadn't eradicated whatever feeling nagged her. Life's great mystery might be learning how to wake up every day and find all the wonderful ways that joy hid itself in: in the sweet, buttery bites of pastries; in the cuddles from animals; in the smiles from friends, and in the nights spent with lovers. Perhaps her greatest feat lay ahead. After a lifetime spent clawing, fighting, tired, broken, and angry, the biggest adventure remained: to allow herself to be happy.

Sulgrave

Acknowledgments

There are so many people to thank now that Nox and
Amaris's story has come to a close. I should be thanking
the readers, friends, editors, agents, artists, demons, Spotify
playlists, manic episodes, bottles of wine, and publishers who
made this possible. I have half a heart to pull a Snoop Dogg
circa 2018 and say "I wanna thank me." But mostly, I want
to thank Brian Helgeland, writer, director, and producer
of A Knight's Tale, for teaching us that anyone—whether a
thatcher's son from Cheapside or a girl who wanted to see
bisexuality, religious trauma, and mental illness represented in
fantasy—could change their stars.

About the Author

Piper CJ, author of the bisexual fantasy series the Night and Its Moon, is a photographer, hobby linguist, and french fry enthusiast. She has an MA in folklore and a BA in broadcasting, which she used in her former life as a morning-show weather girl and hockey podcaster and in audio documentary work. Now when she isn't playing with her dogs, Arrow and Applesauce, she's making TikToks, studying Vietnamese, or writing fantasy very, very quickly.

Website: pipercj.com
Instagram: @piper_cj
TikTok: @pipercj